the dark

V.M. Giambanco was born in Italy. She started working in films as an editor's apprentice in a 35mm cutting room and since then has worked on many award-winning UK and US pictures, from small independent projects to large studio productions. She lives in London.

Also by V.M. Giambanco

The Gift of Darkness

V. M. GIAMBANCO

the dark

Quercus

First published in Great Britain in 2014.
This paperback edition published in 2015 by

Quercus Publishing Ltd
Carmelite House
50 Victoria Embankment
London EC4Y 0DZ

An Hachette UK company

A CIP catalogue record for this book is available
from the British Library

PB ISBN 978 1 78087 899 7
EBOOK ISBN 978 1 78087 898 0

10 9 8 7 6 5 4 3 2 1

Typeset by Ellipsis Digital Limited, Glasgow

Printed and bound in Great Britain by Clays Ltd, St Ives plc

For Valeria Cardi Navach and
Francesca Bellina Giambanco

Ancient trees rise a hundred feet, red and yellow cedars next to black cottonwood and vine maples, their roots twisting out of deep green slippery moss and rotting wood.

Four men walk in single file. Young enough that the difficult terrain doesn't slow their progress too much, old enough to know this is the day their lives have twisted and turned; they don't speak to each other because there is nothing to say.

Their leader wipes the perspiration off the back of his neck with a ragged square of gray cloth; he points at a dead branch that curves out of the dirt, ready to catch their feet; the others step carefully around it. He's not a considerate man; he's a nasty piece of work in a hurry to get his business done and get out of the forest.

The others follow him, wary of his moods and of the uneven ground; they look ahead and never turn around. If they did, they would see the boy held in the arms of the last man in the file, the boy who hasn't drawn breath for what seems like hours. Eleven, maybe twelve years old, fair wavy hair and pale lips. They grip their shovels and walk on.

The man carries the boy and keeps his eyes on the back of the guy in front. The child's thin arms dangle low and his hands brush the tall ferns. Then, as loud as a gunshot, a sharp intake of breath and the boy's eyes open wide. The man recoils and the child slips from his arms onto the soft moss.

The boy doesn't see the others turn as he lies on the cool ground; he's breathing deeply and above him, beyond the highest branches, the sky is so blue it hurts to look at it.

Last night

Homicide Detective Alice Madison tried to find in herself the last shreds of stillness. The woods creaked around her and a puff of breeze soothed the cut on her cheek.

All the time she would ever have was right now. She was frayed with exhaustion and dread, and sanity seemed a lifetime away. It always came down to the same question, over and over: *How far are you prepared to go?*

She pointed her Glock at the man in front of her and wondered if the soft evening wind would affect the bullet's trajectory, whether the small chunk of metal would do what she was asking it to do or the twilight would affect her aim. Precision was all she had, carved out of intent and determination.

Alice Madison had never aimed and shot at a human being before walking onto this field, and this was not what the Police Academy had taught her. Her target was not a threat to her, himself or others. Her target could barely stand on his feet.

Madison squeezed the trigger and in her heart she knew she had a hit like the pitcher knows how the ball is going to curve as soon as it leaves the hand.

Three weeks and five days earlier

Chapter 1

Alice Madison shifted in the comfortable upholstered armchair and adjusted the holster that dug a little into her right side. She stole a glance out of the wide window. Puget Sound shone in the pallid January light, the silver creased white in spots, and Mount Rainier rose from blue shadows in the far distance.

She turned when she realized the silence had stretched for longer than was polite. Dr. Robinson was watching her.

'Don't worry. I know people come here for the sharp psychological insights but it's the view they stay for,' he said.

He had made that joke the first time they had met a few weeks earlier. She smiled a little today as she had then, not entirely sure he was unaware he was repeating himself.

The sign in the lobby said Stanley F. Robinson PhD. The office on the fifteenth floor was smart, the colors muted.

He was early fifties, salt-and-pepper hair in a short cut and big brown eyes. A useful look for a psychologist who worked with cops: fairly unthreatening with bouts of inquisitiveness, she mused.

'How was your week?' he asked her. Dr. Robinson's desk was mercifully free of pads and pens. If he took notes he did so after their sessions.

'Good,' Madison replied. 'Paperwork from a few old cases to tidy up. A domestic incident which turned out to be nothing. Pretty standard stuff.'

'Did you think about the forest incident? I mean, longer than for a few seconds during your day.'

'No.'

'Did you experience any unusual thoughts or have unusual reactions as you went about your business? I'll let you tell me what's unusual for you.'

'No, nothing unusual.'

'Any reaction to chloroform or other PTSD events?'

'No.'

'Anything at all about the last week or in general that you'd like to talk about?'

Madison had the good grace to at least pretend she was pondering the question.

'Not really,' she said finally.

Dr. Robinson mulled over her reply for a few moments. He sat back in his chair.

'Detective, how many sessions have we had to date?'

'This is the third.'

'That's right, and this is what I've learnt: you are a Homicide Detective; you joined your squad last November – that's, what, about two and a half months ago, give or take. You have a Degree in Psychology and Criminology from the University of Chicago – good school, great football team. Your record at the Seattle Police Department is impeccable. You play well in the sandbox and there are no red flags in your private life. Not so much as a traffic violation. With me so far?'

'Yes.'

'Good. Last December all hell breaks loose and once the smoke clears the Department sends you here to make sure you're fit for work and ready to protect and to serve. You are very frank: you admit to a reaction to chloroform as a consequence of Harry Salinger's attack on you and your partner, but that stopped weeks ago. No panic attacks, no incidents of post-traumatic stress disorder. Nothing, after what happened in the forest. The boy, the rescue, the blood.'

He paused there and Madison held his eyes.

'Do you know how long it took me to gain all this perceptive knowledge?' He didn't wait for her to reply. 'Seven minutes. The rest of the time what I got was "good" and "pretty standard stuff" and "nothing unusual".'

'What do you want from me, Dr. Robinson?'

'Me? Nothing. I'm quite happy for you to come up and just look at the view. You can do with the break and I get paid either way. But here's the thing: even though I will certify that you are indeed fit to work and ready to protect and to serve – because you are – it is simply unthinkable that those thirteen days in December left no trace on you somehow. So, these goodies I'm giving you for free: you have occasional nightmares, possibly an exact memory of the event but more likely your own perception of the event and whatever troubles you about the nature of your own actions in it. And, most of all, I'm willing to bet you are careful never to be alone with your godson since you got him out of that forest. How am I doing?'

Madison didn't reply.

'Good meeting you, Detective. Have a nice life.'

Dusk. Alice Madison parked her Honda Civic in her usual spot by Alki Beach. Her running gear was stashed in a gym bag in the trunk but she leant against the bonnet and let the clean salty air into her lungs. The Seattle–Bremerton ferry was going past, seagulls trailing in its wake. Bainbridge Island was a blue-green strip across the water and downtown Seattle shimmered in the distance.

As far as she could remember, even as a newbie officer with her crisply ironed uniform, Madison had come to Alki Beach and run after her shifts. The comfort of the sand under her feet and the rhythm of the tide after a hard day; the sheer physical release after a good day. It had been a constant in her life and Madison knew very well that there were precious few of those, and she was grateful for it.

Then, the last day of the year just gone, after the end of those thirteen days, Madison had come back to the beach, changed into her sweats, started running and promptly slipped into a recall so vivid, so physical, that she had to stop: the sweet smell of pine resin still in her nostrils. Hands on her knees and water up to her ankles, her trainers soaked. *Any dreams you want to tell me about?*

Her arm had healed; the rest of her would take whatever time it would take. Madison changed in the back of her car. Her first strides were hesitant but she ignored the forest floor shifting under her feet, and the sudden scent of blood. And she kept running.

The rush-hour traffic carried Madison into California Avenue SW without any apparent effort on her part; she followed the flow south with the windows rolled down and her faded maroon University of Chicago hooded sweatshirt stuck to her back. She wiped the perspiration off her brow with a sleeve and drove, listening to the local news on the radio and not thinking about Stanley F. Robinson PhD.

We find our blessings where we can and Madison pulled into a parking space opposite Husky Deli and stretched her sore limbs as she locked her car.

Her grandfather had brought her here for an ice-cream cone her first weekend in Seattle. Her grandmother was busying herself in the market nearby. They sat at the counter; he looked at the 12-year-old girl he barely knew and spoke to her like no one had spoken to her before.

'I hope you will like it here – I really hope you will. All I'm asking is that should there be anything troubling you, anything at all, you talk to me, to us. I don't know what happened with your father and I'm not asking that you tell us. I'm just asking that you don't run away, that you don't just leave in the middle of the night. And we'll do our best to help you in any way we can.'

Then he put out his hand. Alice looked at it; no one had ever asked her word about anything. She passed her Maple Walnut cone into her left hand and shook with her right, sticky with sugar. They kept their word, and so did she.

Madison rubbed the sole of her trainer against the edge of the pavement to get rid of a significant amount of Alki Beach that had insinuated itself into the grooves. She mingled with the shoppers and filled a basket with food for home as well as a Chicken Cashew sandwich – no parsley – and broccoli cheese soup that would probably not make it home.

Standing at the counter she was no different from anybody else.

'Whole or half?' the man asked.

'Whole.'

'Cup or bowl?'

'Bowl.'

'Roll?'

'No, thank you.'

The man's gaze lingered for a fraction of a second over the two-inch fine red line across her left brow; it would fade in time, the doctor had said. Madison hadn't cared then and didn't care today. All that mattered was that it made her a little bit more recognizable after the flurry of articles and media reports in early January.

The man nodded; he must have been working there since bread was invented.

'Cone? Caramel Swirl's freshly made.'

Madison smiled. 'Not today.'

She started on the soup in the car, engine already running, and by the time she turned into Maplewood and her driveway, the carton was empty.

Three Oaks is a green neighborhood on the south-western edge of Seattle, on one side the still waters of Puget Sound and on the other patches of woodland and single family homes in well-tended gardens.

Madison parked next to her grandparents' Mercedes and balanced her gym bag on one shoulder; her arm was wrapped around the grocery bag as she unlocked the door, toed the sandy trainers off and gently pushed the door shut with one foot.

She padded into the kitchen and unpacked the shopping. Without turning on the lights she crossed the living room and opened the French doors, letting in the fresh air. The answering machine flashed red. She ignored it, settled herself into a wicker chair on the deck, her feet on the wooden rail, and unwrapped the sandwich.

The garden sloped down to a narrow beach that ran along the waterside properties; tall firs on either side worked better than a fence. In the half-light Madison looked at the plants and the shrubs: soon they would wake up for a new life cycle – the Japanese maples, the magnolias – each one seeded and nurtured by her grandparents.

Madison knew nothing about gardening yet she would weed, water, prune and make sure that everything stayed alive because they weren't there to do it anymore. She worried good intentions wouldn't make up for ignorance. In her job they usually didn't.

Once the stars were bright enough, Madison stepped inside. Her Glock went under the bed in its holster and her back-up piece – a snub-nose revolver – was oiled and dry-fired. Madison peeled off her sweats and climbed into a long hot shower.

The message had been from Rachel: 'Tommy's birthday party is next month. I hope you can make it.' Nothing but love and kindness in her voice.

You have occasional nightmares, possibly an exact memory of the event but more likely your own perception of the event and whatever troubles you about the nature of your own actions in it. And, most of all, I'm willing to bet you are careful never to be alone with your godson since you got him out of that forest.

The nature of your own actions. Madison wasn't exactly sure she understood the nature of her own actions and she was honest enough to admit to herself that there had been moments that night that she probably did not want to fully understand. It had been a blur of fear and rage and she didn't know exactly how much of one or the other.

Tommy would be seven soon. On that awful night she had sung 'Blackbird' to him and he had come back to them, to life, to his red bicycle and his little boy's games. Her godson would be seven and Madison tried hard to come up with an excuse not to go to the party and failed.

As every night since that day in December her last thoughts went to two men: one in jail, locked behind walls and metal doors guarded by armed correction officers, and yet more terrifyingly free than any human being she had ever met; and the other in the prison of his injuries, somewhere deep past the corridors and the silent rooms of a hospital a few miles away. His sacrifice had meant Tommy would have a seventh birthday party. She could not think of one without the other.

Madison closed her eyes and hoped sleep would come quickly.

Under the bed, inside the safe, a neatly folded page from *The Seattle Times* has been tucked under the off-duty piece.

BLUERIDGE KILLER CAUGHT

In the early hours of December 24 the nightmare that had gripped Seattle for thirteen days finally came to an end. Harry Salinger, the prime suspect in the murder of James and Annie

Sinclair and their two young sons, was apprehended by Seattle Police Department Homicide Detective Alice Madison in an undisclosed location in the Hoh River Forest.

Mr. John Cameron, who had initially been under investigation for the crime, and his attorney Mr. Nathan Quinn, of Quinn Locke & Associates, were also present. The former is being held without bail on a charge of attempted murder. Mr. Salinger, an Everett resident, sustained life-threatening injuries and is now under guard in a secure medical facility.

Mr. Salinger has also been charged with the kidnap and reckless endangerment of Thomas Abramowitz, 6, Det. Madison's godson, and with the assault on Det. Sgt. Kevin Brown and Det. Madison earlier in December.

SPD has not made public when Det. Sgt. Brown will come back to active duty.

Mr. Cameron and Mr. Sinclair were first connected by tragic circumstances as children twenty-five years ago when three Seattle boys were abducted and abandoned in the Hoh River Forest, Jefferson County.

Chapter 2

Nathan Quinn held up his left hand and flexed it. It was flawless. No scars, no pain. He stood in the clearing in the Hoh River Forest; he saw every twist in every branch and there was nothing but woods and winding streams for miles. The air was soft on his skin and sunlight slanted through the spruces. A warm, sunny August afternoon. All was well, all was peace.

A whisper through the grass behind him and Quinn turned.

A boy watched him from the edge of the treeline. Twelve years old, fair wavy hair and pale lips. So pale.

'David?'

The boy was barefoot.

'David?'

Nathan Quinn felt the jolt of awareness as the morphine wore off and he remembered that he was in a hospital and his brother had been dead for twenty-five years.

'Mr. Quinn.' The nurse's voice found him through the dull pain that had welcomed his body back. 'There are some police officers here to speak with you. If you feel up to it.'

Nathan Quinn held up his left hand: it was covered in bandages and as he flexed his fingers the pain ran up his arm. In the last four weeks he has seen no one except for doctors, nurses, two detectives from the Seattle Police Department who took his statement and Carl Doyle, his assistant at Quinn Locke & Associates. Everyone else without exception has been turned away. After two weeks in a medically induced coma he had barely the strength to breathe.

'They're from Jefferson County,' the nurse said.

'Yes,' he replied. 'I know.'

It was Saturday and Madison was off duty – a rare event. Her days off had acquired a routine of late: the call, the journey, the exchange of information, the second call. Madison checked her watch – her grandfather's: 8.25 a.m. Enough time to put on a wash; she picked up her sweats from the floor where they'd been discarded and added whatever was left in the hamper.

She pulled on black jeans, a dark blue shirt and short leather boots. Her cell rang as she was adjusting the snub-nose revolver into an ankle holster.

She picked it up from the bedside table.

'Madison,' Lieutenant Fynn said.

'Sir.' Madison froze with her trouser hem stuck in her boot: her shift commander would not call her at home on her day off for chit-chat and giggles.

'Just had a call from Jefferson County. Four days ago park police found human remains about a mile from where you were. Took them this long to recover them.'

Madison knew what was coming before she heard the words.

'A child. The remains are years old.'

'David Quinn,' she whispered.

'Could very well be. County police is getting a new DNA sample from Nathan Quinn as we speak. We'll know soon enough.'

'The kidnap happened in Seattle. It's our investigation.'

'I know. If it's David Quinn they'll ship the remains to our ME and we'll pick it up from there.'

'Thanks for letting me know.'

'It's worse than we thought.'

'What do you mean, sir?'

'The skull bears evidence of trauma.'

Madison's mind raced to recall the details she had learnt from the newspapers.

'No, David Quinn suffered from congenital arrhythmia. At the original inquest—'

'Madison, if that child is David Quinn it wasn't accidental death. He was killed by blunt trauma to the head.'

'It's . . .' She struggled to find the words.

'I thought you would want to tell *him* in person.'

'Yes, I'll be on my way in a minute.'

'Way to spend your day off.'

Fynn had just rung off when the cell beeped again.

'It's Doyle.'

'Carl. How are you?'

'I honestly don't know, Detective. How are you?'

'I've just heard; my boss called me.'

'It will take a few days for confirmation, they said. Do you need to write this down?'

'No, go ahead.'

'Blood pressure normal; the swabs came back clear – no infection; physio was hell this week – as they expected – but it's progressing. Eye test, no difference from before the event. So far, so good. The antibiotics for the partial splenectomy are very strong; they hope to diminish the dose gradually and see how the remaining spleen will react. No temperature, no unusual numbers in the blood work.'

'Thank you, Carl.'

'Are you going for the 10 a.m. slot?'

'I am.'

'Are you going to tell him?'

'Yes, he has a right to know before it hits the news.'

'We'll speak after.'

Madison shrugged on a blazer and locked her front door. The drive would give her time to prepare herself. *Whatever good it will do.*

It had taken them twenty-five years to find him but at last David Quinn was coming home. Abducted with two friends and taken to the Hoh River Forest, tied to a tree with a heavy rope and left to fight for breath until he passed out. Then the men had taken his body and left the other children to the approaching night. No one was ever charged with the kidnap, no reason had ever been found for the abduction. There was no body, no forensics, no chance of a prosecution.

Three children were taken into the woods, two came out alive. One, James Sinclair, would grow up to be a good man, to have a family and to perish one day last December by the hand of a madman. The other would grow up to be something quite different.

Madison drove south on 509, she took an exit west through Des Moines and then crossed I–5, heading fast toward the King County Justice Complex and John Cameron, the last surviving Hoh River boy.

The King County Justice Complex rose from a concrete parking lot, telling the world exactly what it was: an adult detention center for 1,157 inmates, waiting for trial or sentenced as per the Washington State Guidelines Commission instructions.

Madison made sure nothing had been left in view on the car seats and walked toward the Visitors' Reception.

Family groups and single people were also making their way in for the 10 a.m. slot, the sun doing little to warm up the group in the shadow of the 20 ft-high perimeter wall.

Madison could have locked her off-duty piece in the safe at home and avoided the issue of checking it at the Reception Desk but she was a cop. She carried a shield, she carried a piece.

She filed in with the others, a quiet serious group with a few somber children.

A young woman in a delicately patterned dress made a beeline for Madison as soon as she entered the Reception.

'Detective Madison, if you have a moment the Deputy Warden would like a word before your visit.'

Mid-twenties, softly spoken, blonde hair up in bun. She looked like she could have been handing out books and lollipops in a children library.

'Sure,' Madison replied.

'I'm Karen Hayes.' The young woman led her down a side corridor. 'I assist both the Warden and the Deputy Warden.'

Madison had never been inside that part of the jail. It could have been any kind of corporate business: people typing in offices, carpeted floors and water coolers. Still, about twenty-three locked metal doors away from the small geranium pot on Karen's desk men stood, walked and slept, men who had taken lives and done things to their victims that made them wish for death.

These clerks and secretaries organized their days, their dental checks, their parole boards and their menus – all in these brightly lit rooms scented with sandalwood and apple.

Madison, on the other hand, had reached into their thoughts and followed them into dark alleys and, in spite of the sandalwood, she felt their proximity like the touch of gun metal between her shoulder blades.

'Detective Madison.' The Deputy Warden held his office door open for her. He looked like a benign high school principal; a white button-down with a burgundy tie and his jacket hung on a rack.

'I'm Will Thomas, Deputy Warden at KCJC.'

He shook her hand once and waved her to a chair in front of his desk. 'I thought we should – how can I put it – open the channels of communication.'

Madison had no idea what he meant; she felt her own instant reaction to impending governmental speak and hoped her natural courtesy would hold.

'You are here to visit John Cameron.'

And there it was.

'Yes, I am.'

'You're not family and you're not a friend.'

'No.'

'You're not his attorney and you're not here on police business.'

'No.'

'Yet you have visited him regularly since he was brought here at the end of December. He is quite popular. Alleged murderer of nine, charged with assault and denied bail. Since he was apprehended FBI agents from LA have come to interview him, as well as assorted officers from the DEA and the ATF – and I don't know how many media requests we've had. He turned down every one of them. A popular guy apart from one thing.' Deputy Warden Thomas sat back in his chair and regarded Madison.

'He hasn't spoken one word. Not to them, not to anybody. Except,' he smiled briefly, 'to you.'

Madison flashed back to a clearing in the Hoh River Forest in the early hours of the morning: Tommy frozen cold in her arms, Nathan Quinn covered in blood at her feet, and John Cameron standing before her like he was made of the very night around them.

'If you want to leave, leave now. If you stay, do not say anything to me or to anybody at all. Do you understand?'

'John Cameron chose to stay because Quinn was badly injured even though he knew the police were on their way. Quinn was injured saving my godson's life. That's why I'm here.'

'I see. How is Mr. Quinn?'

'Progressing.' Madison replied. 'Slowly.'

'How is Harry Salinger?'

'I have no idea.'

Harry Salinger had torn through their lives and almost destroyed them; Cameron had left him close to death on the river bank that night. The judicial system might hold Cameron on a charge of Attempted Murder but Madison could not put a name to what he had done to Salinger.

'Detective, I like to think of KCJC as a ship, a very large ship. Some people come and go, as you do today, but others, like Mr. Cameron, come to stay for a long time. A long journey, so to speak. I want to keep that journey as smooth as possible. For him, and for everyone else here. You know he's not in the general population, right?'

'I know.'

'Two days after he arrived the incidents of violence between inmates went up ten per cent. Just knowing he was here.'

Madison knew that if Cameron was kept in isolation it wasn't for his own protection.

'There's a long line of men who can't wait to prove themselves against him and that, I'm afraid, is not something we can have. So, since you're the only person he speaks to, I just wanted to make sure that we were on the same page.'

'We don't swap recipes, sir. I barely know the man.'

'Still,' the Deputy Warden said, 'is there anything I should know?'

Not a benign principal, more a science teacher about to dissect a frog.

'John Cameron was not *apprehended*, Mr. Thomas,' Madison said. 'He wasn't *caught*. He's here because he chooses to be. As long as everybody remembers that you shouldn't have any problems.'

'Why would he choose imprisonment?'

'Because he wouldn't leave Quinn while he was fighting for his life.'

'Maybe you overestimate his personal involvement in the situation, and underestimate the security systems of this institution. This is not a bed and breakfast in the San Juan Islands.'

'You might want to ask Harry Salinger about how personally involved Cameron felt when Salinger murdered James Sinclair and his family. As for the security system here, nothing would make me happier than knowing it's as good as you say it is.'

They regarded each other for one long moment and Madison saw a man with graying sandy hair and a desk bare of any family photos, a man trying to keep things running in a place where men would do anything to anyone for any reason.

'Look,' she said. 'For what it's worth, Cameron doesn't feel he has anything to prove to anybody. He's not vain; he's not going to go out of his way to make trouble. But if someone – if anyone stands between him and the thing he wants, he will not be stopped, not without extreme consequences for both sides.'

'What if he changes his mind about staying?'

Madison stood up to leave. 'We can only hope that he doesn't.'

Chapter 3

The first time Madison had met John Cameron she had followed him into a dark wood and waited, unarmed, just to speak with him. The second time he had broken into her home and she hadn't even known he was there. The third time they had chased Harry Salinger, the man who had killed his friend and kidnapped her godson, through the Hoh River Forest.

If John Cameron was out in the world, she would be one of the people who would hunt him down. If she was the one between Cameron and whatever it was he wanted, she knew he wouldn't hesitate to remove the obstacle. If there were words for that kind of acquaintance, Madison didn't know them.

As always, they met in a separate cell, away from the bustle of the visiting room and the brazen curiosity of inmates and strangers. Madison had checked in her shield and her piece, the female guard assessing her like one would an unexploded device.

She had been patted down and cleared and now stood in a bare room made of metal bars inside a larger room; a scratched table bolted to the floor and two chairs made in a prison workshop somewhere in the fifties completed the setup.

The door opened and two armed guards came in, escorting a tall man in orange overalls. It meant he was waiting for trial and had been denied bail; it meant a crime of violence.

Madison turned to face him.

His file told her that he was thirty-seven years old, six years older than she was, and that the four scars that crossed and glistened on the back of his right hand were a reminder of the hours spent tied to a tree with James Sinclair and David Quinn when he was twelve. The numbers were unforgiving: five men on board the *Nostromo*, three drug dealers in LA, one dealer in Seattle. Nine alleged murders: not one of them had ever come anywhere near any charges.

The file gave details and dates and times of death but it couldn't possible give a sense of what it was like to stand in the same room as this man. The fact they were inside a jail was incidental. He was a predator and when his amber eyes met hers she felt the familiar chill in the pit of her stomach.

'Detective.'

'Mr. Cameron.'

He wasn't shackled. The two guards simply withdrew and locked the barred door of the cell with the scraping of metal against metal. Madison could see them in the low light, flanking the exit, their weapons – and their desire to be anywhere else – in plain sight.

His dark hair had been cut jail short but aside from that she couldn't see any discernible changes. He looked as if he had just strolled in, as if he could just as easily stroll out. Only one thing was different, she realized – not that anyone else would notice: she had seen Cameron with Nathan Quinn and there was an ember of humanity there, of warmth. *This* Cameron was completely shut down; the man who had drunk coffee at her grandmother's table had packed up and gone.

They sat. Madison gathered her thoughts. He waited. This visit was going to be different.

'I just spoke with Doyle.' She closed her eyes for a moment and recalled the details. 'Blood pressure normal; the swabs were clear – no infection; physio is coming on, with difficulty. Eye test was positive, no sight loss. They want to diminish the antibiotics for the spleen gradually and see how it will behave. No temperature, blood work okay.'

John Cameron held her eyes. His gaze was very direct and Madison wondered what he had learnt about her during these visits and how he would use it one day, out of this cell.

'Thank you, Detective.' He stood up and was almost at the door in one swift silent movement.

'There's something else.'

He turned.

They had never spoken about it and as far as Madison knew the children had hardly spoken about it at all at the time.

'About a mile from the clearing . . .' there was no need to clarify where that was, not to this man '. . . Park police found human remains. A child. Possibly buried over twenty years ago.'

Something came and went in Cameron's eyes. A thought, maybe hope. Madison couldn't tell yet his focus on her was almost tangible.

For twenty-five years everyone had believed that the death had been accidental. They had been wearing blindfolds, they had heard him suffocate. As if that day hadn't borne enough misery.

'There was blunt trauma to the head, enough for cause of death,' she continued.

John Cameron stood quite still. There were memories there, Madison was sure of it.

'They have just taken a fresh DNA sample from Quinn,' she finished.

There was no need to say anything else and before she could draw breath he was at the door and the lock was clanging open. Visiting hours were over.

Madison sat back in her chair and looked at the ceiling, a thin silver mesh before many layers of concrete. *Way to spend your day off.*

Deputy Warden Thomas looked at his watch. Detective Madison's visits were invariably brief and he wanted to make sure that he had given the correction officers enough time to escort John Cameron back to his cell. And he'd give them some extra time too before he ventured to the secure wings for a routine walk-about.

There was something he had not told Detective Madison. It had started the third day Cameron was there. Another inmate in the same wing saw him walk past and started pounding on the bars of his cell, a quick pulse like a cymbal. Others had joined in; a whole wing, two darned floors of it, hammering the bars with everything they could get their hands on in a steady, hypnotic march that grew in volume and spread like an ill wind from wing to wing.

Every day since, every time John Cameron had left his cell – to go to the yard, to see his lawyer, to the showers, to meet this cop – every single time the wall of sound would start and the inmates would not stop until every shred of energy they had had been burnt out. No voices, just the drumming.

The guards had been trading shifts among each other to avoid being there when Cameron was taken out of his cell, and Will Thomas would fuss over paperwork and look at his watch and dawdle.

Unlike the inmates, the sound would go where it pleased, finding the spot where a guard's nerve was thinnest and piercing deep into the bone.

Chapter 4

Madison called Doyle from her car.

'How was he?' he asked her.

'Are you honestly asking me what the man thinks?'

'No, my mistake.'

Madison wanted to ask him how Quinn had taken it but she didn't. She only passed on the medical report. She had despised and been wary of Nathan Quinn in equal measure from the moment they had met. And still, Tommy will have a birthday soon.

Madison didn't ask how Quinn had felt about the possibility that his brother might have been brutally murdered. He didn't need her concern and she didn't know what to do with it anyway.

She checked the trunk for basics – latex gloves, flashlight, batteries, rain gear and walking boots – and took off North on 509: it would take maybe three hours to get there. The body might not be officially David Quinn yet but she had to see it for herself, the place where the piece of hell Cameron carried had come from.

Somehow Madison managed to make the 12.05 Edmonds-to-Kingston ferry. She grabbed a cup of coffee and found a seat by a window for the thirty-minute journey. It was busy and loud with families, groups, and single travelers scattered in the booths and on the white chairs with navy blue trim, food and drinks spread on the wide armrests like spoils.

Madison was not in the mood for lunch; as she had done almost every day since December, she wished her partner Detective Sergeant Kevin Brown would hurry up and heal and get himself back to work. They spoke often and had met at least once a week but it would have been invaluable to have his perspective today, stalking a twenty-five-year-old crime scene.

She had almost lost him from two gunshot wounds and it was something she tried not to think about. At the time they had been working together only a few weeks – her first in Homicide – but it felt like a lot longer now and her life before it further away. Brown was one of the cardinal points as Madison navigated her course in the Homicide Department: she had decided she would learn from him whether he liked it or not. Then Salinger happened.

With any luck one of the Park Rangers at the Hoh Station would be able to give her the exact coordinates where the remains had been found and her GPS system would get her there. The fact that there had not been a formal identification yet and the case belonged to Jefferson County made her nothing more than a hiker with a badge. She hoped it would be enough.

Madison finished her coffee – the scent so much better than the taste – and ventured out onto the deck.

'*Did you think about the forest incident? I mean, longer than for a few seconds during your day.*'

'No.'

Madison zipped up her jacket, narrowing her eyes against the rush of wind. It wasn't the first time she had gone back into those woods and one day, she knew, they would be just woods again – old-growth trees and valleys and a canopy so thick even the light was green – but not yet.

She leant against the rail, hands deep in her pockets, her gaze already past Kingston, past its pretty main street with the charming cafés, drawn to the line of shadow that marked the mountains of the Olympic Peninsula and their secrets.

John Cameron lay on his bunk. Slowly, one inmate at a time, the sound had died away after he had returned to his cell and the usual calls and shouts bounced back and forth against the concrete walls.

He wrapped himself back in his own personal silence. The outside world was no more than an occasional interruption; his eyes followed the faint crack on the ceiling above him and he ran the tip of his index finger against the rough texture of the blanket. He fell into the memories as if into bottomless waters.

August 28, 1985. Fishing with David and James at Jackson Pond; the blue van and the dirty rags reeking of chloroform. Waking up blindfolded, tied up with rope. *It's not personal, it's business.* Then the awful choking and gasping and the men had left, taking David's body with them. David. It had sounded like death; the men had believed it was; James had believed it, and so had he.

He thought about a vicious man falling into a pit five years later, the spikes Cameron had sharpened going through his body. He thought that it wasn't over, never had been, and Nathan had to go through it all over again, only this time it was even worse. He thought this cell would hold his rage only for so long.

He knew as if he could see her that Detective Madison would be going where David had been found. He would be there too; his eyes remained on the tiny crack until it was all he could see.

Shouts from the next cell along did not reach him; the guard looked in, looked away and walked on.

Madison hit Highway 101 at the full legal speed. The weather was bright; the sun had retreated behind a veil of thin clouds. She looked ahead and asked the deity in charge of crime-scene analysis for as much light as could be spared. The local forensics unit would have already swept the area but Madison needed her own sense of it even if time had washed away everything except the boy's name.

A time would come when she would ask Cameron about that day. She wondered whether it would ever happen, whether the remains that had been discovered, collected, examined and tested held enough truth to launch a proper investigation. Madison's background in forensics was strong and her belief in evidence was sacrosanct. If this had been any other case she would have said that the chances of a prosecution after twenty-five years of Pacific Northwest weather and wilderness were nil. Yet she saw heavy clouds coming in from the west and almost slammed her foot down on the accelerator, weaving around a slow-moving tourist's people carrier with Idaho plates.

She was here because it was not any other case, and whatever trace evidence had been left Madison suspected could not be put in a bag and tagged and would be measured in ways she couldn't even comprehend yet.

She pulled into the parking lot at the Hoh Station, mercifully close to empty this time of year, and dug into the trunk for her walking boots and wet weather gear. The forest was damp and it breathed through a shroud of moist air whether it was raining or not.

Madison adjusted the ankle holster and shoved her small camera and the rest of her kit in a light backpack. She adjusted the straps on her shoulders and suddenly she was adjusting the straps on the ballistic vest Nathan Quinn had just pulled on, her hands trembling from cold and dread, Quinn looking away. She had practically forced him to wear it that night, when she still thought Harry Salinger would come after them with something as mundane as ammunition.

Madison shrugged her shoulders and settled her pack on her back. The Park Ranger, a foot taller and two foot wider than Madison, looked her over.

'You understand the file is with the Jefferson County authorities, Detective,' he said.

'I know. What I need is the location, that's all.'

It was a pleasant office: a large window onto the forest and maps on every wall.

'You're hiking to the spot?'

'I'm planning to, yes.'

'Why?'

'I want to make a few notes, for what it's worth.'

'Jumping the gun a little?'

'Maybe.'

'Why?'

'Because it's my day off.'

The Ranger smiled. 'Let me make a couple of calls.'

'Thank you.'

Madison gave him some space and wandered over to the wall of maps. She traced the network of hiking trails with the tip of her index finger: many she had walked, some she had seen in every weather, most she knew at least a little.

It told her one thing clearly: one of the men who had kidnapped the boys must have known the area very well. Someone had picked the clearing where the boys had been tied up, someone had picked the spot where David Quinn had been buried. Late August hikers around and yet no one had seen them.

Madison followed the winding route of the Upper Hoh Road, almost parallel to the river. They had known exactly where to go and how to avoid gatecrashers at their private party.

Rugged Ridge, Indian Pass, Owl Creek – the trail lines crossed and weaved across the terrain.

Madison was so absorbed by the topographical map she barely heard the Ranger approach.

'I've spoken with my boss. I'll take you,' he said.

For a moment Madison didn't understand what he had meant.

'Thank you, but I don't want to take up your time. I'll just—'

'I'm coming off my shift and there's a weather front closing in. If you want to get there before it, I'm taking you. It's no bother.'

Madison didn't quite believe that but accepted with thanks.

The Ranger – late thirties, fair hair and blue eyes – led the way. They would drive a short while and hike the rest of the way. He introduced himself: Ryan Curtis. He sounded like California with ten years of Pacific Northwest on top. He drove a pick-up truck that made Madison's old Civic look city smart.

'You don't remember me, do you?' he said as they drove west on the Upper Hoh Road.

Madison turned. She had been sure they had never met before.

'I was on duty that night, led the SWAT team to where you guys were.' Ranger Curtis turned sharply into a side road, the paving finishing almost immediately. He didn't give her time to reply. 'A lot of things would have changed in the last twenty-five years – trees, shrubs, terrain shifted by rain, roots, water streams, what have you.'

He engaged the handbrake with a sound like crunching metal and looked at Madison. 'I'm sure I don't need to tell you this but this is not a garden, this is not like they found the remains in someone's back yard. You don't get bears and cougars in your back yard. It's a miracle they were found in the first place.'

The air was clammy and surprisingly warm for January. In spite of his size Curtis moved lightly and quickly through the undergrowth. The trail had disappeared half an hour earlier and Madison had realized why he had offered to take her: where they were going there was no friendly path and pretty views over the streams, no photo opportunities for weekend hikers. This forest did not want to be visited and it did not want to be photographed.

Curtis did not make allowances for Madison: he said at the start that she should follow his steps exactly and then had just pressed on. He was probably part elk, Madison mused, because she needed the joke to distract herself from the coppery scent she knew wasn't really there.

They proceeded under the spruces and the multi-layered canopy, changing direction to go around boulders and ravines. Low branches snagged her pack and the ground grew uneven; jagged rocks protruded through the dirt and tested their footing as the light changed and the silence deepened.

Madison kept herself three feet behind Curtis, glad for her running stamina and the lack of conversation.

'Not far now,' he said without turning ten minutes later.

When the rain started falling it was so light that Madison didn't notice until she felt a single drop on her brow. She looked up: patches of sky through the branches, mostly clouds, some pale blue.

'We're here.' Curtis moved to one side and pointed.

They were in a narrow valley; under a Western Hemlock, tall shrubs around it, a perimeter of yellow crime-scene tape flapped in the breeze.

Curtis had been right to say what he had said in the truck: Madison reminded herself that what had happened here had happened twenty-five years ago. She had been in primary school, her mother had been alive, and she had never been to Seattle. Everything had changed, grown or died away and what was before her was only in part what the kidnappers – the killers, Madison corrected herself – had seen.

She approached the yellow tape slowly: the hole revealed itself, smooth edges and only a few feet deep.

'It was almost on the surface; rain must have washed the earth away over the years,' Curtis said behind her.

It was so small. The impact of what she was seeing hit Madison almost physically: he had been buried curled up and lying on one side. They were in a hurry, they wanted out of the woods quick and they had no time to waste. They dug a hole just about big enough and deep enough to lay the child inside it; they covered it up; they left.

Madison took off her pack and reached for the camera inside. She started taking pictures – the flash working hard in the growing shade – to do something tangible against the flutter of anger in her chest. That pitiful hole told her something else: they had killed a child and they didn't care; it wasn't a burial, it was a dumping site.

She shoved her feelings to one side, took out her notebook and went over the paltry facts.

'Where is the clearing from here? The place you led the SWAT team to that night?'

Curtis pointed west. 'About a mile that way.'

'Terrain similar to the one we crossed?'

'Pretty much. Hard ground to cover fast if you're not familiar with it.'

Madison took notes on the standard issue police notepad.

'It was August,' she said. 'August 28, 1985. No rain that day, I checked. Is there a chance they could drive their van part of the way?'

'There used to be a narrow paved road to a weather station up that way, but when we stopped using the station the road got pretty rough and now it's almost covered over. If they knew about it, it could have taken them almost to the clearing.'

'When was the weather station abandoned?'

'Early 1980s, I think.'

'That's not the way we went. We left the car and hiked a while.'

'It wasn't on the maps. It was an old service track that led nowhere. No reason why you would have known about it.'

Madison felt the frayed end of a thought slipping away and she grabbed at it.

'*They* did,' Madison said. 'The killers did. Do any hiking trails cross the service track or the route from there to here?'

'Not that I know.'

'Which means the children they had left behind would not be found quickly. And if they buried David Quinn far enough from the children he wouldn't be found at all.'

Madison looked around. No footprints, no tire tracks, no tool marks, no shirt fabric snagged on a branch. It was a long list of things they did not have and would never have.

She laid her measuring tape on the long side, took a picture and wrote down the dimensions. The Crime Scene Unit would have already done all that; she did it anyway. Roots pushed out of the side walls and insect life had already begun to claim back the grave.

She stood on the edge of the pit. Had the earth changed because it covered a murdered child? How could that change be measured? Madison crouched on the ground and touched the soil. Cold and damp. The child had become a body and the body had become human remains. Rain and earth had passed through it as it disintegrated. Something, Madison thought – the killers must have left something behind, something that had stayed with David Quinn and waited for them to find him.

'We need to head back, Detective.'

Madison straightened up and nodded.

'Those shrubs all around the pit?' Curtis pointed. 'They're Dicentra Formosa.'

Madison looked blank.

'Bleeding Heart,' he said. 'That's the common name. Flowers are real pretty.'

Madison shouldered her pack and pulled up her hood. Above her and out of sight, beyond the layers of green, a rapid flutter of wings started off and faded into the distance.

The journey back was faster in spite of the coming dusk and Curtis wasn't interested in small talk. They reached his truck and before

Madison knew it he was already pulling in next to her Civic in the Hoh Station parking lot.

'Thank you.' Madison said. 'I mean it. For getting the SWAT team to us as well. I'm sorry I didn't remember.'

'No problem. I'm not surprised really. I had never seen anything like it.'

'You and me both.'

She left the truck, got into her Honda and drove off. The pick-up's lights followed her until the exit to Forks.

Madison felt winded and tired as if she had sat an exam and not even understood the questions. Later, sitting in a booth on the ferry, her hands around a cup of tea she was not drinking, she realized she had taken a vow, whether the child was David Quinn or not.

She was still making notes when the ferry docked.

Nathan Quinn checked the round clock on the wall. Three minutes to go to his call with Scott Newton, Prosecutor, who represented the County in the case against John Cameron. As per Quinn's standing instructions to Doyle, a senior associate from Quinn Locke had represented Cameron while Quinn was incapacitated but there was never any question that he would revert to his original role as Cameron's attorney.

Quinn wanted Cameron out of jail as quickly as possible. Every day he spent inside KCJC was a day in which he was a target and a day in which he might be pushed to defend himself with maximum force to stay alive. It might be something the inmates would pay good money to see, but Quinn just wanted him out of there fast. Even protective custody – who was being protected? he wondered – was barely more than wishful thinking.

Technically Quinn was only consulting on the case: he was still on pain medication and officially the Quinn Locke attorney had to sign off on any deals. However, everybody knew who made the decisions.

Quinn checked the clock. It was time.

'Let me understand,' Scott Newton said. 'Your client attacked Harry Salinger and cut him up like a paper doll, and you think Attempted Murder is an overreaction?'

'I think Assault in the First is an overreaction. Honestly? I think Assault in the Third would be an overreaction. The only thing John Cameron was attempting was to restrain and detain Harry Salinger *after* he had admitted to four counts of murder and one of kidnapping a minor,' Nathan Quinn replied.

'I can see how you'd like this to turn into a citizen's arrest gone badly wrong.'

'No jury is ever going to give you Attempted Murder, Scott. Not when Salinger is about to be declared insane, not when they can look at the photographs of the cage he had built for the boy.'

Newton was quiet. Salinger had built two cages and one had been for Quinn. 'Salinger could have died. Everything Cameron did to him could have led to his death.'

'Do you know how we know that it wasn't Attempted Murder?' Quinn asked. 'Salinger is still alive. It is not accidental.'

Newton didn't want to go to trial: there was too much risk involved in prosecuting the man who had physically apprehended Harry Salinger, the Blueridge Killer, and he had no idea where he would find an impartial jury. On Mars, maybe.

'What are you offering?' he asked Quinn.

'What's on the table?' Quinn replied.

Newton snorted. 'Assault in the First, and my boss will be justified to kick me down to traffic violations.'

'Do you have proof of intent? And by that I mean actual proof of deliberation and intent to cause great bodily harm?'

'I have Salinger's medical reports.'

'I'm sure they are a fascinating read but – I ask you again – do you have intent?'

Newton did not reply.

'Second, do you have a weapon?'

'They are still looking.' He sounded weak even to himself.

'They found Salinger's gun pretty quickly, and the tools he used to set up the cages.' The silence on the line stretched to a long pause. Quinn closed his eyes; his head rested against the pillow and his energy ebbed and flowed unpredictably with his medication. 'Reckless endangerment,' he said.

'I'm not even taking it into consideration.'

'You can take your time and consider what you can prove in front of a jury. They will have to ponder how hard it would be to restrain a man of Salinger's . . . temperament.'

'We're talking about John Cameron here.'

'Who has no priors and did not resist arrest.'

'Nathan, have you looked at Salinger's medical sheet?' Newton asked. 'Have you *seen* what he did to him?'

'Yes.'

'Do you call that "reckless endangerment"?'

Quinn did not know what to call it and he realized that notion applied to much of Cameron's behavior. 'You don't want to take this to trial,' he said.

'I'll do what I have to keep him inside for as long as the law will allow me.'

'Good luck.'

Chapter 5

The man stood by the tall window in the white recreation room and watched as the sun dipped below the trees. Each minute brought a new shadow and the familiar tightening of fear in his narrow chest as the line of darkness stalked the concrete building. He watched and waited. Soon it would be time and he would be alone until the sun rose again.

He felt the room emptying, the television on the high bracket tuned to the news and the steps behind him.

'Somebody's coming,' he said without turning around.

The view didn't let him go until he felt the hand on his arm and slowly, reluctantly, he turned.

'It's getting dark,' he said. 'We should go; we shouldn't stay here.'

'Time for bed.'

'We shouldn't stay when it's dark.'

'Yes, I heard you, same as yesterday and the day before. Come on, my friend, time for bed.'

'It's not personal, it's business.'

'Sure it is.'

He stood by the bed in his room, plain walls around him and a three-drawer chest for all he owned in this world.

From the top of the dresser he picked up the stump of a gray crayon and raised his hand; he closed his eyes and drew a long shaky line all along the white wall; it joined dozens of similar gray lines all over the small cell. Up and down the walls, wherever he could reach.

It was easier to let him do it than take the crayon away and go through the horrendous fits of terror that plagued him.

He brushed his teeth and put on his pajamas. They were white cotton and hung loose on his thin shoulders. He washed his hands; the nails were cut to the quick and yet grimy with garden dirt. He scrubbed them clean and sat down.

'As I lay me down to sleep,' he started, 'I pray the Lord my soul to keep.'

He slid under the heavy blankets and the shivering started almost immediately.

A knock on the door and Thomas put his head around.

'Ready?'

Vincent Foley, forty-eight, shook his head. 'Somebody's coming,' he whispered and rolled himself up into a tight ball.

Thomas Reed, psychiatric nurse at the Seattle Walters Institute, turned off the light and closed the door. A soft click told Vincent that the door was locked. Then again, what was a simple wooden door against what was coming for him?

He hurried to finish. 'If I should die before I wake, I pray the Lord my soul to take.'

In the cell, shadows and lights began to move over the pastel drawings on the walls as if the lines themselves were shifting. Vincent squeezed his eyes shut; all through the night, above him and around him, the drawings crept and crawled.

Chapter 6

In the relative gloom of his hospital room Nathan Quinn listened to his own breathing. Regular and steady. It was still a surprise to him that he was alive when he had fully expected to die. Instead he had woken up to a different world: Jack was in jail and David had been found.

The Jefferson County officers had taken a swab of the cells inside his cheek for DNA-comparing purposes, a swift and routine procedure they had completed in seconds. Now all there was to do was wait.

His waking hours were a combination of pain, boredom and sheer unadulterated fury. His temper, disciplined by years in the courtroom, seemed to elude its usual filters. His body was a prisoner of the injuries but his intelligence was not, and he had argued with the doctors to reduce the painkillers as much as possible because he could cope with the pain but the slow, thick dullness that coated his mind was not something he could bear.

All he knew at that point was that he needed to think and think clearly: the results from the DNA test would come in the next few days and then the world would change again, shift on its axis as it had done at least twice before in his life. This time he would be ready.

If the remains were not David, if there was another boy out there lost in the woods, would that make things better? Quinn didn't know how to feel about it or what to wish for. To have David back meant he had experienced that dreadful moment, that blow that had ended his life. If not, then another child had gone through that horror, another family had been torn apart.

He breathed deeply and realized not for the first time that grief felt like both a weight and a hollow in his chest. He went back to what he knew, thinking like an attorney, like the prosecuting attorney he once was. He closed his eyes and felt a familiar spark of anger. Good. Anger was better than pain.

The numbers were against them: there is no statute of limitation for murder in Washington State; however, he could not remember a single case where a defendant had been successfully prosecuted for a twenty-five-year-old murder without trace evidence, witnesses or confessions.

The officers had been reticent; their chances were negligible. The best they could hope for was a name for the victim. *Breathe in, breathe out, ignore the pain*. A name could be a very powerful thing, even if it was all they had. A name was the beginning: five years after the abduction a man had fallen and been impaled in what hunters call a trapping pit. His name was Timothy Gilman and he had died as he had lived. John Cameron was about eighteen years old at the time.

For twenty years Nathan Quinn had believed that Cameron had killed Gilman – his first victim – because he had met him accidentally and recognized him as one of the kidnappers, maybe even the man who had given him the scars on his arms. Cameron knew that there wasn't enough evidence to take him to court and that that fight would surely kill Quinn's family as if David was to die each day again.

Quinn, then working in the Prosecutor's Office, had found out entirely by chance and one could say that his reading of the events was based on circumstantial evidence. One could say an eighteen-year-old boy does not spend days digging a hole in the snow to lure a man to his death. And so Quinn didn't speak of it; the case stayed unsolved; life went on.

Distant sounds from the ward drifted into the room, voices and footsteps and the chiming of medical equipment. Quinn felt the weight of the blankets; his tall frame had lost weight since December and he was aware of every cell of his body struggling to heal itself.

He thought about fear: what it does to a man and what a man will do under its talons.

Chapter 7

Madison woke up at 6 a.m. on Monday, brewed herself a particularly strong cup of coffee and drove to work with a box of peanut butter Granola Thins and a half-eaten banana on the seat next to her. She had stayed up late preparing her argument and hoped that getting Lieutenant Fynn good and early, before his day became inevitably soured by reality, would help.

She nodded hello to Jenner, the Desk Sergeant, and quickly climbed the stairs to the detectives' room. The previous tour was out and her shift had not checked in yet. The room was a combination of beaten-up desks, worn gray metal filing cabinets, and new computer screens with cables winding under the tables.

Fynn arrived half an hour before the official beginning of the shift, and clocked Madison at her desk. She gave him a couple of minutes and then knocked on his door.

'Thought you might want to speak to me about something,' he said, and beckoned her in.

'I'd like to work the David Quinn case. I know it's a cold case and the Cold Case Team will handle it, but they have a full plate and I could start getting everything together and go over the original kidnap investigation. If the boy is not Quinn I would still like to work the case. Aside from the remains there are no new leads and it's going to be so low on their priorities it will never get a look-in.'

'Good morning, Madison. How was your weekend?'

'Very good.'

'This is when you ask me how my weekend was.'

'How was it, sir?'

'Not bad, thank you. Could have done with another one. What brings you to my office, Detective?'

'I'd like to work the David Quinn case.'

'Okay.'

'Okay?'

'Yes. I spoke with Willis from the Cold Case Team on Saturday. They are up to here right now.' He drew a line up to his chin. 'And the remains will not give us much to work with.'

'I know.'

'Something else.' Fynn gazed steadily at Madison. 'The one surviving witness is not exactly talking at the moment and nobody wants to waste a trip to KCJC to sit in a cell with John Cameron and came away with bupkis.'

'I see. That's why I get handed the case. Because Cameron and I do our nails and braid our hair together?'

'Pretty much. Do you care?'

'Not a bit. If they don't want it, I'm happy to have it.'

'That's what I thought. Did you go to the site?'

'Yes.'

'And?'

'They dug it fast and just deep enough that an animal wouldn't dig him out overnight.'

'Well, here's how it's going to go: we wait for the DNA result – which nobody's in a big hurry to do in the first place since we have hundreds of fresh cases – and if it's Quinn, it's yours; if it isn't, it stays with Jefferson County because we don't know where the child started out from and the forensic anthropologist will have to get to work on an ID before anything else.'

By the time Madison got back to her desk the room was full and buzzing with activity and for the first time she wondered whether she should hope the child was Nathan Quinn's brother. It was a child, and that was all that mattered.

It took nine days for an infinitesimal sliver of mitochondrial DNA to confirm beyond doubt that the human remains found in the Hoh River Forest were in fact David Quinn. As soon as it was official Madison collected the Hoh River kidnap file from Records: she wasn't going to interview Cameron without knowing every detail of the original investigation.

He hadn't spoken about it in twenty-five years, as far as she knew, and the chances of him talking now were less than zero. Then again, the chances of Cameron talking to anyone about anything were generally less than zero. The kidnap was merely one more entry on the extremely long list of no-go subjects. Nevertheless, they had a body and cause of death and there would be an investigation, there would be questions and, somewhere inside the mind of John Cameron, there was the truth.

Thus it was that two days after her last visit Alice Madison found herself back in the King County Justice Complex meeting cell, without her piece and without much hope for meaningful conversation either.

She thought of John Cameron as a twelve-year-old boy, terrified and alone in the woods, and she hoped that boy would want to help her after she told him that the child they found was David.

The cell was warm, unpleasantly so, and it smelled of vending machine coffee from the previous visitors. Whatever the day might be like on the outside, in this room the natural light fell milky pale and ineffective on the sparse furnishing. Madison had gone over her conversation strategy three times when she heard the metal lock of the main door clunk open.

A single guard came in – she had seen him a couple of times before. He looked like he'd seen off a few decades working for the Department of Corrections and was there to stay. The tag said 'Miller, B'.

'He's not coming, Detective,' he said.

Madison stood up, the chair pushed back and scraping the floor. *That* she hadn't planned for.

'He's *not* coming?'

She realized that she sounded almost personally offended but – honest to God – she didn't think she could help it.

'He said he knows the DNA was a match,' the guard continued, 'and to come back when you know something he doesn't.'

Madison kept her face blank; she nodded, put her notebook back in her jeans back-pocket and pushed the chair under the table. Tidy and ready for the next visitors. The guard's sharp blue eyes followed her every move.

'Okay then,' she said.

'Don't feel bad. It's more than anyone else ever got out of him.'

'I know.'

'Unless you want us to haul him in here . . .'

'No, thanks. No need for that today,' she said to the guard's obvious relief. 'I'll just have to survive without the witty repartee.'

'Don't we all.'

Back in her car, in the jail's parking lot, with the windows fogged up and the engine running, Madison allowed herself a good full minute of unrestricted swearing. Once she got that out of her system, she put the engine in gear and drove back to the precinct. It is what it is, her grandmother used to say.

Chapter 8

Carl Doyle waited by the elevator doors, his reflection mirrored in the brushed steel. He looked immaculate in his gray pinstripe, white shirt and burgundy tie. He had been running Quinn Locke from a bench outside Quinn's hospital room – gate-keeper and executive assistant.

Todd Hollis, Quinn Locke's chief investigator, had spent an hour with Quinn and left a few minutes earlier, his mood much bleaker than when he had arrived. Doyle had done what Quinn had asked and now waited by the elevator. He didn't know what this was about, only that Hollis had disagreed and Quinn was going ahead anyway. Doyle was uneasy: Hollis knew his stuff; if he had had objections they would have been to the point and well considered. Doyle straightened his tie, fussed with his cuffs and looked at his watch.

The elevator doors slid open and Benny Craig from Quinn Locke staggered out carrying two silver photography cases and a folded tripod stuck under one arm. Benny had been with the firm six months and looked thirteen. Something in Carl Doyle's demeanor told him to keep quiet and just do as he was told.

'Everything?' Doyle asked.

'Everything,' Benny replied.

Doyle started down the corridor, Benny following. Around them the life of the hospital took no notice as it hummed and bustled in its daily workings.

Alice Madison balanced the plate of chocolate cake on the edge of the desk and raised her paper cup. Detective Andrew Dunne's birthday was an occasion to celebrate and it had drawn officers from all over the precinct.

Dunne and his partner Spencer had been a joy to work with from the beginning. Looking around the busy room Madison spotted Detective Chris Kelly and his partner Tony Rosario, with paper cups in hand. Chris Kelly had not been a joy to work with – in fact Madison believed that Joy would flutter, wither and drop dead if it came within six feet of Kelly. They had ignored each other from the beginning of the year and she hoped it would last.

Spencer raised his cup – fizzy yellow soda under the neon lights – and called for silence. He had known Dunne from the Academy and his toasts were sure to touch on his friend's unmarried status, his Irish red temper and a large number of embarrassing events that had never made it into the reports.

'My name is Nathan Quinn—'

The voice cut through the air and Madison just about jumped out of her skin. Someone shushed the group and increased the volume with the television remote.

'It's the news on Kiro,' someone else said. The room froze into silence.

For the longest moment Madison didn't turn. She knew what they were all looking at: they were looking at the man who had done what Quinn had done and survived. Each and every one of them had wondered about the injuries. There had been no pictures and no tabloid exclusive.

Madison had not been allowed to see him since; now she would have to see him for the first time in a room full of strangers, all of them curious and none of them with any idea about what that night had been really like.

'*My name is Nathan Quinn—*'

Madison turned. He'd lost weight and his dark hair was longer: Nathan Quinn in a head-and-shoulders shot – a blue linen shirt open at the collar, no tie. A hospital room behind him, enough light to see him clearly. A fine red line slashed through his left brow and ran into his hairline, another ran from the corner of his mouth to under his left ear, one started under his jaw and disappeared into the open collar, another smaller line over his cheekbone, his lips. The plastic surgeon had done an amazing job, the best anyone could hope. Yet, for now, Nathan Quinn looked like the Devil himself had kicked him out of hell but not without some fun and games.

'*– a few days ago the remains of a child were found in the Hoh River Forest. My brother David was thirteen when he was abducted together with two friends twenty-five years ago. The men who took him killed him and left his friends in the woods. This is an appeal for any kind of information anyone might have which relates to the kidnap or the murder.*'

Madison had seen appeals before: for children, parents, siblings, wives and husbands. Something in Quinn's tone kept a roomful of cops nailed to where they stood, and she sensed the storm coming because she had seen Quinn in action before and he was not the guy who *appeals* for anything.

Quinn raised four fingers of his right hand. '*Four men took the boys and murdered my brother – two hundred thousand dollars on the head of each one of those men.*' He raised the index finger of his left hand. '*One man, or a group of men, planned it – one million dollars.*' Quinn paused, when he spoke again his voice was low and it crackled with menace. '*They didn't ask for a ransom, they didn't ask for a reward. This is what they are going to get today: a bounty on their heads. Did any one of them tell a friend, a brother, a lover what had happened? Would they trust them with their life today?*' Quinn paused. '*Twenty years ago a man named Timothy*

Gilman fell into a trapping pit and died; there is reason to think he was one of the four kidnappers.' Quinn folded one finger back. *'One down, three to go. The others should know, wherever they are, that they are not safe, they are not out of harm's way, and they will be found.'*

The picture held for a moment, then went to black and it cut back to the news anchor, sitting at his desk and clearly thinking that a degree in liberal arts had not prepared him for this.

The room erupted with sound, voices overlapped and someone muted the television. Madison was still inside the voice and inside the words. It was not an appeal, it was a warning: Quinn had pitched it hard and somewhere out there men had heard the words and understood the message. *And who on Earth was Timothy Gilman?*

It was a chemical change. A catalyst dropped into an otherwise inert solution. *My name is Nathan Quinn.* In offices, in homes, in bars, in television window displays, on ferries, online, everywhere with a screen. People stopped, people looked, and people wondered. After a while it wasn't even necessary to hear the words. Quinn raising four fingers of his right hand, then the index finger of his left. The scars said something about the man that words could not. And in some of those places, where the tourists don't visit and the bartenders know each customer by name and felony type, a few of those customers began to scan the usual crowd and ask themselves who was around twenty-five years ago, who would take three children into the woods, and who would bury one in a shallow grave.

Today is a good day; today there are one million and six hundred thousand reasons to be curious.

Carl Doyle, back in his office at Quinn Locke, had watched the news with the rest of the staff. The camera and lights were back in the stock room and Benny Craig was telling his tale for the nth time to a pretty young secretary with a blonde ponytail.

Doyle didn't want to answer any questions and had closed the door behind him. Now he knew why Tod Hollis had disagreed. He understood Quinn's need to give his brother the justice he had been denied; who wouldn't? What Doyle couldn't even begin to describe was what it was like to stand four feet away from Quinn while he spoke those words. Benny was young; he was a sweet-natured if slightly dull young man who had little or no real understanding of what he had witnessed. But Doyle did, and he picked up a pile of paperwork and began to file, sort and organize because he needed to fill his mind and his hands with the ordinary and the mundane, and because the steel in Quinn's voice had been sharp enough to cut his breath in two.

Dunne, still holding his paper cup, came close to Madison and spoke quietly. 'You asked the boss for the Quinn case, right?'

'Yup.'

'Nice one. Have you looked at the initial report from Jefferson County?'

Madison turned her back to the room so that her words were for Dunne alone. 'There was nothing at the scene. Just the remains and the hole in the dirt they came from.'

'No trace evidence of any kind?'

Madison shook her head.

'Medical Examiner?'

'I'm waiting for Fellman's report. And the forensic anthropologist's – if we can get one.'

Dunne ran a hand through his hair, exasperated by the seemingly inexhaustible ways the world could find to make their work day impossible. 'What is Quinn thinking putting out that kind of reward twenty-five years after the event? About a tenth of it would have been enough to get any information there was to have. All that money is just a beacon for every greedy loser from here to Miami, and each one of them will call *us* to claim it.'

Madison did not reply: everything Quinn did had reasons behind reasons.

'Do you know this Gilman guy?' she asked Dunne.

'No, never heard of him. Twenty years ago my biggest problem was who to take to prom and how to afford a limo.'

Madison looked around: the room was emptying out, everybody back to their duties and Dunne's cake reduced to a few sticky crumbs on a plate.

'Where's the boss?' she asked him.

'With the Chief of D. Can't wait for his delight when he hears about the appeal.'

'Do you call that an appeal?'

'No, I call that a mistake. A big juicy one too.'

Dunne shrugged on his jacket. 'Spence and I are going to Jimmy's for a quick drink before my birthday celebrations with the heavenly Stacey Roberts from Traffic. Are you coming?'

Madison smiled. 'Thank you but no. I need to find out about Gilman before I can go to Quinn and have an argument with him about it.'

'Have fun.'

'Counting on it. Dunne,' she said to his back, 'Stacey has three brothers the size of boulders. Not that she needs them – she shoots competitively.'

Dunne tightened the knot on his tie and smiled. 'Nothing like a date with a woman who can shoot out your tires, right?'

'Happy birthday.'

Madison brought the file back to her desk and the small pool of light from her anglepoise. The room was blessedly quiet; her own shift was over and her colleagues dispersed to the lives they had when they were not there.

In his short time on Earth Timothy Gilman had managed to make few friends and many enemies: what had started as typical juvenile delinquent behavior had quickly graduated to a range of felonies that spoke to her about a deep violent streak. Gilman had cultivated it like another man might work on his aptitude for numbers. Some hard time upstate for Assault in the Second Degree was no doubt a pretty good accomplishment on his personal achievements list.

Madison sipped coffee from a ceramic mug with a wrap-around color picture of Mount Rainier – blue sky behind the grey rocky top and the glaciers. In the end, somewhere in the woods between Seattle and Mount Rainier, in a trapping pit, hikers had found Gilman's body after the first spring thaw, impaled on long spikes. One night the previous winter he had walked out of his local bar and disappeared as so much coal dust in the wind.

Madison ran her index finger down the list of interviews: no one knew how he had gotten from the bar to the woods or even whether he'd fallen in by accident or by design. She read the file twice from top to bottom and all she could garner from it was that the life Gilman had lived in those pages had been infused with blunt destructiveness and willful harm. Having said that, there was no connection that she could see to the Hoh River abduction. The bulk of his issues with law and order had to do with the low-level enforcer work that seemed to fit so well his particular set of skills.

She made notes as she read, feeling that she was reaching back in time half-blind and trying to grasp something that might not be there at all. The thing she went back to – the only thing she had – was the knowledge that Nathan Quinn would not trifle with Gilman's name just as he would not trifle with threats. *One down, three to go.* Quinn *had* something, and it sure wasn't in those yellowed pages she had picked up from Records.

Madison wandered over to the office fridge and found her only contribution: an emergency Strawberry Yoo-hoo left over from a late night stake-out weeks earlier. She unscrewed the top and gulped it down to drown the taste of the percolated coffee. It actually tasted pink.

If Quinn knew the identity of one of the kidnappers it made no sense that he had let it go, that he had not turned Gilman's life inside out and upside down to get to the truth – unless he had found out *after* Gilman was dead. In which case – Madison looked at the meager file – all Quinn had had was the length and breadth of a life spent hurting people, and no answers.

Madison picked up her cell phone and speed-dialed.

'Doyle.' He answered on the second ring.

'It's Madison. Sorry for the late hour.'

'No problem. I'm still in the office and I bet so are you.'

' 'Fraid so. Carl, I need to see him. The sooner the better. Tomorrow morning would be good.'

'Do you have any idea how many media requests I've had since the appeal went out?'

'A good number?'

'Twenty-two. Do you know how many he has granted?'

'Zero?'

'Zero.'

'I'm not media, Carl. I'm on the David Quinn case.'

'I'll speak to him in the morning.'

They said their goodbyes and Madison decided she was done with the day. The drive home went quickly, maybe too much so. The day's work might be done but there was something to be said for the feeling of suspension, for the deferral of any physical action or endeavor that only heavy traffic could provide. She wanted to keep driving to keep thinking.

She drove south past her exit and ended up making a loop around Normandy Park. The dense wooded area was a pitch black pause in the pattern of lights. It was a cold early February night and yet Madison rolled down the window a few inches to smell the salt in the air. Her cell phone on the passenger seat started vibrating just as she was looping back. She saw the caller ID and picked up.

'Sarge,' she said.

'Madison,' Detective Sergeant Kevin Brown replied. 'Did you see it?'

'Me and everyone else with a screen.'

'You picked up Gilman's file yet?'

Madison smiled. Brown might be on medical leave but he was still her partner – her much senior partner – and she missed their conversations.

'Yup, pretty straightforward low-level muscle, some time in jail – not enough if you ask me – and a whole load of nothing regarding how his final hours went. Nothing at all linking him to the abduction – on the surface, that is. Quinn wouldn't put his name out there unless it meant something.'

'I agree. Quinn's message was about greed, fear and that one name.'

'When is the physical, Sarge? When can we expect you back?'

'I have some tests tomorrow. I'll let you know as soon as I'm done. Boredom is worse than getting shot in the head.'

'I'll take your word for it.'

'You're going to see Quinn?'

'Yes, tomorrow.'

'First time since?'

'Yes.'

'Look, that man is made out of some kind of metal we don't even have a name for. You can push him if you need to.'

'Don't worry, I'm not going with flowers and balloons. He's still the same person he was before the forest, and so am I.'

Later, as she was parking her Civic next to her grandparents' car, Madison wondered if she had in fact lied to Brown – unintentionally, sure, but a lie nevertheless. It had slipped out so very easily and

Madison was glad that they had not been face to face. Once Brown was back she would have to accept that the 'all good, nothing to talk about' bull she had delivered Dr. Robinson would go right out of the window.

The file from Jefferson County contained pictures of the boy's remains in situ, the depressed skull fracture evident even before what remained of the body was moved. Madison asked herself if Gilman had been involved what remained of him, what had he left of himself in that hole.

She made herself a grilled cheese sandwich – Jarlsberg and sourdough. She had it on the sofa with a glass of milk, watching *The Philadelphia Story*, and fell asleep just as the *True Love* sailed in the marble pool.

Chapter 9

Manny Oretremos made the sign of the cross once and then, for safety, he made it again. Inside his cell in the King County Justice Complex he sat on the bed – because kneeling would have been too obvious – and prayed for rain. Not just a few drops or a little drizzle – he prayed for the heavens to open and for rain to fall that would bring to mind a flood of biblical proportions. Failing that, a heart attack that would incapacitate him and send him to the medical wing. Anything that would prevent him from having to go and do.

Instead, as the minutes passed, he sat on his bunk, gripping the thin blanket with his sweaty hands and waiting for his yard time, and his doom.

Manny was small, never a good thing if involved with the kind of people he had known all his life, and in order to gain their respect and a modicum of acceptance he had found himself doing a series of things that – as many a high school teacher had predicted – would land him straight into a place with no front door key.

This was only the last of a long list of must-dos, have-tos, can't-get-out-ofs, that pushed him and dragged him to a new level of complete misery.

It had started weeks earlier, it relied on determination and chance, and – one way or the other – it would surely end in disaster.

The vial had been passed to him at breakfast time, small enough to be easily concealed in the brown bag that had contained his take-away lunch. He had eaten his dry eggs and hash from the molded tray like it was radioactive. All he needed to do was carry the vial until the time was right, then use it quickly.

Manny was already doing twenty-five to life; being part of this would be a ticket to make the rest of his life there a little easier, something to be proud of when he was old and frail and still incarcerated.

The plan required a number of people to be in the exact right positions at the exact right time. Opportunity and readiness, they had told him. They had made it sound like a military operation and yet Manny knew that betting money was involved, and a status hike for each participant – maybe up to a dozen inmates. Some of the guys couldn't wait to get out there.

It had been weeks earlier and since then the two-inch glass vial had burned a hole in his mattress. Something, he reflected, the con-tents would have done if any had spilled on his skin.

Manny shut his eyes and prayed for rain.

Madison woke up in her bed and with sudden clarity remembered that she was due in court that morning to be a witness for the pros-ecution in a six-month-old robbery/murder case. She didn't know when she would be called and she might very well be tied up for hours.

She groaned out loud and made a mental note to call Doyle – as soon as courtesy allowed – and the precinct to remind the boss she'd be out of play. This could very well turn out to be a waste of a day, she thought, then promptly chastised herself because her testimony was part of a case and that was how the legal system worked.

Holding a mug of coffee she stood in front of the open wardrobe and picked trousers and a blazer that would be acceptable in court. Nothing to write to *Vogue* about, but they'd do.

Madison had spent an hour with the prosecuting attorney a couple of weeks earlier to prepare for today and go over the details. The defendants had been in the middle of a petrol station hold-up when the victim walked in. The case was based on eye-witness testimony, ballistic evidence, and DNA from both defendants on shards of broken glass. The defendants had hired separate defense attorneys, tried to cut separate deals, failed and decided to claim coercion. Madison hoped Judge Hugo would be in a particularly foul mood and keep the proceedings as short as legally possible.

On a bench outside courtroom E-207 Madison's mind kept going back to Quinn's appeal, to the barely veiled threat and the promise of a financial reward as dangerous as it was irresistible. Madison looked around at the ordered comings and goings of the courthouse: Quinn had set something in motion and dark tides were already churning under the still waters of Elliott Bay. Those who knew something would be dragged to the surface or drown in the process, and the clock had started ticking last night as Quinn's video had faded to black.

After a restless morning, Madison grabbed a bagel for lunch, was sworn in, testified and released, and the sun had already set by the time she walked into the precinct to check her messages.

Lieutenant Fynn waved her over.

'How did it go?' he asked.

'Okay, I think. The evidence is pretty overwhelming.'

Something in Fynn's manner told her that this wasn't about her testimony.

'Boss?'

'Brown passed the physical but failed the firearms qualification test.'

'But . . .'

'I know. He's going to take it again soon; clearly it's a consequence

of the head injury. His hand–eye coordination is out of whack –
medical term – he cannot carry a gun, he cannot carry a badge.'

It had never occurred to Madison that Brown could fail the test.
It had never occurred to her that he could fail *anything.*

'He told me he'd tried to reach you and I explained you were in
court. Look, let him be tonight. You know him – he sounded pretty
calm but I'm reasonably sure he wanted to put his fist through a
glass window, which really wouldn't help the situation.'

'I'll call him tomorrow.'

'Fine.'

Madison went back to her desk and sat down. Brown's desk
opposite hers was clear of papers and suddenly that alien tidiness
bothered her a great deal. The truth was that Brown had been on
medical leave for as many weeks as they had actually worked together. Nevertheless he *was* the job: he had been teaching her; his
questions had provoked her, irritated her and ultimately advanced
her thinking.

She could very well imagine his frustration at this point and,
worse, the sharp bite of that voice that told him he might never
pass the test.

Madison picked up her cell and speed-dialed. One ring. Two rings.
Maybe Fynn was right and he didn't want to talk.

'Hello,' Brown said.

'Sarge.'

'You heard?'

He sounded alright. Contained, sure, but that was Brown.

'Yes, I did.' She specifically did not say 'I'm sorry' because that was
no help to anyone. He knew how she would feel. 'Sarge, you passed
the physical. *That* was the major hurdle. Shooting is technique, it
can be re-learnt. The body can adapt like we correct the sight on a
sniper's rifle.'

'Very well put.'

'When you're ready, let us go down to the range, take apart the technique and build it up again.'

'I heard you were a good shot before you joined the squad. Is that so?'

'Yes,' Madison replied simply.

She could feel Brown beginning to smile.

'How good are you exactly?'

'National Championships good. Twice.' Madison paused. 'With both hands.'

He was definitely smiling now. 'I'll think about it.'

'You do that.'

'You sound eerily positive.'

'You'd better believe it.'

They rang off and Madison let out her breath. *Damn it.*

Her eyes fell on the round wall clock and she realized that although it was pitch black and evening in Washington State, it was much earlier in Maryland and it wouldn't be rude to call. She dug out a piece of paper from the back pocket of her jeans.

'Detective Frakes? This is Detective Madison, SPD Homicide.'

'Glad you called. Let me just find a quiet spot.'

Madison heard voices in the background.

'I'm visiting my wife's people in Bethesda,' he continued.

'Shall I call at another time?'

'No need. Her sister's Italian and we're getting seven meals a day. They can start without me.'

Now there was quiet on the line and the sound of a door being closed.

'Who's your shift commander?'

'Lieutenant Fynn.'

'Your partner?'

'Detective Sergeant Kevin Brown.'

'Brown. Red hair, early fifties, as stubborn as a mule?'

Madison closed her eyes for a moment. 'The very same.'

'I saw it in *The Seattle Times*,' Detective Frakes said finally. 'I figured at some point I'd get a call. I'm glad you found him – been long enough out there, in the woods.'

'Detective Frakes, you were the primary on David Quinn's kidnap–murder case.'

'It was just called the Hoh River case; you said that and everybody knew what you meant.'

'Yes, it's still the same today.' Madison settled herself on the sofa. 'I'm gathering all the information I can find for the Cold Case team; even having the remains might not be enough to kick-start the investigation.'

'No new evidence found at the scene?'

'No.'

'Was it close to where the boys had been tied up?'

Madison realized in that moment that it wasn't just a name in the file: this man she was talking to on the phone had physically been there at the time, had seen the strands of rope still wound around the trees, and had spoken to the boy John Cameron.

'They buried him about a mile from the clearing.'

'You went to see it.'

'Yes.'

A beat of silence between them. Madison followed the pattern of light on the ceiling. She knew exactly how many dozen hours Detective Frakes had spent trawling the woods and looking for David Quinn. Not even the dogs had managed to follow the trail.

'Detective, I wanted to speak with you because a file is a file and that's all well and good, but there might be other thoughts, links, ideas. Anything that might not have made it into the file at the time, that might have seemed superfluous or too unsubstantiated to note down. I'm saying, if you had even a passing thought about the case that didn't make it into the final report, I'd like to know.'

'I still think about it from time to time, you know. Any cop will tell you, in the long run it's the ones you don't solve that stay with you.'

'Yes, I can see how that would be.' Madison had to let him get to it by himself. How long had he been waiting to talk about it?

'This one was just as awful as they come,' he continued. 'When I saw the boys – they had been taken to a local hospital – they looked dead, white as sheets. The little one, who had the cuts on his arms – he could barely speak. It was sheer terror. I'd never seen anything like it before.'

'Or since.'

'That's right. What happened there was a unique incident. A kidnapping where no ransom was asked and no money changed hands. A boy died of a heart condition, another was injured. It made no sense and now it turns out the boy was murdered.'

Madison knew what he meant: it made no sense because if they had wanted money why not ask for it in exchange for the boys' lives? And if the object was the torture of three children, why leave the other two tied up and alive?

'What did your guts say?'

She could almost see him thinking about it: it was the question you can never ask in court, where all that matters is what you can prove.

'I thought the whole business was about the fathers' restaurant. That was the only link between the boys. The fathers had been doing well with the restaurant – it's still going, isn't it?'

'It is.'

'Frankly, I thought *protection.* Seattle then was not New York or New Jersey: it wasn't *mobbed up* in the same way. But there were groups of people who would take an interest in your affairs if your business was doing well in certain areas. Their names are in the file: we looked hard and we found nothing.'

'What did the fathers say?'

'They said no one had ever approached them about it.'

'Do you think they were lying?'

'Absolutely. And I'm not saying I would have done differently in their shoes. They have one kid dead and two kids too terrified to speak.'

'Did any names ever come up at all? People who might have executed the kidnap or others who might have given the order?'

'I know what you're asking me and the answer is no, I had never heard of Timothy Gilman until I saw Nathan Quinn's appeal on television. We looked at some local bosses who might have been involved but we didn't have a shred of evidence. Even the usual informants kept their mouths shut.'

'Gilman was not on your radar for this?'

'Not for a second. I don't know where Quinn got his information.'

'Did you say no informants came forward at the time?'

'None, zero. The case was poisoned. We ran out of leads in days and after that it just got colder and colder. The brother was on the phone to me every day asking about it and I had nothing to say to him.'

Madison heard the anger and the regret in his voice and she saw a younger Nathan Quinn fighting his grief.

'I retired from the force ten years ago,' he continued. 'There's never been a year since 1985 I don't think about the boys on August 28. Did you find the gold chain on the remains?'

'The gold chain?'

'David Quinn wore a little gold chain with a medal around his neck. Saint Nicholas. His father's relatives gave it to him.'

'I thought he was Jewish.'

'Well, the relatives didn't care. Are you Catholic?'

'No.' Madison had no idea what she was.

'Well, Saint Nicholas is the patron saint of children, for what it's worth.'

'No,' she said, 'there wasn't a gold chain there.'

'Murderers and thieves,' he said.

Someone came into the room; she heard a woman's voice speaking softly.

'Thank you for your time,' Madison said.

'Keep me posted, Detective.'

'I will.'

Madison jotted down a few lines in her notebook. *Protection.* She thought about the silence around the murder of the child spreading around Seattle and Elliott Bay as all the informants withdrew into their holes. *One down, three to go.*

She found Rachel's voicemail as she was getting into her car. She must have called while Madison was talking to Brown. 'Neal is taking Tommy to a sleepover at his cousins' and I have the house all to myself. I feel like a movie, chilled white wine and whatever leftovers I have in the fridge. Let me know. If you're coming you won't need to go home and change.'

It was their code for 'no kids in the house, you can come straight from work, with whatever piece of metal is in your shoulder holster'. No one else there: no Neal, no Tommy.

Madison did go home and took off her Glock and her back-up. She walked the few minutes to Rachel's house, and when her friend opened the door all Madison carried was a bottle of Sauvignon Blanc and a family size bag of Kettle Sea Salt and Vinegar Potato Chips.

'I just wish the students were not so obsessed with their grades.' Rachel taught Psychology at UW. They were carrying their plates and glasses back to the family room and catching up. 'As if that was the only true mark of their education and learning. You won't believe the times we have to explain to them that this is not a service industry and they are not clients.'

'Were we like that?' Madison asked her. They had studied together at the University of Chicago what felt like about two hundred years earlier.

'No way. We were bright, polite, engaged, and thoroughly perfect in every possible way.'

'That's what I thought.'

They sunk into the leather sofa and toed their shoes off, plates and glasses on the coffee table in front of them.

'What's going to happen if Brown doesn't pass the test?' Rachel asked.

Madison shook her head. 'If he can't carry a gun he will not be able to be a cop. It's as simple as that.'

'I'm sorry.' Rachel had never met Brown; she was sorry because she knew her friend would be bereft if Brown was forced to leave the department. 'How old is he?'

'Fifty-one.'

'Not a kid but plenty of years left to drive you nuts.' Rachel took a sip of wine.

'I have to fix this. I know I can help him. He's the kind of cop I want to be twenty years down the line and I'm not going to let this happen to him.'

Neither had to say the name, they both knew what she meant: it was a win Madison would not let Harry Salinger claim.

'I saw Mr. Quinn on television,' Rachel said.

'Yes,' Madison replied. Of all the people in the world, Madison would not speak to Rachel of the small pitiful hole where David Quinn had been buried.

'Bad dreams?' Rachel asked.

'No more than usual.'

'At least know you can talk about it with Dr. Robinson.'

'Sure.'

Rachel picked up the remote and pressed 'play'.

'Guess what? My cousin Aaron is in town.'

'Aaron Lever? How is he these days?'

'Divorced, two kids, owns a software company in Saint Francisco. He asked me how you are, if you're single.'

'If I had married Aaron we'd be cousins.'

Rachel snorted into her wine.

As Holly Golightly climbed out of a cab with her coffee and croissant, Madison felt the warmth and the comfort of the house slowly sink into her bones.

Chapter 10

Alice Madison, fourteen, ties her hair back in a ponytail with a pink elastic band and slips her kayak into the water from the rickety pier that juts out of the narrow beach. She raises her arm and waves at her grandmother who's watching her from the deck by the kitchen; her grandmother waves back. 7.30 a.m., Sunday.

Alice paddles south for a few minutes; she sticks close to the shore but that instant of freedom on the water is totally intoxicating. In a world of curfews, homework and general adult supervision – before any of her friends has even begun to fantasize about driving lessons and owning an actual car – sliding into the cool gray and feeling the paddle slice into the water is just as grown-up and independent as it gets. Never mind that she's wearing a red life jacket with matching helmet.

A couple of gulls float by. It feels 'tranquil', as Alice's English teacher would say. She had felt her grandparents' apprehension all week as the day had approached. Father's Day. She wanted very badly to reassure them but didn't know how.

Alice trails the tips of her fingers in the water and lies back as far as the kayak will allow. The sky is like the inside of the shells she picked up last summer on Ruby Beach. Mother-of-pearl. The name made no sense, she had thought at the time.

A mallard flew overhead, the sleek green head almost black against the sky.

'Halloooo! Alice, grab my hand, quick.'

Rachel.

Rachel Lever, fourteen, wears an identical life jacket and helmet; her kayak slides alongside Alice's from the opposite direction. Alice grabs her hand and the kayak stops so that the girls are facing each other, each in her own fiberglass canoe.

'Sorry I'm late,' Rachel says.

'I only just got here myself.' Alice knows why Rachel is late. Breakfast in bed and a Father's Day card for Mr. Lever. *He's a nice man, he deserves breakfast in bed.*

Out of the blue she realizes that she has been waiting to tell Rachel for months.

'I don't know where my father is,' she blurts out. 'And it's probably a good thing.'

Around them there is nothing but water and cool June air. 'The summer I came to live here, I had run away from home. I was traveling for a week before the state troopers stopped me.'

'One week?'

'Yes.'

'One whole week?'

'Yes.'

'But that was two summers ago! You were twelve two summers ago!'

'I was.'

'What happened? Was he mean to you?'

'No, he wasn't mean. He wasn't like your dad but he wasn't mean either.'

'Then why did you run?'

'A few months after my mom died, we were living in Friday

Harbor. He took my mother's things, all we had left of her, and he used them to gamble. Poker.'

'My dad plays poker. He has poker nights with my uncles.'

'My dad plays in Vegas.'

'*Las* Vegas?'

'He's a pro. He taught me.'

'No way.'

'Yes way.'

'Sheeesh, Alice. And he stole your mom's things?'

'I found out and I got so angry I took my baseball bat and smashed pretty much everything in my room.'

Rachel's eyes are wide now. Alice presses on – it's now or never.

'Then I went into his room and he was asleep. He had a switchblade knife. And I stood there with the knife in my hand until a dog barked in the yard next door. I stuck the blade into the dresser, as deep as I could, packed a bag and left.'

They were still grasping each other's hand.

'He didn't put up a fight when my grandfather said he'd bring me here. We haven't spoken since. And sometimes I dream about that night, about the knife.'

There, it was all out now.

The kayaks move gently in the tide. Rachel mulls it over. This is beyond her experience. Life in junior high, her brother's bar mitzvah and Uncle Harold's divorce: those are things that she understands. This is another world. Two things are also clear: Alice has never said this to anyone else before, and if she chose to withdraw her friendship Alice would accept it and she'd slowly become just one more face in the school's corridors.

'He didn't take very good care of you,' Rachel says finally. 'He didn't take very good care of your mom's things.'

Rachel lets go of Alice's hand and flicks a drop of water off the fiberglass.

'My cousin Aaron asked me if you're going out with anybody,' she says and starts a gentle paddle toward the Point.

'Which one is Aaron?'

'Tall, skinny, hair like Taylor Hanson.'

'He looks like Taylor Hanson?'

'No, he *thinks* he looks like Taylor Hanson.'

They continue paddling.

'If you married him we'd be cousins,' Rachel says. 'Then again, you'd be bored out of your skull. All he does is look at his stupid hair and play on his stupid computer.'

'I won't marry him then.'

'Good. Don't you think the water is pretty tranquil today?'

The girls paddle and giggle.

Chapter 11

The cyclist was travelling south on 35th Avenue South West toward Myrtle Street, still warm from the house but feeling the damp chill of the mist creeping in with every breath. The road was deserted. At first he didn't notice it: the sun wouldn't rise for another half an hour and in the shadows of the Reservoir water towers it was only an indefinite patch of darkness.

When he saw it, he stopped, looped around and gave it another pass without getting any closer. Even at that distance he knew that it couldn't be a dummy, that it was a human body sitting on a plain kitchen chair, the top half covered by a black garbage bag and duct tape coiled around it like a snake.

He climbed off the bike, let it fall on the wet grass and called out softly, all the while getting his cell phone out – fingers ready on the first '9'. He called out again as he advanced slowly. The figure on the chair was bent forward as if trying to get away; a puff of breeze brushed the black plastic and the cyclist stumbled back two steps. He looked around, no one else on the street. He took one step forward and the smell hit him straight on: both chemical and human, as if everything that's usually inside a body had been dragged outside of it.

He dialed and spoke quickly, the words getting tangled before they could come out in the appropriate order, and the first blue-and-white arrived in minutes. Two officers with heavy flashlights that cut through the gloom got him out of the way as their car radio crackled and more emergency vehicles arrived, surrounding the Reservoir green with their red lights flashing and, at the center of it all, the man on the chair.

Madison got the call while driving North on 509 and managed a sudden and inelegant exit to Westcrest Park to the displeasure of a number of drivers. She waved her hand in apology and hit Roxbury Street as fast as the Seattle Municipal Code would allow.

Madison saw the crowd and knew she had found the crime scene. She saw their hands in the air and knew each one of them held a phone with a camera, taking pictures and recording, ready for download.

She parked, took a pair of gloves from her kit in the trunk and slipped her shield on a thin chain around her neck.

As she approached the crowd she realized how quiet it was. An outdoor crime-scene can get pretty loud between press, neighbors, law enforcement officers, Crime Scene Unit people, medical teams. Everybody tries to do their job as well and as fast as they can before the scene dissipates in the weather. Here, nobody was talking: no chit-chat with the officers who were keeping the boundaries, no chat amongst the locals. Madison walked through the silent crowd.

'Detective, this way.' A uniformed officer she knew by sight waved her in past the yellow tape.

'Thanks.'

The ground crunched underfoot as she stepped onto the green. A knot of people – Detectives Spencer and Dunne and Dr. Fellman, the Medical Examiner, among them – stood under the water towers with their backs to the crowd, creating a kind of human screen. Madison had made it there fairly quickly and the Medical Examiner and the

Crime Scene Unit officers must have only just arrived themselves. She looked for Amy Sorensen, the senior CSU investigator who had helped her turn around the Salinger case, and did not spot her – occasionally even Sorensen went off duty.

The scene boundaries had been defined and secured and CSU officers were already moving to protect the scene and set up privacy screens. In the dim light, the beams of small flashlights sought out facts and details.

Madison breathed deeply. There it was, the simple rush that came with every call-out, as if all the systems had suddenly turned themselves fully on because driving, eating, shopping and regular human interaction only required a fraction of her attention but this, this was where she lived. She turned on her flashlight.

'What have we got?' she asked.

They parted and she saw him. The training clicked into place and she found herself thinking, speaking and taking notes as if this was not something any human heart should turn away from.

Madison looked on: a man – early to late fifties but hard to be sure – sitting on a kitchen chair, his hands and feet tied to the chair's back and legs with coils of picture wire. The top half of his body had been covered by a black garbage bag, duct tape wound around the chest to bind him to the chair.

The bag had been slit open by the responding officers, who had checked for signs of life and found none; he was leaning forward, the head and neck were out of the plastic and the skin raw and streaked with what looked like chemical burns. On his lips, dried-up gray froth. Madison was glad the man's eyes were closed. He wore pale blue pajamas and his feet were bare. At the moment of death – or possibly before – his body had let go and the smell was foul.

The first thing Madison knew was that they were looking at a secondary crime scene. This had not happened on the green under the water towers: the victim had been moved after the attack and brought here. Somewhere – maybe not too far from where they were standing – was the primary crime-scene. It looked like pain, probably some kind of torture, and pain needed privacy.

Around Madison, the camera flashes from the CSU officer burst dazzling white at regular intervals.

It was Spencer's case and he turned to the ME: 'What do you say, Doc?'

Madison crouched next to the chair, close enough to make her own observations and far enough not to get in Dr. Fellman's way. He placed the tips of his gloved fingers on the man's jaw and delicately tested the movement range.

'I'm not going to untie him here, but judging from the head and neck muscle, I'd say three to four hours ago – rigor is only just starting – but we have to consider outdoor temperatures as well.' He pushed up the man's eyelids. 'No petechias.'

The absence of petechial hemorrhaging meant no asphyxia or strangulation – Madison couldn't see any marks or bruises on the neck. The victim was wearing pajamas, no shoes. He had been in his home, maybe asleep, and someone had overpowered him and bound him to the chair. His own kitchen chair.

'No drag marks,' she said, the beam trailing around the chair's legs.

'Nope,' Dunne said. 'It takes at least two people to lift and carry, three if they have a driver to keep things quick.'

Two, maybe three people. The ground was frosty and hard underfoot; the winter had made the green threadbare. It had kept no footprints for them to find, no tire tracks on the concrete.

She shone the flashlight on the thin silver wire around the wrists: there was blood there – he had tried to break free – but not as much as a long captivity would have suggested. She could not see any wounds on the parts of the body that were exposed, except the streaks on his face. The fabric around the neck was wet; he might be soaked in perspiration. Fear would have done that to him.

'Cause of death?' Dunne asked.

'Painful and unexpected, I'd say,' the doctor replied, systematically going through his routine checks while his assistant carefully placed a bag over each of the victim's hands.

Dr. Fellman held up the man's face. 'I don't want to say anymore out here and I don't want to cut the bag off. Let's just get him back where we can take a good look without every single piece of trace evidence blowing off in the wind. Wait . . .'

He reached in, held the fabric away from the man's skin and undid one button. An inch below the place where the collarbones met, neatly taped to the man's chest with duct tape, a Washington State Driver's License caught the light. Under its laminated surface: a name, a photograph, an address.

Dr. Fellman pushed his glasses back on his nose.

'Meet Mr. Warren Lee,' he said. 'He was restrained for some time – look at the wrists and the ankles there.' He pointed.

'Woken up and strapped to the chair?' Spencer said as he knelt and checked the victim's feet. 'The soles are clean. We need to send a car to the address: maybe he wasn't the only one taken hostage.' Spencer stood and walked off, talking quietly into his radio.

The man had been tagged and branded with his own driver's license and everybody thought the same thing, looking at the picture wire tight around his wrists – let us hope Warren Lee lived alone and let his house be empty.

Madison focused on the raw skin on his face: someone had done that to him very deliberately. It could be burglars out on a rob-and-violence kick, it could be someone already in his life who had reason to be unhappy with Mr. Lee. If it was the latter, unpalatable as that might be, they had a much better chance to find the culprits swiftly;

if it was random, it would be much harder and the outcome much more uncertain.

The ME people started to prepare the man on the chair for transport; a puff of wind brushed his graying hair. Madison zipped up her coat: Fellman was right, they needed to get everything they could out of the scene before it blew away. The CSU investigators lived their lives in a daily struggle to protect and preserve, and today was not going to be a good day.

'Madison.' Spencer turned to her. 'Dunne and I are going to the victim's residence. Can you go with the doc? Anything he finds we need to know as soon as he finds it; we can't wait for the report.'

'No problem.'

The responding officer crossed the green and nodded to Dunne, who knew just about everybody who carried a badge in King County.

'So far no one saw anything,' he said to Spencer. 'The only witness we have is the guy who reported it, and the medic had to give *him* a sedative.'

'We need to know who got home last, who walked or drove past or looked out of the window and saw nothing. We need a timeline of their movements,' Spencer replied.

'Got it.'

Madison looked all the way round. It was getting darker – after a brief moment when it could go either way the day had decided to stay as close to night as possible and the small rectangular screens held by the onlookers looked like pale, unimpressive flares. Nevertheless, Madison thought, it was worth keeping an eye on whatever was downloaded.

'Did we get any footage of the crowd?' she asked Dunne quietly, her back to them.

'Absolutely.'

Spencer and Dunne left, on their way to God knows what. Madison stood in the spot where the chair had been, feeling the chill and looking in the direction where Warren Lee would have been looking had he been alive, and wondered why if you kidnap and kill a man in Rainier Valley you then drive him all the way to Georgetown to leave him under two massive water towers due north-west.

She was crossing the green when the first raindrop hit; nearby a CSU officer swore under his breath.

Chapter 12

After the ordered chaos of the crime-scene, the autopsy room was sanitized air and clean, sharp corners. The man was laid out on the table in a pool of glaring light. The metal instruments clinked against the surfaces as Fellman and his assistant, both suited up and wearing goggles, went through the external examination. Fellman spoke into a mike suspended above the table; his commentary would become the official report.

First they had cut through the garbage bag and the coils of duct tape, which together with the chair and the pajamas had been taken to the lab. Madison – in a disposable protective suit without the face and eye protection – had stood at an appropriate distance.

Lengths of wire were still taut around wrists and ankles. The assistant had snipped the ends off, careful to avoid knots and twists and documenting each step with multiple perspective photographs.

The doctor picked up the man's right hand and peered at it through a magnifying lens. 'No skin under the nails,' he said.

He hadn't had a chance to fight back, Madison thought.

Fellman turned one hand over, examined the palm, then repeated with the other hand.

'Nail marks?' she asked.

'Yes,' he replied. 'Quite deep.'

Madison leant against the wall: nail marks in the palm meant the fists had been involuntarily clenched. It meant a high degree of pain.

The doctor reached for one of the movable lights and pulled it over until it hung above the man's head. The assistant took various samples from the areas of raw skin and collected some of the dried gray froth around the man's lips.

'There was vomit on the pajamas front,' Fellman said to Madison without turning.

'I saw it,' she replied. 'He threw up from the pain?'

'Not sure,' Fellman said, bending close to the man's face and sniffing.

He picked up a small flashlight and opened the mouth. 'The inside of the cheeks and the throat are very inflamed. I think he threw up because he was forced to ingest something. It smells chemical.' He straightened up and turned to her. 'Smells like cleaners.'

Madison nodded. 'I'm going to check in with Spencer about something.'

She had found a message from Dunne on her voicemail as they were starting to cut the garbage bag off, reception being what it was in the morgue. It was good news: the residence was indeed the primary crime scene – specifically the bedroom and the kitchen – and there were no other victims as far as they could see.

Spencer didn't pick up but Dunne did on the second ring.

'You're going to need to print all the household stuff in the kitchen, from the cleaners to the tools to what have you. The doc says they might have forced him to swallow some kind of detergent. Did they keep him in the kitchen?'

'Yes, the bed was a mess. Sheets pulled out, probably happened when they woke him up. The rest of the house was untouched except for the kitchen. We found sick on the floor and they're picking up all kinds of trace evidence.'

'How did they get in?'

'Back door. A neat job. There was no alarm.'

'Does it look like a burglary?'

'Ain't nothing to rob here and, far as I can see, nothing was taken. He must have made a little more than minimum wage, not much more than that. Cause of death?'

'Not yet. I'm going back in.'

Fellman and his assistant were still focused on the top end of the victim's body. Even at a distance Madison could see that the rest of it – except for the wrists and ankles where he had been tied – seemed unblemished. An average man, slightly overweight, whose biological age as given by the driver's license was forty-nine, but who looked a few years older.

Her cell started vibrating and Madison left the room.

'We found a whole mess of drugs in his bathroom cabinet, all prescription. I'm going to send you a picture and you can ask the doc,' Spencer said.

'They didn't touch the drugs?'

'No, left them where they were. The guy had more pills than Walgreens.'

'I'll let you know.'

Madison wandered over to the vending machine at the end of the corridor and got herself a bottle of water. The autopsy room managed to be both cold and suffocating at the same time. It was the smells, Madison told herself. You could build a kind of resistance against the visuals but the darn smells got you every time. She drank deeply and by the time she walked back in Fellman had performed the 'Y' incision and the chest cavity was exposed.

'I think we might have a cause of death,' he said.

Some of the internal organs had already been removed, she noticed.

'He had an enlarged heart. There could be a number of causes, from coronary artery disease to cardiomyopathy, but the result was heart muscle that did not work as it should have done.'

Madison checked that Spencer's picture had arrived on her phone and showed it to Fellman.

'This is his medicine cabinet.'

'Yes, it makes sense. Have a look at his stomach content.' He pointed at a metal bowl on the wall-mounted cabinet.

Madison looked: what was in the bowl made no sense.

'I know,' Fellman said. 'Hell of a last meal.'

'Are you kidding?' Spencer said.

'It was green, and if you check out the sink in his kitchen you're going to find a bottle of washing-up liquid, apple scented. They forced him to swallow it, as well as what could be clothing detergent. Fellman thinks that the streaks on his face were caused by a bleach-based cleaner.'

There was silence on the other end of the line.

'His heart wouldn't have been able to take the stress. The doc said the massive release of adrenaline and then cortisol would have been fatal for a heart as damaged as his was.'

Madison heard Spencer sigh; maybe it was only a background sound.

'We're going to get the entire kitchen packed up,' he said. 'Did I tell you we found a roll of hanging picture wire under the sink?'

'No.'

'Looks like they used what they found lying around,' he said. 'Did the doc say how long?'

'No, he'll tell us more after the tests.'

'I hope he died quickly.'

'So do I.'

By the time the autopsy was finished it was the middle of the afternoon and Madison couldn't wait to be outdoors. She grabbed a chicken sandwich with a coffee in Cherry Street and had both while typing out her notes for Spencer's case-file.

The victim's death had been caused by a pre-existing condition, exacerbated by the situation. Madison wondered if it was at all possible that the intruders had not actually meant to kill him and straightaway excluded that option: they had tied him to a chair with wire; there was no way that the man wouldn't end up on the corner of 35th and Myrtle under the water towers. How much his death had surprised them and how much it had ruined their plans for the night was something the police would only discover in due course.

Warren Lee had never married and didn't have a criminal record; he had driven unremarkable cars all his life and held jobs that had paid enough to live on if you don't like expensive things. His drugs had been paid for by the medical insurance his job provided – stock keeper for a hardware company. Madison realized the picture wire he had been tied with was probably made by the people he worked for.

She left the report on Spencer's desk, her shift long finished, and clicked off her desk lamp.

Alki Beach was deserted. The sun hadn't even made an appearance and the air carried a bite that easily found the spot between her shoulder blades that tightened her whole back.

Madison started running. The sense of falling and the coppery scent rose up immediately and she ignored both. She pushed through, sped up, and inhaled the sharp air as deeply as she could to wash out the faint apple smell from the autopsy room.

Back home she put a steak on the grill pan and had it with some leftover potato salad. She went over her notes from the David Quinn file and sought out the names of the men Det. Frakes had mentioned. Men who would take an interest if your business was successful in certain areas. *Protection.* There were three names: Eduardo Cruz, Leon Kendrick and Jerome McMullen. Madison circled each name.

Chapter 13

John Cameron laid on his bunk and focused his attention on the tiny crack in the ceiling. Folded on the wall-mounted table was a two-day-old copy of *The Seattle Times* sent by Carl Doyle from Quinn Locke. The front page headline was 'Bounty on the heads of kidnappers. $1,600,000 to solve a cold case'.

In the last forty-eight hours Cameron had felt the atmosphere in the jail change like a wild animal senses winter. Those inmates who did not have television privileges or did not read had heard about it from their visitors and the news had spread like an oil spill. The guards, who had so far treated him with wary caution, seemed even more watchful.

John Cameron had known Nathan Quinn all his life: the time before, when he was a boy and the world had been a bright shining thing, and the time after, when the colors had changed and he had thought he would drown in his own rage. And, miraculously, the time after that when Quinn had not turned away from who, or what, he was. Cameron had never entertained any doubts about his own nature but he was glad and grateful that the link with Quinn had never been severed.

Quinn's television appeal had not surprised him; he understood what his friend was doing more than anyone else on Earth. The one thing that had interrupted his train of thought like a stone against a glass window was that name. Because Quinn should not have known; the name should have been Cameron's, and Cameron's alone, to carry. That had been the deal that he had made with himself when he was eighteen: Timothy Gilman would die because he was the man who had taken them into the woods, who had cut him and who was responsible for David's death. He would die by Cameron's hand because there was no way they would ever be able to get him into a courtroom.

Still, Quinn had known. For how long Cameron couldn't be sure. He thought back to a conversation in a diner, eating pie, and how young he had been and willfully deaf to what Quinn was trying to tell him. A few weeks after that day Quinn had left the King County Prosecutor's Office and set himself up in private practice, criminal defense. He had never told him he knew, he had simply waited all those years for a time when Cameron would need him as his nature had always fated that he would.

When two guards came to escort him out for his yard time, the drumming sound started almost immediately. He barely noticed it.

The metal door clunked open and John Cameron was hit by a sudden rush of cold air, air that was not channeled through pipes and conducts. It was damp and gritty and felt wonderful.

Cameron was in protective custody, which allowed one hour twice a week in a walk-alone: a structure in every way similar to a cage, eight feet wide with closely interwoven bars, in a yard that contained a number of such structures. Inside it, he could walk – five long strides would probably cover it – stretch, exercise, or do whatever he pleased while being simultaneously outdoors and separated from every other inmate.

In a jail – a world within a world – yard time was precious: it was a brief opportunity to socialize, strike alliances, and establish boundaries between the groups. Inmates at risk or being disciplined for any number of offenses would have their yard time in the walk-alones.

Cameron had been to a dog kennel when he was a kid: a not altogether different set-up, he thought.

He looked up: a dark sky, heavy clouds rolling in from the west, and no rain.

Manny Oretremos stood by the door of his cell in the appropriate position and waited for the guards to approach. He was perspiring already; there didn't seem to be a moment in the day when he wasn't cold and clammy. He wanted to straighten his shoulders and pretend to himself that he was ready and willing – more than willing, in fact. Instead he wiped his hands on the sides of his trousers and settled for keeping his breathing regular and his mind blank.

'Ready, Oretremos?' the guard asked.

John Cameron stood in the center of his walk-alone. This was the closest he ever got to any other inmate and their energy flowed around him. Some stretched, some ran on the spot, some ignored him, some stared. He was aware of the correction officers guiding each convict and the metal locks snapping shut.

Over the weeks he had had the opportunity to watch them, to become familiar with their routines and their mannerisms. In a place where individuality is taken away with your personal effects when you arrive, every one of those men fought to get it back in any way he could and at any cost.

Cameron was never in the same walk-alone: his position and that of the men around him changed depending on the shift. Today he was in the center of the yard. The cages were at least three-deep on each side. On his right, a young Latino man was hunched against the chill. He stood quite close to the metal mesh and stared at the concrete floor.

He was nervous – Cameron had noticed him on other occasions – and he couldn't wait to get back inside. In fact, he always seemed profoundly relieved when the guards came to collect him to escort him back to his cell.

Cameron understood fear and the boy seemed even more terrified than usual. It was the slightest movement; he caught it almost by chance: the boy had made the sign of the cross. At the same time a call had sounded out in the yard and, like one man, all the inmates had stepped right up to the wall that put them closest to Cameron.

The second yell ripped the silence and he felt more than saw that every man around him was reaching back like pitchers before a hard throw.

Cameron locked eyes with the Latino kid; he alone hadn't moved. Manny Oretremos stood frozen where he was, in his right hand a two-inch vial filled to the brim with sodium hypochlorite in a concentrated form strong enough to disintegrate skin on contact.

Cameron took one stride up to the wall nearest Manny – the long side of his walk-alone – while around them the yard exploded in a hell of sounds. The guards hollered as they rushed through the maze of cages, the inmates shouted at Manny to throw, and above all was the sound of the tinkling, crashing and hissing of the vials dropping like rain around Cameron.

He heard the first warning shots of the guards and all the inmates dropped to the ground, but Cameron knew that the safest place for him to be was standing right by the side closest to the kid. His amber eyes held the boy whole, only a few feet between them. Vials hit the roof of the cage; some shattered on impact, glass shards and their contents dripping onto the ground; others rolled and fell through the gaps in the bars. Something bounced and broke on his shoulder and he shrugged off his jacket, pain like a bee sting through his orange coveralls. Cameron never broke eye contact.

Pale green drops of the solution fell from the top of the cage and fizzled on the concrete as they burnt through. The guards reached the door of the walk-alone, fumbling with the lock, yelling their instructions as they beckoned him out – no one going inside – and the alarm sounded high and wide.

Cameron walked the stretch to the door as the last of the sodium hypochlorite trickled down from the ceiling mesh. As soon as he was over the threshold two guards clasped him above the elbows – their touch curiously hesitant – and started to lead him to the yard's exit. He turned: every inmate in every cage was lying flat on the concrete, watching him, dead eyes following him as he went past, except for the Latino boy who was still standing – guards shouting their orders at him – until he finally lay down and the glass vial rolled away from his hand.

Inside the walk-alone Cameron's Department Of Corrections jacket rested in a heap against the mesh as the scent of bleach reached the corners of the yard and the crackle of the guards' radios was the only living sound.

'I want to know *how*,' Will Thomas said, trying to keep calm. 'I want to know *how*, and *who*, and *when*.' The Deputy Warden of the King County Justice Complex had been briefed about the 'event'. The Warden was on his way back from a conference.

The supervisors of each wing of KCJC, including D wing where John Cameron resided, were assembled in his office; the guards who had been present stood at the back; the doctor on duty hovered by the door.

'We recovered one of the vials completely intact,' the supervisor of D Wing said; he had aged five years since he'd gotten up that morning.

'We're talking about "vials". Not a sharpened toothbrush or a shiv or a shank.' The Deputy Warden looked around the room. 'Vials,' he repeated.

The 'event' was still only one hour old and the jail was in lockdown.

'What's the situation, Harry?' Will Thomas asked.

Dr. Harry Norringer looked at his notes. 'We have a number of inmates with various injuries. Nothing that warrants a hospital transfer. Small lacerations mostly, and a couple of contact burns no bigger than a pin head where the solution touched them.'

'They were flinging the vials with some kind of elastic-type, home-made catapult and they had to get it through their own bars first. Some of them didn't manage it and it bounced right back,' one of the guards, Miller, said.

'What was in it?'

'Some kind of bleach. The smell is still all over the yard.'

'Cameron was smart to stay where he was,' the doctor continued. 'He has a burn on his shoulder the size of a dime; the skin is raw but it didn't go deeper than that. His jacket caught most of it. The injury was bandaged and I put him on a course of antibiotics. His blood pressure is better than mine and his heart rate was practically at coma level.'

'How many inmates were involved?' the Deputy Warden asked Miller.

'We think at least nine, maybe more. We'll be looking at the CCTV to confirm. And then there's Manny Oretremos – the kid who had the vial and didn't throw it. By now he's on the "bad news list" and he'll have to stay in protective custody. For the rest of his life, I think.'

'The inmates never go into the same walk-alones, right?' Thomas asked.

'No, they rotate in a non-repeating pattern,' Miller replied. 'Just so that what happened today cannot happen.'

'But it *did* happen. And what it means is that they waited, for weeks possibly, so that he would be in the middle.' Will Thomas ran his hand through his hair. 'We've been lucky today.'

No one said anything; it was a conclusion they had all already reached in the privacy of their own minds.

An ill wind, Will Thomas thought, *an ill wind through my jail.*

Chapter 14

Madison held her cell in her hand for a long minute after Doyle had rung off. KCJC had called Cameron's legal representatives to report the ambush on their client; Doyle had called her as he was driving to the hospital to tell Quinn in person.

It was not unexpected, Madison reasoned. In fact it was the very thing KCJC had tried to avoid by having him in protective custody from the start. Yet there was something repulsive about a targeted attack where the prey had no chance to defend himself. Even against a con with a shiv, Madison's money was on Cameron and that was the problem. There was something unsettling about the amount of preparation and patience that had gone into the attack; it was the one piece of their life that got those inmates up in the morning: wondering if that was going to be the day and how much damage they could do before the guards stopped them.

Madison left her desk and went outside for a few minutes. People didn't smoke anymore – Madison had never smoked in the first place – but she missed the pretext to stretch her legs and feel air on her face. It sounded silly to say 'I need to breathe different air for a little while,' and yet occasionally that was precisely the case. A few minutes were enough.

The day had been about canvassing Warren Lee's neighborhood

and the area where the body had been left by the killers – forensics seemed to indicate that at least three men had been present in the victim's kitchen. They had boot prints by the back door, though as yet nothing to match them to and no witnesses to the abduction or the dropping off.

Madison had been supporting Spencer in his investigation but the whiteboard with the list of Homicide Detectives in black marker and the names of the victims in red said that she would be the primary on the next one. Soon Spencer and Dunne would have to look after their dead because Madison would have her own.

She automatically reached for her cell to call her partner and then decided not to: it was up to Brown to decide when he was ready to go to the range with her, and the worst thing she could do was to put him under pressure at a time when he was already feeling its heavy load.

'We got something,' Dunne said from his desk, where he had just replaced his receiver. 'A resident on 35th Street came home at 3.10 a.m. and he could swear the victim was not there yet.'

'It makes it a three-and-a-half-hour window when they could have left him there,' Spencer said.

'Do we know why "there" was there?' Madison said. 'I mean, did Warren Lee have any connection to that spot? Far as I could see he never worked at the reservoir and no one around there knew him.'

'No connection to his life that we can see,' Spencer replied.

Madison went back to typing up her interviews. Lieutenant Fynn was waiting for Spencer to come up with motive and suspects, and for the moment they had neither. What they had was a brutal home invasion that had finished with the victim dropped off in a spot known for its water towers. Madison had not read the Medical Examiner's report sitting on top of Dunne's desk – she didn't need to. It had taken a very long hot shower to wash off the Autopsy Room from her skin.

*

The man on the chair had found posthumous fame if not fortune at the hands of the press. Quick to catch the details that mattered, online and in print, the media grabbed the story and shook it hard for all it was worth: a sadistic murder, the torture of a defenseless man taken from his own home, the body dumped in an unusual manner. The words had been picked up by the search engines and YouTube; crime-scene footage shot with telephones – grainy and shaky but perfectly clear – was all over the net. The words were *torture, murder, Seattle* and, Madison found out to her surprise, *chair*.

The city reacted as it did when a person who is not involved in a life of violence meets a violent death: it held its breath, waiting for law enforcement to comfort and reassure. *The killers were known to the victim, possibly a drug deal gone wrong, possibly retribution, leads are being followed and arrests will be made*. And when no reassurance was forthcoming – because Warren Lee had no ties to gangs and not so much as a parking fine to his name – still the city held its breath.

Chapter 15

Madison finished typing the interviews, printed them, and left the pages on Spencer's desk; Spencer was in Fynn's office, having what was no doubt going to be a very brief conversation on the Lee case.

She checked the wall clock, turned off her anglepoise lamp and shrugged on her jacket.

As she was leaving the Detectives' Room she noticed that Tony Rosario's table had been cleared of papers – the man must be on yet another medical leave. She had never seen him looking anything other than stick-thin and gray-faced; maybe that's what fifteen years in Homicide do to you.

She had found out what she could reading the reports on Cruz, Kendrick and McMullen – the three men Det. Frakes had identified in the David Quinn file. At different times, they had individually been charged with a variety of felonies from insurance fraud and corruption to all colors of assault, malicious harassment and coercion, which fit with the potential *protection* motive for the abduction of the children. Eduardo Cruz had died in 1987, a hit-and-run which first left him in a coma for three days. The driver was never found. The second, Leon Kendrick, had withdrawn from the business and moved to California in 1998, never to spend a single day in jail. The last of them, Jerome McMullen, was doing time in the Bones, the McCoy State Prison north of Seattle, for extortion.

Files and reports were useful but, as always, there was much that hadn't made it onto the page. If Madison wanted to find out about what things were like on the street in 1985 she had to go to someone who had been there. Before internet, before email and text messaging, before the dozens of ways in which information was acquired or dispersed, encripted or straight, before all this there was Jerry Wallace, who always knew who was doing what, where, and for how much, and would be happy to share that information for a fee. He didn't take sides and was consulted by all, the Switzerland of the West Coast crime scene.

Det. Frakes had said that after the boys' kidnapping a shroud of silence had fallen on the informants' community in the city but now, twenty-five years later, there was no harm in trying for a chat with Seattle's retired information bureau chief.

Wallace lived off Highway 165 just before the bridge that led into Burnett, in Pierce County. Madison didn't want to call: this was a conversation that needed a face-to-face and if Wallace was not in the mood to converse, even his reaction would be some kind of response.

The drive on 165 was uneventful. There were strips of bright February sky between the clouds and yet darkness fell quickly after the middle of the afternoon. By the time Madison arrived she had turned on her headlights and they swept across the dense copse as she almost missed the turn. Wallace's bungalow was 300 yards off the highway and Madison could see lights at the end of the narrow lane as she drove under the low branches.

It was a rural part of the state and Madison was not surprised to see a four-wheel-drive pick-up truck parked by the front door.

She pulled in at the end of the drive and closed her car door without slamming it, but making it clear for anyone who was listening out that she wasn't interested in stealth.

Jerry Wallace had lived out here for fourteen years, give or take; however, she was reasonably sure that the inbuilt habits of a lifetime hadn't quit the moment he had retired. The front door light came on courtesy of a motion sensor as Madison approached and she rang the bell.

The two-story wooden house looked neat and well-kept; Wallace hadn't made millions trading information but he had made enough to live comfortably in a town with two shops and one church.

There was a clear semi-circle of bare dirt in front of the house and Madison felt the woods would claim it back just as soon as Wallace looked away. Something small scuttled through the undergrowth and she tracked it as it moved deeper into the gloom.

A couple of minutes went past. Madison could hear muted voices from inside, maybe a television. Her breath puffed white before her. She rang the doorbell again and looked around. No pretty flower pots by the door, no second car tracks on the ground.

She stole a glance inside the pick-up: it was old, the cabin was clean, and there was no sign that anyone but the driver ever sat in it.

When it became clear that no one was coming to the door Madison decided to follow the house around on the right hand-side. Wallace was sixty-nine years old and it was perfectly possible that he hadn't heard the doorbell above the television.

The lights were on downstairs and the sounds from inside became louder as Madison walked down the side – a brief memory of another house and blaring music came back to her, a case from a lifetime away, and she paused.

Maybe it was the darkness of the woods pushing against the house, maybe it was the memory of a fresh-faced police recruit who had found herself in a situation they don't teach you about at the Academy – Madison's hand went to her holster and she flicked off the safety strip on her piece.

She proceeded and the first window looked into a living room that ran the length of the house: she saw the French doors into the yard and the dining table in one corner, and on the television someone was interviewing someone else about something and they were both having a wild time of it. And she saw a four-foot floor lamp that had been knocked onto the rug, the lampshade rolled to one side and the light bulb in pieces.

Damn. In one gesture Madison cleared leather, settled into a two-hand grip with the Glock pointing at the ground, and stepped quickly around to the French doors. Even in the gloom she could see that the yard was empty.

She grabbed the door handle and turned. It was unlocked.

'Mr. Wallace,' Madison called out. 'Mr. Jerry Wallace.'

The television continued its bouncy chatter. Madison stepped into the living room.

'Mr. Wallace, this is Seattle Police.' Madison's eyes went over the room. The table was set: scrambled eggs, bacon and a slice of white toast on plain white china. A tumbler lay flat on its side, a few drops of milk still in the bottom. A white paper napkin was on the floor by the chair.

'I'd like to ask you a few questions if you have the time.'

The eggs were congealed and the milk had become a stain on the cotton place mat.

'Mr. Wallace . . .'

It would have taken some hours for the milk to dry; the glass was upturned but not broken. The lamp, close to the French doors, had been knocked to the floor on the way in or on the way out.

Madison noticed the remote control on the table near the plate, picked it up and pressed the 'mute' key.

Now there was nothing except for the quiet breathing from the trees finding its way in through the chimney. Madison stilled, listening to the house and to every unfamiliar creak and scrape from the heating pipes.

'Mr. Wallace . . .'

Everything else in the living room seemed to be in place: the sofa cushions were plumped and the landscape was hanging straight above the fireplace. Under the table, though, abandoned on its side, rested a single navy woolen slipper, as if Jerry Wallace had been lifted clear out of it and out of this house.

Madison walked to the kitchen and leant on the door; it opened slowly and revealed nothing more than a saucepan on the stove where someone had cooked the eggs and bacon.

The hall led to the stairs. Madison turned on the lights. There was no sense now in calling out, only in paying attention to whatever the house wanted to tell her.

Madison peeked as she climbed each step. She reached the landing; her heart beat a fast steady beat. Maybe cars were streaming past on Highway 165 but there and then, in Jerry Wallace's house, there was only silence and Madison's soft steps on the carpet.

The bedroom was empty; a man's black leather wallet was on the bedside table. She checked the closet and under the bed.

Who hides under the bed? Monsters. Monsters hide under the bed, her six-year-old self answered instantly. But not in this bedroom, not tonight.

Perhaps they didn't wait for me, she thought, but something had definitely come into the house. The bed was made, she noticed. How long ago, she couldn't say.

A quick look into the bathroom and the second bedroom confirmed to Madison that she was alone.

Jerry Wallace was sixty-nine years old; there were high blood pressure pills on the kitchen counter and an herbal solution for insomnia; he was not the guy who goes off on a whim and leaves upturned furniture and his wallet by the bed.

The telephone.

Madison looked around in the living room and found it on a small table by the sofa. The handset sat on a gray box with a red LED light that told the world that seven messages awaited Jerry Wallace.

Something in Madison hesitated to play the messages even as she lifted her hand toward the box. What was she doing inside a stranger's house in the first place?

From the stale warmth of the house she came out into the clean early evening chill and stood on the back steps. The line of trees that circled the small yard was almost completely indistinct. Had someone stood there and watched while Wallace went about his life? Was someone watching now?

Madison's eyes followed the low branches that almost reached the ground, the curve of a root jutting out of the earth, and right then she saw something that was neither tree nor ground.

She crossed the yard in long running steps and there it was, caught by a twisting root – a navy woolen slipper. She didn't touch it. It was sitting on the damp earth, on the edge of the impenetrable darkness. Madison, her piece in her hand, stood stock still and searched the shadows for movement or sound. It was a wall of black and the rustle of the top branches, shifting and swaying, was all there was and, she suspected, all there ever would be. She paused there, one hand against the rough bark and the other holding the Glock.

Then the telephone was ringing deep in the house, and Madison, startled and swearing under her breath, ran back and managed to grab the handset.

'Hello,' she said.

'. . . who is this?' a woman's voice replied.

'Detective Madison, Seattle PD. Who am I speaking to?'

'Katy Wallace. I think I have the wrong number.'

'No, you don't. This is Mr. Wallace's home number—'

'Is my father there? I've been trying to reach him for the last two days.'

Madison looked around the room, at the muted television and the eggs on the plate. She passed the receiver to the other hand.

'Miss Wallace . . .' she started.

Officers from the Pierce County Sheriff's Department arrived in their whites with full lights and sirens thirteen minutes after Madison's call and took over the scene. Jerry Wallace's daughter, Katy, was on her way from Portland with her boyfriend. She had said 'yes' a lot during their conversation, as dread became reality and panic took hold.

Madison and two deputies swept the woods behind the house with the beam of their heavy duty flashlights but, as one officer said, it was blacker than a bag of crows out there and all they were achieving was trampling the crime scene.

He turned to Madison. 'There's a trail five–ten minutes that way.' He pointed ahead of them. 'Someone doesn't want to be seen approaching the house could park there and walk through no problem in day light.'

Madison nodded. Jerry Wallace was gone. Jerry Wallace, who knew everything and everyone, had been lifted clear out of his own life.

Madison drove back to Seattle, her thoughts chasing one another in circles, and by the time she got home she was bone tired. She dug out some leftover roast chicken in a Tupperware container and didn't even bother with a plate. She ate it thinking about two-day-old eggs and bacon on white china.

Four a.m. Madison woke up with a start. Her heart was drumming fast and she was covered in perspiration in spite of the chill in the room. She wrapped herself in her duvet and waited for her breathing to go back to normal. She had been due a bad dream in the last few days and there it was. *You have occasional nightmares, possibly an exact memory of the event but more likely your own perception of the event and whatever troubles you about the nature of your own actions in it.*

Dr. Robinson had been right, of course, and yet Madison knew that he had been wrong about the most important part of the dream. Post-traumatic stress disorder events like her sensitivity to chloroform were born out of fear: the fear the victim felt in the precise moment of the attack which was then triggered by any of a list of sensory perceptions. Madison's dream – the long run in the pitch-black forest, the smell of blood in the clearing – was not about being attacked, it was not about being a victim, it was not about being defenseless.

She slipped her feet into a couple of woolly socks at the bottom of the bed and padded to the kitchen to make herself some hot milk. It didn't really help; it never had. And yet it was what her grandmother had done when Madison was a girl and that was the comfort, that memory.

She crawled back into bed and stared into the darkness above her. She started to think of ways in which the inmates could have smuggled the vials into KCJC, how many of them it would have taken to make sure enough of them had surrounded Cameron, and her last thought as she fell asleep was that the inmate who had frozen during the attack was in as much trouble as Cameron right now.

Chapter 16

Ronald Gray sat in the waiting area of the coach station; the long strips of neon lighting gave him a headache and the seating – row after row in metal mesh – bit into his back. The clock said 8.22 p.m. Almost half an hour to go. His bag, a black American Tourister with four spinner wheels, rested against his leg. He had bought the ticket and then grabbed a bite – more to kill some time than out of real hunger – and now he wished he hadn't.

All he wanted to do was to get on that coach, rest his head against the cool glass and fall asleep. He didn't know how long it would be before they let the passengers on board; he had never travelled by bus. His car, a 1998 maroon Lincoln Continental, sat in front of his apartment.

Ronald Gray was fifty years old, looked fifty years old, and today felt a hundred and seven. He was wiry and capable but his nerves were in shreds and he was exhausted. He stood up and looked around: at least he could visit the restroom before the journey. He wheeled his suitcase behind him and tried to get through the dozens of passengers waiting in the cramped station. A man behind him took offense at the vending machine and started kicking it. Ronald Gray jumped at the sound but the security guards were already moving.

Chapter 17

'Jerry Wallace's gone,' Madison said to Dunne, both of them standing by the coffee machine. 'I went by last night and the house looked like someone had come in and just snatched him off the chair he was sitting on and dragged him into the woods.'

'Some weird burglary-type felony gone wrong?'

'Not really. The house was untouched. No big valuables that I could see but his wallet was in plain sight. Plastic and cash inside.'

'Was he kidnapped?'

'We don't know what happened yet: the daughter couldn't get hold of him for a couple of days but there were no calls and no ransom notes.' Madison took a sip. 'He was just *taken*.'

The call came in at 9.27 a.m. and Madison, being the primary for the next homicide case, got up to get her things and go to the crime scene.

'Madison,' Lieutenant Fynn said from the door to his office as he beckoned her.

Madison stepped in. Detective Chris Kelly was slumped in one of the visitors chairs with a face like a big dog at the groomer's. He looked up and she knew what Fynn was about to say and the sheer inevitability of it hit her with full force.

'Boss . . .'

'No way round it, Madison. Your partners are out on medical and you both need a partner for the next few weeks or whatever. This is how it's going to be.'

Kelly was speechless in his obvious misery. They had disliked each other from the moment Madison had joined Homicide. She thought he was mean, obtuse and proud of it; he didn't need a reason, he just plain disliked her. Nothing to do with gender, history in the force or anything else that could pass for a reason. Kelly's disregard had been immediate, absolute and unreserved.

The one positive thing – if one tried very hard to be positive – was that they both knew where they stood, which at the present time was in a corner and without a hope in hell of changing Fynn's mind.

It was Madison's turn to be the primary on the case. She slung her bag across her shoulders and nodded to Fynn. 'Okay,' she said.

The ride to the Industrial District passed in complete silence. Madison drove under the spitting rain, the day promising just as much light and blue skies as the previous one had. She spent the first ten minutes kicking herself for not having considered the possibility that this could happen until after it had actually happened. The last time they had gone head-to-head Rosario had stepped in and defused the situation; this time it was the two of them riding in the same car and forced to share a case and no one left to step in as needed. Madison decided she'd call Brown the first chance she had and drag the man to the range whether he liked it or not.

Madison had already worked cases in the Industrial District, the depots and workshops area on the edge of the Duwamish Waterway. It consisted of row after row of identical washed-out single-story buildings, the gray interrupted only by occasional patches of rust. It was built on a grid and unremittingly miserable on a cold, wet February morning.

Madison ignored Kelly, who sat shotgun with his linebacker arms crossed, and her thoughts went back to the remains in the Medical Examiner's morgue and David Quinn's last day on Earth; no one from the Cold Case team had approached her yet and as far as she knew no one had been looking into Timothy Gilman's death in the last twenty years. *One down, three to go.* The chances of getting a forensic anthropologist to look at the remains with any urgency were slim. The question was what did Quinn know that they didn't. She remembered the first time they had met in Quinn Locke's smart offices in Stern Tower, Brown and Madison bringing the news of the murder of James Sinclair and his family like harbingers of the doom the following thirteen days would bring. Quinn had kept his secrets until the end, risking his life in the process, and Madison wondered what was he prepared to risk now that his brother's killer was the ultimate prize.

The flashing lights of the blue-and-whites at the top of the road told them they had arrived. Madison had decided during the ride to sit on her doubts and wait for Kelly to make the first move. Fynn had been right, they *had* to work together; that is to say that as Homicide detectives they had to be able to work with anybody and make the best of it. The case couldn't suffer because two cops would rather lose a limb than talk to each other. And so Madison would wait, hoping to discover that Kelly had reached the same conclusion, and maybe they'd both make it alive until either Rosario or Brown could get back to work and the universe would be right again.

Kelly had not said a word. He unfolded his large frame from the passenger seat and hooked the badge on the chest pocket of his overcoat. Madison looked him over quickly like she would a witness to assess his reliability. Late forties, married, put himself through college on a football scholarship. He had probably passed as good-looking then but now his dainty features looked lost in his wide face and, since his nature had given shape to it as much as genetics, there was a bright hard light in his eyes and furrows in his brow. He was several pounds heavier than he should have been and wouldn't catch you if you ran fast, but if you stopped and he did catch you, he would do a lot of damage and enjoy it immensely. Madison looked away.

The warehouse, the last one in the long road, was evidently not in use at present; old metal signs discolored by the weather hung by the doors – a wide one for trucks and a narrow one for people – and made their statements in peeling red paint over white.

The metal shutter in the large door was still intact but the smaller door next to it had been forced open; the wood had splintered and the cheap lock had simply given up.

Madison understood that security was expensive, and for companies going bankrupt it was cheaper to replace the lock and fix the door of an empty warehouse than to pay for an alarm that needed to be set up and monitored, and for a security guard to go past every night. Squatters, vandals, and anybody who needed a discreet place for a questionable deed were quick to find those places. It was her victim, her case, her questionable deed. A small spike of adrenaline hit below her sternum.

Three patrol cars outside, two officers by the door, the others inside.

Madison knew one of them and they nodded hello.

'First officer?' she asked him.

He pointed to the entrance to the building. Madison walked in, Kelly a few steps behind her, and her eyes adjusted to the low light. Feeble strips of neon overhead threw a sickly pale glow over everything. A vast space, bigger than she had expected, and bare except for a few stacks of discarded pallets here and there. The floor was concreted and stained; it had been a while since anyone had taken care of it; the air felt grimy with dust and the memory of engine oil. Three uniformed officers stood at the other end, the beams of their flaslights running over the walls and the floor.

Madison smelled the body before she saw it and for an instant she thought of the man on the chair under the water towers: it was the same foul scent of fear and the beginnings of decomposition. The officers turned when they heard them approach, their steps clicking on the concrete.

'Madison, Homicide. Who's the first officer?'

'Here.' A tall woman with short fair hair and a plain face stepped forward.

The body lay several feet behind them; a man was curled up against the wall in a corner, his knees up against his chest and one arm over his head. One shoe was missing. Even in the dim light Madison could see the pattern of dirt on the floor had been disturbed: the man had dragged himself, or had been dragged, into that corner. *Like Jerry Wallace, dragged into the woods, kicking and screaming.*

She turned to the officer. 'What do we know?'

'One of the workers in the next warehouse along saw the door had been forced and called it in – third time in three months, they have the owners on speed-dial – and they sent a clerk to check and call the locksmith. Anyway, the guy comes over, turns on the neon lighting to assess the damage, and sees . . .' the officer turned and pointed . . . 'him in the corner there.'

'Where's the witness?'

'Having a cup of strong sweet coffee nearby – my partner took him. No witnesses to the break-in or the attack. We asked the offices nearby but they were all shut for the night. The owners had a CCTV camera but it was stolen a year ago and they didn't replace it. Usually it's kids breaking in for a dare: once they found chicken feathers everywhere – don't ask. But this is a first.'

'For him too, I bet,' Kelly said, nodding at the victim.

The beam of Madison's flashlight travelled over the body as she went closer, his left arm giving the impression that he was shielding his eyes from the light. She stepped carefully around the marks left on the ground. She wouldn't touch him until the Medical Examiner had arrived but she didn't need him to fathom the cause of death: two bullet wounds to the head. Instinctively she swept the floor nearby for the casings with her flashlight.

'No casings that we could see,' the responding officer said.

Madison nodded. The holes were small and she couldn't see blood spatter on the wall or on the concrete from where she was. A .22 perhaps. Brown's voice came to her then. *Tell me what you see.* Madison froze everything else – the pit in the woods, the nightmares, vials of acids through metal bars – and did just that. 'Male, Caucasian, possibly fifties, two GSWs to the head. I can't see his face well but there's dried blood on his chin and streaked down his shirt collar and front.'

The victim was wearing trousers and a shirt, the fabric quite thin considering the weather. There must be a jacket or a coat somewhere as well as the other shoe – no one would leave the house dressed like that.

'There might be some clothing around,' she said.

'We're looking,' the officer replied.

The socks were dark and plain, nothing special, and the remaining shoe was black leather with Velcro straps, comfortable and inexpensive. The sole of the sock was dusty, a small tear in the material. The longer Madison's beam shone on the folds of the fabric the more she saw of the last hours of the man's life: blood droplets from being repeatedly hit, dirt and grime on the clothing because he had tried to crawl away, and in the palm of his right hand, open and slack, half-moon nail marks.

Madison stood up and wished the ME would get there quickly; the victim was curled up tight and she wanted to see his face. There had been violence, sustained violence, for a period of time, and then, when they had what they wanted or maybe because of the opposite, someone had stood at the exact point where Madison was and shot him in the head twice.

'We've got something,' one of the officers hollered from behind a stack of pallets at the other end of the warehouse.

They all gathered there, everybody wearing gloves and no one touching anything. In a bundle on the floor a suit jacket, a coat and, to the side, a small travelling suitcase with wheels, overturned but still locked.

'I've got the shoe,' another officer called out from the half-light.

The coat's inside pocket was visible through the jacket's folds. With extreme care not to disturb anything Madison reached in with thumb and forefinger and extracted a brown leather wallet.

At least they would have ID, she thought. She flipped it open and a Washington State driver's license told her his name: Ronald Gray.

Half an hour later the inside of the warehouse was brightly lit by the Crime Scene Unit's portable lights, reaching into every corner and every imperfection in the uneven flooring.

The lights had warmed up the air considerably. Doctor Fellman expected they would and had taken the body's temperature as soon as he had arrived.

'Rigor?' Madison asked him.

'Still coming on,' Fellman replied as he gently lowered the arm and revealed the man's face. Pale stubble, sallow skin under the discoloration from the bruising, a broken nose and dry blood in sticky flakes. Madison took in every detail. The low temperature in the warehouse had impeded the progression of rigor mortis and the doctor could still move the arm.

The victim's face, as Madison had predicted, bore the marks of an awful end.

Fellman looked it over. 'Beaten about the face with a blunt object. I see splinters embedded in the skin.' He turned to Madison. 'There might be a piece of wood around here, maybe coming from one of the pallets.'

The forensics officer standing next to Madison nodded and went off.

'He was beaten,' the doctor continued, 'but not strongly enough to kill him, as you can see. I'll know more after the X-rays.'

Madison tried to read through the discoloration of the bruises. 'Did you notice the marks on the palms of his hands?' she asked him.

'Yes. It was a prolonged attack. Once I get him out of his clothes we might see extensive contusions to the rest of the body.'

'And yet . . .'

'And yet the cause of death is two GSWs to the head.'

'Looks like .22.'

'That's what I think.'

'How many attackers?'

'I couldn't tell you now. Maybe later. If they held him down we could have palm prints.'

'Any defensive wounds?'

The doctor examined the man's hands. 'Hardly. Judging from fingers and nails he only tried to crawl away. And didn't really manage that either.'

'How long do you think the attack lasted?'

Fellman thought it over. It was too early to get a precise time of death but he could make a rough evaluation considering the time it took for bruises to develop.

'I'd say they had him for at least an hour. That is to say the attack lasted an hour; they might have had him for longer.'

Madison looked around: if they had spent one whole hour there they were bound to have left something behind.

Amy Sorensen, the Crime Scene Unit senior investigator, had been taking photographs and making diagrams of the blood-spatter patterns: the dazzling lights had quickly revealed droplets on the walls and floor. Each had been marked and snapped. Sorensen's people worked like a quiet army in protective suits, collecting and preserving, as they progressed through the warehouse.

Under their suits some of them wore the T-shirts Sorensen had given each member of her team: navy blue, the lettering in bold white: *I ♥ Locard.* Edmond Locard's exchange principle: every contact leaves a trace. She had given Madison one of the T-shirts too.

Sorensen had trained her people well and there was no one else Madison would rather work with at the evidence table. Sorensen pushed a lock of red hair behind her ear.

'Here.' She pointed at the floor. Madison looked where she was pointing and nodded. Sorensen knew that Madison had at least three courses in Evidence Collection and Analysis on top of the basic ones required and she wasn't going to spell it out for her.

What she was pointing at was a collection of blood drops on the concrete, perfectly round.

'And there.' She made a sweeping gesture with her right arm toward the wall.

Madison stepped up to it and narrowed her eyes. 'Yes, I can see that.'

The blood drops on the wall had a tail and it told them which direction they came from and at what speed they flew through the air. Once they had collated all the evidence Sorensen would be able to tell her how tall the aggressor had been and how the blows had been struck.

From what Madison could see the warehouse was the primary crime scene. The victim had been brought there and attacked. No blood had been found anywhere near the door. Madison looked at the round drops like shiny coins on the dirt. That was where the attack had started: the man had been standing right there and the aggressor had been raining blows down on him, the weapon creating the pattern of drops on the wall as the arm travelled back and forth, over and over.

'I'd like to see the inside of the suitcase,' she said to the CSU officer standing next to it; the black American Tourister was already sealed in a large evidence bag to be opened at the lab.

'If we start taking things out here we might contaminate—'

'I understand. I just need to see inside. We don't even need to touch the contents.'

'Why?' He started to undo the plastic evidence bag.

'Because the victim's wallet contained plastic and two hundred and fifty-seven dollars and twelve cents.' Madison thought of the half-moon nail marks on his right palm. 'It wasn't a robbery,' she said. 'We need to know if he was in a hurry.'

The CSU officer placed the suitcase on a sheet under one of the lights. He had hooked what looked like a bent paperclip in the hole on the pull tab and moved it gingerly backwards as the teeth came apart. Madison knelt close to it, aware of the hectic work around her but focusing only on this one thing. *How quickly did you pack, Mr. Gray? How quickly did you get out of the house last night?*

The officer's gloved hands turned over the flap and moved back. Madison stilled and stared, then she turned and looked at the Medical Examiner zipping up the body bag.

No, not for 'travel' – the suitcase had been packed for 'running'. A jumble of items of clothing thrown together, balled up and crammed into the small space without any care except for speed. As much as could be carried of the man's life was in that bag. She could almost see his frantic hands grabbing shirts from a drawer and papers from a table and shoving everything into the case until it could hold no more. There was something unspeakably ugly in the way things were twisted and molded into each other. Fear, Madison thought – fear had made him move fast but, in the end, not quite far enough.

'Packed in a hurry,' the officer said.

'With good reason,' Madison replied and stood up. 'Thank you.'

'Here. We found these in the coat's inside pocket.' A CSU officer showed her two thin plastic bags: in one, Ronald Gray's passport; in the other, a coach ticket in his name to Vancouver. The coach would have left the previous night just before 9 p.m.

She needed air. Madison edged out of the door as two forensics officers were taking off the lock. It had started to rain in earnest and it was eerily dark compared to the blazing light inside. The clouds were rolling in from the sea, heavy with rain, their edges black with it.

A patrol car had been dispatched to the address on Ronald Gray's license: the residence had been empty, the front door secured. Madison would get there as soon as she could. Her unmarked car was parked just beyond the blue-and-whites and, she realized, Kelly was sitting inside it in the passenger seat, possibly talking on his cell phone. She hadn't even noticed when he had left and couldn't see his face behind the windscreen. Maybe *that* was his first move.

Madison breathed deeply. He could do what he damn well pleased as long as he stayed out of her way.

The body bag was loaded on the Medical Examiner's white wagon and they left. Cars and trucks came and went on the road, unloading their cargos and picking up deliveries. *Cars.* Ronald Gray had a driver's license in his wallet, not somewhere lost in a kitchen drawer or under last year's bills. He had a driver's license in his wallet because he had a car he drove every day, and yet he had bought a coach ticket to Vancouver. Madison, a fast driver even on her slowest day, could make it in three hours, maybe two and a half if traffic was on her side. She turned and considered the suitcase, already re-packaged in plastic and ready for the lab. Gray had been on his way to the coach station. Maybe he had already made it there when he was picked up by his killer.

*

Madison drove toward downtown, her brain making a list of what they had and her body reminding her that it was past lunchtime. Kelly sat next to her, looking ahead, observing the traffic flowing around them as if words and language had not been invented yet. Madison realized that they had not spoken since leaving Fynn's office: Kelly had wandered through the warehouse, fixed the body with his small blue eyes, listened to the Medical Examiner and taken his own notes. More than anything he was an absence sitting next to her in the car and Madison regretted her desire to reach out and talk to him, start the conversation, get him talking. She reminded herself of every single instance when he had been condescending, aggressive or quite simply yard-dog rude, and her desire to make peace was slapped down by her appreciation of his silence: a quiet Kelly was someone she could work with.

There were some facts in the case – not many, but enough to get them started. They had an ID, they had a primary crime scene and the ticket to Vancouver. They had who, how and where; what they did not have was a reason for the attack and any clue to the number or identity of the attackers. Madison wanted to let the evidence guide her thinking and was wary of giving a meaning to the packing of the suitcase, a meaning that might mislead her reasoning. Her gut told her Ronald Gray was on the run, her head told her to wait and use the suitcase to confirm a scenario, not to create one. The man had been found in a corner, curled up and trying to shield himself from two bullets to the head; he might not have been afraid when he was packing but he sure had been in that warehouse. Why had he been beaten and then killed when nothing on his person had held any interest for the murderer? Was it all about the violence itself? Madison wondered and her gaze brushed past Kelly. There are reasons why police officers work as a pair: you need a partner to back you up and to talk things through. But more than anything you need a partner because you spend your days asking those questions. *Was it all about the violence itself? Was that seventeen or eighteen blows before the guy was shot twice in the head?* Madison saw a gap in the traffic and hit the accelerator.

The coach station downtown was housed in an unremarkable building the color of milky coffee. They walked through the glass doors and Madison eyed the CCTV cameras fixed at various angles. It was just as shabby and depressing as the last time she had been there. At any time of day there was a constant stream of travelers arriving and departing through the dank hall; if there had been witnesses to anything they might very well be halfway across the country by now.

Madison was instantly aware that the second they had come in four homeless men had gotten up from their metal seats and discreetly left, two guys had stopped talking and moved to different parts of the room, and one woman had made her way speedily toward the restrooms. You couldn't exactly be incognito while with Kelly – the man shouted *cop*. The crowd practically parted in front of them and she knew without looking that Kelly had enjoyed it like an iced drink on a hot day.

Madison showed her badge to one of the security guards and in less than five minutes they had established that last night's 8.50 p.m. coach to Vancouver had left without a hitch and arrived when it was supposed to. Madison had taken a picture of Ronald Gray's driver's license photo on her cell phone and she showed it to all the personnel who had been on duty the previous night. None of them remembered him.

'How about CCTV footage?' Madison asked the head of security, a lanky thirty-something with a diamond stud in his right ear and a short, untidy ponytail.

'We have everything you need. What time are you interested in?'

'Let's start with immediately before boarding time and go backwards. We know our man didn't make it onto the coach but he might have been here. Can you see on your records how and when the ticket was bought?'

'I'll just need a minute.' He set them up with two chairs in front of the monitor. The office was not elegant but at least it didn't smell as bad as the ticket hall and she didn't feel she had to sanitize the chair.

The quality of the picture was grainy black and white; somehow the technology in the office had stopped evolving around 1972. It was a four-way split screen: two angles of the main ticket hall, one of the restrooms corridor and one of the exit to the coaches. It was entirely possible that Gray had not even made it to the station, Madison thought. She sat on the edge of the chair as the time code flew backwards and the previous evening unfolded in front of them. Kelly sat slumped in his chair, blinking at the rapidly moving images and missing nothing.

They saw him at the same time and for an instant forgot themselves and exchanged a look.

'There,' Madison said and froze the image. Ronald Gray, wearing his coat, sat on the metal seating, his suitcase by his feet. He was looking at his wristwatch. Madison suddenly remembered it; it was still on his left wrist.

'I'm going back to the beginning,' she said, as if there had been any kind of conversation between her and Kelly.

She rewound the tape until the moment when Ronald Gray came into frame at 7.47 p.m. He had sat down and waited; every so often he would look at the main entrance then look away. He seemed exhausted – edgy and exhausted. Around him people came and went, sitting and standing, and no one paid him any attention.

They were running the footage at normal speed and it was maddening: something was about to happen and Madison could do nothing to stop it. A little after 8.20 p.m. Ronald Gray stood up and wheeled his case out of the frame just as a small commotion around one of the vending machines had started. He was picked up by the camera facing the restrooms corridor. For a few seconds nothing happened, then two men walked into the restroom behind him. Two minutes later two men walked out, walking fast and close, one almost propelling the other forward. Then a third man came out wheeling Gray's suitcase, except that it wasn't Gray. He was taller and broader and made sure the camera didn't get a good shot of his face.

Madison rewound the tape. The two men who had walked in after Gray were wearing dark winter clothes: hat, scarves, gloves, coats. Their faces were indistinct and they had been looking away from the camera anyway. The two men who came out were also bundled up.

'Shoes,' Madison said.

Kelly grunted.

Both men were wearing black boots going in, but on the way out one of them was wearing black shoes with Velcro straps. The guy who came out with the case wore boots.

Madison sat back in the chair: they had swapped coats and clothes and forced him to go with them. Actually, nothing on the screen told her with absolute certainty that Gray had left against his will. For all they knew, he had voluntarily exchanged coats with one of the men who had followed him into the restroom and decided against going to Vancouver, decided that maybe Seattle was the place to stay after all. Madison snorted. That moment frozen on the screen in front of her – *that* was when Ronald Gray's life had ceased to belong to him.

Madison played it again. On the way out the man with the boots had placed one hand in the middle of the back of the man with the Velcro straps, the other hand gripping his arm above the elbow. When the third man appeared, wheeling the case, he cut through the crowd and just before reaching the glass doors he turned. Madison appreciated for the first time in her life the subtle and timeless beauty of a four-way split screen: the instant the man had turned and looked across the ticket hall, the guy who had created the commotion kicking the vending machine had somehow calmed down, raised his hands in apology and made his way out. The guards had just stood there, managing to look both menacing and relieved, totally unaware they had just witnessed a kidnapping.

It was a lot of energy to expend on a man like Ronald Gray: three men in the station and – Madison could have sworn to it – one waiting in a car outside, motor running, eyes in the rearview mirror. Four men to grab an unarmed, unremarkable fifty-year-old guy, take him to a deserted warehouse, beat him with a piece of wood they found there – Sorensen had called to confirm the find – and then shoot him in the head twice. A lot of energy, Madison considered. She did not try to shape the facts into a story; for now all she had was a sequence of events – the story would come later.

She got busy with station staff again, this time with pointed questions and the position of each of them as the kidnapping had occurred. Kelly did the same.

Practically all of the people in the ticket hall had been watching the exchange between the guards and the guy with a grudge against the vending machine. His actions had been perfectly calibrated: enough noise to draw attention but not enough damage that the guards would attempt to hold him when he wanted to leave. And when that moment had come he had made it out of the room very swiftly. A black baseball cap and turned-up collar had made sure his face was not identifiable.

Frank Lauren and Mary Kay Joyce arrived with their kit; they were Sorensen's best and brightest. As they stepped through the glass doors, Madison went to meet them.

Lauren didn't bother with greetings. 'Please tell me it's not the restroom,' he said to Madison.

'I'm sorry, Frank,' she replied.

'Oh, man. Is it the ladies' restroom at least?'

'Nope.'

They sighed. Madison led them down the corridor; she was already wearing a double layer of gloves. She pushed the door open with the toe of her boot; so far she had managed not to touch a single surface except with her shoes, which she might have to burn at the end of the shift. Lauren and Joyce, already wearing their suits, snapped on face-protecting masks. There was ancient dirt and grime coating every inch of every surface, as if mops and scourers had barely brushed against the tiles and no detergents had ever crossed the threshold. The smell was indescribable.

'Of course you realize we're going to pick up everything and anything here. The last time they cleaned this place – we're going to pick up Jimmy Hoffa's prints off that sink over there.'

'I know. We don't know what they touched or if they touched anything but whatever you can find would be gold.'

'*Gold* ain't what we have here, Detective,' Joyce replied.

Ronald Gray's apartment was downtown, a 1930s building with some but not much of the old charm. The super let them in, a short man in his early thirties with a neat blond buzz cut and pale eyelashes. He had started working there only ten days earlier and didn't know anything about Ronald Gray except that he lived on the fourth floor, at the back. The super wore very bright T-shirts in layers, was glad to help and sorry for the reason they were there. Climbing the stairs, he ignored Kelly's bulk and directed his conversation to Madison. She could see he was pleased to leave them by the threshold.

The light on the landing was not enough for their needs: she shone her small flashlight on the lock and around it. Untouched. No one had come visiting after or before Gray had left.

Madison turned the key in the lock and they walked in.

The apartment – one bedroom, living room, kitchen and a small bathroom to the side – had been left in haste. Kelly wandered from room to room but Madison stayed by the front door and took it all in. The dishes had been washed – white china with a fine green line;

the plain blue covers on the bed had been pulled up over the pillow; the surface of the dining table – beech, big enough for six – was not polished but clean and dust-free. A broom cupboard held domestic cleaning products, some white paint with a brush, and a roll of wallpaper. In spite of all that, or maybe because of it, it felt as if a gust of wind had spread things all over the place, things that normally would have been tidied away: bills, letters, a couple of picture frames with no pictures, two drawers that had not been shut properly and stuck out a couple of inches. Then there was the smell. The smoke alarm was high in a corner of the room, quietly manning its post. However, the scent hung in the air, acrid and sharp.

'Do you smell it?' Madison asked.

Kelly grunted.

The kitchen was an IKEA knock-off and Madison found what she was looking for on the stove: a tall saucepan, the kind used to cook pasta. She lifted the lid and found the source of the pungent smell: floating in four inches of grayish water, a black mass which once had been ashes with something fused to it, a form that had once been plastic and had melted into the burning paper.

Ronald Gray didn't have a fireplace: he had a smoke alarm in the living room and a kitchen stove. If he needed to burn something that badly, he didn't have many options. Madison looked at the pattern of disarray in the rooms. Part of it had been generated by packing the suitcase as quickly as his hands would allow him; part of it had been the result of his searching for something, maybe a number of items, which once found had ended up in the saucepan and been set alight. Once he had achieved the required level of destruction, Gray had poured in the water and replaced the lid.

Madison pulled out a cheap digital camera that she kept in her bag and started taking pictures. There was a trail, she could almost sense it, in Gray's frantic comings and goings from room to room.

It might tell her what he was trying to obliterate. It was the first thing she had in her hand that whispered *motive*.

It didn't take long to go through the apartment and nothing else held Madison's interest as much as the saucepan and its contents. As she was locking the door, Lauren and Joyce walked up the stairs.

'How did it go?' Madison asked.

'As predicted,' Joyce replied.

Madison handed her the keys. 'The saucepan on the stove. He used it to set fire to something very recently.'

'You owe us breakfast, Madison,' Frank Lauren said as the detectives were leaving. 'In a place with napkins made of cloth.'

'Don't I know it.'

Madison knew just how good they were, undaunted by circumstances: if there was something useful to the case in that restroom Lauren and Joyce would have found it, no matter how many layers of crud they had to go through to collect it.

The afternoon had slid into an early night and the road was slick with rain. It was past the end of their shift but Madison wanted to go to the morgue to see what the autopsy had revealed. She turned to Kelly, sitting in the passenger seat, his face barely lit by the street lights' orange glow.

'I'm going to see Fellman,' she said. 'Would you like me to drop you off at the precinct first?'

Kelly turned. It was their first conversation of the day. 'Why?'

'Because it's past the end of our shift and I'm not familiar with how you like to work.'

Kelly nodded. 'So you can tell the boss you stayed on and I clocked off?'

'No, I couldn't care less about the hours you keep. I will miss you but I'll survive,' she replied. 'Honestly, Kelly? I don't care. We made it through the shift without killing each other and that's an achievement. Maybe due to the fact we exchanged three words in total. So far, so good. I'm asking you again, do you want me to drop you off? It's not a trick question.'

Kelly thought about it for a second. 'Let's go to the morgue.'

'Wonderful.'

They found Dr. Fellman in his office, still wearing his scrubs and typing a report.

'Nineteen blows to the body,' he said, 'including three to the head. The lab has the piece of wood they used. It was about this wide.' He held his fingers three inches apart.

'We saw the men on CCTV; they picked him up at the coach station. We saw three; we think four on the whole.'

'It would make sense. There was bruising on the arms where they restrained him; the way the fingers were splayed I'd say large hands. At least two people, plus another who was doing his work with the wood.'

Madison tried not to think about how Ronald Gray must have felt, how terrified he must have been. She tried to keep it a sequence of events and still there was something about *fear*, about that sheer overwhelming panic that she had seen in his home, that kept coming back to her.

'What can you tell from the blows?' she asked.

The doctor sighed. 'They didn't want him unconscious, this much I can tell you. The blows were designed to hurt but not to kill: his internal organs were intact and there were no breaks except for his nose. There was dirt and grit under the fingernails – he had dragged himself into that corner with the last shreds of energy he had. He would have survived if not for the GSWs.'

'Anything else?'

'He had Vietnamese soup before they grabbed him.'

'There's a restaurant just by the coach station.' Madison nodded. 'Thank you, Doctor.'

Back in the precinct, Kelly gone home and her legs stretched out under her desk, Madison picked up her camera and examined the photographs she had taken in Ronald Gray's home. Details of his last hours on Earth and the mundane routine of his every day. They had found payslips from his employer – a transportation services company – where he had been a booker for seven years. Kelly had knocked on various neighbors' doors but either people were at work or they didn't know anything about him.

Madison sipped her coffee as the pictures scrolled in front of her. There had been no trace of a female visitor to the apartment – no clothes in the closet, no second toothbrush in the bathroom – and yet someone in his life was bound to miss him at some point. After twenty-four hours no one had claimed Ronald Gray. Madison looked at the picture of the dark watery lump at the bottom of the pan. Tomorrow she would visit his employer and see what kind of person Ronald Gray had been and why no one had missed him yet.

Madison drove home, and even before taking off her weapon and holster she crouched by the fireplace, added two logs, prepared the kindling and put a match to a long rolled-up strip of paper. The fire took up straight away, the fluttering light so much gentler than the lamps.

She toed off her boots by the sofa and sat back with a glass of Sancerre, while a dubious slab of leftover penne warmed up in the oven.

When she was done she put the dish in the sink, made herself a cup of coffee and spread all her notes and the newspapers clippings on the Hoh River case on the dining table. At the end of August and the beginning of September 1985 the press had still been full of speculation on the murder of a Washington State senator on one side and the Mariners' records of eleven games won and seventeen lost in one month on the other, the lost New York Yankees games being particularly chewed on. Senator Newberry had been due to testify in a federal investigation about corruption and racketeering in the Seattle docks: he had disappeared at the end of June before the day of the testimony and his body was found six weeks later in Lake Washington. Without his testimony the case against the defendants, *family* men from the East Coast, had collapsed. The Hoh River boys' pictures were laid out between the dead senator and Gorman Thomas in his Mariners uniform.

Madison smoothed out the clippings with her hand: there were lines that ran from the boys to their fathers and to the men who had taken them. After twenty-five years the lines might be almost invisible and yet somehow Madison knew they had not been erased by time because Edmond Locard was right: every contact leaves a trace.

Chapter 18

The television in Nathan Quinn's hospital room was muted. He lay back on his pillow and his black eyes tracked the figures on the screen. A reporter stood by the water towers on the corner between 35th Avenue South West and Myrtle Street. He pointed to where the murdered man on the chair, Warren Lee, was found days ago, the crime scene tape even now in place. Quinn didn't need to hear the words to know the police had made little progress on the case.

Very slowly he pulled himself up to a sitting position and swung his legs off the side of the bed. He breathed deeply, wishing away the dizziness. Holding most of his weight on his arms, he gingerly edged himself forward and stood up, his bare feet on the cold floor.

The noises from behind the door had settled down into their night rhythm and Quinn did not expect a nurse to come in and interrupt his work. He took one step, holding on to the side of the bed, and reached for the stick the physiotherapist had left behind for him. His right hand – the good one – closed around it and he put most of his weight on it. He took another step and another after that, the exertion depleting his energy faster than he was prepared to admit.

The partial splenectomy had been done with open surgery and the incision was only one more scar that slowed down his recovery;

in this plush room he wore his body like a prison sentence he had to get past. He took another step.

They had told him that twenty-five per cent of splenic preservation might be adequate to preserve its function. The doctors had left him forty-seven per cent of his spleen and so far infections had been kept at bay by medication and sheer bloody-mindedness. He took another step.

On the screen, the photograph from Warren Lee's driver's license appeared for a few seconds, then it cut to a car accident in Everett. Nathan Quinn walked inch by inch across the room and back, his eyes on the screen.

His thoughts, so unlike his body, had been travelling fast and moving back and forth in time as the memories had thickened around him like tall grass. He didn't offer any resistance as feelings he hadn't experienced for years washed through him whether he liked it or not. The doctors had told him that the kind of trauma he had gone through was likely to affect his sense of balance, not merely from a physical standpoint. They had warned him to expect a rush of emotions that might be unfamiliar to him as his body and his mind tried to give meaning to what had happened. The counselor from the Psychology Department had spent twelve minutes with him a few days after he had first woken up and then had left, never to return. She had very quickly, and quite correctly, come to the conclusion that Nathan Quinn was not the kind of patient who was eager to overcome his present difficulties with an open and frank discussion of his state of mind. *Polite but frosty*, she had written in her report.

On the table, next to copies of Cameron's defense case, lay a pile of letters and personal notes that Carl had delivered that morning, among them a letter from the U.S. Attorney for the Western District of Washington State – an old friend from the days of the King County Prosecutor's Office – who wrote to wish him well and to convey her yearly invitation to leave his practice and join her in her fight against the tide of brutes that threatened the land. It was their private little joke: she always asked, Quinn always declined. There was also a kind, sweet card from Rabbi Stien, who remembered his parents and wished him well in his recovery; when the time came, he would support anything he decided to do about David.

Quinn had not formulated the thought in so many words, nevertheless the notion was there and probably had been there since that first visit by the Jefferson County police: David would not be laid to rest next to his parents until his killers had a name. He wondered if Rabbi Stien would have understood: in his note he had spoken about Quinn's courage, resilience and inner strength. Quinn knew he had resilience, knew that now for sure if he hadn't known it before. The other two he wasn't sure about; he could still taste the fear as he tried to free Madison's godson from his cage and the relief as Jack held his hand, tethering him to this world, when all about him was darkness.

Maybe resilience was enough to get him through this, he thought – resilience and rage. Rabbi Stien might favor one over the other but Quinn recognized that he needed both and you can only use what you have.

Chapter 19

July 4, 1985. John Cameron, twelve, lies down on the back seat of his father's car. His legs stretch out and his feet, in his cherished red Converse trainers, rest against the rolled-up window pane. From that position he can see the sky and the wisps of clouds that foretell another hot July day – like they haven't had enough of those this year. It makes the journey more interesting than sitting up even though his mother will tell him off and get him to 'sit properly' as soon as she notices.

They are driving to the Locke estate, out of Seattle and somewhere east, where they will spend the Fourth of July with friends – running around in the wooded grounds, cooling off in the pool and stuffing themselves with barbecue. Heaven. Though all that was only the prelude to the highlight of the day: the fireworks over the lake. Jimmy and David would be there too, of course, which was good, as well as Bobby Locke, which was less good – he was in their year in junior high and no one could stand him. Hopefully there would be enough people that they could lose him and do their thing. The fact that it was Bobby's house they were going to and his pool they would dive in took the edge off Jack's delight a little but not too much. There was a gloss to that day that made you feel as if every atom in Creation had been polished to a shine, like his father used to say – and he felt generous, even toward a ratty little sneak like Bobby Locke.

'Jack, sit up straight, honey.'

'Yes, Mom.'

His father is a fast driver and they're making good time. Jack leans his cheek against the glass pane, keeps an eye on his Casio wristwatch, and practices holding his breath like a swimmer under water.

Nathan Quinn, twenty, wakes up in his bedroom and it takes him a second to realize where he is. All summer he's been slaving away as an intern at a law firm in Boston and he arrived back home in Seattle only yesterday.

His old bedroom seems hopelessly childish to him this morning and – still not entirely awake – he resolves to take down his Springsteen poster and replace it with a CND one. When he graduates he will apply to Harvard Law and this internship – making coffee and carrying files for divorce lawyers in suede slip-ons – will seem like a distant nightmare.

'Don't they pay you enough for a haircut?' his father had asked him last night, his tone gentler than the words.

'I like the curls,' his mother had said simply.

The internship paid hardly anything, but it looked good on the résumé, and anyway it had paid enough for David's present. The silly kid had practically squealed with joy when Nathan had given him a 35mm Nikon camera. It still made Nathan smile: he had felt grown-up then and his brother, seven years younger, impossibly young. He had spent hours showing him how to use the aperture and the zoom. It had been a long time since they had spent any time together; David was growing up and Nathan was missing it, coming home from college or his summer jobs and driving off to see his friends, just about saying hello and goodbye to the little kid who had trailed behind him as soon as he had started to walk.

David's thirteenth birthday had been in May; Nathan had made it to the barmitzvah and had left quickly after.

'He misses you,' his mother had said and he had easily found a dozen reasons why study, work and social commitments had prevented him from spending time with his brother. Nevertheless, his mother knew that her words would stay with Nathan better than any reproach.

'God knows how he's going to be a lawyer,' his father, an attorney himself, would say to her. 'You can see every single thought in his face.'

The expensive camera was an apology. Maybe David understood that, maybe he didn't; Nathan couldn't tell and he didn't care. They were sitting on the kitchen steps, the sun was setting in the purple sky, and his brother's small hands fumbled around the back of the Nikon as he changed the roll of film.

'Show me again. I'm afraid I'm going to scratch it,' David said.

'Give it here. First, look at the sprockets . . .'

As a concession to his mature years he had been left to sleep late while the rest of the family drove to Conrad Locke's estate for the Fourth of July celebrations; he would join them at some point later, depending on how his 1973 Ford Pinto decided to behave.

Chapter 20

Madison had spent the morning interviewing Gray's colleagues and getting nowhere – a quiet guy, kept to himself, never spoke of his private life. She typed up her notes, however little value they held, while so far the day's only blessing was that Kelly had been wrapped in his usual scowling silence.

The apartment and Gray's body were both free of any traces of drug use and his bank account, modest as it was, spoke of a life lived within its means.

Her phone rang and she picked up.

'Homicide, Madison.'

'It's Sorensen. Is Spencer there?'

'Sure – they put you through to me by mistake. I'll transfer you—'

'No, I need you both. Could you get him over and put me on the speaker?'

'Hold on.'

Madison turned. 'Spence . . .'

Ten seconds later Spencer and Dunne were there and Amy Sorensen was on the speaker.

'Spencer, you're the primary on the Warren Lee case, right?' she asked.

'Yes,' he replied.

'Okay. What I have here is flakes of paint recovered from the clothing Ronald Gray was wearing which matches the paint on the chair that Warren Lee was tied to when he was found by the water towers.'

'Gray was one of the men who carried the chair? That's how it got transferred?' Madison asked.

'No. Judging from how the flakes were grouped on the cloth I think it was transferred from the shoe of one of the men who killed Lee when he kicked Ronald Gray.'

Madison sat back in her chair.

'Let me start from the beginning,' Sorensen continued. 'Lee was tied to the kitchen chair with picture wire. As you can imagine there was a lot of friction there; the wire went through the first and the second layer of paint. The flakes were all over Lee's pajamas and one or more of the killers were close enough to the chair that they transferred to their clothing, their shoes. Lee was transported with a garbage bag over his upper body – that limited the transferral a little but they couldn't avoid it altogether. When they attacked Gray, some of the flakes transferred on to him. We're testing them for blood as well; it should be a match to Warren Lee's.'

'Silly question, Sorensen, but—' Spencer said.

'Am I sure it's the same paint?' Sorensen interrupted him.

'Yes.'

'Absolutely. The chair had been painted twice in different shades of the same color. I used a stereomicroscope. It's the same paint, coming from the same chair, sliced off by the same picture wire, on both your victims. They couldn't have chosen a better kind of ligature from our point of view.'

'It's what they found in the house,' Spencer said.

'Thrifty as well as vicious. A charming combination.'

Madison leant forward. 'Do you have any news on the lump of ash and plastic found in the saucepan?'

'So far, I can tell you it's a lump of ash and plastic. I'll tell you more when I know more.'

Sorensen rang off.

'It's a twofer,' Dunne said.

'I don't know what "it" is,' Madison said, then she remembered. 'You need to see the coach station footage. I really don't think they picked Gray at random and the man was on the run; chances are Lee was not picked at random either.'

'I guess he didn't know he was supposed to run,' Spencer said.

At his desk, near enough to hear every word but clearly not interested enough to participate, Detective Chris Kelly kept on typing his morning interviews.

Madison left her desk for a few minutes in the early afternoon. She snuck into a deli and grabbed a smoked salmon bagel and a black coffee, sitting at a window table and looking out at the street. She ate thinking about the cases and hardly tasting the food. Outside the rain was thin and gritty, more urban traffic than heaven-sent.

She missed Brown's insight and dry wit for sure but almost more than any other time she missed him at lunchtime, when more likely than not they would sit in silence and think their thoughts about the Salinger case and the shadow it had thrown over the city.

Madison, a Psychology graduate, didn't need to dig deep into the mind of someone with no father to speak of who had connected with an older, much respected colleague. Still, she didn't know what to do with that knowledge: awareness of how the mind worked didn't change the end result.

Back in the detectives' room, the teams swapped files so that Madison and Kelly would go over the Lee case while Spencer and Dunne would catch up on the Gray murder. Fynn joined them after a while. It was an informal briefing; Fynn leant against Brown's desk and looked over Gray's autopsy report.

Ever since Sorensen's call, notions and facts had been shifting in Madison's perception and finding new positions, as if one map had been overlaid on top of another and dry land was even further away than they had thought. The two constants so far were a deliberate and prolonged attack and, though in different circumstances, the death of the victim. In essence, torture and murder.

'Do we have a timeline yet?' Fynn asked the group in general and no one in particular.

'It started sometime on Thursday night,' Spencer said. 'Three, possibly four, intruders break into Warren Lee's house; they wake him up and tie him to a chair in his kitchen with picture wire. The ME's report says they used what they found lying around – cleaners, detergents – to inflict a considerable amount of pain on the guy. He has a medical condition and his heart gives out. They wrap him up in a black garbage bag and leave him still tied to the chair by the water towers on the corner of 35th Avenue and Myrtle.'

'Any witnesses?'

'Not at Lee's house. What we do have is a witness who could swear the body was not there at 3.10 a.m. Friday and the cyclist who called it in at 6.52 a.m. And to make it easier for us, the victim driver's license had been taped to his chest.'

'Neat,' Fynn remarked.

'This takes us to Friday morning.' Madison picked up the narrative. 'Then, thirty-six hours later, Saturday evening, the CCTV at the coach station tells us Ronald Gray was followed into the restroom by two men and marched out. A third was creating a diversion for the security guards. Patrol called us Sunday morning just before 9.30 a.m.: Gray had been taken to an empty warehouse, hit nineteen times with a blunt object – the piece of wood is at the lab – and then shot in the head twice with a .22.'

'We recovered the bullets?'

'Yes, Ballistics has them.'

'And the paint flakes are telling us we are talking about the same men who attacked first Lee and then Gray?'

'So it seems,' Spencer said.

'What about the families?'

'Both unmarried. Lee has a sister in Tennessee; they hadn't spoken in thirteen years.'

'Gray had no next of kin we can see from the records,' Madison said.

'Do the victims have anything in common at first glance?' Fynn asked. 'Acquaintances, work histories, anything at all?'

'If they do it's not immediately evident but we have only just been told about the connection,' Spencer replied.

'Different day, different cause of death, same killers.'

'Yes and no,' Madison said as her eyes travelled over the autopsy reports, thoughts aligning. 'They *already* have something in common: during the attacks the killers used what was present at the scene. Chemicals for Lee and a piece of wood from a pallet for Gray. Both attacks lasted between forty-five minutes and one hour. Lee would have survived the assault and Gray would have survived the beating but both died – one of a stroke and the other as a result of the GSWs to the head.'

Madison had never worked a case where torture had played a part. It happened from time to time, and those who investigated such cases would carry them quietly at the back of their minds for a long time and not talk about them at home.

'They didn't want to kill them,' she said finally.

'Mr. Gray would disagree, I think,' Kelly interjected.

'I mean, yes, they wanted to kill both of them, and Lee might very well have been shot like Gray if his heart had not been compromised. But if the object of the exercise was cruelty and pain, why did they shoot Gray? Considering the injuries, they could have gone on for hours. They just *chose* not to. The reason for the assault was not necessarily to kill the victim.'

'I agree,' Spencer said.

'Maybe they got what they wanted out of them and that was enough.' Kelly undid the collar button of his shirt under a patterned green tie.

'And they wanted the police, and everybody else, to know very quickly who the first victim was,' Madison continued.

'I'm liking this more every minute,' Dunne said.

'Is Sorensen in charge of this at the lab?' Fynn asked.

'Yes, she is,' Spencer replied.

'Good, because after three days all we have right now is *paint flakes* and the clock's ticking. Also, I don't want to tell the press about the connection between the murders. Let the killers think we don't know. We *don't* have motive and we *don't* have suspects,' Fynn said, straightening up. 'We really don't have to work very hard to look like we're treading water.'

Nobody said it but they all knew that the media would seize the story and spew out the same headline: *Everything comes in threes.*

Madison was making notes of Gray's early employment records – sparse and unsatisfactory – when the call came in.

'Homicide, Madison.'

'Hello, may I speak with the detective investigating the Ronald Gray case?'

'That would be me. How can I help you?'

Madison had the handset in the crook of her shoulder while she kept typing.

'I'm calling about his brother.'

Madison stilled for a moment, then took the phone and spoke

into it. This had better not be a joke. 'Mr. Gray had no siblings on record, sir. Whom am I speaking to?'

'Dr. Eli Peterson, at the Walters Institute.'

Madison's mental rolodex flipped to the appropriate page: residents at the Walters Institute had psychiatric problems ranging from the moderate to the very serious and most of them lived there longterm and did not expect to leave. Most of them, reflected Madison, might not be entirely sure of their surroundings in the first place.

'Please go on, sir. Our records show Ronald Gray had no next of kin.'

'The relationship between them was not one of blood, Detective. They were foster brothers; they grew up together. And his brother is a resident of the Walters Institute.'

'I'm sorry for his loss,' Madison said. 'Has he been told?'

'I think it would be best if we spoke about it in person. Do you think you could come over sometime today?'

'Did you know Ronald Gray, Doctor?'

'For years.'

'We'll be right over.'

The Walters Institute, a red brick building from the early 1900s, sat at the center of its private grounds, lined by tall firs and by a perimeter fence almost as tall. The iron railings were painted black and well maintained, and even though they were a world away from the concrete and barbed wire of the King County Justice Complex, Madison observed that they were certainly not making it easy for someone to leave the grounds without authorization.

She gave her name and Kelly's at the intercom by the main gate and waited; two cameras had her car in view.

Chapter 21

Alice Madison, fifteen, sits in the school's counselor's office and looks around. Some of the posters on the wall have changed since the last time she was here, three months ago. She is about to miss PE and would rather they got on with it but the woman is poring over a file with her grades, occasionally looking up with a smile, and then back to the file.

Having run out of leaflets and posters to examine, Alice focuses on the woman sitting on the other side of the desk and, before she realizes what she's doing, she reads her like her father taught her. The woman is in her mid-thirties, unmarried – no ring, if that means anything – and her clothes are more expensive than a part-time school counselor would afford. Although they are not brand new: Alice notices that the maroon cashmere twin set is beginning to pile a little and the pumps are beautifully kept, though the leather is slightly scuffed by wear.

Miss Harley genuinely likes working with teenagers – many of Alice's classmates have confided in her and let her help with their troubles, but not Alice. For some reason Miss Harley has always been a tad uncomfortable with her, and thus tried ten times harder to get the girl to like her and open up.

Alice appreciates the effort and yet has kept her own counsel, which the older woman has begun to feel is her own personal failure as a professional.

'Your grades are very good.' A flash of the Harley smile.

'They're okay.' Alice shrugs.

'You plan to do college courses at some point?'

'I think so, yes.'

'Good, that's good.' Miss Harley closes the file. 'And how are things generally?'

Alice shifts on her chair. She runs with the track team and swims with the swim team; she goes out regularly for burgers and milkshakes with Rachel and a group of classmates and she has gone out on the odd date. Still, as immersed as she is in the life of Three Oaks High, Alice feels like an odd number where there should only be even ones.

'Okay,' she replies.

Miss Harley's magic might not be working with Alice; however, it doesn't mean the woman doesn't see a troubled teenager when she is sitting right in front of her, even though being troubled is pretty much a synonym for being a teenager.

'Look, Alice, you're doing really well in school and from what I hear you have lots of friends and are involved in extra-curricular activities as well. Brilliant.' Miss Harley doesn't go for the smile this time; she fixes Alice with her pretty hazel eyes and cocks her head to one side. 'Sometimes being smart doesn't make things easier. Being fifteen is already fraught with all kinds of issues that have to do with growing up, and you are a very smart fifteen-year-old who has dealt with a lot. I just want you to know that it's okay to feel . . .' Miss Harley waves her hand and waits for Alice to finish off that sentence with whatever word pops into her mind, which would be more appropriate than anything she could supply.

Alice nods, as if a great truth has just passed between them.

'And I'm here,' Miss Harley continues. 'For anything you want to talk about, anytime.'

Alice is well aware that her file on the desk says that her mother died three years ago and she lives with her grandparents. Maybe this well-meaning woman thinks it's easier to open up to someone closer to her age than to her grandparents.

Alice stands up and picks up her heavy backpack from the floor. She needs to get to the track fast and start warming up or Coach Lewis will throw a hissy fit.

For a long time she thought that a *psychologist* like Miss Harley would be able to see right through her and spot the thing, whatever that was, that made Alice feel different, like a metal detector would pick up a gun. It took her a while but finally she had to admit that Miss Harley was just as much in the dark as she was, with one difference, though: Alice believes it has nothing to do with being fifteen.

She reaches the track – thank God she is already wearing her sweatpants – dumps her pack by the bleachers and starts a gentle jog.

'Good of you to join us, Madison,' Coach Lewis hollers from across the field. 'Ten laps and put some mustard in that stride, will ya?'

Alice half-raises one arm in assent. Maybe it's just that they haven't yet invented the metal detector that works for her particular thing. Maybe a proper psychologist or, even better, a psychiatrist who works with lunatics would be able to take one look at her and say, *Yup, girl's wired up wrong; no need to put her with the crazies but let's keep an eye out, for everyone's sakes.*

The sweet spring air is a balm after all the hours cooped up inside and Alice takes it in in big lungfuls. Only time will tell.

Chapter 22

The gates swung slowly open and Madison put her foot on the accelerator; as they locked shut behind them she felt Kelly bristle at her side. They had been inside countless jails and yet a residential home for the mentally ill was a slightly different game, however lovely it looked in its landscaped gardens.

'Be good to know how Ronald Gray could afford this place,' Madison said.

'It's prettier than *my* house,' Kelly replied.

Both of them had forgotten that they were not supposed to talk to each other.

The silver sky brought out the deep green in the firs that dotted the grounds; Boston ivy would make the red brick building even lovelier in the fall. They followed the drive that wound around the lawn and parked in a visitors' parking lot to the side of the main building; it was Monday and it was almost empty.

As Madison locked her door she noticed a solitary figure looking out from one of the windows on the top floor, staring at the line of trees. For some reason she turned, but there was no one there, only the growing darkness pooling between the branches.

Kelly seemed troubled.

'What's wrong?' Madison asked him. They had already spoken that day; she figured another couple of words wouldn't hurt.

Kelly rolled his broad shoulders under the coat. 'Ever feel if you walk into this kind of place they're not going to let you back out?'

He wasn't being prickly, he was being honest.

'Every single time,' she replied without hesitation.

He snorted. 'One day it might just happen.'

The reception was brightly lit and friendly, more a country hotel than a clinic whose residents couldn't leave.

Dr. Eli Peterson was waiting for them. He was late thirties, a little gray in his copper hair and a couple of inches taller than Kelly. Her grandmother would have said he was *a fine-looking young man*. The receptionists, Madison noted, gazed at him like he was the Second Coming. He didn't seem to notice. From their phone conversation Madison had imagined an older man in a tweed jacket; Eli Peterson wore pressed jeans and a white button-down with a tie. He introduced himself and they shook hands.

'Let's go to my office; I'll explain once we're there.'

He punched in a code and led them through a door and corridors to an office wing. The inside of the Walters Institute, what they could see of it, was as pleasant as the outside and Madison wondered if any of the people who had nodded hello to them were longterm residents or just doctors and nurses.

The office of the institute's director turned out to be the same size as the ones on either side; it was simply decorated with antique furniture and bookcases crammed with tomes. There were diplomas on a wall but that was as far as Peterson's ego went. He motioned for them to sit but he himself went to stand by the tall window behind his desk; the view of the grounds ran uninterrupted to the line of firs.

He had hardly made eye contact on the walk there and now he seemed to be struggling with whatever it was that had made him pick up the phone and call them. Madison hoped Kelly would let him come to it in his own time and heard the squeak of leather as her colleague shifted in his chair.

'I first met Ronald Gray ten years ago,' Peterson said suddenly, as if they were already in the middle of a conversation. 'That's when I started working here. Ten years ago: three as associate, five as deputy, two as director. By then Ronald had already been coming for years, of course, and inevitably we got to know each other on his visits.'

'His visits to his foster brother?' Madison asked.

'Yes.'

'Dr. Peterson, what you said on the phone earlier—'

'I spoke with Ronald the day he died – the day he was murdered – and he was terrified.'

'What did he say?'

No one – not at work, not one of the neighbors – had spoken with Gray the day he died.

'He said he was going out of town for a while and that we shouldn't expect any visitors for Vincent. In fact, if anybody came looking for him we should be very wary. He stopped short of saying we should call the police because that's not our remit here – we're not a jail – but that is what he meant. He said I should keep Vincent inside and not let him out in the gardens either. He seemed exhausted and paranoid.'

'Was that unusual?'

'Very. Ronnie was a quiet kind of person – reserved. I asked him if he wanted to come in and talk about it. He said there wasn't time but that I should look after Vincent while he was gone.'

'Did he say why he was going away?'

'No.'

'Did he mention names, situations, someone who was after him and Vincent?'

'No. He just said he had to go away immediately and his car's transmission was dead.'

Madison and Kelly exchanged a look: that was why Gray had been at the coach station.

'Let's start from the beginning. You said Gray had been coming since before you started working here?'

'Vincent Foley became a resident in the 1980s; he's our longest-staying-resident, in fact.'

'What's . . .?'

'What's *wrong* with him?'

'Yes.'

'Are you familiar with the Wechsler Adult Intelligence Scale?'

'Yes.' Madison refrained from mentioning her Psychology Degree and that she had spent weeks writing about W.A.I.S.-III, K.B.I.T. and even K.T.E.A. As a student she had given enough tests to teenagers and adults to see the block-shaped designs even in her dreams.

'Vincent Foley, who's forty-eight years old, was tested as a teenager and as a young man – before coming here – and his IQ score was put at sixty-nine which is below average, in fact borderline low.'

'Was he tested here?'

'No.' Peterson shook his head. 'By then he couldn't be tested. He's not here because he has an IQ of sixty-nine; he's here because something happened to him one day and his intellect did not have the resources to deal with it and effectively shut down. Nobody knows what happened and he has never been able to speak of it. He had been living his life – as best he could under the circumstances – being looked after by Ronald and with a degree of independence. Then one day Ronald got back from work and found him in a catatonic state. He came out of it eventually but he hardly spoke; when he did he didn't make sense, and there were fits and terrors and suicide attempts. Ronald couldn't look after him anymore and brought him here.'

Something occurred to Madison just then. 'Doctor, you are putting aside doctor–patient confidentiality.'

Peterson sat at his desk. 'Vincent Foley doesn't have anyone else; he's *my* responsibility now in every way. And I thought Ronald was paranoid; I wanted him to come in for a *chat* . . .'

Madison nodded. She could well imagine the conversation and the doctor thinking quietly to himself that maybe Gray needed to lighten up and have a Happy Meal.

'He was a volunteer here,' Peterson continued. 'He visited Vincent once a week and a few days a month he would do some filing for us. He had his own volunteer staff ID.' He closed his eyes. 'When he called and said no one should visit Vincent, that he should be kept inside, I thought he was high or intoxicated.'

'Had that ever happened?'

'No, never.'

'Has Vincent Foley ever had any other visitors except for Gray?'

'No.'

'You're sure?'

'I'm positive.'

'Then you saw the news . . .'

'Yes.'

It's the oldest joke in the book: just because you're paranoid it doesn't mean they're not out to get you. Gray had not been high, he had been right on the money.

'How could he afford this place?' Kelly asked out of the blue.

'We're a non-profit organization. All our patients are here on that basis.'

'Why was Gray afraid for Vincent Foley?' Madison asked.

'I don't know. I have no idea. Vincent is in his own world and he has no contact with the outside.'

'We need to speak to him. Has he been told about Gray?'

'I haven't told him yet.' Peterson straightened the papers in front of him, a small gesture of self-comfort. 'Vincent doesn't interact with people with ease; he has fixations and compulsions and he lives every second of his life in a state of acute anxiety, but he recognized Ronald and he was always calmer after his visits.'

'What is he afraid of?'

Madison regretted the words as she said them: Vincent Foley's horrors lived this side of the walls and had no reach and thus no bearing on the outside.

'The sun going down,' Peterson replied. 'He's afraid of the darkness at the end of the day. He thinks someone is after him and they will come at night.'

It was a simple, straightforward fact: someone had done something to him in the past, someone might come again.

'Was the original assault reported? Was there a police report?'

'No. Ronald told me long ago that he couldn't get him to speak of it and there weren't any physical injuries. He wouldn't have known what to put on the report. By the time Vincent was admitted here it was months after the event. We tried Cognitive Behavioral Therapy, we tried pretty much anything we could, but nothing helped. Vincent used to stack shelves in a supermarket; he would come and go from work alone. He would have been an easy target.'

'Have you ever seen this man before?' Madison produced Warren Lee's photograph from his driver's license.

'No.'

'His name is Warren Lee. Has Gray ever mentioned him?'

'No.' Something shifted and clicked in Peterson's mind. 'It's the man who was found days ago.' He didn't say *the man on the chair* and yet the words hung in the room all the same.

'Yes.'

The news had reported enough details, enough facts that even a man who wasn't interested in the particulars of such a violent death knew what had happened and how.

'How did Ronald die?' he said finally.

One of the few positive aspects of the Gray case was that the primary crime scene had been the deserted warehouse: his body had not been photographed huddled in a corner by casual walkers with phone cameras and internet, and the specifics of his murder were still, at least for the moment, not in the public domain.

Madison wanted to say *quickly, he died quickly and painlessly*, because Peterson seemed a kind man who already felt guilty for not taking Gray's fears seriously. Even so, a lie was a lie and in a double homicide investigation the weight words carry is measured in long tons.

'We are still gathering all the facts,' she replied.

'I understand,' Peterson said, and he did.

'What color was it?' Kelly asked.

Madison and Peterson both turned.

'What color was what?' Peterson said.

Madison snapped to the idea and kicked herself for not thinking about it. Or not thinking about it *first*. 'His staff ID. What color was the plastic volunteer staff ID Gray had?'

Kelly nodded.

Peterson held up with thumb and forefinger the black plastic sleeve that hung from his neck on a strap. It contained a card – on it a photograph, his name and a barcode; it was barely bigger than a driver's license.

'It was like this one.'

It was a piece of black plastic, nothing more than that, and yet what Madison saw was Ronald Gray rushing through his apartment, grabbing clothes and packing them in his small wheelie case. They had gone through it, through drawers and cupboards and the small desk, and there had not been one single item that had led them to Vincent Foley. They wouldn't even have known about him if Peterson hadn't called because, as he was running for his life, Gray had dug out every letter from the Institute, every medical report, every scrap of paper and every picture taken in the last however many years and had turned them into ashes, including his own volunteer staff card, now a melted lump on the bottom of a saucepan on a table in the lab.

Ronald Gray's body had been found as life had left him, cowering in a corner of a desolate building, and yet his last act had been to shield and protect another human being.

'If you want to meet Vincent, I should first check how he's doing today. I haven't seen him yet. I'll be right back.'

They were left alone in the office. Kelly stretched his legs, rested his head on the back of the leather chair, and stared at the ceiling. Madison went to the window; beyond the trees and Lake Washington, Kirkland would be getting itself ready for the evening.

The heavy clouds had finally let go and the rain fell in sheets. Madison's gaze followed the line of trees. This must be the worst time of day for Foley. It was possible that he actually knew something: the man had been inside these walls for a very long time and the only thing he might conceivably know something about was what had happened to him before he was admitted. Maybe there was more to it than an assault on a vulnerable individual. Still, the paint flakes linked Gray to Lee, and whatever threat had panicked Gray into leaving town also connected Lee and Foley.

She turned; Kelly was still staring at the ceiling, without any inclination to share his thoughts.

'We need a timeline,' she said.

'We have it,' he replied without looking at her. 'It still starts with the Lee home invasion.'

'If Foley is connected and he's been here this long, it must start way before then.'

Chances were that it was the news of Lee's murder which had scared Gray.

'If Foley has been here this long,' Kelly said. 'And he wasn't that bright to start with – after all the meds his brain'll be mush and you'll get more out of talking to a lampshade.'

Madison wanted very badly to disagree and yet, however crudely put, Kelly had a point.

'Maybe so,' she said. 'All the same, Gray is dead and there's a significant chance Foley is in danger too.'

'Right now, he's nice and snug in his white straitjacket. I wouldn't worry about him.'

'What would you worry about?'

Kelly didn't get a chance to reply.

'Vincent is okay; not his best day but not his worst either,' Peterson said, standing in the doorway. 'If you want to meet him I have to ask you not to say anything about Ronald's death or anything that might upset him in any way.'

'Would he even understand it if we told him?' Kelly said.

Madison hoped that the doctor had not heard Kelly's earlier comments.

'We don't know exactly how much he understands or how much his mind is able to process. Vincent understands about fear, about pain. That's all you need to know.'

Peterson's eyes measured Kelly and found him lacking, and Madison knew then for sure that he had heard him.

Kelly stood up.

'And you're going to have to check your weapons,' Peterson said as he turned away.

Madison wrapped the leather strap around the holster, its weight so familiar in her hand, placed it in the locker and turned the small key in the lock. The visitors' room had rows of cubbyholes; most of them stood empty, the doors open. Kelly was doing the same.

'Doctor, when was the last time Gray visited? The last time you saw him?' Madison asked as Peterson led them down a corridor.

'I saw him a couple of weeks ago, but I don't know if it was the last time he was here. I'll have to check.'

'Do you remember anything unusual on that visit?'

'No, I'm sorry. We might have exchanged a couple of words but I can't remember anything strange or different about that day. I thought about it after I heard the news.'

'How many patients are here full-time?'

'Thirty-nine.'

The doctor took his ID card out of the sleeve and swiped it through the side of the elevator's call box.

'Without one of these you can't go anywhere,' he said.

'How do visitors get in?'

'They're brought in by a nurse or a nurse's assistant.'

'Each one?' Kelly asked.

'Each one. Visitors have to call before coming, as the patient might not be well enough to see them on that day.'

The elevators' doors slid shut and a slight lurch told them they were moving. Madison felt a tiny spike of adrenaline.

'What kind of security do you have here?' she asked.

'A couple of people monitoring the grounds, a couple near the reception and the exit. We don't need guards. Our doctors, nurses and assistants are more than capable of dealing with any situation.'

Madison wasn't thinking about somebody who wanted out; she was thinking about somebody who wanted in, and how easy it would be to get to the floor where Vincent lived.

'What kind of meds is he taking?' she asked. *Would he be too out of it to defend himself if someone came at him? Not that being drug-free had helped Warren Lee or Ronald Gray.*

'Sertraline. It helps with the post-traumatic stress disorder episodes. The problem is that there haven't been many studies on PTSD in people with learning disabilities.'

Kelly stood stiffly with his back against the elevator's wall. Madison believed in that moment he could not possibly care less about studies of post-traumatic stress disorder in people with learning disabilities:

he just wanted to be elsewhere, out of that building, away from the faint scent of hospital disinfectant that seemed to wrap itself around you and squeeze. She was glad it was not chloroform.

They walked out into a windowless landing with another heavy-duty door and a swipe box. Madison took mental note of each security measure. A small camera on a high bracket followed them as they went through.

'This way,' Peterson said. 'Vincent is in the day lounge.'

It was a long bright corridor with patients' rooms on both sides, most of the doors open though Madison did not even glance inside; they just nodded to a few doctors and nurses who went about their business.

They reached the end of the corridor; a nurse in blue scrubs stood by the door to the day room, keeping an eye on its sole occupant.

'Thank you, Thomas,' Peterson said. 'I'll take it from here.'

Vincent Foley didn't stir as they approached. He stood framed by the tall window looking out. Lines of rain streaked the thick glass, what was beyond it made invisible by the light inside.

'Vincent . . .' Peterson said gently.

Vincent Foley turned.

Madison didn't gasp and her face didn't change; it took all she had not to react. The man before her, impossibly pale and as slight as a boy, didn't look a day over twenty. Livid shadows under his eyes spoke of sleepless nights; his short hair, baby soft, stuck out in straw-colored clumps with some gray in it, the only sign that Vincent Foley was forty-eight years old. He couldn't defend himself if a third-grader swatted him, Madison thought.

'Hello, Vincent,' she said.

Vincent's eyes were piercing blue and wide; they focused on Madison for the first time and she noted that while he seemed still he was in fact vibrating with tiny shakes that coursed constantly through his whole body. He blinked twice.

'Somebody's coming,' he said.

A long cold shiver uncurled itself down her back; his voice, reedy and frail, fit so well with the rest of him that she sensed Kelly recoil a little.

'Somebody's coming; it's getting dark,' Vincent murmured. 'We should go, we shouldn't stay here.' The shaking was getting worse.

'It's okay, Vincent,' Peterson said, in the tone of a loving father with a scared child. 'There's nothing to be afraid of. You're safe here.'

'No, I'm not safe. Nobody's safe.'

Madison overcame her first response and examined him objectively as the only living, breathing part of their investigation. How in the name of all that's holy were they going to have a conversation with him about anything?

'Why are we not safe?' she said, aware that the doctor was ready to interrupt this little get-together any time he wanted.

Vincent looked at Peterson for reassurance.

'Go on,' the doctor said.

Vincent shook his head. 'It's not safe after dark and it's not personal, it's business.'

'What is not personal?' Madison asked him, her voice matching Peterson's, glad that Kelly had held back, his bulk like a boulder behind her.

Slowly Vincent held out his right hand open between them, then lifted the other and ran his left index finger over the back of the right, tracing the strained tendons, over and over again. His hands, smooth and delicate, were scrubbed clean, even though a line of grime had settled under the nails.

'What does it mean, Vincent?'

But he had turned away to face the window.

'Vincent?'

He didn't turn back.

Peterson motioned with his head and they left the room; the nurse was waiting in the corridor.

'He's all yours,' the doctor said to him.

Madison wasn't entirely sure of her own feet as she followed him down the corridor, as if part of her had stayed in the day lounge.

'Here,' Peterson said. 'This is his room.'

'What . . .'

Every inch of the white walls was covered in meandering gray crayon lines, over and under the bed, around the dresser and as far up as his arm would reach.

'May I . . . ?'

'You can go in. It'll take Thomas a few minutes to persuade him it's time to get ready for bed.'

Madison stepped inside and her eyes tried to read a pattern in the chaos of intersecting marks; they weaved and tangled and came apart. This was what he saw every night when he closed his eyes and every morning when he awoke.

If there was a part of Madison which had hoped against hope that it would be possible to get any kind of information from Vincent Foley, standing in this room surrounded by this madness made visible put an end to that pretty quickly.

'It's one of his compulsions,' the doctor said. 'At the beginning we attempted to stop him but it just made the episodes worse. The hand movement he does, that's another of his regular gestures.'

'What he said . . .'

'He says that every day, Detective, every time the sun sets. For him, no place is ever safe.'

They ran to the car and by the time they got in their shoulders were damp. Madison turned on the heater and the windscreen wipers as the engine warmed up. The Walters Institute loomed through the rain in the headlights, altogether less pretty now. In the visitors' room they had strapped on their holsters without a word.

'Don't tell me that he didn't creep you out,' Kelly said finally as he buckled his seat belt. 'Say what you want, just don't pretend that you weren't creeped out.'

'I don't know what I was,' Madison replied. 'There's something about him that's unnerving and—'

'He looks like a *child*. He's my age and he looks barely older than a boy. The lights are on but there's nobody home. He's a weird little creep and, frankly, he's no good to us or to the investigation.'

Kelly was angry because Vincent Foley had unsettled him and that was rare; Madison let him vent. Not weird, she thought, but eerie. Foley was *eerie*, like the relic of some Grimm fairy tale that didn't want to get back into the book it had come from.

'Is he in danger?' Peterson had asked as they were leaving.

'I don't know,' Madison had replied because she didn't want to lie to him one way or the other.

Back in the precinct, Madison dug out the relevant records and learned that Ronald Gray and Vincent Foley had been fostered by the same family – Mark and Vivienne Bell, four decades of fostering children in King County – since they were twelve and thirteen years old respectively. She could hardly imagine what Vincent would have been like as a boy and that other children might have been less than kind to him in school. Maybe Ronald had become his protector then. Neither had a juvenile record or anything to do with the law; that they had ended up being fostered after a series of different and yet similar events meant they had no one else but each other.

Madison wondered what Vincent had been like before that day, that moment when reality had ceased to make sense and his mind had splintered, and whether the haze of fear and damage that cloaked him like a shroud was a remnant of that day or had always been there.

Her hand hovered next to the phone: it had to be Brown's decision to go to the range with her, and calling him with the pretext of talking about the case looked just like what it was, a pretext. Even if she'd rather talk to him about it than anyone else.

The phone rang; Madison almost jumped; it was Sorensen.

'I have a few more goodies for you. They'll be in the report but I wanted to give you a heads-up.'

'We always welcome goodies here,' Madison replied.

'Well, you'll like these ones for sure: we have a footprint from the warehouse, recovered near the body. Working boot, size 11. Also a small amount of powdered detergent that matches the mess on the floor in Warren Lee's kitchen. And we have fibers from what looks like car upholstery, enough to match it to a car if you ever find one . . .'

'I'll do my best.'

'Honestly, the warehouse was dusty and dirty and full of what will probably turn out to be useless trace evidence; however, I'm told Lauren and Joyce hit the jackpot with the coach station restroom.'

'I hope they found something worth their time in that hell.'

'Another footprint, same boot as before.'

'Excellent.'

'And a smudged handprint . . .'

'Don't toy with me, Sorensen.'

'Do I ever?'

'A handprint . . . with fingers?'

'Yes, palm and fingers. It was low, about one foot from the ground, on the tiled wall. Someone tried to wipe it off but we might find enough points of similarity on it. I have no idea why it was there and it might be unrelated. Judging from the muck around it, it could be quite recent.'

'They swapped coats.'

'What?'

'The two guys who went into the restroom after Gray and grabbed him. One of them swapped his coat with him. He must have taken his gloves off to put it on Gray.'

'It was a pretty small restroom . . .'

'You bet. Easy to lose your balance, and then you put your hand out on the tiles to steady yourself. He realized what he'd done and attempted to wipe it off. Are you running it?'

'Yes, it's going through every system known to man. Just don't hold your breath – we still don't know for certain that it's relevant.'

'With what I have, I'll take every grain of detergent you've got.'

Madison briefed Fynn and Spencer on the day's developments and then turned off her desk lamp. She wanted to go to Alki Beach and run. In a day that had given her more questions than answers she longed for the simple, straightforward joy of pounding her feet on the sand and letting everything go. The forest might come back unbidden and with it the scent of blood, but she could deal with those, she could run through those.

In her car, though, the rain still falling heavily over the windscreen, Madison decided to go home, and cook, and eat, and think things over. Maybe not think too much, maybe not think at all. Vincent Foley's presence was like a bitter scent in her cold, damp car. *Somebody's coming.*

Chapter 23

Vincent Foley, twenty-three, stood by the door of Ronald Gray's bedroom. He was quiet and yet his misery was evident. Ronald ignored him; he knew what was coming and wanted none of it.

'I don't want to go,' Vincent said.

Sweet Jesus, his voice could be so annoying. Ronald continued dressing, buttoning up the cotton shirt that would no doubt become a sweat-fest as soon as he set foot outside the house.

'I don't want to.'

Ronald sat on the bed to do up his shoes.

'I don't—'

'It's work, Vin,' he said. 'We all go to work, right?'

'I know, but I don't like it.'

'It's going to be alright, you'll see.'

Vincent leant against the doorframe; at twenty-three he looked barely fourteen. He could certainly sulk like fourteen, Ronald thought.

'I don't like *him*,' Vincent whispered finally.

Ronald looked up. He wished he could say something to make him feel better. Vincent had always been afraid of this thing or that thing, ever since he had known him. He seemed to have a direct connection with terror every God-given day and, with the benefit of experience, Ronald knew there was precious little he could do to help him. Some things always worked though.

'Why don't we go for an ice cream tonight? Would you like that?'

Vincent shrugged but there was a faint smile there.

Chapter 24

John Cameron had measured his cell in KCJC in every way it could be measured: how many steps it allowed him to take in any direction, how many of the sounds around him would reach him if he wanted to block them out, how much of himself would stay within those walls if, from time to time, he wanted to leave. The answer was *not much*: if he wanted to leave he could, anytime he so wished. His body, ostensibly asleep, lay utterly still on the bunk, and yet he was sitting in a deep leather chair, watching the pinpoints of light that were cars in the far distance, driving along the Alaskan Way Viaduct. It was the view from his home and he had done some of his best thinking there – mostly at night, always alone.

The burn on his right shoulder was an inconvenience, nothing more. The pain had been sharp; the painkillers had taken care of it quickly and what remained was a sense that the nature of his time there would be determined neither by the Washington State justice system, nor his own. As much as Nathan was doing all he could to get him out, there was much that was not in his hands. Cameron had followed the rules of the house so far; what would happen if anybody came at him with another one of those tiny little vials he couldn't say. He would defend himself, and that would be the swift and final end to any bail appeal and plea-bargaining conferences.

While he was in his cell he was safe, and so were they.

Under his pale lids, he tracked the pinpoints of light and the ferries all lit up as they crossed Elliott Bay. Ever since Madison had told him about David's body he had spent more time in 1985 than in the present. He had been so young when he had run into Timothy Gilman; he wondered what Gilman would have told him if he had met him today. Everything, Cameron thought. He would have told him everything about the kidnap, who paid him to take them and why. It was maybe his one regret, that he had been too young and too inexperienced to do what needed to be done, and had let Gilman die without getting each and every truth out of him.

That one day, July 4th 1985, was the last time they had all been together at the same time and in the same place. It was a comfort to go back to it and it was etched on his skin.

John Cameron, twelve, ran the length of the diving board and leapt, grabbing his knees close to his chest and yelling his delight for all the world to hear. He swam to the bottom – his ears let him feel the pressure – and looked up: the stone edges of the pool were distorted and so were the people standing near. He tried to lie on the bottom: it was difficult but he managed it, and for just an instant above him all was sky.

After a few moments his lungs begun to burn and he followed the air bubbles back up; the surface of the water was full of light as he flicked the hair off his eyes. He loved the Locke estate, he just *loved* it: acres and acres of woods it was safe to explore, and the parents let them roam as they pleased. Conrad Locke had started from nothing and married money, his father had said, which John hadn't quite understood at the time, and knew everyone from the local sheriff to the governor. But what mattered to John was that they were going to get dry and go for a wander. And please God let Bobby Locke stay by the pool because it would be impolite for the three of them to tell him to get lost in his own backyard.

John lay on the recliner and closed his eyes. Nearby he heard Nathan's voice calling out to David.

They sneaked away from the pool area as soon as they could: John's hair was drying in short little spikes and Jimmy's shorts were still damp over his trunks. They gave him a couple of *wet-pants* though they were more out of duty than serious ribbing, and they proceeded toward the dense woods behind the house.

'It's not a house,' Bobby Locke had said in the tone that explained why nobody could stand him. 'It's a ranch.'

To which John, David and Jimmy had rolled their eyes as far back as they would go. Now Bobby was inside with his cousins, busy with a videogame.

'He's *in the ranch*,' David had said, and they'd all laughed like hyenas without quite knowing why.

'What are you three little thugs laughing about?' Nathan had asked, and David had told him.

John thought Nathan was alright as older guys go – dorky but alright. One day he had been in high school, the next he was a grown-up with a starter beard and a summer job across the country. Still, David was the only one with a sibling and that made Nathan okay – better than okay, in fact. The way John saw it, seven years was a good age difference: distant enough they wouldn't compete for the same toys but close enough to tag along if he was doing anything interesting. There had been Sonics games in the past and fishing trips; in the last year though they had barely seen Nathan, and anyway they were old enough to go fishing at Jackson Pond by themselves.

The ground under their feet was hard and almost dusty in the July heat. The spruces gave some shade and they meandered for a while without too much thought. Jimmy had a penknife and he was using it to sharpen a stick, David pointed his new camera and snapped everything that moved, and John picked the pebbles off the path and threw them into the bracken. They didn't need to talk and when Jimmy broke the silence the others stopped and turned.

'I heard something the other day,' he said. 'I don't think my dad wanted me to hear it.'

It got their attention faster than any other opening line.

'He was on the phone and I don't know who he was talking to – could have been your dad,' he pointed at John, 'or yours.' He pointed at David.

'What did he say?' David asked.

Jimmy looked around and dropped his voice: 'He said, "I will pick up my bat and personally put a dent in their future if they ever come back to The Rock."'

David and John looked at each other; those were serious words for Jimmy's dad, who was the kindest, mildest guy you would ever have a chance to meet.

'Who was he talking about?' John said.

'I don't know; he must have heard me outside the door and changed the subject.'

'His *bat*?' David said.

Jimmy nodded.

'And he wasn't kidding? He wasn't, you know . . .'

'No way. He was deadly serious.'

The Rock, the restaurant owned by their fathers, had been in their lives for as long as the boys could remember.

'Has anything happened at the restaurant?' David looked at John, who just shrugged.

'Don't think so,' he said. 'I haven't heard anything.'

'And you're sure he meant business?' David asked Jimmy.

'No doubt about it. He sounded really mad.' What Jimmy didn't want to say was that his dad also sounded a little scared and *that* had frightened him more than anything, though he couldn't say that to the others either.

They mulled it over for a moment – three boys with their T-shirts stuck to their backs trying to work out if real, grown-up, honest-to-goodness violence was going to pass. Jimmy drew shapes in the dirt with his stick. What they all knew without saying was that anything to do with The Rock involved them all.

They walked on because moving was better than standing still, the heat suddenly more oppressive than before. The ground rose and fell and normally it would be one of the day's joys to scramble up and down the ditches and gulleys and pretend they were alone in a wild and unexplored land. Today though the mood had turned to muted worry: they were familiar enough with the usual middle-school disputes – mostly resolved by trash talk and the occasional lunch-break stand-off. This, one of their own fathers talking about hurting somebody with a baseball bat – this was a foreign land.

'I say we just keep our eyes and ears open and see what happens.' Only David could manage to make the only possible course of action sound like a smart plan. Yet once there was a plan in place, everybody felt better.

The inmates in the D Wing of KCJC were hollering a call-and-response chant, the guard telling them to cool it and shut it. In his cell, John Cameron breathed in warm July air and felt the heat of the sun on his cheeks.

Chapter 25

Dr. Eli Peterson had slept badly and the drive to the Institute did little to improve his mood. The previous day's rain had morphed into drizzle so pervasive that it was like mist; it took the edge off all the colors, especially the greens: through the driver's window, the grass was washed out to a dull gray and for a moment he wondered if that wasn't exactly the outcome of most of the meds his patients were given. Was he seeing what they saw every day?

He parked and walked to the main door without bothering with an umbrella. The receptionist gave him his mail, his messages, and a smile that would have sent a diabetic into shock. He didn't notice – he never did – but it didn't stop her.

He was about to swipe his card when he picked up and unfolded the small yellow square of paper with his deputy's scratchy handwriting. He read it once, and then read it again. Somehow he managed to use the swipe card and push through the door and run to his office without dropping anything. He dumped all he carried on the armchair in front of his desk, dug into his pockets and found what he was looking for: a key ring with three small silver keys.

One of those fit the lock in the bottom drawer and he opened it. He grabbed a single key which rested on a plastic folder and locked the drawer again.

At the end of the corridor there was a windowless room with a tall dresser that had been outfitted with thirty-nine drawers, one for every patient. The yellow scrap of paper had told Eli Peterson that the last time Ronald Gray had visited Vincent Foley – the previous Thursday – he had placed something in Vincent's box. The box had been empty for over twenty years. Peterson fumbled with his master key and finally managed to get it open.

Madison's day off had started with Carl Doyle's call as per their routine. She sat at the table in the living room gazing out at the water. The view was blurry and she felt a little blurry herself – maybe another bad dream, she couldn't be sure.

'How is he?' she asked Doyle as she took a sip of nuclear-strength coffee. *He* was Quinn – no need to explain.

'Quiet,' he replied. 'He's been really quiet since last Wednesday.'

The night of the appeal, Madison thought.

'Not that he's particularly expansive at the best of times . . .' he continued.

And this is definitely not the best of times, Madison thought.

'Everything's progressing: the blood work looks good, whatever spleen he has left is working to compensate for the bit that's gone. He's getting restless. Will you be going to visit Cameron today?'

Madison had been asking herself that very same question since she'd woken up. She hadn't seen him since the attack in the walk-alone: half of her wanted to check on him and the other wanted to ignore him after his no-show at her last visit. The choice was between anxious and petulant.

'I don't know, Carl.'

'Fair enough. Is there any news on David Quinn?'

'We still haven't managed to get a forensic anthropologist to have a look. Do you know how many of those there are in the US? I mean, how many certified by the ABFA?'

'A few hundred, I guess.'

'Ninety-two. I checked.'

'Ninety-two?'

'Yes, and David Quinn is a low priority right now.' Madison thought of the small hole and the men who had put the body of a child inside it.

Six days had passed since Quinn's appeal and still they had not spoken.

'Let me know if you decide to go,' Doyle said.

'Will do. Nothing says *day off* like correctional institute coffee and a chat with Deputy Warden Thomas.'

'Glad you're living the dream, Detective.'

After they hung up Madison, still in her pajamas and bunny slippers, padded to the French doors, leant her brow against the cool glass and closed her eyes. She might as well admit it: she was both anxious *and* petulant. *So be it. Who cares ultimately?* The man had been attacked with bleach; she had to see him. She was turning to call KCJC and book her visit when her cell started beeping.

'Madison.'

'Detective, it's Eli Peterson from the Walters Institute.'

From the end of the conversation, it took Madison nineteen minutes to leave the house – including a shower, another gulp of coffee and getting her off-duty piece out of the safe. She didn't want to call Fynn until she knew exactly what they had in their hands.

The drive felt excruciatingly slow and it wasn't until she pulled in at the gates that she realized it hadn't even occurred to her to call Kelly.

The message to the doctor had been brief and clear: *Whatever it is, do not touch it until I get there.*

Once again Peterson was waiting for her by the reception desk.

'It's in my office,' he said.

He didn't attempt any small talk on the way there and she was grateful for it.

'Can you tell me about the boxes?' she asked him.

He spoke as they strode down the corridor. 'Every patient has one. If someone has a few objects that are dear to them but cannot be kept in their room for their own safety . . .'

'A necklace, a chain, a brooch, that kind of thing?'

'Exactly. They go into their box and they can have them when they want them. It's a comfort for them to know their things are here—'

'And it makes it easier for you knowing they're not going to be used to self-harm.'

'It's a balance between a person's emotional well-being and their physical welfare.'

'What about Vincent's box?'

'It's always been empty. Until last Thursday, that is. Ronald asked my deputy to put something in it for safe keeping because it was something that belonged to their foster mother and had special meaning for Vincent.'

'Those were his exact words?'

Peterson gave her the note; the door to his office was open and Madison saw the bundle wrapped in silk blue fabric on Peterson's desk.

'Look,' he said, 'maybe I asked you to come for nothing. Maybe it's just . . .'

But Madison had already crossed the room, almost forgetting he was there, to stand behind his desk. She turned on the anglepoise lamp and directed the cone of light straight on to the oblong swaddled in what looked like an inexpensive scarf. From her jeans she took out a pair of latex gloves and snapped them on.

It looked like a smallish box. Madison picked it up to feel the weight of it and its contours.

'It's a book,' she said as she started to loosen the fabric around it.

It turned out to be a volume three inches thick with yellowing pages. Madison stared at it. 'It's a Bible.'

'I'm sorry,' Peterson replied. 'I thought it might have been something to do with the case.'

Madison picked up the yellow scrap she had dropped on the table.

'Your deputy wrote that Ronald gave him this to keep for Vincent,' she said, 'because it had belonged to their foster mother.'

'Yes.'

Madison opened the book to the front page. 'It's a King James Bible.' She turned each page carefully, looking down one side first and then the other.

She was halfway through *Genesis* when Peterson spoke. 'Detective . . .'

Madison looked up. 'Mark and Vivienne Bell were Jewish; Ronald Gray's and Vincent Foley's foster-parents were Jewish. This,' she held up the book, 'is a Bible. Whatever Gray wanted with it, I doubt it was a family heirloom. I'd like to speak with your deputy, please.'

She went back to *Genesis*.

The pages were printed on thin paper – almost translucent – and so far, deep into *Exodus*, Gray had not underlined any passages or made any notes in the margins.

'He's just gone off shift. I'm sorry,' Peterson said, coming back into the office. 'I'll write down his number. He's done the night – and it was a heavy one – so he might be a little punchy. Anything?'

'Not yet.'

A part of Madison, the dark tinny voice that whispered to her of mistakes and uncertainty and, occasionally, wickedness, spoke now and said that the book in front of her was nothing but a book; it might be a good book – even the best of books – and yet it was nothing but a book, and thus worthless to the investigation. I don't think so, she thought. *Ronald Gray knew what he was doing.* She would go through it word for word if necessary. Madison flipped through the thousand-plus pages and the tips of her fingers felt the irregularity before she saw it. She didn't even have time to think: the book fell open and it was clear that a number of pages had been glued together. Something had been purposefully trapped between them as if inside an envelope. It was invisible if you looked at it from the side but once you reached that point . . . there it was. Madison gave the smallest of smiles.

'What is it?' Peterson asked.

She showed him. Ronald Gray had chosen well: whatever he was hiding was nestling inside the Book of Revelation.

Madison speed-dialed Sorensen as she wrapped the Bible in the silk scarf.

Eli Peterson watched as Madison drove off at speed. She had thanked him and he had felt a little better about doubting Ronald, but only a little: the lawn was still pale gray and indistinct, and they all lived in a world where Vincent Foley was right.

Chapter 26

Sorensen's lamp was the brightest light Madison had seen that day and it shone directly on the blue silk. The bench had been cleared, disinfected, and covered by a sheet of clean paper.

'Who handled it?' Sorensen asked Madison; she wore an immaculate lab coat and her red hair was pulled back in a ponytail.

'Ronald Gray, Peterson's deputy, Peterson and yours truly, as far as I can tell. We don't know yet when Gray bought the book or if it was already in his possession. We don't know anything at all about the book.'

'We'll get to that later; first I'd like to *liberate* whatever is held between these pages.' Sorensen put on a head-mounted magnifier. She examined the book from each side and finally peered at the pages bunched together for a long, silent minute.

Madison fidgeted quietly, leaning against the wall. She knew Sorensen – hurrying her would produce no results except for a thorough lecture on the life-enhancing benefits of patience. On the drive to the lab Madison had had time to think about Gray and what he had left for them to find. An explanation would have been nice and yet somehow she didn't think that was how things would play out. Whatever it was, Gray thought it had *meaning*, something so valuable it had to be kept safe in the only place he could find which the men who were after him could not reach – the men who were after Vincent.

Sorensen swabbed the side of the book and smelled the spatula, then offered it to Madison. She leaned over and sniffed it. Nothing. Madison had come to believe the crime-scene unit investigator had developed the olfactory system of a hound.

Sorensen smiled. 'What kind of kid were you, Madison?'

'That's an interesting question.'

'Did you ever do stuff you were not supposed to do?' Sorensen had turned and was looking for something inside a wall cabinet.

Madison had absolutely no idea where they were going with this. 'Amy . . .'

'Did you ever *steam* open a letter that was not addressed to you?'

'I see . . .'

Madison had indeed never steamed open a letter that was not addressed to her; however, she understood the notion very well. The steam alters the adhesive properties of the glue and an envelope can be opened or pages separated.

Sorensen made brief work of getting the steamer up to the required temperature and aimed the narrow nozzle at the edges of the book. It took less than two minutes. Her tweezers picked up the corner of the first page and turned. Gray had done a reasonably good job: Sorensen had turned six pages when she hit the jackpot.

'Here we go . . .' she said and Madison leant forward, ready for anything.

A white paper coin envelope, about 4 x 6 inches, had been placed in the middle. Sorensen lifted it with her tweezers and something behind it caught the light: at first it seemed as if a minute pool of gold had taken shelter in the small print of Revelation.

She laid the envelope next to the book and delicately teased their find out of the niche Gray had scraped into the paper.

'It's a medal,' Sorensen said.

A neck chain unraveled as Sorensen lifted the delicate oval to her eyes. 'There's the image of a saint and some words: "Saint Nicholas – pray for us."'

Madison stepped forward.

'On the other side I have initials – "D.Q." – and a date—'

'April 14, 1972,' Madison said.

Sorensen looked up. '4–14–72. How did you . . . ?'

Madison stared at the droplet of gold that held all the light in the room. 'It's David Quinn's date of birth, and that's the medal his father's relatives gave him. He was wearing it the day he was killed.'

Madison heard Detectives Frakes' voice. *Did you find the gold chain on the remains?*

Sorensen was never speechless and this was a first. For a moment they both just watched the medal as it swayed lightly with each heartbeat.

'The envelope, Amy . . .' Madison blurted out.

'Yes,' Sorensen said. She laid the medal to one side.

The woman reached inside with the tweezers and slid out the contents: a thin yellowish scrap of paper folded in half. Sorensen spread it.

The scrap was the top corner torn off a page; someone had ripped it very precisely to get exactly what they wanted.

'Photocopy,' Madison said, her eyes on the shaded blacks and grays of the image.

'Yes,' Sorensen replied.

'Yearbook?'

'Looks like it.'

On the scrap of paper, grinning as if he'd just heard the silliest joke, David Quinn in his school yearbook picture, around it a faint but unmistakable pencil line.

Chapter 27

Madison walked out of the lab and into the veil of rain. She resented the necessity of getting back inside her car; she needed to be outside, where at least she had the illusion of breathing more easily. They were *connected*, all of them, starting from Gray in the warehouse and Lee tied up to the chair with picture wire, going all the way back to the boys blindfolded in the woods. And Jerry Wallace, who had known so much about so many people, had gone missing just as she had needed his counsel.

Madison called the precinct to make sure Fynn was in his office and left word for Spencer and Dunne too. There was one more call to make and when it went to voicemail Madison could have whooped with joy.

'Kelly, it's Madison. Ronald Gray left a Bible in Foley's safe-box at the clinic. Inside it, he had hidden a neck-chain that belonged to David Quinn and a scrap of paper with his picture. I'm on my way to the precinct to brief the boss.'

No hellos, goodbyes or see you laters. If he wanted to come in he would, if not she had told him what was going on and that was enough for the moment. That was plenty.

One of the things she missed about working with Brown was that they could develop ideas and argue about them and eventually come to a conclusion, more often than not a shared conclusion. *Brown*. She'd call him later; he would want to know about this. And Detective Frakes too – he deserved to know.

In the end, whether Kelly had listened to the message or not, he had decided not to be a part of Madison's day. She briefed Fynn and the others in the lieutenant's office – door closed and blinds drawn.

'We seem to understand less about the Lee and Gray murders every day,' Dunne said once she had finished. 'Shouldn't it be the other way round?'

Madison replayed in her mind the conversation with Peterson's deputy; she had called him on her way in and though groggy with sleep he was very clear about the sequence of events.

'Gray took the Bible to the clinic last Thursday. He looked beat and edgy as hell,' she continued. 'He delivered the medal for safe keeping the day *after* Quinn's television appeal and *before* Warren Lee was attacked and his body found.'

Madison remembered Gray's apartment: the disarray left behind, the haste and the fear.

'The timeline begins with the appeal,' she said. 'He saw Quinn on television and he knew he was holding something that could get him into serious trouble. He wasn't going to come in, testify to whatever he knew and claim the reward. He was getting out of town as fast as he could.'

'What would you do if you had information that could net you in excess of a million dollars?' Dunne asked the room.

'I'd come in, testify, and pick up the cheque,' Spencer replied.

'What if the information Quinn was after is about what *you* did twenty-five years ago?'

One down, three to go. Three to go.

'I'd get out of town.'

'Not just Gray,' Madison interjected. 'He managed to destroy any link to Foley before he left. If they didn't know about him, they probably still don't know.'

'How about interviewing Foley? Is he anywhere near sane?' Dunne asked.

Madison shook her head. 'Not really, no. It doesn't mean he doesn't have anything to contribute though. There might be something there.'

'Great. Two dead guys and one certified psychiatric patient. That's three perfect witnesses.'

'Okay, starting point for the rest of the day,' Fynn said. 'What was Ronald Gray doing on August 28, 1985? I don't care what he was doing two weeks ago, I want to know how he got hold of that neckchain and why he left it for us to find. Madison, the photograph is being processed?'

'Yes. Sorensen is trying to pick up as much detail as possible from the photocopy, see if there is anything that can be matched to an original.'

'Spencer, is Foley in danger?' Fynn asked.

'Once they know Gray was protecting him, yes, definitely.'

'Dunne?'

'Maybe, but we still don't know what they're after.'

'Madison?'

'He will be in danger the minute they find out Gray was protecting him.'

Spencer and Dunne left.

'Aren't you off today?' Fynn asked her.

Madison shrugged. 'That's not how the day played out. I'll be around.'

'Kelly?'

'I left him a message.'

'How's it working out with you two?'

'It's delightful, sir.'

'I thought it would be.'

Madison had officially given up on having a day off. Then again, if she hadn't been at the precinct she would have been home thinking about the case or experiencing the charms of prison visits. Even if she had wanted to take out her kayak, the rain would have made it not impossible but thoroughly unpleasant and ultimately a waste of time. It was a pretty accurate description of her relationship with Kelly, Madison reflected as she sipped her coffee.

The Gray autopsy report was open in front of her; the photographs, stark and bleak, were fanned out on the desk.

They hadn't said it because they didn't need to: the obvious reason why Gray had the medal might be that he was one of the men who had taken the boys into the woods, one of the men who had dug a hole in the dirt and put David Quinn in it.

Madison looked at the autopsy pictures: the bruises were horrifying. She didn't know how to feel about it. Was this the fate Gray believed had been stalking him and Foley?

It required a change of perspective and Madison had felt it in Fynn and the others. For them Gray had started out as a victim; now he was possibly a kidnapper and a murderer, and yet he was still a victim. Madison replaced the pictures in the report and shut the file.

As lunchtime came round, Madison's thoughts were batting against the precinct's walls and she needed to get out and stretch her legs. The sky was overcast, the rain had decided to give up for at least a few minutes, and she resolved to walk down 5th Avenue toward Pine Street. She passed the Public Library on the corner with Spring and resisted the sudden impulse to go inside and spend the afternoon reading instead of going back to the precinct and looking at pictures of dead men who might or might not have been murderers.

She had always enjoyed ambling down 5th Avenue: the trees were doing their best in the winter chill and it was so much more pleasant than going from A to B in her Honda, even for half an hour. Other people hurried past Madison in the bubble of their own lunch break.

She reached Nordstrom on Pine and turned left. The Food Court on the third floor of the Westlake Center was as busy as always and that was exactly what Madison needed: watching people leading their lives, shopping, eating, and generally getting on with things. The smell of food being cooked or, more often, simply reheated was as sharp as it could be in a world of air con and ventilation. The warm air was heavy with jostling spices.

She silently apologized to her grandmother and queued for a burger and the fries to go with it; she found a spot at a large table and picked at her food. It was predictably awful and yet sometimes that particular kind of awful can be perfect. Half of the patty disintegrated in her hands and she wiped the mustard and ketchup off her fingers with a small paper napkin that wasn't really up to its job.

Something had unsettled her in a day rather crowded with unsettling things and she couldn't quite put her finger on it. She understood as she was washing her hands in the restroom by the Food Court: it was the pencil mark around David Quinn's photograph. Someone had drawn that line to make sure the kidnappers abducted the right children, because the kidnappers did not know what they looked like and did not know them personally.

It's not personal, it's business. Vincent Foley's reedy voice came back to her. The water ran cold on her hands and she saw him, standing in the white day room in his scrubs, holding his hands out to her and running his left index finger over the back of his right hand. And Madison knew then what she had seen. *It's not personal, it's business.* And why Vincent Foley was terrified of the sun setting each day. *Somebody's coming.* Damn right, Vincent, Madison thought as she hurried down the escalators and out of the building. She hailed a cab and got dropped off at the precinct – no time for pretty walks under the winter trees now. She found Fynn at his desk, a plastic container with a salad in front of him and the fork halfway up to his mouth.

'Gray left the medal in the Bible,' she said. 'He left the medal and the picture in case someone came looking, in case the killers caught up with him. He knew Peterson would contact the police on behalf of Vincent and we would go chasing after clues, and sooner or later the Bible would turn up. And if he made it out alive, nobody would ever find it. The Bible was insurance in case he didn't make it.'

'How did he get the medal?' Fynn sat back on the chair, the fork abandoned amongst the leaves.

'It's what we thought: three men plus Timothy Gilman. One down, three to go. Lee, Gray and Foley.'

'We have the same evidence now as we did an hour ago.'

'Foley showed me the hands.'

'He what?'

'Let me call Peterson.'

'Go right ahead.'

Madison dialed from Fynn's landline and put Peterson on the speaker. Spencer and Dunne came in.

'Doctor,' Madison went straight to it. 'Could you tell me the exact date Vincent Foley was admitted to the clinic?'

'Give me a second,' he replied and they heard the tapping of computer keys. Madison stared at a spot on the oatmeal-carpeted floor: if it was before August 28, 1985, her theory was all the way dead.

'September 17, 1985,' Peterson's voice came back.

Madison felt the spike of adrenaline hit and the coppery taste in her mouth. 'Thank you, Doctor. One more question: you mentioned that Vincent has a repeating pattern of gestures and actions, like the hand movements he did when we were there. Are there others? Are there any other similar – what did you call them – compulsions that you could mention?'

'This has nothing to do with Ronald.'

'Are there any other similar compulsions?'

The line went quiet for a long moment and Madison hoped to God Peterson wouldn't decide to claim doctor–patient privilege.

'There is something else, yes,' Peterson said after a while. 'He goes into the garden with the other patients – you know, it's a positive environment for them to be in . . .'

Madison waited. She could almost hear Peterson thinking and trying to measure the weight of his words. 'Doctor . . .'

'He digs, Detective. Vincent has to be supervised every time he is outside in the grounds of the clinic because he will run to the same spot and dig a hole in the dirt with his bare hands as hard and as deep as he can.'

Madison closed her eyes; she had seen that hole in the Hoh River Forest. 'The same spot?' She asked. *Vincent's hands scrubbed clean with dirt under the nails.*

'Yes.'

'Can you describe it to me?'

'I don't understand . . .'

'Please, Doctor, could you describe to me the place Vincent goes back to?'

'Well, it's right under a very tall fir. There's a shrub just nearby. The first time Vincent saw it in bloom he became so agitated he needed to be sedated.'

'It's called Bleeding Heart,' Madison said quietly.

'Detective . . .'

'I'll call you back as soon as I can, Doctor. Is Vincent okay today? I mean . . .'

'He is how he always is.'

'Thank you, Dr. Peterson.'

After she replaced the receiver, Madison took a deep breath. 'Vincent Foley has a tested IQ of sixty-nine; that is, that was the score when he was tested as a young man. When he was admitted to the Walters Institute, Ronald Gray said that months earlier Vincent had been the victim of some kind of assault – the details were unclear because Vincent could not explain. In essence something dreadful had happened to him and his mind had shut down. He suffered episodes of PTSD and still does to this day. I don't think that's what happened.'

'He digs . . .' Dunne said.

'The pit in the forest was dug under a Western Hemlock and a shrub of Dicentra Formosa.'

Spencer sighed. 'Bleeding Heart.'

'We have to prove the connections,' Fynn said. 'Who gains from their deaths? Who stands to gain from Lee's and Gray's everlasting silence? We need to work both ends of the case: find out who gave the order twenty-five years ago and we find who ordered Lee's and Gray's executions last week.'

Picture wire and the Book of Revelation.

'What about the hands?' Fynn asked Madison as she was almost out of the door.

She turned to him. 'The cuts on John Cameron's hand,' she said. 'Foley saw it happen – he saw it all.'

Chapter 28

Madison sat at her desk. The life of the shift flowed around her – phone calls and conversations and computer clinks – but she heard nothing. The notion that she had been standing two feet away from one of the men who had done that dreadful thing, that awful act that had changed so many lives in the space of a single missed heart-beat – it was almost too much to bear because wherever Vincent Foley was he could not be reached, he could not be taken down by the law, he could not be touched. What do you do with that? How do you begin to live with that?

Madison's hand reached for her phone; there was much she needed to tell, there were people who deserved to know what was happening. *Not now, not yet.*

She straightened the Gray file, first aligning the edges of the various reports inside it with the tip of her finger, then the small pile of notes and paperwork that seemed to have taken residence on her desk. She straightened the pens, the pencils and the orange Day-Glo marker. She straightened the pale pink eraser and the pencil sharpener. And finally, when everything was at a ninety-degree angle – even the yellow square Post-it pad – the sounds from the world around her found their way back into her consciousness and Madison flipped her notebook open, and began to write.

The details of the people involved might change – their motivations, the particular twist of their heart – however, the questions asked remain the same: who did this? Why did they do it? There were two bodies in Dr. Fellman's morgue and the questions had to be answered, and answered quickly.

They did not have all the links yet but they were working on it, because Nathan Quinn had been right: four men had taken the boys, and one man – or a group of men – had given the order. Where were they today?

Twenty years ago a man named Timothy Gilman fell into a trapping pit and died. There is reason to think he was one of the four kidnappers.' Madison grabbed her coat.

She dialed the call as she was leaving the precinct. 'I'm on my way now and it's not a social visit,' she said.

She remembered from Gilman's file that he was already in his early forties at the time of the kidnap. Neither Lee nor Gray had a record; in 1985 they would have been no match for Gilman, who had already done a stretch upstate for Assault in the Second Degree. He had to be the ringleader and he would not have taken orders from some fresh-faced twenty-year-old or someone like Vincent. *There is reason to think he was one of the four kidnappers.* Madison drove automatically and found herself pulling into the parking space before she knew it. She turned off the engine and gathered herself. The streaks of rain on the windscreen shielded her from view.

What had happened that night in December in the Hoh River Forest had left some kind of impression on her core not entirely unlike the whorl of a fingerprint on a lump of soft clay; she knew it was there even though she had hardly begun to understand it or measure its reach inside her. She couldn't even fathom the mark it had left on Nathan Quinn. Some religions believe that pain – physical and spiritual – has a purifying effect on the soul; Madison believed that pain was pain and you got out of it only what you brought in, and Quinn had had bagfuls of it.

It was only the belief that there was no way she would ever feel ready for this particular meeting that got her out of the car.

Madison knew where she was going, she knew the floor and where the room was placed in the corridor. She knew because she had come every day when the cuts and grazes on her face and hands were still healing, when Tommy was recuperating in his mother's arms and Nathan Quinn slept peacefully in the blank empty darkness of a medically induced coma.

He had been many things: the attorney who protected an alleged murderer; the man who held a small plastic tape with the potential to kill her career; he was the brother who had buried the memory of a thirteen-year-old boy in an empty grave. He had been many things, Madison thought as the elevator doors slid open, and she didn't know what he was now.

He's a relative of the victim, she told herself, and was glad for the sudden scents of the hospital and the paltry distraction they offered.

The door was closed and she knocked.

'Come in.'

Madison pushed the door and Nathan Quinn stood to meet her.

'Detective . . .' he said.

The scars were dark red lines that traversed his fine features. *So pale.* Tall and thin and stubble on his cheeks.

'Counselor . . .' she replied, looking and not looking at the same time.

'Carl let me know you were coming.'

'*What are you going to tell him?*'

'*The truth, Lieutenant, but as little of it as I can manage. What I don't tell him he will guess.*'

'I didn't know I was coming until then.'

'I'm always home,' he said with a small wave at the room.

Madison took it in: her university apartment hadn't been as large or as smart. Quinn wore linen – a charcoal shirt over navy blue drawstring trousers. He was barefoot and leant on a stick he grasped with his right hand. The room smelled of the fresh flowers arranged in a vase on a table – Carl's work probably.

'Not always,' she said. Doyle's gatekeeping in the worst days had been fierce.

'No,' he conceded.

'Things are happening, Counselor,' she said. 'Things are happening fast and I need your help and your advice. Shall we sit?'

He nodded and there was the smallest amount of relief as he sat in one of the chairs; Madison pretended not to notice it. She wondered briefly if he was on painkillers and whether they would affect his focus and his concentration. *Don't underestimate him. Bare feet and a linen shirt don't make him any less dangerous.*

In their acquaintance she had never lied to him and her honesty had been dearly bought. She wouldn't lie today and the truths she had brought were blades sharp at both ends.

'Something has happened,' she started. 'We have new information about the men who took them.' Madison let him absorb it; she didn't need to explain what she meant.

He was very still.

'I need you to tell me what you know about Timothy Gilman.'

Quinn sat back. 'This *thing* that happened, was it because of the appeal?'

'Possibly. We can call it an appeal if you like, but we both know you put a bounty on their heads.'

Quinn's eyes were black and held her.

'Did it work?'

Madison hesitated. 'We still don't know,' she replied. 'At this stage we are building the case, making the connections.'

'What can you tell me?'

A little pool of gold surrounded by small print. 'I can tell you that we found David's medal,' she said.

A pause. It was the first item ever recovered that had belonged to his brother and it would be the last.

'Where?'

'It was left for us to find as part of another investigation.'

'Another cold case?'

'No.'

Quinn nodded. 'The something that happened because of the appeal?'

'Yes.'

'I see.'

'That's why we need all you have on Gilman. We need to put him in the forest. Nothing in his record suggests his involvement.'

Quinn said nothing.

'Who told you about him?'

Quinn said nothing.

Gee, doesn't this bring back memories.

'Mr. Quinn, this is how I see it: the appeal was like a hand grenade – you had to throw it hard and far to get things moving. But Gilman, Gilman was the pin of the grenade. You put a bounty of over a million dollars on the heads of the men who killed David and you're just a brother doing what he can to bring murderers to justice. You say *Gilman*, and the people who did it, and those who paid them to do it, know you've got something real. And they scatter.' Madison took a deep breath. 'You wouldn't waste that opportunity with a name that wasn't gold, which means you had full confidence in the information. Gilman died twenty years ago. If you had found out while he was alive, you would have crucified him – figuratively speaking – and that means you found out *after* he had died.'

Quinn didn't seem in a hurry to join in the conversation and she remembered another day, another conversation, Cameron speaking to her and Quinn listening at her grandmother's table. She knew his silences.

'How did you find out about him?'

'I just did. How that came to be is irrelevant.'

'How can I verify the information?'

'You can't.'

'But you're betting the house on it?'

'Your assessment was right on the money. Would I use that name unless I was completely sure?'

'*Completely sure* is very nice but it doesn't really cut it with the King County Prosecutor's Office unless we have proof.'

'Then you might have to go another way.'

'There is no other way, and you know it. Gilman would have been the leader, he would have been the one giving the order. If I can't prove Gilman's involvement I can't get to the people who paid him to take them.'

Quinn leant forward and Madison knew that painkillers or not, his focus was as sharp as ever.

'Be. Creative,' he said.

'I can only work with what I have.'

'All evidence to the contrary. You believed John Cameron was innocent *in spite* of all the evidence you had.'

'Okay, I'll give you that one. What *can* you tell me?'

'Ask me and we'll see how it goes.'

'Was it an informant who told you about Gilman?'

'No.'

'Did you find out yourself?'

'Yes.'

'How?'

He shook his head.

'What makes you absolutely sure it was him?'

'It was him.'

'Was there an informant at any stage? Are you protecting someone?'

'You're asking the wrong questions, Detective.'

'Then you tell me, what are the right questions?'

'Someone left the medal for you to find?'

'Yes.'

'Perhaps one of the two men found murdered in the last week?'

What she wasn't saying he would guess. She chose her words carefully and gave him what truth she had.

'Mr. Quinn, I didn't come here to tell you that there is a very strong chance that two of the men who took the boys are dead. That's what I think, yes. And it's the trail I'm following. But I have no solid proof and you are the last person on this planet to whom I would ever say anything like that if I couldn't back it up.'

'You went to the place where they had buried him?'

Madison didn't even know how he could bear to say it, and Brown's words came back to her: *That man is made out of some kind of metal we don't even have a name for.*

'Yes, I went there. It was about a mile from the clearing.'

One day, when he left the hospital and when he could walk without that damn stick, Madison was certain he would find his way there too. Maybe by then Vincent Foley would have given up his secrets.

'Warren Lee and Ronald Gray,' Nathan Quinn said quietly.

'That's what you wanted,' Madison said. 'You knew we had less than nothing to work David's case: no new evidence, no new witnesses. Still, if the men who gave the order felt sufficiently threatened by your "appeal", they might very well decide to tidy up all the loose ends, and in the process they would give us something real to pursue. New evidence, new leads and new bodies,' she said. 'And somehow we'd follow the trail back to David.'

'Not everyone, no. Just you. I knew *you* would follow the trail back to David.'

Madison didn't know what to say to that.

'I'm only a brother doing what he can,' Quinn said.

'Don't underestimate yourself.'

'Do you have new leads?'

'Yes.'

'Then,' Nathan Quinn said, his voice coming from a dead place, 'it worked.'

'Two men were killed. Another might have been hurt.'

'I regret that. I had hoped for life-long imprisonment, one wretched day after the other.'

'Not a death sentence?'

'Have you ever tried maximum security with a child-killer sign around your neck?'

'We don't know for sure yet they were involved, and I still need Gilman.'

'Gilman is long dead.'

'Yes, and I'm sure we all regret his early demise. I still need to find out about him though.'

'I can't help you there, Detective.'

'Can't or won't?'

'Does it matter in the end?'

'Are you willing to stake the success of all this, finding those men and bringing them to justice, on that single piece of information you will not share?'

His eyes were bright – maybe it was fever, maybe not. 'Absolutely,' he replied.

What we choose to say, what we hold back, how the cards are held in the player's hands: Madison had been to countless poker games by the time she was old enough to realize there was something unusual about it. She didn't know exactly what she had now that she didn't have before; however, something in her guts told her that Nathan Quinn had inadvertently given her a small truth. Maybe the larger one would follow later.

'Where is he?' he asked her. The hospital around them had all but disappeared and Madison dreaded his next words.

'Who?' Madison replied. *One down, three to go.*

'The fourth man. The one you're not looking for. The one you haven't mentioned. Where is he?'

It was her turn to be quiet.

'You said you need Gilman to go after the men who gave the order, but there was a fourth man in the forest that day.'

'Yes, there was.'

'If you're not looking for him, it means you already know where he is. Is he dead?'

I don't know *what* he is, Madison thought. Was she really going to tell Quinn that there was a flesh-and-blood human being walking this Earth who had dug the hole in the ground his brother had been buried in? The world was not this hospital room – one day he would be out of here. One day he might stand in the same white day-lounge as Vincent Foley, who had garden dirt under his nails.

'Do you believe I could reach him from here? That Jack could reach him from where he is?'

'I don't want to lie to you,' Madison said simply.

'An admirable sentiment.'

'He's alive and he's not going anywhere.'

'You *have* him?'

In that moment Madison was grateful that Quinn was a sworn Officer of the Court and Cameron was behind a number of locked steel doors.

'We know where he is and, where he is, he's already in his own jail.'

'Where is he?'

'Where he can't be reached.'

'Have you spoken to him?'

'He's not in any condition to help with the case.'

Quinn took that on board. 'What happened to him?'

'I don't know. As far as I understand it, he was a witness. I can't tell you anymore about him for now – I hope you understand. We're still trying to put it together ourselves.'

Quinn nodded. 'He's not going anywhere?'

'He's in custody.'

'Will you bring charges?'

'It will be very difficult, practically impossible.'

'Where is he?'

'He's in a clinic for psychiatric disorders. Has been there since September 1985,' Madison said. 'One wretched day after the other.'

She stood to leave and started toward the door. Quinn stood with her.

In their acquaintance there was no room for those words, nevertheless they had to be said. 'How are you?' Madison asked him.

'Alive, Detective.' He unconsciously touched the place where his spleen would have been. 'More or less.'

'Yes,' she said. 'You're alive, and so is Tommy.' Sometimes *thank you* is pitifully inadequate.

'Carl says he's doing well,' he said.

'He is,' she replied. 'You asked me if I believe you could reach the fourth man from here. Truth is, I believe you could do anything you put your mind to; I know that for sure because Tommy will be seven in a few weeks.'

Madison's hand was already on the door when he spoke.

'Your ballistic vest saved my life.'

Madison nodded and left.

Chapter 29

August 28, 1985. It was a hot day coming at the end of a hot month; standing in the concrete parking lot on the corner of South Lander Street and Utah Avenue South, Ronald Gray was aware of the perspiration between his shoulder blades and how the fabric of his shirt stuck to it in patches. He had promised Vincent an ice cream at the end of their working day but he could do with one himself right now, with an iced beer chaser – actually, make that two. He squinted in the full morning glare and looked around: shoppers, passers-by and Vincent, hunched and unhappy.

The work would be straightforward: he had done something similar three times before, though never with kids. It would be easier than with adults, he thought. Kids can be handled without danger, they scare easy, and parents think twice before talking to the cops. The money today would be pretty damn good too – and that's where Vincent came in. He was a cheap pair of hands and didn't talk back.

He had taken Vincent on a couple of jobs before, as a lookout. The thing about Vincent was, he always did as he was told. If he told him to stand on that corner and wait for him until hell froze over . . . there he would stay, waiting, icicles dripping off his hair.

The blue van turned the corner and Ronald said to Vincent, 'You know what to do, right?'

Vincent nodded.

'Good man. Stand up straight,' Ronald said, as the van pulled up to them and stopped.

Timothy Gilman was driving. He should have been pretty relaxed considering the job ahead and yet he looked like something nasty was already curled up in his guts. Ronald knew Gilman well enough to know that he was a violent bully and nothing should please him more than a chance to lean on somebody and get paid for it. The fact that it was a bunch of kids was neither here nor there: Ronald didn't know anything about it except that their daddies had to get the scare of a lifetime. If they were so stupid they'd left themselves open to people like Gilman it wasn't Ronald's fault. He was there to do his job, and Gilman wanted Vincent because he was cheap. All in all, it should be a light day.

Warren Lee hopped off from the passenger side and Ronald sighed: he had met Warren a few times and he disliked him and despised him in equal measure. Warren was cut from the same cloth as Gilman but where Timothy had an honest-to-goodness temper that could strip paper off a wall, Warren was merely a little weasel with a taste for occasional violence.

'Hey, boys.' Warren grinned.

The blue van weaved its way through traffic. Ronald sat in the front between Gilman and Lee, and Vincent rattled around in the back. Warren had wound down his window and his bare arm was halfway out, catching the sun and the breeze. Ronald could feel his glee at the afternoon's endeavor and was vaguely repulsed by it. He was in it for the money – no more, no less. Gilman had said maybe three words in all, which was unusual; there was a grim determination about him that invited a respectful silence.

From a golden oldies station the Ronettes sang 'Be My Baby' as if it was all they needed for the world to be perfect. The sky was blue and the van was on its way to Jackson Pond.

Two hours later, Gilman drove the van as fast as the law would allow, Warren sat in the passenger seat – the window rolled up all the way in spite of the heat – and the radio was turned off. Nobody spoke.

In the back, Ronald Gray and Vincent Foley sat and crouched around the small bodies of three boys. The kids were blindfolded and unconscious, their hands tied at the front. In the gloom the smell of chloroform and sweat made Ronald's throat sting.

Vincent's eyes were huge as he gazed at the sleeping children. Ronald kicked his foot lightly. 'Don't watch them. They're not going anywhere,' he whispered.

Vincent nodded and looked away.

It had been so easy: Gilman knew where they'd be and when. Jackson Pond was a spit of a pool, hidden in a thicket of trees, and the road could take them almost right up to it. The traffic in both directions was light in that part of the park and nobody noticed when the van pulled up fifty yards before the trail to the pond.

Gilman dug out a scrap of paper from the back pocket of his jeans: it was the picture of a boy. He stared at it for a minute, then folded it and shoved it back in his pocket; he left them in the van and disappeared into the copse that lined the road.

Warren prattled on about some job or other he'd done for him and Ronald wished they would just get on with it: if he had to spend one more minute squeezed into that seat next to Warren he might just have to punch him into silence. Behind them, Vincent had not uttered a single word since they'd been picked up.

Gilman reappeared suddenly out of the woods. 'They're there,' he said.

He drove the van down a narrow trail, and when he turned off the engine all that was left was the sound of their breathing and the odd car going past in the distance.

He gave them masks to wear; he gave them dirty rags for blindfolds and rope to tie the children's hands. He told them exactly what to do and they did it. The kids didn't stand a chance.

The cigarette smoke rose and curled in the afternoon heat beating down on the clearing; above them, a patch of sky; around them, the old growth trees of the Hoh River Forest. It had been a long drive but the job was almost done. The men smoked, leaning against the van, and watched the boys, each blindfolded and tied to a different tree.

They had reached the clearing through an overgrown trail that had once led to a weather station; it was secluded and the men knew their work would not be disturbed. They smoked because they had all the time in the world and because in that world they had all the power they would ever need. Warren's eyes glittered as the children slowly began to stir.

The first boy – dark hair and slightly shorter the others – whimpered as he came to and felt the ropes that bound him to the tree. The second – dark hair, but taller – was awake and quite rigid with fear. The third – fair, curly hair and taller than the others – was trying to find his bearings, breathing hard under the blindfold and turning his head in the direction of the others. Gilman watched him.

In the stillness of the clearing there was nothing but cigarette smoke between the children and the men who had taken them. One by one, the boys smelled the scent of cheap tobacco and became quiet. A bird flapped and cawed.

It was time for the message to be delivered; Ronald turned to Gilman – he should have been moving now, talking, pushing and bullying and doing what he did best. Instead Gilman lit another cigarette, his eyes hardly ever leaving the blond boy. The silence stretched and Ronald waited. He knew without checking that Vincent was at his left – eyes blank, expecting instructions.

When Gilman spoke, Ronald felt a sense of relief: soon they'd be out of there.

'Boys, I want you to listen to me and listen good. Say yes.'

Nobody spoke.

'Say yes.'

Three faint voices did as they were told.

'This is a message for your daddies, I want you to remember it. The message is: it's not personal, it's business. You got it? Repeat it.'

The boys could barely get their voices out. Gilman paced back and forth between them and yet Ronald noticed that he kept an eye on the blond kid.

'Repeat it.'

'It's not personal, it's business.'

'Again.'

'It's not personal, it's business.'

'Hey, little guy. You heard me, right? You want to go home?' Gilman strode up to the boy tied to the first tree – the shortest and youngest, it seemed – and screamed right in his face. The kid's voice was caught in his chest and he could hardly breathe, let alone speak.

Ronald Gray thought of the money they would be paid and the down-payment on the car he wanted. By tomorrow at the latest the kids would be found. *No harm, no foul, message delivered.* He pretended to ignore the fact that Vincent had frozen as if Gilman had been screaming at him.

Gilman yelled, the boy shrunk against the tree and Ronald missed nothing – like the fact that while he was putting the fear of God into the little one, it was the other kid Gilman eyeballed every few seconds.

Finally, the little kid yelled out the words and Warren sniggered. 'Ooh, this one got a set of lungs on him.'

'Good job. Now, we are going to let you go home in a while but I want to be clear about something: you ever, ever tell the cops about this and I'm going to come back and take you. You ever tell anybody at all about this and I'm going to come back and take you, and I will hurt your mom and dad too. You understand? You saw nothing and you heard nothing. You just pass on the message to your daddies and everybody stays alive. You understand?'

'Yes.'

'See if you can get louder than that, you little girl.' Suddenly there was a blade in Gilman's hand and he slashed at the boy's arm.

'The hell are you doing, man?' The words left Ronald's lips before he could call them back.

'Shut up. Don't make me do this, boy. Let's hear it.'

The boy yelped as the blade cut his arm again.

'Hey,' Warren said to no one in particular. He was a coward and a fool but even he could sense that this was moving into a whole new direction and it meant bad news for yours truly.

'Get into the van and shut the fuck up,' Gilman said calmly.

'C'mon man, let's get out of here,' Ronald said.

'What are you doing?' It was the blond kid's voice and Ronald could have sworn – man, he could have bet all he had in the bank that there was a dark delight in Gilman's eyes as he turned to him.

'Leave the kid alone. Let's go,' Ronald repeated.

'Don't make me do this, you little shit. Let's hear it.' He cut the boy again.

'Stop it!' The tall kid was straining at the ropes.

'What did you say?' Gilman moved toward him.

'He's just a little kid. We'll do what you want – just stop hurting him.' The boy sounded out of breath.

'If you want to go home in one piece, boy, you're going to have to shut up right now.'

It happened right then: one second the blond kid was okay, the next he couldn't catch his breath. Under the grimy rag they had used as a blindfold, he was straining to get air in his lungs.

'What's wrong?' Warren said.

'He's not breathing. Cut him loose.' Ronald stepped forward.

'Don't touch him – he's going to be fine.' Gilman put out his arm, the blade of the knife pointed squarely at Ronald's chest. 'Touch him and I'll cut your hand off.'

'There's something wrong with him,' Vincent whispered.

'We can see that, you moron. Cut him loose,' Warren said.

'No.'

The breathing was fast and shallow and becoming fainter by the second.

'Dave?'

'Dave?'

That was all that Ronald could register, the boy's name as his friends called out to him and Timothy Gilman as he stood with his knife out, staring each one of them in the eye and meaning *their* blood should they come closer.

Then, the longest silence. The kid had slumped against the ropes, his head hanging forward.

'We're done here,' Gilman said.

'What happened?' the little one cried out.

Warren started to work through the ropes, loosening them. 'This shit we hadn't signed up for.'

'Just do it,' Gilman said.

'What we're going to do with him?' Ronald asked.

'He's coming with us.'

'What are we going to do?'

'Shut up and start the van.'

'This is not—'

'Shut the fuck up and start the van.'

Gilman went back to the little one. 'You remember what we talked about.'

'How's David? What happened?'

'You and your friend don't say anything to anyone. Not to the cops, not to your father, no one.'

'What did you do to him?'

'Not to the cops, not to your father, no one.'

'What did you do to him?' The thin voice cracked.

'Maybe I should make sure you do remember.'

The last thing Ronald saw, as he was climbing back into the van, was the light catching Gilman's blade.

Chapter 30

Madison walked out of the hospital glass doors and let out a big breath. So far every conversation she'd ever had with Nathan Quinn had been less than straightforward, and today's had been no different. Somehow, in their brief acquaintance, they had relentlessly managed to be both truthful and oblique, their words slanted by circumstance, respect and slights given and borne with the same unease. And taking shelter in those words there was a burden of secrets; Madison had first glimpsed it as Quinn had given up his position as the Sinclairs' next of kin to be Cameron's attorney, his faith in his friend wrestling against evidence and common sense.

After the dry heat of the hospital, Madison shivered in the chill: Quinn had created another trail and trusted her to follow it to the end, wherever it might lead. Beyond the layers of cloud cover, the sun would soon set and Vincent Foley – who would be watching and waiting – was, for all concerned, the end of the trail.

'We need to protect him,' Madison said to Lieutenant Fynn. Her engine was running and the windows had already fogged up.

'I'll take that into consideration,' he replied.

'Sir, how long do we have before someone puts two and two

together and works out what cases we were working on when we went to the Walters Institute?'

'I'm not disagreeing with you. I'm saying we don't have enough warm bodies to scatter around the grounds. You've seen the place. It's massive.'

'I know.'

'What they already have is a half-decent security system and hopefully that will be enough.'

'Sure. Then again, their main concern is to keep their patients in, not to keep professional killers out.'

'We're going to have to take this one day at a time, Madison. Any news from Quinn?'

'Nothing concrete about Gilman. No surprise there.'

'Have you told the doc his Rain Man patient could be a murderer?'

'Not yet. And Foley is not autistic. He's borderline low IQ with PTSD and God knows what else thrown in.'

'You're going to talk to him? I mean, will you try to get something out of him anyway?'

Madison rested her head back and closed her eyes. 'I'll try.'

A rustle of papers on the line. 'Something else,' Fynn said. 'Do you remember Warren Lee had a sister?'

Madison dipped into her mental archive. 'Tennessee. They haven't spoken in years?'

'Right. Thirteen years to be precise. Spencer called her back because, as luck would have it, they were still talking twenty-five years ago.'

'In 1985?'

'Exactly.'

Madison sat up. 'What did she say?'

'As far as Spencer could see, there was no love lost between them. She thought he was trouble and didn't want him anywhere near her husband and kids. However, she remembers that Lee had a girlfriend in the 1980s. Spencer is tracking her down.'

'That's good news.'

'I sure hope so.'

While Spencer and Dunne were left working on Lee's and Gray's work records to find points of contact, Madison scribbled the girl-friend's current address and phone number on her notebook. Paula Wilson lived in Bellevue, across Lake Washington, and her social security number had told them that she was a nurse in a medical practice.

When Madison had called she didn't sound particularly happy to dredge up the very long past and yet she hadn't been surprised by the call: she had seen the news, she had recognized the name.

'My husband will be back from work soon. Can you try and make it here before he does?'

Madison didn't question it; she drove fast on I–90 and took the north exit to Bellevue Way SE.

The two-story brick house was pretty and stood a little way off the road in a residential street. Madison was walking up the short dri-veway when Paula Wilson – her married name was Kruger – opened her front door and gazed past her, as if something unwelcome was trailing behind the detective.

'I think I might have given you the wrong impression,' the woman said as Madison took a sip of coffee from the hand-painted ceramic mug. 'My husband knows all about Warren. It's just that it was a difficult period in our lives and he would be upset for me . . .'

Paula Wilson Kruger was a handsome brunette who looked her age and took care of herself. Madison knew that she was forty-seven years old, two years younger than Warren Lee. The home and everything in it told her about a stable family life in a quiet neighborhood. They sat in the living room – a patterned three-seat sofa and matching chairs – and Madison could smell the pot roast in the oven.

'What can you tell me about Warren Lee?' she asked, treading carefully and not knowing where this might lead.

The woman smiled and then it went away. 'He was cute when I knew him. He was cute and mean as a snake.'

Madison had the good sense not to interrupt.

'I was 20 years old, that's all I can say in my defense. I met Warren in a mall, he chatted me up, we started dating and we moved in together after a few weeks. My parents were unhappy about it but I thought I knew everything.'

The woman sipped her coffee. 'It was the worst two years of my life,' she said finally. 'I'm a nurse, have been for a while. Did you know that?'

Madison nodded.

'I can always spot the girls who are in trouble, the women. It's not about age really. Sometimes they let me help them, sometimes they don't. But I can always see it – the ones who are afraid, ashamed, so deep inside the hole they cannot see out. That was me with Warren. We had two perfect months and then things changed. He was wonderful one day and angry the next. After a while, he didn't bother with wonderful anymore. There was occasional violence, but mostly it was fear, constant fear.'

'Did you work? Did he?'

Madison already knew the answers but wanted to hear her side of things.

'I dropped out of community college and I was waitressing in a restaurant over in Kirkland. Warren worked part-time in a club but he always had more money than he should have had. I didn't ask him where it came from, he didn't tell me.'

The woman hesitated. 'I haven't seen Warren in over twenty years.

Why would you be interested in something that happened such a long time ago?'

Madison turned the words around in her mind before speaking. 'We are trying to understand the kind of person he was, to understand what happened to him and why. Did you meet any of the people he worked with?'

'Some. People from the club mostly.'

'Do you remember any names? People he knew, or he saw regularly, even people he just talked about from time to time . . .'

The woman sighed.

'There was Henry Dee and his girlfriend, Lisa – they were nice to me,' she said. 'Bill Morris, the other bartender.'

Madison wrote down the names.

'Richard Lucas and his brother Paul.' She hesitated. The memories were coming to the light like stowaways.

'Does the name Ronald Gray mean anything to you? Or Vincent Foley?'

'No.'

'Did Warren ever mention a man called Gilman? Timothy Gilman?'

The woman ran the palm of her hand over a cushion on the sofa – a soft quilted square had been embroidered on the top: robins over cherry blossoms. 'Lisa was a sweet girl; she was a lap dancer at the club. I have no idea what happened to her,' she said and stood up. 'I need to check on the oven.'

Madison waited as Paula Wilson Kruger busied herself in the kitchen for a few minutes. She knew that an answer would come and if the woman needed time to get herself together and feel the comfort of the life she had built, Madison would let her have it.

'Is he dead?' The woman asked her from the kitchen door. 'Gilman, is he dead?'

'You knew him?'

'I met him. Once. Is he dead?'

'Yes. Twenty years ago.'

'Good. That's good,' the woman said.

There it was: Quinn had been right. They knew each other.

'Please tell me about him.'

'He came to our house. He had found the job at the club for Warren and Warren talked about him all the time. The things he'd done. He was like a puppy around him.'

'And you met him?'

'Once was enough. He came to pick up Warren one afternoon, June or July that last summer, and I had heard so much about him already. He didn't come inside, he just stood by his car.'

'Did you speak with him?'

'No, I watched him through the screen door. Warren was rushing around getting his things.'

'What happened?'

'Nothing. He was just standing there, next to his car, and these kids were playing football on the street. Little kids, ten or twelve years old, and he stared at them.'

'That's all?'

'That's all,' the woman said. 'He stared, and all I wanted was for him to leave. He was waiting for one of them to throw the ball a little too close, a little too hard . . .'

'And?'

'Nothing. Warren ran outside and they left.'

'Will you come to the precinct and sign a witness statement? Tomorrow maybe?'

The woman nodded.

'When was the last time you saw Warren?'

The woman didn't need to think about it. 'February 14, 1986.'

'And you were still living together in 1985?'

'Yes, for most of that year. I moved out in the summer, went back to my parents.'

'In the summer . . .'

'Yes.'

'Were you still together in June '85?'

'Yes.'

'July?'

'Yes.'

'August 1985?'

Paula Wilson Kruger set her mug on the coffee table between them. 'I left him at the end of August,' she said.

'What happened?'

'I took the car keys and drove to my parents in the middle of the night and never came back. My dad came for my clothes and things a few days later.'

'What happened?'

'He came home late one night and said he'd run over a deer.'

'A deer?'

'He came back late, after midnight. He smelled like smoke – not cigarettes but like bonfire smoke – and his clothes were filthy. He said to put them in the machine and wash them straight away. There was dirt and mud, there was blood all over his jeans and T-shirt. I saw it and he said he'd run over a deer and had to drag it off the road.'

'Did he say where it had happened?'

'I was too afraid to ask. I'd never seen him so terrified and angry and I thought anything would set him off.'

'What did you do?'

'I washed his clothes, went back to bed, and when I was sure he was asleep I left.'

'I know it's impossible to remember the details of something that happened so long ago but–'

'It was August 28, 1985,' the woman said, 'if that's what you're asking me.'

'How can you be sure?'

'Some days you just don't forget. I never went back. He came to look for me but I wouldn't see him. He came the last time on Valentine's Day, February 14, 1986. By then I was already back with Martin – he had been my high-school sweetheart – and we married eighteen months later.'

'Why did you leave that night?'

The silence between them stretched and Madison found herself listening out for the husband's car and hoping they wouldn't be interrupted.

'Why did you leave?'

'Because it wasn't deer blood,' the woman said. 'I just knew it wasn't. And that's why you're here, isn't it?'

Chapter 31

Nathan Quinn was exhausted. His meeting with Detective Madison had left him drained and yet, after she had left, he had paced the floor for all it was worth: he couldn't bear to lie down and the room was too small to contain his brittle energy. Three weeks ago they had nothing, today they had names. His knuckles were white as he leant on the stick; he knew he would have to stop soon even though his mind would keep its restless vigil.

They had *names*. He sat down on the edge of the bed and speed-dialed the fourth number on his list. Tod Hollis, the chief investigator for Quinn Locke and Associates, picked up on the second ring.

'Warren Lee and Ronald Gray,' Quinn said. 'The third one is in a psychiatric clinic. We'll find out who he is soon enough, I'm sure.'

'What do you have in mind?'

'The full works. Every little scrap of information that the police will not have time to go after. Gilman chose these men but somebody chose him. Somewhere in Gilman's connections is the man who ordered the kidnap.'

'I agree, this is not someone who went up to him cold. I'd say you'd have to have done business with a guy before you asked him to abduct three children.'

'Lee and Gray don't have a record.'

'Just because someone doesn't have a record it doesn't mean they haven't done very questionable things.'

'If they have, I trust you'll find them.'

'I'll be in touch.'

They rang off and Quinn went back to the pile of mail that Carl Doyle had delivered that morning. He picked up one envelope – heavy paper and his name in the black ink of a fountain pen. No address was needed: the envelope had been handed to Carl by the other senior partner in his law practice. *Conrad*.

Quinn read the card inside, written in a familiar scrawl.

> *Dear Nathan, I hear that you are confounding the doctors' expectations and healing faster than they anticipated. They might be surprised but I'm not: I know what you're capable of, my boy. Once you are well enough to go home you might like to come and spend some time with us at the estate. It will be peaceful. Grace wants to spoil you and bake that pie she knows you love.*
>
> *Let me know if there's anything I can do with regard to John's case.*
>
> *Take care of yourself,*
>
> *Conrad*

John's case. No other attorney would refer to it as such except for Conrad Locke. He had been a friend of Quinn's father's, had run a thriving law practice and, most of all, knew Cameron since he was in elementary school. There was still someone in the world who remembered him as he was then and it was an unexpected source of comfort. And no one else would dare to call him 'my boy'.

Quinn had no real desire for company and even Grace Locke's blueberry pie held no attraction; however, he picked up a blank card and started writing a reply because their kindness and their concern required paper and ink.

September, 1985. Nathan leant on the wooden banister and breathed in the salty air. David's funeral had come and gone and somehow he was still walking and breathing when he'd thought he couldn't possibly live through it.

The ceremony had been brief, the rabbi himself almost in shock, and they had all gathered at the restaurant, which was going to be closed for the rest of the week.

The fathers were in the kitchen, everybody else was in the main room, and Nathan had escaped to the narrow deck that ran along the building. *So this is what hell is like.* He felt empty. A photographer had intruded into their grief as they were leaving the cemetery and only Jack – his arm still in a sling – had reacted and attacked the guy with all the strength and the madness of that day. Everybody else, including Nathan, had been too numb and dazed.

The sky was a shade of gray barely lighter than the water, cloudy and yet so bright even without the sun. Too bright. Nathan looked away from Elliott Bay and took off the velvet yarmulke he was still wearing. He couldn't go back inside, not yet.

'Nathan.'

He turned to see Conrad Locke standing there in his dark suit and black tie.

'How are you, my boy?' He said. 'Forget it – stupid question. May I keep you company for a moment?'

Nathan had nodded and they had stood companionably in silence for a while, looking out at the view as the gulls did their best in the wake of a fishing boat.

Twenty-five years had passed and Quinn still appreciated how the older man had not tried to talk away his grief. Years later, when Quinn's law practice had become so successful that he needed to expand it, joining forces with Conrad Locke was the logical thing to do. Locke had spent most of the last ten years in San Francisco, semi-retired and busy with his charity foundation, and Quinn had run the most successful legal practice of the Pacific Northwest.

Tod Hollis would find something – Quinn was sure of it – and there was much that he himself could do, starting with Cameron's bail and the plea bargain situation.

He looked around the room: the monitors were still there, reminders of a time when his life had been measured by the fluid ounces of the IV drip. This room, both comfortable and featureless, was where he had found his way back from the jagged metal cage in the forest. He had no idea how the rest of his life would be measured. *Time to go home.*

Chapter 32

Amy Sorensen sat in the darkness of the lab and studied the image projected on the portable screen. It took up most of the wall and was blessedly archaic in a world that was dominated by digital technology. It couldn't be simpler than that: the scrap of paper recovered in Ronald Gray's Bible had been carefully unfolded, straightened, and placed under the keen eye of an overhead projector.

Amy Sorensen was a great believer in 'simple', and she thought that the most important thing that she could do at that point was just *to look* at the darn piece of paper and see what it would tell her.

They already knew it was standard copy supply – the kind you buy in Staples in boxes of 5,000 sheets – 20 lb weight, 92 US brightness. Good for heavy-duty, high-velocity copying. If you wanted thicker, stronger paper you had to be ready to shell out a good deal more.

So far, so good. Someone, probably Gray, had taken very good care of the scrap over the long years: he had kept it in paper, not plastic, and had not handled it a great deal. Maybe he knew that paper would preserve it, maybe he didn't. Sorensen didn't care. Like an archeologist standing at the edge of an ancient grave, she was merely grateful for the find.

On the wall, light against the gloom around it, David Quinn in his middle-school yearbook photo. Sorensen's sharp blue eyes swept the firmament of tiny dots and imperfections in the paper; they followed the contours of the fragment: it was the top right-hand side corner of the page and it had been torn to make a triangular shape that included the Quinn picture. *Torn*, she noted, not cut: the edge was neat because someone had folded down the corner, pressed, and then carefully ripped that piece. If the person had used scissors or any kind of blade the edge would have been more than neat, it would have been perfect.

Sorensen picked up a small yellow bottle of chocolate milk she had filched from her daughter's stock and took a long swig. *Perfect* was no good to her; her whole life was about the individual, the unique, the anomaly in the pattern. This was what she was looking for now.

One of her crew put his head around the door. 'I'll fume it for prints once you're done,' he said.

'Yes, thanks,' she replied without looking away from the projected image.

'When do you think . . .?'

'Not sure.'

'Anything I can help with?'

'Not really.'

'Would you prefer it if I–'

'Left? Yes, thanks, Nick. I'm better at this on my own.'

'Sure thing.'

Sorensen focused her attention back on the bright image. There were ways and means to identify a printer and a copier, and they used those methods on a regular basis to track down alleged terrorists, counterfeiters and all kinds of felons. However, modern techniques that exploited a printer's individual intrinsic and extrinsic signatures were pointless when the image was twenty-five years old and the machine that had created it was in all probability laying on a heap of garbage somewhere. The notion that a piece of plastic and ink from the 1980s was still churning out copies was ridiculous when anybody could buy a new one for $59.99.

Although there was a point to getting the latent prints off the paper as soon as possible, Sorensen wanted to track the origin of the page. Who had held the yearbook down on the copier and pressed the start button? If the picture had been used to identify one of the boys it was certainly something worth pursuing.

The Quinn picture was not complete: the angle at which the corner had been torn meant that a little had been lost – a little of his right shoulder. It also meant that a very small portion of the top of the photograph below Quinn's had been caught. Sorensen sat forward in her chair.

The pencil line around Quinn had obviously been drawn on the photocopied page, the depression still visible on the other side after all these years. And yet . . .

'Oh my . . .' she said to herself as she grabbed her head magnifier and slipped it in place.

They were small but they were definitely there, and Sorensen thought of her own yearbooks and what she used to do as soon as she had her own copy in her hands: you get them signed. You write on the glossy photos and in the margins, you forever and irreversibly alter the pristine beauty of the book with adolescent scrawls. *That* was the point of a yearbook.

Sorensen reached for her cell.

Madison was driving back into the precinct from Bellevue. Paula Wilson Kruger had asked her about Warren Lee's death and she had tried to be truthful without giving her too many details – the tabloid press and the internet had done enough scavenging around it. The traffic on the bridge was moving at the usual rush-hour speed and she was about to hit the tunnel when her cell phone beeped. She pressed the speaker button and left it next to her on the passenger seat.

'Madison.'

'It's Sorensen. I've been looking at the paper. I think we have something.'

'Go on.'

'You know there's the pencil mark around the boy, and it was made on the scrap of paper we have?'

'Yes, made before it was torn off from the rest of the page.'

'Right. Well, there are two further identifiable marks which are clearly not dust on the copier or a paper imperfection.'

'Pencil marks?'

'No, it's *pen*. I'm thinking ballpoint, biro type marks . . . but they're not on our scrap,' Sorensen said, her voice crackling through in spite of the bad reception. 'They're *on the original*.'

Madison's brain – up to that point still in Bellevue, dealing with memories of blood – lurched forward and caught up with her.

'*On the original?* Do you mean that if we had the right yearbook in our hands you could match them to it?'

There was static on the line as Madison drove fast through the traffic. There was crackle and a beat of silence.

'Yes,' Sorensen said finally. 'Now I have safety copies to make and prints to lift.'

'Thank you, Amy.'

Madison reached for the cell without taking her eyes off the road, pressed the button and rang off. Sorensen was right to go hunting for latents but they had to expect that the only prints lifted would be from Ronald Gray, and a lot of good that would be to them.

On the other hand, the yearbook was the breadcrumbs trail to the man who had wanted to mark David Quinn for kidnap and, ultimately, death.

Madison drove automatically while her thoughts chased a sea of numbers: how many yearbooks had been made that year, how many they could check against Sorensen's mark, and how long it would take to gather them. There was another point, no less important: whoever had made that photocopy was looking closely at the investigation into Warren Lee's and Ronald Gray's murders and they could not simply roll up, knock on doors and demand to see decades-old yearbooks. She groaned; they would need to find a very good excuse to go trawling through people's basements and it wouldn't be dozens, it would be hundreds of books that they would need to get hold of and check.

Madison checked the time on her dashboard – Fynn would still be in the office. They had to come up with a really good story and go lie to the general Seattle public as soon as possible.

She saw an opening in traffic and hit the accelerator. Two men dead by the same hand, nineteen blows including three to the head, two GSWs, three men in the CCTV footage, twenty-five years in psychiatric care. *One down, three to go.* A sea of numbers.

Sitting at her desk, Madison dialed the call to the Walters Institute, and even before the receptionist asked her to stay on the line, she knew that Dr. Peterson had not gone home yet.

'We are trying to fit all the various pieces of the story so that they tell us what happened,' she told him. 'But, the way things look, Vincent Foley witnessed something awful, something his mind could not deal with. He was a witness because he was with the men who instigated the crime. He wasn't a victim, not in the sense that something was done *to* him. And we still don't know to what extent he participated in the crime that was perpetrated. However, the fact that Ronald Gray tried to protect him by destroying any evidence in his house that might lead to Vincent, and the things he told you when you last spoke, indicate that Vincent was as involved as he was.'

'What kind of crime are we talking about, Detective?'

'Kidnap and murder of minors.'

Madison saw Peterson in his office, the white day room where his patients came together, the pretty grounds where they walked on a sunny day. It wasn't a facility for the criminally insane.

'The men who killed Ronald,' Peterson said, 'will they come after Vincent too?'

'I think they will,' she replied, 'once they know where he is.'

Fynn was already on the phone with the Chief of D. to work out the kind of protection Foley could expect. Madison could see him through the blinds of his office, standing and talking. Fynn always stood when he was displeased.

'I'll need to speak with Vincent, Doctor. The sooner, the better. Tomorrow if we can manage it.'

'I understand,' he replied.

After the call Madison wondered if he really understood, and knew that she would have to ask Vincent about his memories of burying a murdered child and the blood on his clothing. Her degree in Psychology and Criminology seemed a rather slight tool to go panning for gold in Foley's mind.

Dunne came over, grabbed a chair from an empty desk and slid it close to Madison's desk.

'We have a confirmation of address for Gilman from 1978 to 1983,' he said as he sank into the chair. 'East Howell Street.'

'That sounds—'

'Same block as the couple who fostered Ronald Gray and Foley. They lived two doors away from each other.'

'He knew them,' Madison said. 'He knew them since they were kids.'

'Yup.'

Dunne's red hair was in a constant state of rebellion however short he had it cut; now it stuck out at the back, as if he had just woken up. He leant against the chair's upholstered back and closed his eyes.

'We're going to order take-out,' he said. *We* was always understood to mean Spencer and himself. 'Are you in?'

Madison realized she couldn't even remember whether she had eaten that day.

'Definitely,' she replied.

'Pizza?'

'Extra anchovies.'

'Got it.'

By the time Madison left the precinct the evening had settled into an uneasy chill that carried neither rain nor a clear sky. The low clouds reflected back the orange glow from the city and the only patch of true black was the expanse of water before her on Alki Beach.

Madison had already changed into the sweats she kept in a gym bag in her trunk. She leant on her car with one hand and stretched one leg behind her, shook the tightness off her shoulders, and repeated with the other leg.

The first steps were stiff and her muscles felt like heavy rope, cold and unyielding. She pressed on, running along the edge of the tide and waiting for the running to trigger the memory of the forest. It first came to her as a change in the ground under her feet: the sand gave way to a slippery trail, rocky under the thin dirt. Then came the scent – resin and the layers of damp leaves. *Here we go.*

For an instant Madison felt the warmth of Salinger's torch on her cheek and then she lunged forward, running through the empty darkness, her body existing on the beach and in the forest at the same time.

Her feet found the unsteady ground and she pressed forward, and again she sensed the man running ahead of her and she hastened her step. The beach was all the way gone now and Madison could smell the forest around her and feel the low branches brushing her face. Her heart was punching its way out of her chest and a coil of fear wrapped itself tight around her gut. The chase was almost done and she knew what would happen because that was what always happened, and neither Dr. Stanley Robinson PhD nor anyone else could stop it.

She caught up with Harry Salinger, who had just told her that he'd killed Tommy, and fell upon him, both of them rolling onto the pebbled bank of the Hoh River. John Cameron was nowhere to be seen and Nathan Quinn was faraway, back in the clearing, slowly dying inside a metal cage.

The knife was in her hand before she knew how it got there and it fit her hand so well because it was meant to be there. There was nothing else to do and no one else to do it. With neither joy nor anger, Alice Madison ran the blade under Salinger's throat and saw the dark line widen and the man become nothing but a blurred pool of red that covered her hands.

Madison woke up with a start and sat up in bed, tears streaking down her face. She choked as she ran to her bathroom and threw up whatever was left of the pizza dinner she had had hours earlier with Spencer and Dunne. She hesitated and waited a few seconds to see if another heave was coming; then she went to the sink, filled it with ice-cold water and dunked her face in it.

Her heart was still racing and yet she could already feel it going back to normal. Was that her *normal*? Was that what she should expect for all her time to come?

She thought about her conversations with Dr. Robinson. He was a good man but he'd gotten things the wrong way round: her PTSD episodes were not about being a victim, they were about being the killer. And she was pretty sure they don't let you keep your detective badge once you tell your shrink you have nightmares about killing suspects.

She looked up, water dripping off her face, and though her heart had slowed down, her eyes were still wide with fear.

Madison slipped on a pair of thick socks she had found on the floor by her trainers and went to the kitchen, turning on lights as she went. The ice-cold milk in the fridge was as soothing as her throat was raw; she drank from the carton. Her gaze fell on the kitchen chairs by the nook and with 4 a.m. clarity, when the thin dark voice speaks too clearly to ignore, she knew why Warren Lee, tied as he was to a kitchen chair, had been left under the water towers between 35 Avenue SW and Myrtle Street, with his driver's license taped to his chest.

She headed for the living room and the cupboard in the bookcase that her grandfather had stocked with all kinds of maps. Madison knew what she was looking for and found it easily. The dining table was large enough to accommodate it. She unfolded the map and her fingertips found the intersection of the two roads. Warren Lee had been carefully positioned due north-west: she could still picture him clearly and had stood right there where he had been to see what he would have seen had he been alive. Now, she knew: had Warren Lee been alive he would have been looking – from miles away – at the exact spot where twenty-five years ago the Hoh River boys had met their destiny.

The message had been clear to anyone who knew anything about the event. *Your silence and your life: don't even think about Quinn's reward money. However you've come to know about what happened, this is where it ends. This is where everything ends.* And Ronald Gray had understood the message.

She left the map on the table and went back to bed. Wrapped in her comforter, lights off, she wondered what Cameron dreamt about.

One person had nightmares for sure, and she'd get to spend more time with him soon. *Somebody's coming.*

Chapter 33

All day the chaos of sounds shunted against the concrete walls of KCJC; at 4 a.m. the relative silence was almost eerie. In a densely populated wing it was never completely quiet as the bodies of dozens of incarcerated men turned and twisted on their cots, coughed and occasionally called out. Nevertheless, there were a handful of hours – always too few and always too quickly gone – when a person could almost pretend to be somewhere else, and sometimes believe it.

A guard was walking down the gangway and his steps were unusually soft. John Cameron recognized the man before he reached his cell. *Miller, B.*, doing his best to be stealthy as he approached at a time when no one else stirred in D Wing.

Miller reached Cameron's door and looked inside. After their eyes met, and he was quite sure Cameron was awake, the lock-release clicked open.

Cameron's interactions with the guards had been a marvel of non-verbal communication, polite distance on one side and watchful wariness on the other. All the same, a visit in the middle of the night was neither expected nor welcome, especially since Miller had done his darnedest to tiptoe around so that the whole wing wouldn't start the ritual banging on the bars.

Cameron stood up and slipped on the regulation black leather sneakers with Velcro straps; he remained standing near the back of the rectangular cell, facing the door and watching Miller with neither hostility nor concern.

Miller was waiting for him to make a decision. *They were going someplace. He either would go or he wouldn't. Simple as that.*

Miller stepped back and Cameron joined him on the gangway; the lights were low and whoever saw them thought, quite rightly, that the best thing to do was to keep quiet and let them pass without fuss or bother. Should it then transpire that Cameron had been taken to one side to be told what's what by a friendly group of officers, well, that was just the way things went sometimes.

They reached the first set of doors that would lead them out of D Wing and the locks clicked open for them. It was a pleasant surprise that the building would allow its entries and exits to operate in ticks and snaps at night while the daytime was all about clanging metal.

KCJC was deep into the night shift and the corridors belonged to the wall-mounted cameras and the convex mirrors. Somewhere in the concrete structure careful eyes followed their progress along the pale green corridor, so bright after the dim cells.

After a left turn and a third set of doors – two prison officers staring as they went past – they left behind the blueprint of KCJC, such as it was in Cameron's mind, and stepped into uncharted territory.

Cameron and Miller walked companionably side by side as if a 4 a.m. stroll was part of the routine, but Cameron was well aware that the guard measured his every step and breath and if he so much as sneezed, a squad of COs in riot gear would materialize in a nanosecond. Aside from the irritation of being physically bound by those walls, it was sort of funny.

Cameron had no intention of giving them the opportunity to throw on their full-face corrections helmets and stampede out of their rec room. He was curious and unafraid, but if trouble was about to tap him on the shoulder he would return it threefold and gold-plated. Weeks earlier, as he was becoming familiar with the lay of the land and the people that, at least temporarily, would be part of his daily life, Cameron had observed Miller and read him like a doctor holds up an X-ray against the light. He was experienced and older than most of his colleagues, though what he lacked in fitness and strength he made up for in common sense. He slightly favored his left foot, ate too much red meat at weekends, and tonight his back was acting up.

Cameron would not start a fight but he could end one, and he knew – as someone might know how to gift-wrap a present – that from where he stood he could break Miller's neck in two seconds, should it become necessary.

Many years ago reflections on death and killing would have been noted down in a different color ink from the other thoughts that coursed through him. For a long time now though, they were the same color and font as everything else and John Cameron no more noticed them than he would a consideration on the weather.

The corridor opened into a hexagonal foyer with a door that looked different from the others. Another officer was waiting for them and he gave Miller a dark bundle.

He nodded and extended his arm toward Cameron: he was holding out a heavily lined denim winter coat, Department of Corrections issue. Cameron's previous coat had been left on the pitted floor of the walk-alone on the day of the attack and he had not received another: he had not needed one because he had not been outside since it had rained bleach.

Cameron stepped forward and took the jacket. Miller shrugged on his coat and nodded to the camera whose single eye was trained on them. A click told Cameron the lock had been released. Miller put his hand on the handle and – just like that – they were outside.

The space between the wall and the chain-link fence was narrow, six feet at the most, and they followed it to the entrance into the main yard. Miller unlocked it with a key from a bunch at his belt and with an old-fashioned arm gesture invited Cameron to go inside.

Cameron stayed where he was.

'One hour or less, should you get frostbite,' Miller said and he pointed at each of the four towers, one at every corner of the yard. 'They have their rifles scopes trained on you and will follow every skip and every step. Aside from that, knock yourself out – it's all yours.'

Cameron stepped inside and the chain link door was locked behind him. He turned to the guard. 'Why?' he said.

'It's easier to do this than screw up the schedule of the walk-alones for hundreds of people. Apparently you don't have many friends here and most inmates want to either kill you or help you sustain a very serious injury. Enjoy the fresh air.'

Miller stepped away and re-entered the building; no doubt the guards in the towers would keep in radio contact.

Cameron walked to the middle of the yard – it was large enough for a couple of football fields – and bathed in the glow of the 400-watt HPS lights mounted on 30-foot steel poles. Since December 26, when he had transferred into KCJC, he had never had that much space, that much emptiness around him; and the silence, with no other human being intruding on his perceptions, was blissful.

The cold air was sharp on his cheeks and he filled his lungs with it in ragged breaths. The damp chill found him quickly enough and crept under the layers of clothing. He could see the white puffs as he exhaled and felt his chest shudder. None of it mattered as John Cameron looked up. A person who has never spent time inside a prison cannot possibly understand what the sudden and unexpected exposure to the wide night sky can do to a man who has.

'TD-4 to TD-3: you there, D-3? What's he doing, Billy?' The voice came strong and clear though his headset, and in the darkened tower

William G. White blinked as he adjusted the rifle's butt against his shoulder and peered through the scope.

'I'm seeing what you're seeing, D-4. He's just standing there looking up.'

'It's been a while, D-3.'

'What do you want me to do about it?'

'He's going to have to move soon or he'll freeze on that spot.'

'How about a little wager, D-4?'

The scope was powerful and the cross hairs traveled up Cameron's back, to his raised collar and his bare head.

'How about—'

'TD-1 here. Would you gentlemen care to keep your eyes open, your mouths shut and your scopes where they should be?'

'Copy, TD-1,' both men replied, and alone in their tower each man thought that this shift they had volunteered for out of curiosity was turning out to be a mighty big yawn.

'He's on the move,' a voice, maybe TD-3, said in the gloom and the others shifted their feet and adjusted their positions.

John Cameron started a gentle jog along the chain-link fence. He waited until his body had responded to the rhythm of the run, and warmth was slowly coming back to his limbs, before he allowed himself to start thinking about this odd and unforeseen opportunity.

If he had been in the general population, just one inmate among the many hundreds who used the yard every day, he wouldn't have had the chance to look around properly and take measure of the place. His attention would have been focused on potential threats rather than the fine points of correctional architecture.

The glow of the powerful lights kept him easily in the sights of those charged with baby-sitting him but it also illuminated the structure around the yard: the 20-foot-high perimeter wall beyond the chain-link fence, the roofs of the various wings rippling off the round central section.

John Cameron saw everything, and as he picked up a little speed the blueprint in his mind was adjusted. The one thing that the Department of Corrections had proven beyond reasonable doubt was that they could not protect him, and Cameron was not about to let them fall asleep on their watch again. He had pretty much volunteered for this ridiculous confinement because it suited his needs; however, things were changing fast and once Nathan was well enough to go home, Cameron would be ready to leave.

They hadn't spoken since that night in the forest but he knew what Nathan would say: he'd talk about plea bargaining and reversing the bail decision.

Cameron's feet hit the dirt hard as he sprinted and slowed down, sprinted and slowed down, his body reveling in the expense of energy.

Nathan's reasoning would always follow the lawful path, Cameron reflected, while his own might just have to go right through that perimeter wall to get to the other side. In his loop, he passed the yard's locked door and in one smooth movement he took off the coat, dropped it on the ground and kept running.

If he took another man's life to get out of KCJC – which was more than likely to happen – he would never be able to stand in the same room as Nathan again. He would be a fugitive with his prints and his DNA in the system, and while none of it worried him unduly – most of his properties and assets had been set up under different identities – he would have to shed this name he carried and all of his life and past in Seattle, because it would be a felony for Nathan to merely speak on the phone with him and not report it to the authorities.

Cameron felt the scopes following his movements as if he could see them. He imagined those men standing in the murky observation decks, in the middle of the night, and wondered what he would have to do for them to take aim and shoot, how far up the chain-link fence they would let him reach before they stopped him.

He had no intention of behaving in such a crass manner and yet there were unavoidable choices in his near future that would affect how he would live the rest of his life.

He saw the side door open and Miller step outside to take him back to his cell. That was the only thing that worked ultimately: in a place like KCJC the fastest way out was to let people unlock the door for you and walk through.

'Show's over for tonight, boys.' TD-1's voice came through the headsets and the other men laid down their weapons for a moment, stretched their sore limbs and then resumed the watch. Below them, housed in the sprawling buildings, over a thousand men slept on narrow cots and dreamt their dreams.

Back in his cell, as his skin cooled down and he drifted into sleep, John Cameron thought he heard the trees that surrounded the prison shiver and murmur in the gloom. He might not have seen them behind the perimeter wall but he knew they were there all the same.

Vincent Foley wrapped the blanket tight around his slim shoulders. He had curled up under the bed and peeked every so often to check if a sliver of dawn was travelling across the walls.

The white day room of the Walters Institute was the only place that allowed him moments of brittle peace; he longed for the light that flooded in through the tall windows and hated the clouds that deprived him of his only protection.

He tried with all his might not to fall asleep again because dreadful creatures infected his dreams – men who spent the night whispering and hollering in a pit dug deep into the earth. He knew their faces but their names had crumbled away over the years. And yet, their words were always the same, and although Vincent couldn't tell anymore what they meant, in his dreams they trailed like claws over his skin and during the day they were the rustle of the trees around the brick building.

Vincent saw the first light slide over his crayon drawings. As it reached them they trembled and stilled, watching him and waiting for nightfall.

Chapter 34

Madison opened her eyes. There was enough light slipping in through the curtains that she knew it was early and little enough of it to tell her that sunshine would not be a part of her day. Her throat was still raw from the previous night and she knew for a fact that she had drunk all the milk in the fridge. Cranberry juice would have to do.

In the kitchen, she put on the stove-top coffee maker and drank the juice. Her fridge was beginning to look desolate. She brought the cup of coffee back into the living room, saw the map unfolded on the table, and remembered her thoughts from the previous night – the significance of the chair's position, the message it sent to anyone who knew the truth.

She sank into the sofa and rested her feet on the low table, waiting for the caffeine to kick in and her brain to gear up and get going. Whatever direction her thoughts were heading they seemed to twist and turn and go back to Vincent Foley. She was sure he had been there on August 28; he had seen everything and it was all rattling around in his ruined mind, beyond their reach.

Madison had met a good numbers of cons on and off the street, and men like Vincent, who would be vulnerable in any area of human interaction and field of work, were utterly exposed in a world where predators made the rules.

It was very doubtful that Vincent would have been entrusted with any information; he probably just turned up and did the job that was required of him, following Ronald and doing what he was told. And yet he might know something, anything that might give them a little push in the right direction.

Madison finished her coffee and stood up as the flat silver of the bay was becoming visible in the French doors: it was possible that it was Vincent Foley who had murdered David Quinn. If that was the case, what measure of justice could be exacted from that wreck of a human being?

The men who had slain Warren Lee and Ronald Gray were not interested in justice or how it was measured. They had tortured their victims to extract what they knew about the kidnap and whether they'd told anyone about it, Madison was sure of it. She was fighting for all of the dead, for all of those whose voices had been silenced – the boy and the men who had killed him – and that knowledge rested heavily on her heart because she had knelt by the pit in the forest and had seen with her own eyes the hole Vincent Foley had dug.

They arrived at the Walters Institute with their unmarked cars and their badges and Dr. Peterson showed them to a comfortable observation room. Spencer and Dunne, Madison and Kelly, together with the department consultant psychiatrist Dr. Jennifer Takemoto, crowded into the airy space with a view of the gardens. Peterson looked like he'd hardly slept and Madison could imagine the long line of bleak thoughts that might have kept him awake.

Dr. Takemoto was in her forties and dressed like a smart senior manager; Madison had met her a couple of times and was very glad they could count on her skills. She had seen her help a traumatized hostage recollect a four-day ordeal and send the perpetrator to jail for life. If there was anything left of Vincent's memories of his time before the Walters Institute, she'd be the one to find them.

'This is where we'll bring Vincent to sit and talk,' Peterson said. 'I was told he had a good night, or as good as his nights ever are. I'll also be present during your interview. It will be a comfort for him to have someone he knows in the room, and I will stop the interview at any time should he become distressed.'

Dr. Takemoto nodded.

'He's always *distressed*, isn't he?' Kelly interjected. 'I mean, how will you know when he is unusually distressed?'

It was a good point.

'You'll have to trust my judgment. I've been his doctor for many years and I'll be able to tell when he's had enough.'

'Doctor,' Madison said, 'the likelihood is that he will be very upset and *enough* might come pretty soon, but we need to find out what he knows because – aside from everything else – that's how we can protect him.'

'I understand.'

Madison wondered if he did and – if it came to that – whether he would come between them and Foley. In the last twelve hours the doctor had had to adjust an assessment that had taken years to develop and yet, in the swift tide of changes, the one immutable factor was Vincent. Their perception of the man might change with every piece of information they gathered; however, the man himself had not altered his behavior and the way he related to the world since he had set foot in the Institute. Whether they liked it or not he was their constant, the beginning and the end of the nightmare, forever stuck in that awful day while time had flowed on around him.

The detectives went into a side room with a one-way mirror while Peterson briefed Takemoto about the patient. A video camera had been set up to film the sessions from behind the glass. There was much to say and Madison had had a chance to talk to Takemoto herself about what they needed from Vincent and the circumstances of the case.

Then, flanked by the nurse they had met before, Vincent Foley shuffled into the room and every other thought faded away.

The day was overcast and although the light coming through the windows was barely more than timid, Foley was immediately drawn to it. He lifted his hand and touched the glass – the people in the room might very well not have existed at all.

He wore scrubs and they hung on his slight body like a boy wearing a man's shirt.

'Hello, Vincent,' Peterson said.

Foley turned and his piercing blue gaze slid over the doctor and Takemoto without apparent interest or recognition and went back to the view from the window. Every cell of his body seemed to shiver as his fingers traced the glass. His nails had been cut as short as they could be.

'How old is he?' Dunne whispered. Their room was soundproofed but that was just about as much voice as Dunne could muster. Spencer said nothing at all.

'Forty-eight,' Madison replied quietly.

They had all read the file and knew exactly how old he was; however, to see Vincent in person was something entirely different. Kelly had been utterly silent and yet Madison saw in the way he held himself that he was pleased Spencer and Dunne were as spooked by Foley as he had been.

No one had ever asked Vincent the right questions because no one had ever known what the right questions were.

'Hello, Vincent,' Jennifer Takemoto said.

*

The detectives watched as the psychiatrist began to interact with Foley, speaking to him in a series of short statements – friendly comments on the view that required no response from the patient but allowed him to become used to her presence. She now stood next to him by the window; framed against the dark sky, their silhouettes were only a foot apart. Peterson watched every step and weighed every word.

Madison's cell vibrated in the inside pocket of her blazer. She reached for it and when she saw the caller's number she pressed the key and left the room.

'Madison,' she said

'Detective, it's Fred Kamen,' the man said. 'From the FBI.'

Madison allowed herself a small smile: as if there could be another Fred Kamen in her acquaintance. Weeks earlier, when she was deep in her war against Harry Salinger, Kamen – one of the best and brightest of Behavioral Analysis Unit 4 and the Violent Criminal Apprehension Program at the FBI – had given her invaluable support. He was also an old friend of Det. Sgt. Brown, Madison's partner, and that more than anything else – made him a good man. *Was he calling about Brown? Had he heard Brown had failed the firearm shooting test?*

'Mr. Kamen, it's been a while. How are you?'

'It's twenty degrees outside, Detective, that's how I am.' The tone was still more East Coast academic than law enforcement.

'I see.'

Kamen was not the small-talk type. 'I have something on my desk. It was flagged up for our possible interest and it came back to you.'

'What is it?'

'You were looking to match a latent handprint on a homicide case? The victim was a Ronald Gray.'

The smudged handprint on the tiles of the coach station restroom.

'Yes, I certainly am. How—'

'Because the match is someone I have known about for a number of years. Peter Conway. And he's *organized crime*.'

'Organized crime?' Madison's mind started running through possibilities and scenarios.

'Yes,' Kamen continued. 'Your print has turned up twice in homicide investigations connected to racketeering, fraud and extortion. Never enough points of similarity to do anything about it, mind you, but enough to get flagged up.'

'How many points do we have for my case?'

'Seven.'

Madison sighed: the courts handled anything between eight and sixteen points of similarity in their trials but a defense attorney would tear a hole right through a seven-point match.

'How did you get the original prints?' she asked Kamen. 'Was Conway ever charged with anything?'

Kamen hesitated. 'No, we have his prints courtesy of an undercover agent who gave us the glass Conway had drunk from. We have his DNA too. That investigation is still open and the agent died in suspicious circumstances three weeks later.'

'Conway's work?'

'Very probably. His prints are not in the system but should they ever turn up anywhere, we take an interest.'

'I understand,' Madison replied. 'Mr. Kamen, what we're looking at here is a homicide that is connected to a twenty-five-year-old kidnap and murder. The kidnapping – three children – was in all probability tied up to threats of extortion related to a restaurant. It would fit the organized crime model and explain why Conway turned up in Seattle and started a clean-up operation.'

'Yes, most of his work has been on the East Coast. It's a very specialized crew. I joined the early investigations because they needed a behavioral analysis angle: the killings are always different;

there is no identical pattern that makes them stand out on the Violent Criminal Apprehension Program database. Except for one thing, and once you know it that's how you keep track of them: they use what they find on the crime scene against the victim.'

Madison closed her eyes and saw Warren Lee's body on the autopsy table. 'I know what you mean. I have seen their work here in Seattle in the last week. And I don't think they're done yet.'

'Madison, sometimes the victims just disappear. No bodies, no trail and no evidence.'

Jerry Wallace.

'Witnesses and informants have not fared well. I'm going to send you everything I can on Conway and his crew,' Kamen said.

'Any other names? Biometric information for any of them?'

'They don't have records. What we have is what our agent had managed to collect before he was killed.'

'How did that happen?'

'A hit-and-run in Vegas. The car had been stolen two days earlier and was found at the bottom of a lake.'

'I'm sorry.'

'These men have not done the work they do for this long without being extremely good at it. If they're in Seattle to clean up some-body's mess that's exactly what they'll do until they are stopped irrevocably and conclusively. They are motivated by money and money alone. They charge a very high fee but get the job done – whatever the job happens to be.'

'Thank you for this, Mr. Kamen. I'll wait for the file.'

Kamen paused for a moment. 'You speaking to Brown much?' he said.

'Some. Saw him too.'

She didn't know whether Kamen was aware about the failed test and it wasn't Madison's truth to give.

'Keep an eye on him,' Kamen said.

'I will,' she replied.

Madison walked back into the small room. The detectives were silent. Through the glass, Jennifer Takemoto sat on the gray carpeted floor opposite Vincent, who stared straight at the detectives as if he could see them.

'Anything?' Madison whispered to Spencer.

He shook his head.

'We just got a break,' she said, and motioned for them to join her in the corridor.

Chapter 35

Nathan Quinn sat on the edge of the bed in his hospital room and waited. The results would be ready soon: blood tests, MRSA swabs, what have you. In the last few hours he had been checked every which way – the partial splenectomy scar had been examined by the surgeon and judged *satisfactory within the parameters*, whatever that meant in the real world. And now, all being well, he would be finally discharged and allowed to go back home. Dr. Toyne would have preferred to keep him in for another few days but there was no real need for him to stay. As long as he continued a steady increase of physical activity, there was no reason why he could not finish his recovery at home.

He looked around the room. He wouldn't miss being here; he wouldn't miss the weeks spent attached to monitors and IV fluids. The only thing he would miss, among the depths of pain, was that the morphine had given him David back and those brief hallucinations had been as real to him as the soft satin bedspread under his fingers.

His bags were packed and Carl Doyle would arrive any time. Soon Dr. Toyne would give him his blessing and he would get to breathe fresh air for the first time since last December. He was almost out of there; next it would be Jack's turn.

*

Nathan Quinn left the hospital with very little fuss compared to his arrival there. He thanked the doctors and nurses who had managed to save his life every day for the first two weeks and was taken to the exit on a standard wheelchair. Outside, he stood up and his skin tingled in the sudden chill: he felt weak and insubstantial in the February cold but also exhilarated – dangerously so. Given what he had survived, anything was possible, and as the truth gradually revealed itself Nathan Quinn felt he could almost reach into the past and wrap his hand around the throat of the man who had ordered the abduction of the boys.

All in good time, he thought, and reminded himself that the doctor had said his energy and his moods would be 'up and down with the tide' for the next few weeks and had suggested he speak to a counselor about the trauma of his injuries. They both knew it wasn't going to happen but the poor man had felt obliged to say it.

The chauffeur-driven Lexus pulled up to Quinn and Doyle and he was soon on his way home to Seward Park. He leant back with his head against the seat and watched the city go past. A part of him hoped that the dangerous clarity he was experiencing was simply a consequence of all that his body and his mind had endured; a part of him knew that it might not be.

The ride was pleasant because any time spent out of a hospital room would be, even a dreary car ride under overcast skies.

The house was a beautifully kept wood and stone building with a deck in the style common in the Pacific Northwest. The exterior paint had started as flinty gray but rain and the salt in the air had weathered it into washed-out pewter.

The driver brought his bags to the door as Quinn turned the key in the lock, and the alarm beeps told him he was finally home.

Doyle had been coming in once a week or so to keep an eye on things and check his mail; he had even stocked up his fridge the last time he was there; nevertheless, when Quinn reached for the alarm box in the half gloom to punch in the code, the familiar gesture felt alien and a gust of icy wind swept into the darkened house.

The driver left and Doyle closed the door behind him.

Quinn leant on the stick in his right hand and took in the space he knew so well. He had expected to feel relief and yet there was something not quite right. A long time in a space awash with chemical scents had left him very sensitive to the delicate balance of smells in his own home. There was something rancid and sour in the stale air, something that did not belong.

'Are you alright?' Doyle said.

'I don't know yet,' Quinn replied.

He walked to the living room – each cautious step born out of stubbornness and determination – and he noticed it: the semi-pro Meade telescope that stood mounted on a tripod next to the French doors to the garden. Quinn stared at the ground where the tips of the tripod legs met the parquet flooring. Years earlier he had found the perfect spot for the telescope and it had remained in the same place ever since – three small indentations in the wood marked its usual position. It was quite clear that the tripod had been moved about five inches to the left.

'Carl?' Quinn said over his shoulder. 'When where you last here?'

'Four days ago,' Doyle replied.

'Since I've been in the hospital, have you ever come anywhere near this telescope? Looked through it? Moved it perhaps?'

'No. Usually I just pick up the mail, put the flyers in the garbage, and that's it. I don't even walk to that part of the room.'

'Did you go into the study?'

'No, I didn't need to.'

'I just have to check something.'

Bookcases covered every wall; a mahogany desk sat in a corner; a thin film of dust had built up over the green glass banker's lamp that reminded him of his college library. Nathan Quinn remained by the threshold and examined the room: his eyes went over the small, significant objects of his past life: pens, papers, a framed photograph of his parents' wedding day, an antique carriage clock.

On a bookshelf, the hourglass and the three nineteenthth-century nautical compasses that had belonged to his father laid where he had placed them. Quinn's eyes held them whole: *almost* where he had placed them. Our life and its minute parts are an indistinct landscape to others, but to us even the smallest detail has its own precise coordinates and any change, however infinitesimal, is obvious.

'Someone was inside the house,' he said to Doyle, proceeding to the alarm box fixed on the inside wall next to the main door. He had it installed seven years ago and at the time it was top of the range.

'I don't understand,' Carl said. 'The alarm was set, there was no . . .'

Quinn keyed in a number combination and a list of dates and hours appeared on the box's screen. All the times were during daylight or early evening.

'Are these the days and times when you were here?' he asked Doyle.

Doyle looked, he nodded.

Quinn took out his cell from his coat pocket and dialed the telephone number on the alarm box. He gave his name, a password, and an eight-number code. 'I need you to email me the last twenty entries in the log. Thank you.'

Doyle tried to remember the last times he had been in the house – all those times had blended into a blur of repeated actions, and he could not think of anything that had looked amiss because nothing had.

'Nathan . . .'

'There's nothing you could have done, and there's no way anyone but me would have noticed.'

'Did they take anything?'

Quinn looked around. It had been a nearly immaculate job because they weren't there to rob, they were there to examine and analyze the enemy.

'Come with me,' he said to Doyle.

The safe was 15 x 12 inches of steel and was concealed behind a panel in the linen closet. Quinn ran the combination quickly on the electronic locking device and opened the thick metal door. The contents – various papers and some antique jewelry boxes – seemed intact. Quinn took them out, then reached inside and pressed a hidden switch that revealed a secret compartment within the safe. He looked inside.

'Nothing has been touched,' he said to Doyle.

'Do you understand what happened?'

'I think so,' Quinn replied.

The alert pinged on his phone. Quinn opened the email from the monitoring company: the last entry in the log was their arrival at the house, the second from last entry indicated that the previous night someone had disarmed the system at 3.10 a.m. and alarmed it at 3.57 a.m. Quinn showed it to Doyle.

'Nathan . . .'

'They deleted the entry from the box here but it had already been registered in the central database. They spent forty-seven minutes inside and then they left.'

Suddenly the house seemed quite different.

'There's nothing you could have done,' Quinn repeated. He knew Doyle well enough to understand that he was as angry as he was mortified that this breach had happened on his watch.

Quinn thought quickly. 'We must treat this as a crime scene,' he said as he dialed Tod Hollis's number.

He needed to make sure that nothing had been taken but he needed to make just as sure that nothing had been left.

Chapter 36

They left Dr. Takemoto with Vincent Foley and returned to the precinct. Sorensen at the lab had been alerted to the possibility of a match to Conway's DNA from the samples recovered at the Lee and Gray crime scenes and Lieutenant Fynn had been briefed.

Madison read the Conway file at her desk. It was a catalogue of brutality that had begun eleven years earlier and swept its way across both coasts and the mainland. Kamen had been right: Conway and his crew had been involved – allegedly involved – in every kind of violent felony bar very few, and they were good at their job.

Madison had printed out Kamen's notes and the tip of her finger ran down the long list. *Murder of a witness in a racketeering case, murder of a local boss, kidnap/murder of a drug dealer, suspected murder of a journalist (victim never recovered/probably deceased), suspected murder of a made man in Jersey (victim never recovered/probably deceased).* And on and on.

It wasn't difficult to imagine those men breaking into Warren Lee's home, torturing him with whatever they had found in his kitchen, and then leaving him under the water towers. Madison checked the list of alleged felonies: bodies had been recovered in some cases, not recovered in others. They had wanted them to find Lee and Gray just as they were, and Wallace . . . Madison hoped that there was another explanation for the disappearance of Jerry

Wallace, though she held little hope. He had been the equivalent of a walking, talking Wikipedia of West Coast crime. No wonder they wanted him gone. *They.* Nathan Quinn's appeal had sent out a question; these men were the answer.

I hope to God you know what you're doing, Quinn.

Her cell started vibrating. It was Dr. Takemoto.

'Detective, I just wanted to let you know that we're done for the day here. I've kept it pretty light and breezy for Vincent but Peterson stopped the session when he thought he was getting tired.'

'What do you think? Can you recover anything from his memories?'

'Are we talking about Vincent's mind as if it were a hard drive?'

'In a way, yes. A fabulously complex and unspeakably damaged hard drive.'

'I see. The only person he had any meaningful interaction with was his brother. Everybody else here, kind as they are, didn't really make a dent. I think Vincent's memories have been *corrupted* by the trauma but they are there, even though he might not know the meaning of what happened. And maybe the only one who could have accessed those memories was his brother.'

'What about his relationship with Ronald?'

'Mr. Gray was very loyal; he visited him frequently and spoke to him all the time. Apparently he could keep him calm without recurring to drugs. It will take me some time to be able to get through to Vincent, if I ever do . . .'

Time was what they did not have. Madison closed her eyes – the brightness of the anglepoise lamp still shone through behind her lids.

'Doctor, assuming that Vincent knows something, anything that comes out of his mouth we have to treat as gold. Peterson said his mind is locked inside that day, frozen during those hours. We are going to need a complete account of every single word he utters because we should assume everything is related to that day.'

'I'll mail you a transcript after each session.'

'Thank you very much.'

There was a pretty black iron railing around the Walters Institute, two security guards who patrolled the grounds and a couple inside to keep an eye on things; there were well-meaning and well-trained nurses who made sure the patients didn't harm themselves or each other, and there were doors with magnetic locks and swipe cards. And all these measures would count for nothing if Peter Conway wanted in.

Madison closed the file, her palm flat on the card cover that contained such horrors. There were things that they could do – must do: information to sift through, traffic cameras' footage, trace evidence that had been recovered and might perhaps be matched to this crew from hell. And yet all Madison could think about was an empty house at the end of a long narrow lane and the darkness pushing in through the windows.

Madison's cell started vibrating as she was going through the traffic footage from the coach station abduction. She recognized the number.

'Detective.' Quinn's voice was soft.

'Mr. Quinn.'

'I thought you might like to know that my house was broken into last night, and the burglars didn't take anything; they just had a good snoop around.'

'How . . . what happened?'

'I came home late this morning, I noticed something, the records from the alarm company agreed with my theory.'

The first thing Madison thought was that Quinn had been discharged, he had finally been discharged; the second thing was that no one in that house should touch anything; better still, he should wait in the car while she called the crime lab and they processed the house from top to bottom.

'I'm on my way,' she said. 'And—'

'I know. I'll try not to wreck the scene.'

Kelly buckled his seat belt and sighed; he could have stayed behind at the precinct but he had come, Madison knew, mostly out of curiosity. He had lifted a solitary eyebrow when she had called Sorensen at the lab and he had expressed his doubts that this was any of their business – an attempted burglary, the intruders had been disturbed and left before taking anything. However, a chance to look at Nathan Quinn up close was not to be wasted and so there he was: a silent, surly presence that Madison tried her level best to ignore.

It wasn't a coincidence, it wasn't an interrupted burglary, it wasn't Father Christmas coming late to Seward Park. It was Conway and his crew paying Quinn's house a visit because of a single piece of information they did not have: how did Quinn know about Timothy Gilman?

Madison drove fast through a haze of rain. She couldn't bear to think about what would have happened if Quinn had been discharged a day earlier.

Seattle was surrounded by water: the long strip of Puget Sound to the west and the large expanse of Lake Washington to the east; salt water and fresh water holding a ribbon of land between them.

They arrived in Seward Park just as the sun broke out of the cloud cover and the sudden light found every last raindrop on the thick stretch of green that surrounded Nathan Quinn's house. Madison parked next to his Jeep. She had never been to his home before: their dealings had been mostly about courts, precincts, and dark woods in the middle of the night. A home was almost too mundane.

At the bottom of the sloping garden Lake Washington lapped at the lawn and a long pier jutted toward Mercer Island.

Stone and wood, seasoned by the Pacific Northwest: though there were other much larger houses in the same road, there were probably none as quietly striking.

The door opened and stayed open.

'You met him since?' Kelly said as they got out of the car.

'Yes, once,' Madison replied.

Kelly grunted something that she didn't catch.

In spite of the brief sunshine the ground was still soaking wet after days of rain; they wiped their shoes on a mat and walked inside.

Quinn met them in the hall; he was talking on the phone and said goodbye to someone.

'Thank you for coming, Detective,' he said.

They dispensed with the introductions as quickly as courtesy would allow – Quinn had never met Kelly – and moved on to the intricacies of breaking and entering into a house with a top-of-the-range alarm system.

'When did you notice something was not right?' Madison asked Quinn.

'The telescope had been moved from its usual place,' he pointed. 'And two small objects on a bookshelf in my study.'

'That's all?'

'It was enough.'

'While you were in the hospital only Carl came over?' Madison turned to Kelly. 'Carl Doyle is Mr. Quinn's assistant,' she explained.

'Just Carl,' Quinn replied. 'And he didn't even go near the telescope or the study.'

'What about the alarm company records?' Madison was aware of Kelly's eyes taking in Quinn and the dark red lines that crossed his features, watching him as if he were some kind of exotic creature.

'They were good,' Quinn replied. 'They erased the record of the entry but it had already been registered on the central database at company HQ.'

'What time were they here?'

'Between 3 a.m. and 4 a.m. last night.'

'You're positive they didn't take anything?'

'They didn't take anything, I'm sure.'

'Left anything?'

'Hollis swiped the whole house and found nothing.'

Madison nodded; she remembered Hollis from the Salinger case. If Hollis had swiped the house and found no bugs, it meant there were no bugs to be found. It also meant that another person had been in the house to add to the trace evidence that the Crime Scene Unit would have to process. They were standing just inside the living room door now, trying to limit the contamination of the scene.

'Is that why you waited to call us?' Kelly asked. 'You got the house swiped first and called it in after?'

'Yes.'

'That's really not the way to go about it, Counselor.'

'At that point I didn't know whether I would call it in at all,' Quinn replied.

Madison understood what he meant: if Hollis had picked up a device they might have left it in place and used it to their advantage. It would have been the most dangerous course of action and absolutely typical of Quinn.

'Perfect,' Madison said.

'They just had a look around and left?' Kelly said.

'Yes,' Quinn replied.

'Let me understand, our little theory here is that this –' Kelly gestured at the house around them – 'is connected to the whole mess started by your television appeal, right? So if they didn't come for your television and your hidden gold, what were they looking for?'

'Information,' Madison interjected, and her eyes found Quinn's. 'The single piece of information that made the appeal dangerous for the killers: how you found out about Timothy Gilman's connection to the abduction and who else knows.'

'I imagine so, yes,' Quinn replied.

They had been over this at the hospital and he didn't seem any more inclined to reveal his source.

'You're absolutely sure they didn't manage to find your notes, your documents, whatever in the name of all that's holy you've got hidden away, then copied it and left it for you to believe they didn't find it?'

'That information is not to be found on any paper and never has been.'

The Crime Scene Unit van rumbled to a stop in the drive and Quinn left to open the door for them.

'I have to make a call,' Kelly said and went back to the car.

Frank Lauren and Mary Kay Joyce walked in carrying their equipment, nodded hello and began their sifting and their sieving.

'A B and E – how refreshing,' Joyce commented, looking around. 'No blood-spatter chart for once, Madison.'

'Don't get used to it,' she replied.

Madison and Quinn went out to a side deck and left them to it. The pale sun offered little warmth and they were both wearing their coats with the collars up.

'I'm not even going to say anything about you not calling this in straightaway; it would be a waste of breath,' Madison said. 'But this you should know: have you ever heard of a man called Jerry Wallace?'

Madison told Quinn about the phone call from Kamen, about Peter Conway and his crew, about the file sitting on her desk and what it contained.

'There's every reason to believe these are the men who went after Lee, Gray and, in all probability, Wallace. We're hoping that the evidence will link all the crime scenes,' she concluded.

'And you are protecting the fourth man?'

'Yes, protecting and *interrogating* him, as far as his condition allows.'

It was to Quinn's credit that he had not asked her to let him meet Vincent Foley. Technically speaking, Foley was still merely a patient in a psychiatric facility.

'I have to ask you about your parents,' she said, treading lightly in a territory that was both unfamiliar and perhaps difficult to navigate.

'What about my parents?' Quinn replied evenly.

'At the time of your brother's abduction, and also before and after, did you ever hear them mention the names Eduardo Cruz, Leon Kendrick or Jerome McMullen?'

'No, they never did mention any names, not once. Not at the time or ever,' Quinn said. 'Years later, when I was working in the Prosecutor's Office, I made my own enquiries and read the file and came up with the same names, for what good it did.'

'If the men who broke in last night didn't find what they were looking for they might very well come back for it,' Madison said. 'And they might be inclined to ask you personally.'

'Last night's was a subtle job, Detective; they didn't want to attract attention to themselves. I've been in a hospital – without any security or protection – for long enough that if they wanted to pay me a visit they could have done so at any time of their choosing.'

'Don't take this lightly, Counselor.'

The view was lovely, the water reflecting the bright sky for those brief moments when the sun was showing itself, while they spoke of the ugliest things a person can do to another. A small sailboat with three young sailors in bright red life jackets bobbed past; their voices floated up to the deck.

'This is how it works, Detective,' Quinn said, his eyes following the boat. 'You have to kick the tree to see what falls out of it.'

'That you did, Counselor,' Madison said.

For a moment it was alright just to stand out there in silence.

'How's your partner?' Quinn said after a while.

'He's . . . he's getting better. Slowly.'

A text message pinged on Madison's cell. She read it twice; it was from Spencer. *Jerome McMullen could be out on parole in seven days.*

'McMullen,' she said to Quinn. 'He's up for parole.'

It meant that the last thing he wanted was for a twenty-five-year-old kidnapping gone wrong to flare up and disintegrate his chance at freedom; it meant *motive*.

A burst of laughter from the small sailboat drifted up and died away.

Chapter 37

The rest of the afternoon passed in a blur as the detectives tried to connect McMullen to the murders and continued the hunt for Conway's crew. Madison concentrated on finding a connection between Gilman and the soon-to-be-released convict; she examined records of past convictions, addresses, known acquaintances – everything and anything that makes up the life we lead, that connects us to the people we know. The fact that Jerome McMullen had a potential motive to want the Quinn kidnap/murder to disappear forever was absolutely no good to them if they could not prove he had ordered it, paid Gilman to carry it out and, twenty-five years later, made sure that Peter Conway and his men wiped out anyone still alive who could testify against him.

Madison stood up and reached for her coat: she would nip out and grab a coffee nearby and bring it back to her desk. The detectives' room was peaceful, as her team had left, and the current shift was out in their daily duty to protect and to serve.

Her cell started vibrating.

'Madison,' she said as she shrugged on her coat.

'Are you still in the precinct?'

Brown. Madison smiled.

'Yup, one of those days. How's it going, Sarge?'

'Swell,' Brown replied. 'If you're still kicking around in the precinct, do you want to meet at the range?'

'Can think of nothing better.'

'See you there.'

Madison slipped her cell back in her jeans back pocket and gazed out of the window. It was pitch black. Detective Sergeant Brown had called her late enough in the day that she might have already gone home or made other plans, maybe hoping she had, and still he had reached out to her.

Madison had no illusions about the situation: if Brown didn't get his shooting up to the level required by the examining board he would hand in his badge and that would be that. He wouldn't be a civilian on the force, he wouldn't finish his last ten or however many years pushing papers from one side of his desk to the other. He would be gone. Madison took a deep breath and rubbed her hands on her face. She couldn't allow that to happen.

The range was quiet at that time and blessedly deserted. J. B. Norton, the chief instructor, had already left for the day and Madison was grateful for that small mercy. Norton was the kindest soul who had ever taught human beings how to shoot each other but Brown needed privacy.

The cool air whispered through the pipes as Madison lifted her Glock in the MI stance. She aligned the sights – the gun in a comfortable two-hand grip – and listened to her breathing. At the end of the exhale she squeezed the trigger and the shot ripped through the silence. She allowed herself two breaths with the weapon lowered and then repeated the sequence. Her six rounds found the center of the target and disintegrated it.

She wasn't there to show off, and almost put one round out of the target's core on purpose. She turned to Brown, who was leaning against the wall behind her. Detective Sergeant Kevin Brown, her partner, who weeks earlier had been her main ally in the war against Harry Salinger and in the small daily battles of a rookie detective in a Homicide unit.

He looked as he always did: a crisp shirt and a smart tie, even his ever-present raincoat folded neatly on a chair nearby. His ginger hair had a touch more gray in it – that was all the change the past few weeks seemed to have brought. Madison knew better though: the fear of not being allowed to do the one thing that you are truly good at would have been overwhelming, like an oil slick that rea-ched into every corner of a person's thoughts. She understood and didn't dwell on it, and thus they both ignored the actual reason why they were meeting at the range and instead talked about the case, about the joys of partnering Detective Chris Kelly, and about the latest from Cameron's jail.

This was her second set; she had gone first, then Brown had taken her place, and now that she was done it was his turn again. Madison watched him and assessed him carefully.

There's always more to an injury than the mere physical side of it. How has pain changed us? How has it changed the way we live inside our bodies and inside the world at large?

Brown's shots tore through the range. Her eyes had followed the line of his shoulders, his grip on the weapon – he favored a Modi-fied Isosceles stance as she did – and saw his chest rise and fall with each breath.

They took turns for a while. Brown had taken the obligatory reme-dial lessons after the two fails on the same day.

Madison examined the target still in place: Brown's score was on the narrow line between failure and success. Tonight he had barely made it; a hair's breadth difference on test day and he would fail – no doubt about it.

'What do you think?' he asked her, the directness of the question almost startling.

This was not the time for the cosmetic version; Madison pressed the button that retrieved the target and in the half gloom the paper cut-out flowed toward them like an ungainly spirit.

'The technique is there,' she started. 'And so is strength and breathing. However, just before you shoot you lock your shoulders and become rigid.'

Brown nodded. 'Go on.'

'There's a small flinch there when you get locked, and sometimes it's not so small and it affects your aim.'

'It's been improving but not fast enough.'

'Yes, I can see that. Also you peaked a couple of turns ago, and now you're tired and it's getting worse.'

They both leaned against the wall, their ear mufflers around their necks and the eye-protectors back on the shelf. The smell of cordite was sharp in their nostrils.

'What do you suggest?' he said.

Madison didn't want to cheapen the moment with some half-assed psychobabble – she'd run away from that kind of thing herself – and yet the answer was not merely physical.

'It's not about how you're holding the weapon or the angle of your feet,' she started. 'You are controlling your breathing without holding it and you're doing everything right.'

'Except that . . .'

'You're over-thinking it. You're not using your muscle-memory. Every shot you take it's like the first one you ever took, and it's using up all your energy to make sure every single element is right. Which it is. But the tension is pulling your body apart and you're barely making the score.'

Madison took a breath. Their relationship had always been about honesty and Brown would not have asked her the question if he didn't want the answer. His eyes were still on the target trembling in the air conditioning.

'What do you suggest?' he said after a moment.

'How good are you at mental Math?'

Brown snorted. 'Let's just say I've never been to Math camp.'

'Perfect. What you need to do, Sarge, is occupy your rather large and complex brain with some six-digit additions while letting your muscle-memory do the job it's there for and hit the darn target.'

'Additions?'

'Multiplications, if you prefer. Anything that's going to keep your mind from becoming too involved in shooting could work.'

'You ever use this trick?'

'All the time.'

'You're kidding?'

'Nope. When I was competing I'd get very nervous and J. B. suggested it.'

Neither needed to say that the reality of the street was extremely different. Harry Salinger had not given them time to count anything when he had attacked them in near darkness.

Madison clicked the release and the loader slipped out of her Glock – such a familiar gesture. They were working on a B-27 target – a human silhouette in black, with the elliptical target areas in white. In the past Madison had also trained on a G-64 – a human silhouette with every organ clearly marked and assigned points for importance. She had done it a couple of times, then stopped and never used it again.

'I'll come back tomorrow, fresh and full of numbers,' Brown said. 'Do you have time for a beer?'

'Absolutely,' Madison replied.

Jimmy's was a cop's bar with a meatloaf that had nourished and raised the cholesterol levels of generations of cops. It wasn't meatloaf night but the chef found them two chicken salads and piled them

high with extras, just to let them know how pleased they were to
see them there after so long.

Brown and Madison sat in a booth a little off from the main area,
eating and drinking chilled long necks from a local microbrewery.
It could have been the end of a normal shift.

Madison enjoyed their silence as much as their conversations.
Brown wasn't the chatty type and she didn't mind. On the Salinger
case he had kept his thoughts close to his chest and had let her reach
her own conclusions. In the end they had both arrived at the same
theory, roughly fifteen minutes before he had been shot in the head.

'I met Jerry Wallace in 1987,' Brown said after a while. 'There were
good reasons he did what he did and didn't get involved in anything
heavier than information. He was a little guy with a talent for speaking to anybody on any side. One of Conway's crew could have just
carried him out under his arm.'

Madison took a sip of her beer. 'This thing, it goes all the way
back to August 28, 1985, and every time I feel I'm getting close to
seeing the shape of it something else happens and it shifts into a
different animal.'

Her frustration was evident. Brown was silent for a beat.

'Do you know how they measured the Great Pyramid?' he said
finally.

'What?'

'Do you know how the ancient Greeks measured the Great
Pyramid? In essence, how did they measure the height of an inac-
cessible object?'

Madison was struggling to find a connection.

'There are objects that could not be measured by conventional
means,' Brown continued. 'Because their shape made it impossible.'

'I don't know how they did it.'

'Shadow reckoning,' Brown said. 'They measured the shadow the
object cast, how far and how wide the shadow would reach.'

Madison nodded. *Shadow reckoning.* It was the only way she could measure that single day in August and the impact it had on all those lives. The dark coiled inside, that shadow had stretched out for decades and killed or somewhat maimed everyone it had touched.

Chapter 38

Nathan Quinn listened to the wind disturbing the trees around the house. He hadn't heard it for weeks. From the hospital room he couldn't see the waters of Washington Lake darken and still. It was a specific kind of sensory deprivation where the only sounds allowed were the ticks and beeps of the machines and even the silence had an aseptic quality. He breathed in the chilly air out on the deck and his eyes tracked the indistinct shape of Mercer Island. He was home.

The break-in – not even twenty-four hours earlier – was only one more sign that the right people were feeling under pressure and making mistakes. He welcomed their mistakes and should they decide to visit the house again, he'd be so very glad to meet them in person.

After Detective Madison and the Crime Scene Unit had left, Tod Hollis had returned with an acquaintance who dealt in biometric technology-based alarm systems and the house had been wired up. The alarm worked on a combination of iris and fingerprint recognition and by the time the technicians left it was probably easier to break into Bill Gates' mansion on the other side of the lake.

Nathan Quinn had never owned a firearm license in his life and there were no weapons in the house. He was not afraid, and looking at the healing scars on his hands, he couldn't imagine ever being afraid again.

Inside, Quinn poured himself an inch of bourbon – the first alcohol he had touched in weeks. He took the glass with him as he climbed the stairs to the first floor and then to the attic. Step after step. It wasn't as easy as he would have wished and he was exhausted by the time he reached the top of the house. He leant on the door frame, took a deep breath to steady himself, and turned on the light.

He hardly went up there; it was a whitewashed room under the eaves filled with stacks of boxes and a couple of armchairs under dust sheets – his parents' chairs.

He had the first sip of bourbon and placed the glass on the table; the warmth in his chest was as sudden as it was welcome.

The box he was looking for was on top of a pile; he put his arms around it and lifted; every muscle in his body was aware of the movement as he placed it carefully on the table. It was the only box in the attic that had not been marked by a black marker scrawl to signify its contents because it didn't need it. Quinn took another sip. The last time he had opened it John Cameron and James Sinclair had been by his side. *David's things.*

He pulled the string connected to the bare light bulb above the table. He didn't even know why he was there except that without the morphine he couldn't see David, and the idea that he existed in this world only as remains kept in a morgue's drawer was unbearable.

He removed the box's lid. Everything was present and accounted for: the baseball mitt with the ball still cradled in it, Jack Sikma's Sonics jersey with the number 43, the yearbook, the camera, four seashells, a strangely shaped piece of wood from Ruby Beach collected when he was ten – and more objects and more memories than he could handle just then. He replaced the lid and began the long climb down the stairs. The house creaked around him, small noises as familiar as his own heartbeat. The alarm had been set for the night and a tiny red light pulsed on the box beside the front door.

July 4, 1985. The sun was still high in the sky and the voices of the guests splashing around in the pool were competing with the music from the speakers in the garden. David Quinn had appeared out of the wooded area and made a beeline for Nathan, who was standing to one side and talking to one of the Locke cousins, a blonde girl about his age. Now they were inside, the pretty girl was gone, and Nathan – still feeling generally guilty for months of neglect – was trying to change the roll of film on David's camera.

'It's stuck,' David said. 'I tried to do it myself but I thought I was breaking it . . .'

'Don't worry – let me see. Do you have a new roll?'

'Here . . .'

The roll was indeed stuck and Nathan was doing his best to look like he knew what he was doing.

'Tell me,' he said, hoping to distract him from his own clumsy hands. 'What pictures did you take? Did you change the shutter speed like we talked about?'

'Yes, I took a bunch of Jack diving, and lots of people too: Mom talking with a lady, Dad talking with Mr. Locke, Mr. Locke and a man, Bobby being an idiot, and a whole bunch of squirrels in the woods. I got two deer too, over by the east side fencing.'

'Sounds good.' Nathan's fingers managed to finally remove the old roll. He offered it to David with a flourish and deftly inserted the new one in the camera. It clicked shut with a pleasant snap and he gave it back to his brother. 'All done,' he said.

David took it and held it. 'If there was something . . .' he started. 'If there was something serious, something big, and I told you about it, would you promise not to tell Mom and Dad?'

'Yes,' he said. 'But if it was really serious than *you* would have to tell them. Is it about school? Are you in some kind of trouble?'

'No, it's not me. It's just something . . . I don't know . . .' he shrugged. 'It could be nothing.'

'You can tell me.'

David looked around: there were too many people about and anyone could walk in on them at any time. 'I'll tell you later.'

'You're sure?'

'Yup.'

'Okay.'

David left and Nathan went back to find the pretty blonde girl. He left soon after to join some friends back in Seattle; he missed the fireworks by the lake and never had a chance to talk to David about the phone call James had overheard. By the following morning he had left for a one-week holiday in the San Juan Islands.

Nathan Quinn laid down on his own bed and closed his eyes. He had placed the walking stick to one side. In the books he had read as a boy a walking stick might hide a dagger or a sword. The one leaning on the side of his chair had been made in China and held nothing more inside its coils than cheap manufacturing and mass production. If he was going to keep using the darn thing he'd have to buy himself something more suitable. Something with a concealed sword maybe. Quinn sighed and hoped sleep would come soon, deep and empty. He felt the blackness take hold and drifted toward it: as always there was the memory of music, the memory of a hand holding his through the pain. And for an instant there was only the song, then all was darkness.

Chapter 39

Madison sat up in her bed, her brain thick with sleep and slightly disoriented. Her cell phone was ringing in the back pocket of her jeans on the floor. She managed to turn on the bedside lamp and lunged for it.

It was Sergeant Jenner from the precinct.

'I have a note here saying that you want to be notified in case of any emergency calls from the Walters Institute . . .' he said.

'What happened?'

'Emergency call eleven minutes ago. I don't know any more than that.'

'Thank you. I'm on my way.'

Madison had had three hours' sleep since she had left Brown. She made do with a two-minute cold shower and left the house ten minutes after the phone had rang.

At 3 a.m. there was no traffic to speak of and she hardly touched the brakes. Her mind was a jumble of thoughts, none of them good. An emergency call could mean anything from one of the patients having a heart attack to Conway's crew breaking into the clinic to get to Vincent Foley. She tried to reach Dr. Peterson but the call went to his voicemail.

Madison drove through the thin drizzle and hoped that someone had slipped and sprained an ankle.

The journey was brief yet long enough for all the worst scenarios to present themselves.

Madison arrived at the Walters Institute and through her windscreen wipers she saw that the wrought iron gates were wide open and inside the grounds lights blinked through the trees. She attempted to drive up the lane that led to the main building and didn't make it all the way: a number of emergency trucks were parked, leaving just enough room for other vehicles to get through.

One of the Fire Medic One vans sped past with lights flashing and sirens blazing. *Okay, so it's not a sprained ankle.* Madison pulled up, parked on the grass and ran the rest of the way. She smelt it before she saw it: a dark acrid scent that found its way into her throat and squatted there. *Smoke.* She reached the end of the lane and once out of the canopy of the trees she saw the beautiful red brick building. *Fire, the building is on fire.* Dozens of people had repaired to the lawn: doctors and nurses in scrubs, patients in their pajamas and dressing gowns, some already lying down and strapped to gurneys with IVs connected to their arms.

The firefighters were tackling a blaze that had taken hold of the East Wing and was crawling up and down the floors like something alive and angry. It was concentrated on that side of the clinic but some bricks on the ground floor had been scorched black by an earlier burn; the windows were shattered and the water was still dripping where the hoses had waged their war.

Madison tried to remember what Peterson had said the first time they'd met. Thirty-nine patients who would have been asleep, plus the medical staff who took care of them, the night cleaning team and the security guards. It was a lot of people to get out of the building in a hurry.

A couple of people dashed out of the main door: a firefighter with his arm around a woman in nurse's scrubs. People were still coming out. Madison swore under her breath and headed toward the group of doctors and patients, hoping to see Peterson among them.

Firefighters hollered instructions at each other as they directed the hoses at the blaze; a police officer and the fire chief were trying to get a head count from one of the doctors to know for sure exactly how many people had been in the building at the time. Some patients were wailing and others sat quietly on the cold ground, hugging their knees.

'Where's Dr. Peterson?' Madison yelled above the din.

'Over there.' The doctor pointed.

Peterson was kneeling next to a patient and injecting him with something. He looked up and spoke to his deputy who was with the fire chief: 'Thirty-two here, three taken to Harborview, two to the Swedish, one unaccounted for.'

'What about doctors, nurses and the rest of the staff?' the fire chief said.

'One unaccounted for?' Madison asked him, dropping to her knees and helping him wrap an elderly lady in a blanket.

'Two staff are still missing: one doctor, one nurse. Everybody else is out.' Peterson looked pale under the smudges of dirt on his face. He was going from patient to patient, checking heart rate and temperature.

'One patient unaccounted for?' Madison repeated.

'Your staff are all out,' the fire chief said and pointed at the front entrance. Two of his men were bringing out two women in scrubs.

'Where's Vincent Foley?' Madison asked Peterson, looking around at the group gathered on the lawn.

'We have one patient still missing,' the fire chief told one of his team, who started at a trot toward the fire engines which took up most of the parking lot.

'Vincent is missing,' Peterson said to Madison. 'He should have been evacuated with all the other residents on the fourth floor but he's not with them. They're all here. The head count said we had everybody when we left the floor . . .'

'Peterson,' she said, 'look at the fire.'

He turned.

'It's on the opposite side from the patients' rooms, right? It's where you have all the offices, right?'

He nodded. Madison pointed at the windows on the opposite corner on the fourth floor.

'Is that the day room?'

He nodded.

'What does Vincent do when he's scared?' She stood up.

'He hides,' Peterson replied after a beat.

Madison lifted his ID card from around his neck. He didn't object.

'Officer,' Madison approached the uniformed officer who had been talking to the fire chief. 'Madison, Homicide. There's a real strong chance that this is arson and the men who set the fire are still on the grounds. They're after one particular patient and right now he's missing.'

'What's going on, Detective?'

'There could be people here who are looking to harm somebody.' She looked around at doctors running around, patients, other officers, firefighters. 'Watch out for anyone who doesn't belong, who's not emergency services.'

She started moving toward the entrance. 'Call my boss, Lieutenant Fynn, Homicide. Tell him what's going on.'

'Hey . . . where the hell . . .'

'Seattle PD.' She waved her badge to the firefighters but they were too far away to stop her, and in seconds she had entered the building. It was eerily intact, just dark and empty, and the carpet felt soaking wet under her boots – the odd drop of water still dripped from the sprinklers. The air was plain, fairly clean and with a bitter tinge of smoke. It would have to do.

The blaze was well contained in the East Wing; someone had made sure of that. How much did they know about Vincent? Did they know where his room was?

Madison crossed the reception – no young woman to smile politely this time – and reached the door to the stairs. The light was blinking green on the magnetic box: when the fire had been discovered the locks had been released, which is great if you need to rush out and even better if you're trying to break in. She pushed the swing door and she was in the stairway: the emergency lights were on, bathing everything in pale orange. Madison looked up – a quick peek and then back against the wall: no one there.

She flicked the safety latch and unholstered her piece. The sounds from outside were dulled by a series of walls and doors. She heard nothing from the inside of the building except the muted ticking of the lights' emergency battery on the stairs.

She had to start from the fourth floor. She climbed the stairs at a run, stopping dead at each corner to make sure the course was clear and then moving on. The higher she climbed the warmer the air became. She passed the entrance to the second-floor corridor and glanced through the glass door as she went past. No one there.

Her heart was drumming fast as she reached the third floor and peeked. No one there. Madison paused. If Vincent was anywhere, he would be on the fourth floor. If the killers were anywhere, they would be on the fourth floor. She climbed the stairs with her weapon held at eye level and made a swift mental inventory of the contents of her jacket pockets: she had a small flashlight and a penknife – the police radio had been left in the car, forgotten on the seat. On her ankle she had her back-up piece.

A window shattered on the other side of the building and Madison froze. She was four steps away from the door to the fourth floor corridor; the sound had come from the East Wing. She wiped her right hand on her jeans and resumed the grip. She tried not to think about the whimsy of shooting paper targets only hours earlier, when in minutes she might have to shoot a human being.

Madison glanced through the window's reinforced glass – her eyes skimmed the corridor and saw no movement, only a half-light and the flicker of overhead neon strips trying to come on.

Madison had been there in daylight and was grateful for that tiny bit of luck. She leant on one side of the swing door – her gun hand ahead of her – and stepped inside. The doors to the patients' rooms were wide open and the floor was littered with the debris of a quick evacuation.

It would have been nice to call out to Vincent; however, that was probably not the best way to go about it. Madison crouched behind a medicine trolley, flat against the wall. She reviewed the situation and it didn't look promising: Vincent was missing; he could still be on the fourth floor or he could be anywhere on the grounds. They suspected Conway's crew was a four-man unit; it meant two on the outside checking faces and two on the inside checking rooms. At least that's what she would have done.

Madison stood up: there were four rooms between her and Vincent's. The first was empty; the bed covers had been strewn on the floor. The second was also empty. The door of the third was ajar and she pushed gently with her left hand: it had been left in hurry – a drawer had been half pulled out.

Madison paused by Vincent's door; it was nearly closed. The searching beam of light from the firefighters swept the corridor's ceiling and the building creaked under the pressure of the fire and the water hoses, but in her wing there was only silence.

Madison pushed Vincent's door open with the tip of her finger and immediately saw the body curled up on the floor by the bed. She dropped to her knees by the unmoving shape.

'Vincent.'

The body faced away from her and in the gloom she could only see that it was a man wearing scrubs.

'Vincent.'

Madison felt for signs of life and found none. She turned the body delicately and looked into the face of Thomas Creed, Vincent's nurse. His eyes were open and his chest was a vast red slick.

Madison resisted the impulse to close his eyes; her fingers went to the place where the carotid pulse should have been to make sure. One shot in the chest had spun him almost under the bed. *Under the bed.* Madison leant in and peered. A blanket was bunched up under the cot. Vincent might have slept there but he wasn't there now. She heard it too late, a soft step coming close and the click of the door locking her inside.

SHIT.

Madison was on her feet, slamming her shoulder against it a fraction of a second too late.

SHIT.

She squinted through the small window in the door as shadows shifted in the corridor and the search beam made another slow pass. The spike of adrenaline in her chest was a stabbing pain. She grabbed the handle and turned, knowing that nothing would happen and yet not being able to help herself.

Calm yourself, calm down and think, breathe, just breathe.

Madison backed away from the door without turning her back to it until she reached the opposite wall and leant against it.

Calm down and think.

It was a locking system created for people's safety – this wasn't a jail. Madison looked at the full clip in the Glock: she'd have to shoot her way out of the door. She had to hit the lock in exactly the right place. She tried to remember if there were sliding bolts on the outside.

Time had stretched inside her mind as if one minute of thinking was merely one second of action. *I'm getting out of here.* Madison gathered herself: the shots would be incredibly loud in the small cell and her hearing would be compromised for minutes. No way around that one, she thought, if she wanted out. She lifted the Glock and took aim and a movement in the window froze her where she stood. A pair of eyes stared at her through the glass: dead eyes, empty eyes like marbles in a doll's head. Eyes that held her whole as she raised her weapon above the lock and straight at the window. The eyes didn't look away but stared at Madison as she stared back and aimed the gun squarely at them. There was no flicker of life or recognition or even a moment of doubt. It was a blank void and the muzzle of Madison's piece trembled as she kept it trained on the face she could barely see. One breath, two breaths – heart thumping in her throat. Dead eyes, empty eyes. And then they were gone.

Madison puts three shots in the lock. Loud, so darn loud she could hardly think. Yet now they knew, the cops on the lawn – now they knew there was trouble for sure. Arson, and a cop shooting up the clinic. Madison kicked the door hard with the heel of her boot and it swung open. Those three shots were an alarm bell and, Sweet Jesus, she was glad all those patrol officers downstairs were wearing ballistic vests.

The corridor was empty on both sides and the ringing inside Madison's ears blanketed every sound. The man had gone but he couldn't be far. On her right: the door that led to the stairway and all the way down to the reception and the main entrance – where cops were probably flooding in, weapons out and tempers rising. On the left: more patients' rooms, the day lounge and the door to the back stairwell. Madison ran left. They knew she was out of the cell. Hell, her shots could have been heard across the lake in the quiet of the night. The time for bashful was well and truly gone. She glanced at the day lounge as she went past, but no Vincent there, standing and gazing out at the trees.

Whoever had locked her in wouldn't want to stay for introductions, and they must know there were officers outside who were on their way in. They needed to get out and fast.

Madison reached the back stairwell door. It was wide open – no elevator's shaft, just plain stairs going up and down. *Up.* She hadn't realized there was a fifth floor.

Something made her climb up instead of heading downstairs – maybe it was the thought that the man with the dead eyes wouldn't want to rush into the arms of incoming police officers. She wasn't sure exactly, she just found herself flat against the wall and following the steps that led to the floor above. And she would have given anything to hear something other than the flat drone that pounded inside her head.

Cold air brushed her face – a chilly breeze mixed with the tang of the fire nearby. No, she thought, not a fifth floor but roof access, and the door had been kicked open.

From faraway she heard sirens approaching, their top notes finding their way through the hum. *Good. That was good.* They needed all the lights and all the people they could throw at the clinic to smoke out Conway's crew. Even if more people would mean more bodies on the grounds, more cover for those who wanted to slip away unnoticed.

A narrow walkway followed the edge of the roof. The way was clear – wherever he was, he must already have turned the corner to the other side. Madison stepped out: beyond the low railing the roof fell away into nothing and the ground was a long way down.

The angle of the roof meant she couldn't see the walkway on the other side; then again, he couldn't see her either. Madison covered the distance as fast as she could and turned the corner to the back of the building: two dark shapes moving ahead of her, the distance between them nearly the length of the clinic. *Two men.* Dead Eyes had a friend. Madison flattened herself against the side and continued; hopefully the gloom would give her some protection. The men stopped and the unmistakable clanging of metal against metal rang out in the night. Too far for anybody else to have heard from the lawn but it cut through Madison's fog like a bell. She leant on the railing, narrowed her eyes, and saw the outline that stood out like a metal trim. The fire escape. They were already on it and climbing down. Madison ran fast and low and reached the platform in time to see them edging between the fourth and the third floor.

She didn't like the idea of climbing after them and being a perfect target; however, her options were limited. She swore, stepped on the platform and then onto the metal stairs, holding the guard rail with her left and the Glock with her right, pointing at the fast-moving shadows below her. This was not about calling out and giving notice, this was about catching up and laying down.

Their steps clanged on the metal and Madison was sure they'd heard her. In a few seconds they'd reach the ground. What then? She climbed down as fast as she could, once or twice losing her footing and gripping the rail with all her strength to keep from falling.

Madison didn't want to shoot blindly at the men below her, and clearly they had decided that taking a shot at her was a small gain against the major drawback of attracting the attention of the other cops.

Madison's feet hit the ground and she spun around. The men were already heading for the trees.

'Stop!' she yelled. 'Seattle Police Department.' The muzzle of the gun tracked the silhouettes but Madison didn't squeeze the trigger. Too dark to know what she'd be hitting. She pointed her piece at the ground a few feet away and let out one shot – just a quick warning to let everyone else know where the action was.

She was about to follow them into the darkness when she stopped.

Her priority was Vincent. Vincent, who was not in his room, who had been missing from the head count. Madison needed to think clearly and the chase had scrambled her logic. Vincent. The perspiration was cooling on her skin now that she had stopped; her clothes clung to her and her chest rose and fell. Vincent.

Madison had been inside and had seen the rooms. The doctors had gotten everybody out carefully, head counts every step of the way. What if? What if Vincent had gone walkabout once he was already out of the building, once the doctors had relaxed for a moment because the grounds were safe and help was on its way? And poor Thomas Creed had gone back to look for him. Vincent, Madison thought, with grime under his nails even after his hands had been scrubbed clean.

Madison looked around and tried to orient herself, to remember the structure of the clinic and the gardens as she had felt it from Dr. Peterson's office, and she took off at a dead run.

She had no idea where the men were or where anybody was but she had a rough idea of where she might find Vincent. The fire was still blazing on the first floor of the East Wing as she turned around the side of the building and her hearing caught up with her.

The light from the fire played among the shadows of the firs as the cool scent of the damp earth mixed with the smoke. At first the glow showed her the way as the path meandered away from the open and further from the brick structure. After a few seconds Madison reached into her pocket and twisted the cap of her flashlight; it wasn't ideal but she had to see where she was going. She kept the pool of light right in front of her feet; her steps were overly loud and clear to her returned hearing.

She heard him before she saw him: a low keening and shuffling only yards away from her. The beam of the light found Vincent crouching in the dirt and digging with his bare hands by the bush of Dicentra Formosa. The hole was already a couple of feet wide and a foot deep. For a moment Madison couldn't speak. Vincent's high-pitched wail rose through the air and fluttered with each breath he took.

Madison came back to herself. 'Vincent,' she whispered.

He looked up and she wasn't sure whether he really saw her or anything else around them: his face was smudged with dirt and the wide blue eyes shone with purpose. He went back to raking his fingers through the ground.

'Vincent,' Madison repeated.

His hands never stopped and the soft whimpering resumed like a chant.

Madison turned toward the building: orange light flickered through the shadows, dimmer now than it had been before. The firefighters were winning their battle. Occasionally a vehicle, invisible in the undergrowth, would roar past on the nearby driveway.

She had to make a decision about what to do with him now that she'd found him, and she had to do it quickly.

'It's not safe,' she said.

Vincent looked up and for the first time his gaze flitted around her, found Madison and focused on her.

'No, it isn't,' he replied. 'It isn't.'

'Who are you afraid of?'

'The man.'

'Which man?'

'The man.'

'What happened?'

'I don't know.'

The very act of digging seemed to ease his anxiety, as if the compulsion was relieved by the action; however, it only lasted for a moment and though he kept checking, it wouldn't keep the darkness around them at bay for long.

'What are you doing, Vincent?' Madison asked him.

She examined the circling shadows. Was it safer to keep Vincent there when four men were searching for him? Should she bundle him into her car and just drive him to the precinct?

'What are you doing?' she whispered again, trying to keep the conversation going and aware of every noise around them.

'Over and over,' Vincent replied in a similar whisper, his reedy voice barely carrying the words.

'What's over and over?'

'Ronald said "Hit".'

'He did?'

The weak pool of light from Madison's flashlight danced on the bottom of the fresh pit.

'What else did Ronald say?'

Ronald lay inside a morgue's drawer and wouldn't say anything to anyone, anymore and Madison felt like a thief prying nuggets of gold from this man who couldn't begin to grasp that the only person who had cared for him in this world had been murdered trying to protect him.

'What else did he say?' she repeated.

'The trail is the wall,' Vincent said, digging and patting the sides of the hole.

What?

'The trail? What trail, Vincent?'

He stopped and raised his muddy right hand into the beam of light. The index finger traced a line in the air between them.

'The trail,' he said.

And Madison saw his bare cell and the intricate lines that traversed every inch of wall that he could reach.

'The drawings on your walls? Is it the trail?'

She didn't quite understand what it meant, or even if it meant anything at all. 'What trail? Where does it go?'

Vincent dug and patted, dug and patted, with a pattern of

repeating gestures. He spoke without looking up. 'It's not safe. Over and over.'

The icy coldness from the damp earth reached into Madison's bones. She shifted on the ground but stayed close to the slight man.

Had Ronald told him to hit David Quinn over and over? Was that how the boy had died?

The snap of a dry branch rang out only yards away. Madison fumbled with the flashlight, turned it off, and they were instantly wrapped in darkness. Even the glimmers from the blaze had all but gone.

She stretched out her hand and touched Vincent's shoulder. There he was. He stiffened but did not shrink from her touch. She sidled up close to him and whispered: 'It's not safe, Vincent, like Ronald said. It's not safe right now. Don't make a sound. I will protect you.'

They were ridiculous, inadequate words and fell like stones from her lips.

Madison crouched next to Vincent: her left arm went around his bony shoulders, her right in front of her holding her piece. The muzzle tracked the muffled sounds approaching them. Someone walked lightly between the trees; someone placed his feet carefully and avoided making too much noise.

Madison thought of the dead eyes in the little window and how the man hadn't blinked when she had pointed her gun at him.

Vincent was a taut ball of wire tucked in by her side, vibrating with fear. The beams of two flashlights blinked through the bushes and then appeared as they crossed and parted on the uneven ground, suspended in the gloom.

Two men. Not cops. Not calling out to Vincent or to anyone else. Not here to rescue and protect.

If it came to it she could aim at the light, but chances were their other hands held a piece and her muzzle flash would tell them where they were.

The men approached slowly and steadily, a gap of eight feet between them. The slender light beams crawled over the ground and the roots of the evergreens; sometimes they made a quick pass at waist height.

They made hardly any noise at all, as if they had been absorbed by the chilly air that stank of smoke and the trailing fingers of the flashlights were all that was left of them.

Vincent whimpered. It was a tiny bubble of sound that resonated like a gunshot in Madison's ear.

The beams stopped where they were, about twelve feet away from Madison, and she took aim at the closest. She had hoped that the gap between the men would be enough for them to stay unseen, but their chances were getting slimmer by the second. If it happened, if it really happened, all she had going for her was precision and speed. *Shoot at the light. If they see you, shoot first one, then the other. Those two seconds is all you can count on.*

And even then the men would probably get a few shots off themselves.

A burst of sounds and lights from the edge of the lawn startled Madison. People calling out, hollering and coming closer: doctors, cops, all looking for the missing patient. Had they found the dead nurse yet?

The two men had also heard them and stepped closer, closing the gap between them and walking faster, bearing straight down on Madison and Vincent. Stealth was not necessary anymore now that the noise from the search party covered their steps.

Madison grabbed Vincent and inched backwards, putting her body between them and him, keeping low, careless of the rustle of clothes and Vincent's yelps.

A car drove past, the engine picking up speed as the siren came on. Madison continued backwards: they were sandwiched between the men and the wall that surrounded the property and in a few yards they would find their backs against the iron railings, and the search party was pushing the men right onto them.

A car pulled up and stopped on the driveway, engine still ticking – she could glimpse the headlights through the bushes. Suddenly the flashlights moved sideways and away from them, and after a beat two car doors opened and closed. The car – Madison had not seen what it was – sped away.

Madison let go of Vincent, who crumpled on the ground behind her, and she quickly searched her pockets for her cell phone. The small square screen lit up her face and told her exactly what time it was. *Traffic cameras, there are traffic cameras all over the darn road.*

Vincent was slumped against the railings, his hands opening and closing around fistfuls of earth. Madison sat down next to him.

'It's alright,' she said. 'They've gone – the men have gone. We're safe now.'

Vincent shook his head as if she'd missed the whole point. 'It's not personal, it's business,' he said.

Uniformed officers of the SPD made a cautious sweep of the grounds and found no trace of the intruders. The body of Thomas Creed was carried out on a stretcher before Health and Safety could snap into action and declare the building a no-go area until it had been checked for structure failings due to the blaze.

Madison gave her statement to an officer of the North Precinct, who took her piece – standard operating procedure when a weapon is discharged – and watched Vincent Foley as Dr. Peterson checked him and gave him a mild sedative.

Most of the patients had been temporarily dispersed among a number of institutions and no one knew when and if they would be allowed back inside the place they called home. Peterson looked drained and pretty close to collapse himself; the rest of his staff wondered from patient to patient, trying to make themselves useful and not think about Thomas Creed.

As Madison had imagined, Vincent had been evacuated with everybody else and then slipped away in the confusion. Creed had gone back – into a burning building – to look for him.

'You'd said they'd come,' Lieutenant Fynn said. He was unshaven and wore no tie.

'Not like this,' Madison said. 'I never thought . . .' She gestured at the blackened, ruined East Wing.

'Was it Conway?'

'Yes, I'm sure of it. I saw his eyes and I'm not going to forget them in a hurry. But any lawyer five minutes out of law school would be able to get a jury to doubt: it was dark, there was a reinforced glass window in between, and it lasted seconds.'

'Still . . .'

'Still . . .'

'Where are they taking Vincent?' she asked him.

'Peterson's deputy is going to chaperone him and two uniforms will stick to them like glue. They're still looking for a secure, appropriate environment. We can't exactly drop him into a B and B.'

Madison nodded.

'Are you alright? Do you need to get checked over?'

Madison looked at herself: her clothes were muddy and her hands had a few nicks and scratches from the run down the fire escape but nothing that needed a bandage.

'No, I'm fine, sir. I need a cup of coffee, a shower, and my piece back as soon as humanly possible, but aside from that I'm okay.'

'Did Foley say anything useful?'

'I honestly don't know. I need to write it down and think about it. It's difficult to sieve what's relevant from the rest. One thing I know is that Ronald Gray spoke to him and Vincent retained some of it.'

Among the police officers and the firefighters Madison spotted

Kelly. They had not spoken, though he'd let her have one long somber look from a distance as if at some point, somehow, he knew this mess would turn out to be her fault.

'It's almost dawn,' Fynn said. 'And you look like death warmed up. Go home, grab some sleep, and get to the precinct when you don't need to spellcheck your name.'

Madison waited until she saw Vincent climb into a Fire Medic One truck, together with a doctor and two police officers.

'How many people know where they're taking him?' she asked Fynn.

'Not as many as those who knew he was here. Go home, Madison.'

Chapter 40

August 28, 1985. Ronald Gray put one foot in front of the other and tried to hold on to the very small pool of calm and common sense he still possessed. The air was heavy, thick with humidity and the scent of earth and undergrowth that the sun never reached. They had been walking for a while with their shirts stuck to their backs and a growing sense of panic crawling in their guts.

They walked on because there was no alternative but to follow Timothy Gilman: he had brought them there and he would lead them out of that nightmare.

It had been ridiculously easy to grab the kids – they were like puppies. And yet even then, even in that moment which should have been an easy day out for men used to that line of work, there had been a dark focus in Gilman's eyes that – if Ronald was going to be honest – had scared him a little.

He had watched Gilman closely as they had swooped on the boys, afterwards in the van and in the clearing, as he went from one boy to the other, delivering his own brand of threat and evil. And all the time Ronald was sure – even as he was taunting and yelling at the little one – that Gilman had kept an eye on the blond curly-haired kid; and when the awful thing happened and the kid choked and stopped breathing, Gilman watched it happen without blinking.

Almost, Ronald thought, almost as if that was exactly what he had wanted to happen.

It made no sense. Still, there they were: four men walking in a line in the deep green of the Hoh River Forest. Gilman was first, then Warren Lee – the grinning idiot whose jokes had died on his lips an hour ago, then Ronald, and last Vincent – bewildered and mute with fear. And Vincent carried the dead boy in his arms. Warren had refused to do it but Gilman had turned to Foley and said, 'Do it,' and he had picked up the child from the mossy ground because Vincent always did what he was told.

Gilman knew where to bury the body; all they had to do was to get there, dig a hole in the ground, and then they'd go home.

Ronald's middle ached as if his inside had been filled with acid. *The shovels.* All of them except for Vincent were carrying a shovel. Ronald walked and stared at the soil – all those rotting leaves and dead roots – because he didn't dare lift his eyes as his brain tried to grasp the reality of the situation. *Gilman had put three shovels in the van. He had packed shovels in a stolen van with a stolen plate to go snatch three boys for a simple intimidation job.*

In that instant he knew Gilman's look, he recognized it for what it was: a killer setting the scene, making sure his intended victim fell into the pit he'd dug.

Ronald felt the old familiar fear coming back like a ghost as the sun set above them and the woods turned dark. It was the fear of being pushed, shunted and shoved by someone harder, colder and stronger into doing something he didn't want to do – slap someone or be slapped, cut someone or be cut.

The sound behind him, a sudden gasp followed by Vincent's yelp, froze them all and, as they turned and saw the boy's eyes wide open and the kid breathing – breathing for Chrissake – on the damp dirt, all Ronald could think of was, *No, please God, no.*

Years later, for as many years as were given to Ronald on this

Earth, he wondered how different things would have been if he had said something or done something in that moment when Timothy Gilman, with neither doubt nor hesitation, stepped forward and thrust his shovel into Vincent's hands.

'Kill him,' he said.

Later, their clothes caked in sweat, grime and blood as they travelled in silence toward Seattle, Gilman pulled the van off Highway 101 outside Port Angeles into a dirt track.

'We're switching cars,' he said.

They staggered out of the van; Gilman emptied a petrol can inside it, making sure all the rags, ropes and shovels were covered, and lit a match. It went up like kindling. They were already driving away in the maroon estate when the tank exploded.

Ronald wasn't sure how they'd made it home. He had helped Vincent undress and had put him under the shower.

'Wash it all out, Vin. There's a good boy.'

He had peeled off his own clothes and crammed everything in the washing machine, hoping it would take care of the worst stains. Tomorrow he'd put the whole load in a garbage bag and drop it in a dumpster downtown – one of those in the alleys behind the busiest restaurants.

Vincent had spent the journey back with his head leaning against the car window, staring at the pitch-black darkness and the blurry lights. He had not said a word for hours.

Once they were both clean, Ronald dug out a tub of strawberry ice cream from the back of the freezer and they sat down at the square kitchen table under the strip of neon lighting.

'Here.' He scooped out the ice cream into a bowl and passed it to Vincent. The younger man's eyes could not rest on anything; his gaze flitted about the room and his hands trembled in his lap. Under his nails a line of grime and dirt from digging the grave had managed to escape the flannel.

'Here,' Ronald repeated, his voice gentler than he thought possible.

Vincent looked at the bowl as if he had never seen anything like it before. After a minute, he picked it up and ate the ice cream.

The round clock on the wall said it was 1 a.m. The boys were still in the forest, Ronald thought. The plan had been that Gilman would make an anonymous call after the message about payment for *protection* had been delivered and the kids would be found before nightfall. *Three kids.* No harm done. Except that was not really the plan, was it?

Ronald waited until Vincent went to bed, he waited until he could hear his slow regular breathing, and then he laid it on the table – the thing he had saved from the van as it caught fire.

'Hold it, Tim. I've left my jacket in there.'

'Make it quick.'

He had noticed Gilman stuff the piece of paper under the rags and had left his jacket in the back on purpose. He placed the scrap of paper on the cracked Formica table. He had known what it would be and it didn't surprise him: a photograph of the fair, curly-haired boy circled by a pencil mark.

He opened his hand and a golden chain with a medal unraveled and pooled next to the picture. He had seen it come away from the boy as they were lowering him into the grave and he had pocketed it, his mind already jumping ahead to guilt, blame and consequences.

He wanted a drink so badly his eyes kept wandering to the fridge where three cold ones were waiting for him. Yet he couldn't – wouldn't – take a sip until he had managed to make sense of what had happened and had made a plan, because as things were, Ronald thought, looking around their simple kitchen, they were well and truly screwed.

I'm no child killer. Still, three boys had been grabbed and one had been murdered. Washington State had the death penalty and there was no question where the blade of justice would fall. He could very well repeat *We were only told to scare them* like a mantra all the way down the corridor to the electric chair or whatever they were going to use. It wouldn't matter. People would line up from Seattle to Walla-Walla to cheer their stupid, miserable deaths.

Gilman had made sure they thought it was no more than a bit of work on a summer day, no more than putting the fear of the everlasting into some rich kids who'd tell their daddies to pay up and shut up.

He knew they were no child killers, none of them, and the only way it would work was if they all thought it was an accident. They'd keep their silence and he would have his hit.

Ronald stood up, went to the fridge and opened it. The beer mocked him but he grabbed a bottle of cream soda and drained it where he was standing. He was horrified at what had happened and at his part in it. He felt sorry for the kid, sure – no one should die like that – but he had bigger problems of his own now and his priority was about protecting himself and Vincent. *Vincent*. Ronald took a deep breath in the stifling heat.

There were things that he could and should do, things that would protect them in case the worst happened, things that would allow him to make a deal with the King County Prosecutor's Office and keep them both out of the chair – if it ever came to that.

Ronald had no illusions about why Gilman had chosen the three of them for the job: they had done similar work before, didn't balk at using a little muscle when necessary and they were cheap. And yet Gilman had been chosen too – someone had given him a picture of the kid and said, 'This one, not the others, just this one.'

Ronald knew where Gilman lived and where he drank his beer. He would follow him like the shadow of hell that he was and find out who had ordered the hit. Whatever he'd done, that kid's father must have really pissed off somebody who didn't forgive or forget.

It would be an early start and Ronald checked the clock. 2.17 a.m. The ice cream in his bowl had turned into pink goo. He took one bottle of icy cold beer from the fridge and twisted off the cap.

Chapter 41

'Cameron, your lawyer's here,' Officer Miller said, and John Cameron regarded him through the bars.

He had not received any visitors since he had turned down Detective Madison's conversation days earlier, and she had not been back. He knew enough from their meetings to know that petulance wasn't a natural part of her make-up: if she had not visited it meant she was busy and the case was progressing. A lawyer – indirectly – was an emissary of Nathan's.

Cameron stood up and approached the door to his cell.

Officer Miller took a step back. Their 4 a.m. walks through the silent jail and Cameron's yard time in the middle of the night might have become routine, and yet he didn't let himself get too comfortable – like the trainer who gets mauled by his favorite big cat because he forgot himself and what he was dealing with.

The drumming started straightaway, metal against metal. If the jail had a soul that was what it sounded like. Officer Miller braced himself against it and escorted his charge out of D Wing.

Nathan Quinn ran his fingertip against the rough grain of the table. The visiting room in KCJC was spartan and, like everyone else there, the furniture had been serving its own life sentence.

He was wearing a suit and tie for the occasion – the first time since the night in the forest. His client, Quinn knew, couldn't have cared less one way or the other; however, the job had its duties and its uniform. *His client.* Quinn did not know what those weeks of incarceration had done to John Cameron, how far back into himself he'd had to retreat to survive. Even though Quinn had been expecting this moment for most of his life, he didn't know how they would navigate what was coming. This was uncharted territory. It was their first meeting since he had uttered the name of Timothy Gilman, since Cameron had found out that Quinn knew, and had always known, about his first kill and about its reasons. And it was the first time that Quinn had seen with his own eyes what Cameron was capable of: the photographs of Salinger's injuries should not – must not – be seen by a jury. It was Quinn's job to make sure that the case was pleaded out of court and he might have just received the best news he'd had for months.

He heard the lock clang open and stood up: it was a small thing but he wanted his friend to see him standing, even if his walking stick was leaning against a chair.

John Cameron walked into the room flanked by two guards and saw him by the table. Cameron blinked: it was maybe the only show of emotion he was ever going to allow himself in KCJC, and the guards missed it. Quinn didn't. He knew all too well where they were and the boundaries that drab room imposed on their communications.

He extended his hand. 'Mr. Cameron,' he said.

'Counselor,' his friend replied as he shook it, 'it's good to see you back to work.'

'I'm a medical miracle.'

It was the smallest of smiles. 'You certainly are,' Cameron said, and Quinn was aware his friend was watching him and evaluating the price he had paid in the forest.

A look passed between them and they both knew that, had Cameron been aware at the time what Salinger had had in store for Quinn, he would now be facing a charge of Murder in the First instead of Attempted Murder, and Quinn's job would be that much harder. Not impossible, no, just trickier.

'I'm still part of the prosecution case against Salinger as a victim and a witness but I am *consulting* in the case against you, and our side has had some rather good news today: three independent experts have declared Harry Salinger legally insane.'

'Is that his defense?'

'No,' Quinn replied. 'He has pleaded guilty to four counts of Murder, one of Kidnapping of a Minor in the First Degree, and two counts of Attempted Murder.'

'How long will it take for the appeal?'

'The hearing for the bail appeal will be in days and I'm negotiating with Scott Newton about the plea. Salinger's insanity status is a very bad hit for them and there's nothing they can do about it. He absolutely doesn't want to go to trial with it: their plaintiff would not look good in court.'

'A trial could be a long way away,' Cameron said, and it hung between them as the statement of intent that it was.

If it was going to go to trial Cameron would have to hang around in jail waiting for more bleach vials to break over his head or perhaps a time-honored 'shiv in the showers' assault. Quinn nodded – message received.

'The hearing will be in *days*,' he repeated, his tone terse and allowing no argument. *You will manage a few more days in jail and I promise I will get you out of here. You will not look for trouble or conjure it out of nowhere.*

Cameron acknowledged Quinn's promise. He would do his best.

There was too much that could not be discussed in a visiting room – the cogs and gears of the Department of Corrections were whirring around them all the time. Still, there was one subject that could not be avoided.

'Your appeal,' Cameron said. 'Timothy Gilman?'

'Yes,' Quinn replied, and his gaze never left his friend's. 'A violent man who found a suitable death in a hunter's trapping pit.'

'How long have you known?'

'A very long time.'

'You didn't share that knowledge.'

'No.'

'Until now.'

'Now the case is moving forward.'

Cameron missed nothing: Quinn wasn't talking in general, there were specifics there – names, facts and case numbers. 'What can you tell me?'

'We might have three names.'

Gilman and his colleagues.

'Three?'

'Two are very recently dead, one is alive.'

It was a dark irony that at the precise moment when they could finally talk about what had happened on August 28, 1985, the restrictions imposed by their surroundings made it seriously inadvisable.

'It's a start,' Cameron said. 'It's a start.'

To sit there and talk in riddles seemed ludicrous, but no more so than many other aspects of their friendship.

'Do you need anything?' Quinn asked him, aware of how ridiculous the question sounded.

Cameron smiled a crooked smile and for the first time he looked like himself.

Quinn nodded. 'Days,' he said.

As he left the jail from the visitors' entrance, Quinn made a quick call to his driver who had been waiting nearby – the regulations being that he could not wait for him in the jail's parking lot during the visit – and decided that he'd have to go back to driving himself as soon as possible. He'd have to go back to whatever *normal* was for him as soon as possible. And for the first time ever in his life he wondered what that was and if it meant anything anymore.

November, 1985. Nathan had not gone back to the East Coast after David's funeral. He had stayed in Seattle watching over his parents as reality had dimmed to a never-ending wake with neither color nor relief. The police were doing what little they could and he felt a constant weight on his chest that would not let him breathe.

The Camerons were in the process of selling their house and moving to the Laurelhurst neighborhood. They wanted to create a whole new set of memories for Jack in a place that bore no connection to the life before August 28 and Jackson Pond.

Nathan had volunteered to look after Jack that Saturday afternoon and leave the parents free to pack. It was a glorious Fall day and he was thinking about a movie, ice creams and a pizza too if Jack was hungry.

Jack had seemed to be recovering very well physically – the cuts on his arms and hand were healing – however neither he nor Jimmy had ever really talked about what had happened and, watching the slight little boy, Nathan saw slow changes like roots digging into soft earth and the odd flash of rage that Jack – always aware of his parents' concern – was quick to cover.

After *The Goonies* they walked to Pike Place Market and then two floors down to the home of Golden Age Collectibles. Jack seemed to be in good spirits and Nathan felt like a very young, very ill-equipped parent. More than anything, he felt Jack's sharp eyes watching him and knowing that he was measuring his every smile and every joke. Their companionable silence was a comfort to both and Nathan wondered for a moment whether he was looking after Jack or vice versa.

The comics in the shop were always a good diversion and Jack used some loot left over from a birthday to buy a couple of new ones. They both marveled at the price of the collectors' editions in the glass case and went to pay. Jack's school's picture had been splashed all over the newspapers in the last ten weeks but, whether out of courtesy or genuine ignorance, the clerk ignored him and rang up his purchase without a second look.

It was the first time since August 28 that Nathan had been alone with Jack. Sitting in the Athenian Restaurant at a table in the back – one with the view over the bay – Nathan felt he had to say something, do something, or he might not bear another day. And it was that understanding as he watched Jack slowly demolish his cheesecake that pushed him to speak. Was that why he had offered to take him out today? So that the boy would be alone with him?

'Jack,' he said, trying to keep his voice soft, 'you know that you can tell me anything, right?'

It was so awkward that it made him wince; Jack looked up.

'I mean,' Nathan continued, 'if there was anything you couldn't say to anyone else, you know, about what happened, you could tell me . . .' The words had just burst out, so rough and crude compared to the subtle phrasing Nathan had turned over and over in his mind.

Jack froze.

Nathan wanted to be there to comfort him and protect him in a way he couldn't be with David, and yet his voice shook as he spoke and the sudden bubble of grief caught him unprepared.

'If there was ever anything you'd like to say about what happened, anything that could help us find the men who did it . . . would you tell me?'

Jack nodded.

'Is there anything?'

Jack shook his head.

'Anything at all?'

Jack shook his head.

Nathan wiped his face with his hand and looked out to the piers and the ferries for a few minutes. Jack let him, and when their eyes met again he seemed to Nathan impossibly old.

'I'm sorry,' Nathan whispered. 'I'm so sorry.'

Chapter 42

Alice Madison ran the shower and then stepped under it, washing away mud and the scent of smoke from her skin. She had driven home at dawn and peeled off her clothes. Her shoulder holster was empty and she missed the familiar weight. Fynn meant well but there was no way she could grab a few hours of sleep unless she knocked herself out with a sedative. Which, she reflected, after that kind of night, was probably what doctors were doing to each and every former patient of the Walters Institute.

Madison wrapped herself in a towel and lay back on her bed. The uncertain light was chasing the shadows of the magnolia tree on her ceiling. So much death, so much destruction. It seemed there was little Conway and his crew were not prepared to do. Kamen's file had painted a terrifying portrait: they worked for anyone who could pay for their services and were driven by twin hungers: greed and cruelty. Thomas Creed had been shot in the chest: they knew he wasn't their target, it wasn't mistaken identity. They killed him because he was there. *He* killed him because he was there. *Dead Eyes*. And he could have shot her too. One day she would have to ask him why he didn't. One day there would be a conversation about what had happened last night and Madison would make sure he knew just how close they had been to Foley.

She didn't feel lucky to be alive, she felt ticked off and wired and buzzing with restless energy that had absolutely nothing to do with rest and a good night's sleep.

Madison threw on some clothes and got back into her car. Her neighborhood, Three Oaks, was slowly waking up to a colorless morning and she wished for hard rain or a blue sky. Anything but the pale, washed-out nothing that seemed to drain all the energy out of the world.

C.J.'s Eatery on 1st Avenue opened its doors at 7 a.m. for the early breakfast crowd and Madison found a table to herself. She ordered a lox, egg and onion scramble with toast and a large black coffee, and took out her notebook. People around her were beginning their day – some would go to an office nearby, some would spend some time in Pike Street Market and enjoy their holidays – and Madison watched their flow as her thoughts arranged themselves and the memories from the previous night slotted into place.

The food was the fuel she needed and the coffee helped somewhat to clear off the cobwebs from the lack of sleep; she jotted down everything Vincent Foley had said and filled five pages of notes. When she reread them it seemed that most of them were questions.

The shift was present and accounted for, and everybody looked like three hours sleep and too much caffeine. Madison had great hopes for the traffic cams: they must have picked up Conway's vehicle speeding away from the Walters Institute, and if they were extremely lucky he wouldn't know he had been spotted and torch it.

Health and Safety had been crystal clear about processing the building and there was no way that the Crime Scene Unit would be allowed in to seek trace evidence to link Creed's murder to Lee's and Gray's. It had been too dark on the roof; however, Madison was reasonably sure that the men she had seen were wearing black clothing and probably gloves: there would be no fingerprints from the doors or the fire escape. If the gods were smiling on them Ballistics might connect the bullets that killed Ronald Gray and Thomas Creed. Then again there hadn't been a whole lot of smiles lately.

Madison put in a call to the Pierce County Sheriff Department to keep the line of communication open and find out whether any evidence had been recovered at Jerry Wallace's place. Conway's crew had had a busy week.

'Nothing much,' Deputy Walbeck said, sounding brisk and capable. Madison heard her flipping through a pile of reports. 'The house was clean: no prints, no evidence, locks intact on all exits. They probably saw him through the windows at the back and took him before he could so much as make a peep. Must have kept the back door open.'

'Yes,' Madison said, 'I think that's what happened too. Any trace evidence from the victim?'

'No, but South Prairie Creek is very close. If they wanted to get rid of a body they had ways and means. We've been searching the banks in both directions.'

Madison thanked the Deputy and left her her cell number. Did Jerry Wallace see Dead Eyes through the glass as she had done, just moments before his death?

Madison saw Kelly approach. Everybody looked tired today but he also added a twist of sullenness to it that worked better than a 'Keep away' sign.

'You talked to Quinn, right?' he started.

'You were there.' Madison replied.

'Yesterday, sure. But before that you also went to speak to him in hospital.'

It was a statement.

'Yes, I did.'

'Did you tell him about Lee and Gray? That we're probably looking at the creeps who killed his brother?'

'Yes, I did. They're dead and they're not going to get any deader because Quinn knows.'

'This is an ongoing investigation, an open investigation, and you have shared information with the family of the victim about our suspects. Not only that, I'm willing to bet you also told him about Foley, and where he could be found. I'd be surprised if you didn't give him floor and room number.'

'By all means, Kelly, share your thoughts and don't hold back. What's troubling you?'

Kelly pulled up a chair and sat down.

'You're way too close to Quinn and his *client*. What makes you think that information was safe to share? Why would you tell a victim's relative anything about the suspect before we had a chance to cross the Ts and dot the Is?'

'I told him because he deserved to know that we found his brother's gold chain. He's very much part of what's happening and he needed to know about Lee and Gray. Quinn's appeal started the ball rolling—'

'And we're left picking up the pieces. Did you know Salinger was declared legally insane?'

Madison moved back a fraction of an inch. *A smudge of dirt and a slick of blood on Salinger's shirt that night in the woods.* 'I didn't know.'

'Yup, three separate independent experts – not that we needed them to tell us, by the way.'

Kelly let Madison absorb the news, then continued.

'Do you have any idea how fast the whole of Quinn Locke is working to get John Cameron out of jail? And what do you think will happen when your pet serial killer is out on the street, fresh from incarceration, eager to get busy on the last surviving member of the gang who took him and beat his friend to death? What I don't understand is whether you're painfully naïve or simply too arrogant to follow procedure.'

'Quinn needed to know and the break-in proved that point. He doesn't know Foley's name or where he was. I told him he was in a psychiatric institution and had been since 1985, and that's all. And John Cameron is many things – most of them unfathomable to me – and I deal with him sensibly and cautiously because that's better than not deal with him at all. Foley is not the last surviving person who was in the forest. Cameron was there too and I have to be able to speak with him about the case.'

'He will go after Foley the minute he's on the street again and we'll be looking back at the good old days when all we had to protect him from was Conway's crew.' Kelly stood. 'You will screw this up. Sooner or later. And it will be measured in body bags.'

Madison let him have the last word and he returned to his desk. No one else had heard the exchange and she felt like punching a hole through a wall. She had to get busy and do something to cool off: traffic cams, reports, witness testimonies. There must be something that could engage her and keep her from letting Kelly's words soak into her mind. Madison picked up the tapes from Traffic and checked the location/time tags. Still, the thin dark voice spoke to her and whispered that Kelly was right and, when it came down to it, body bags was the only measurement that mattered.

A black Subaru Outback had been picked up by three traffic cameras in quick sequence. At that precise time the only other options were a white pick-up, a motor bike, a delivery goods van and a supermarket chain truck. It had to be the Subaru. The light and the reflection on the glass made it impossible to see who was sitting inside, but it had to be the Subaru.

The car had a squeaky clean Oregon plate, and given that that type of vehicle was one of the most common in Washington State it was bound to be almost invisible.

Madison thought back: had she noticed a black Subaru on the grounds last night? No, she hadn't, and the uniformed officers had not been posted at the gates until later.

Dunne was in charge of tracking the car as far as possible using Automated License Plate Recognition technology. It was a standard tool and Madison hoped for a quick result and a call to the Special Weapon And Tactics unit to be on standby.

In the meantime they still had Jerome McMullen, counting down to his parole date, and Leon Kendrick, sunning himself in California. Madison started reading: their files were inches thick and full of ugly. She felt a wave of tiredness wash over her and left the detectives' room. She washed her face in the restroom and her steps found the way to the outside of the building for a few moments of fresh air. The connections were there if only they could see them. The trail was there, ready to be found. That word made her think of Vincent Foley and his drawings. *The trail is the wall indeed, Vincent*, she thought. *Just give us a break, will ya?*

The break came half an hour later: Jerome McMullen might be in jail waiting for a parole, which would give him motive, but Leon Kendrick had known Gilman personally: they were pals from way back and had been arrested together for a felony charge. It was a 9A.36.140 type felony and Madison didn't need to look it up: it was Assault of a Child in the Third Degree. A boy. The victim had changed his statement, a witness had changed his statement, and the charges were dropped. At nineteen Gilman had attacked a twelve-year-old boy and got away with it: Kendrick knew it and maybe, when the time came, he knew he could count on him to do what he needed done because Gilman would have no trouble abusing little kids.

Madison sat back in her chair. Yes, she could see how Jerry Wallace would be a threat to both Kendrick and McMullen. She turned to Dunne. 'Do you know anyone in California we could ask a favor of?'

Dunne shrugged: 'What department?' he replied.

Andy Dunne was better than whatever social network regular people use to get in touch with each other. He called a guy who called a guy and forty-three minutes later Detective Nolan from La Jolla called them back. They put him on speaker and Spencer pulled up a chair.

'We sure know Leon,' he said. 'Unfortunately not well enough to put him away for anything, but he was flagged to us when he moved to California from one of our contacts in your Vice Unit – just a friendly call to let us know who was coming into our neighborhood. We kept an eye out; however, he's been clean ever since – rumors, sure, but nothing ever came to anything. He's a pillar of the community and all that.'

'What's he up to now?' Madison said.

Detective Nolan chuckled. 'He owns a golf club. Pretty slick too from what I hear.'

'Ever been?' Dunne said.

'I have four kids under twelve. Any free time I get I lock myself in my car and sleep. Why the sudden interest in Kendrick?'

'He might have been involved in a murder twenty-five years ago while he was still in Seattle. The investigation has just been reopened with new evidence,' Madison replied.

A beat of silence at the end of the line.

'Is this the Hoh River case?'

'Yes.'

'Well, if even the smell of a connection blew anywhere near his classy set-up it would definitely spoil his day.'

They said goodbye and Nolan offered to chaperone should they ever need to travel south and have a chat with Kendrick in person.

Spencer did a quick internet search and pulled up a few items on the Golden Oaks Golf Club. He printed the articles and passed them to Madison.

'Snazzy,' she said.

'Gets even better,' Dunne continued. 'It says here they're in negotiations with a Japanese company who wants to buy it and invest in it. How's Leon's motive looking now?'

In his home in Seward Park, Nathan Quinn sat in his office. His desk was covered with the files Tod Hollis had brought to him. Some of them were good old-fashioned research on the subject at hand, others he had come by in a less straightforward manner.

Detective Madison had mentioned two names: Leon Kendrick and Jerome McMullen. Quinn turned the page: Hollis had printed a pretty picture of the Golden Oaks Golf Club and a description of the facilities for the members. Quinn couldn't stand golf. He read the background check on Kendrick and calculated how big his share would be if the Japanese company bought the club, and how much he could lose if it didn't.

Quinn stood up and walked about; his strength was slowly coming back. He would have to buy some ridiculous device like a stationary bicycle to use it up and build his stamina. He went out onto the deck to breathe, calm down, and focus on the most important job he had to do that day.

The water was dappled with light and rain, the weather unsure from one moment to the next what was required. There was a hint of warmth in the air and he stayed out there for as long as he could, sleeves rolled up and tie undone.

After a while he went back to his office, put away Hollis's files on Kendrick and McMullen, shifted the pile of mail that had begun to accumulate, and started to write the argument that needed to get Cameron out of KCJC.

Chapter 43

Vincent Foley sat on the cot that was his new bed and stroked the pale blue woolen blanket. This room was almost the same size as his previous quarters. He sighed and lay down on his side. His slippers were neatly arranged on the floor and the room was bare of possessions.

He wasn't afraid, not really. For the last ten hours he had been sedated and the familiar spike of fear that usually pulsed through his whole body was today only a dull ache in his chest. Two police officers stood just outside his room – he could see them if he stood on tiptoes. He didn't know where this room was and he didn't know why they had left his old room. The previous night was a blur.

In spite of a nurse's best efforts, earth from the grounds of the Walters Institute still lined his nails. From his reclining position he saw something under the small dresser, something that could easily roll away from vacuum cleaners and mops. He crouched and stretched his arm until he could wrap his fingers around it. He retrieved it and opened his hand. What a treasure – a green crayon barely two inches long, dusty from its stay on the floor but perfectly intact.

The memory floated up through the mist of sedation: it carried a sense of urgency and the illusion that Ronald was close by and speaking to him. Over and over. Vincent reached up as high as his arm would go and traced a single green line. It snaked around the room and curled around the door. It travelled over paint and brick and wood. It travelled from the coils of Vincent's mind out into the world.

By the time Vincent was back on the bed and had whispered the '. . . my soul to take' part, five lines crept and twisted around each other.

Chapter 44

Madison closed her eyes. In the late afternoon the street below the windows of the detectives' room was already a haze of headlights and flashing signals. So many times on Alki Beach, pausing after her run and breathing hard with her hands on her knees, she had gazed at Seattle across Elliot Bay: the water seemed to capture each and every light and throw it back up in the air for those who cared to notice. Where was Conway's car? Madison thought of it as a dot of light moving among the other identical dots along the highways, the overpass and the busy city streets. Just one dot among thousands, carrying its own burden of death and destruction.

Kelly's words had hunkered down and shot out roots. Even her perfectly reasonable reply now seemed paper-thin and inadequate. She didn't particularly care about his good opinion; however, that accusation had cut to the quick: she considered herself neither naïve nor arrogant, and yet there was a connection to the two men in question that she could not explain away as sensible strategy and good planning. Maybe it was Harry Salinger's true legacy and it couldn't be filed and dispensed of in a police report.

Madison sipped her coffee, hours old and heated out of all recognition. Maybe, if they were lucky, the water would catch that one dot of light that was Conway's car and single it out for them to catch.

Madison dialed Dr. Peterson's cell number. He picked up on the second ring. She already knew where Vincent Foley was: a cell in a secure wing inside an institute for the criminally insane, checked in under an assumed name. It was an observation cell and as comfortable as those can be. The sequence of walls and locked doors around him were for his protection. Hopefully he wouldn't have to stay there long.

'My patients have been spread about a dozen or so institutions, my staff is in shock and I have no idea if and when we'll ever be able to go back . . .'

He didn't say 'home' although that was what it sounded like.

'I'm really sorry,' Madison said, and she meant it.

'I know. And here you are calling me about one patient in particular.'

'Yes, Doctor. In spite of what happened I have to ask you this. When will Dr. Takemoto be able to interview Vincent again?'

'Did *you* speak to him before we arrived? When you were alone with him?' The stress was on 'alone'.

'Yes, I did. He was digging and I asked him about it.'

'Anything useful to your investigation?' Peterson's tone was bitter and felt entirely unlike him.

'I don't know yet, Doctor. Possibly.'

A beat of silence on the line.

'Thomas Creed had two daughters in middle school. He went *back* in to search for Vincent.'

'I know.'

'Your Dr. Takemoto could go back in a couple of days if Vincent continues to improve and he doesn't need sedation.'

'Thank you, Doctor. I'll let her know.'

'He can't stay in that place forever; you understand that, right? He needs to be able to walk about, have other people around him, look through windows and see natural light.'

'I understand.'

Nevertheless, if there was a place for Vincent Foley in this world, Madison sure had no idea where it might be.

The call came in at 8.17 p.m.: the black Subaru had been picked up on I-90 driving east toward Bellevue, coming off exit 10. Not hours earlier but just now. Madison and Dunne were already putting on their coats when Lieutenant Fynn stopped them in their tracks.

'No time to run after them. It's Bellevue PD's patch; they are dispatching a SWAT team to assist their plain clothes officers – not a uniform in sight.'

'Have they been told what to expect?'

'I've just briefed their Chief of Ops. The car has been clocked pulling into a motel, the Silver Pines. Two hundred and thirty-seven rooms, business travelers and conference heaven.'

Madison thought quickly. 'I'm the only one who has seen any of them; we have Conway's picture but it's not that great.'

Fynn nodded. 'I'll call the Chief and tell him you're on your way to ID Conway.'

Spencer shrugged on his jacket. 'Perfect end to a perfect day,' he said.

They had all been up since 4 a.m. or earlier.

There was little conversation during the drive to Bellevue. Spencer drove and Dunne rode shotgun with Madison in the back. Kelly had already left by the time the call had arrived.

Neither of her companions had clapped eyes on Conway or any of his men but there was no question that they would come along.

Madison relaxed into the seat because she was well aware that soon she would need all the focus and whatever smarts she could muster.

She knew without seeing it that the motel was being steadily

surrounded by units, that only plain clothes were on the ground
and visible, that a SWAT team commander was telling his people
about the FBI agent Conway had slain and about Lee and Gray and
last night's fire. She could see the men and women in their heavy
gear nodding and taking in the catalogue of murder and evil, and
their expressions become more somber as they understood what
they were dealing with.

Madison wasn't sure whether she had fallen asleep for a few minutes.
She remembered dots of light moving behind her lids. The car pulled
to a stop as they were intercepted by a plain clothes detective who
waved them in the direction of the parking lot of the small commercial center next to the motel.

The Chief of Ops, Captain Hegarty, was waiting for them. He was
in his forties and looked ready to chew a hole through a steel blanket.
Muted crackle and the voices of his units reporting came in gusts
through the radio.

'We're eyeballing the Subaru, but by the time the first officer got
here whoever was driving it had already gone inside.'

Madison looked around. The commercial center – dentists, veterin-
ary clinic and a yoga studio – had shut for the day. The driver had
to have gone inside the motel.

'We're checking the client list for a group of three or four businessmen who arrived in the last few days.'

Madison nodded.

A woman in sweat clothes, wearing a bulky fleece top, came out
of the motel and jogged out into the street. She made a quick turn
and trotted up to them. She acknowledged Madison and the others
and spoke to the Captain.

'Four men, four rooms on the second floor, back of the corridor,
near the fire exit. One has returned forty minutes ago, the others
are still out.'

'How many of them can you ID?' the Captain asked Madison.

'Just Conway. And as much as I saw him he saw me too and he did take a good long look. No chance he wouldn't recognize me if he saw me.'

'Fair enough.'

'We're going to pick up nice and easy whoever it is who's in the room and wait for his friends,' Captain Hegarty said. 'You need to get yourself in position to spot Conway if he sets foot in the hotel. Here.' He handed Madison an earpiece and a mike the size of the nail of her little finger. She tested them both and then made her way to the motel's entrance. *Come home, little bird, come home.*

Madison settled on a plush chair with full view of the entrance and the three lifts that led to the five floors. The motel's signature colors were oatmeal and maroon and the designer had made ample use of both in the guests' lounge and the patterned upholstery.

Madison had pulled her hair up in a hurried ponytail and borrowed a navy blue Huskies baseball cap from a plain clothes officer. *Go, Dawgs.* She was screened by a large plastic potted plant that would give her maybe a five-second advantage if Conway came straight at her. She had picked up a magazine from the reception desk and tried to look fascinated by a season of conferences and leadership seminars in the Pacific Northwest. Her body however was a taut ball of wiring and cable held together by adrenaline.

In her ear, the steady clear monotone of the officers reporting status: 'Red Ford estate pulling into parking lot. Family of three: man, woman and child coming out.'

Five seconds later the family entered the hotel.

'Silver Honda Civic pulling in. Single woman passenger.'

A woman in her fifties in a business trouser suit came in and stopped at the reception.

'Unit 3 in position,' a soft voice whispered from her earpiece.

Madison breathed in. Unit 3 was on the second floor, getting ready to take down the guest in Room 237. She shifted in her chair and tried to keep her focus on the main door.

'Unit 3 is go,' the response came.

Voices tumbled through the earpiece: someone issuing commands, someone giving a count to three, quick heavy steps and the rustle of the stiff navy blue material against the mike.

Madison was utterly still.

Silence. Five seconds. Ten seconds.

'He's down,' the disembodied voice said. 'The target is down. Tasered, breathing, and with healthy life signs.'

Madison exhaled.

'Captain? We had to Taser him but he managed to hit a panic button. It's a wireless system connected to the hotel Wi-Fi and he activated it before we took him down.'

A black van with darkened windows, which had just come off Exit 10, signaled right, took a sharp turn, and rejoined the Interstate due west toward Seattle. Inside it, Peter Conway was not happy man.

The prisoner lay face down in the middle of the room. A wiry man in his late thirties wearing jeans and a gray T-shirt. He was barefoot and cuffed, and from the moment the Taser's wires had been retrieved he had not said a single word.

Technically speaking he was Bellevue PD's prisoner, but the paperwork was already being sorted and a van was on its way. He'd spend the night, and quite possibly longer, as a guest of the Seattle Jail on 5th Avenue, where the signature colors were not oatmeal and maroon.

Chapter 45

The Silver Pines Motel was not inclined to have the normal flow of its life interrupted by something as mundane as the SWAT arrest of an – alleged – dangerous felon: the portion of the second floor that included the four rooms that the Conway crew had rented for the last three days had been cordoned off and the SPD Crime Scene Unit had been called with the understanding that, even though the motel was in Bellevue, any findings would have to be shipped over to Amy Sorensen and her team. Thus it might be convenient for everyone if – with the blessing of the smaller though equally dedicated Bellevue CSU – Sorensen took a ride across the Memorial Bridge and came to collect her evidence herself.

As they were piling into their vans Sorensen had warned her people: four rooms and four men who were not keen on being identified or tracked down. Short of hospital appointments that included actual emergency surgery, they might want to cancel their private lives for the next few days.

Madison stood by the threshold of one the rooms and looked inside. Unfortunately the motel's cleaning service had already done their job for the day, which in this case included wiping away prints and hoovering hairs, epithelials and other biological trace evidence.

Madison suspected that the room would have been tidy even without professional help: there were hardly any personal possessions that she could see – just a few leaflets on a desk for local attractions and a change of clothing in the wardrobe. Conway's men travelled light. *Arson and murder in the evening and breakfast in Pike Street Market in the morning.*

She didn't know which room was Conway's; hopefully the cleaners had not entirely eradicated his presence. One Bellevue PD detective had been allowed in each of the three empty rooms to look for weapons that had been stashed or items that might require an immediate response, though she had found nothing of use.

'No itinerary then?' Dunne commented.

The detective had smiled politely and moved on.

On the other hand, in the room of the presently detained Henry Sullivan – no one believed for a second that it was his real name but he had booked into Room 237 under that name and they had to call him something – the detectives had recovered the following: one Beretta 92FS 9mm with three spare magazines, one hunting knife with a 7 inch stainless steel blade, one military-style boot knife with a rubberized aluminum handle and a 3.5 420HC blade with a fiberglass sheath and, stripped down inside its modified leather briefcase, an M24 sniper rifle with ammunition in a separate case.

Madison looked at the hoard as an officer photographed it where it had been found. It was bad enough to have had first-hand experience of what Conway and his men could do up close and personal, and the thought that they had come prepared to do some long-distance target practice made everything much worse.

By the time Spencer pulled into the precinct it was almost midnight and Henry Sullivan was somewhere nearby on 5th Avenue getting his picture taken and his fingerprints detected by sensors. Lieutenant Fynn had been briefed, and the general consensus was that

Sullivan should be interviewed as soon as possible. Spencer would do the honors with Dunne in the box and Madison observing behind the one-way mirror. She had no ego about this: Spencer was much more experienced than she was and she was happy to observe the prisoner and draw her own conclusions.

'No hits on AFIS yet,' the uniformed officer told them when they arrived; it meant that so far the prints collected and put in the system had drawn a blank, and for the time being Henry Sullivan would have to remain Henry Sullivan. 'He hasn't said one word, by the way,' the officer added as he left them at the door of the interview room.

Madison was glad to be the only person in the observation box. At a different time of day there might have been someone else there, even – God forbid – Kelly, and for what she had to do she preferred privacy and no distractions.

Henry Sullivan sat at a metal table screwed into the floor. He was cuffed and an orange jumpsuit had replaced his jeans and T-shirt. Madison watched him. Her eyes, unseen from the other side, found his – dark, birdlike – and stayed there. He was calm and uncommunicative, almost bored. It was quite possibly an act, then again maybe not. He would be aware that he had not been identified and all they had on him was what they had found in Room 237. If the bullet that had killed Thomas Creed in the Walters Institute turned out to have been fired from his Beretta it would be an unexpected bonus for the case although Madison – without a logical reason for it – believed that it had been Conway's work.

What was Sullivan thinking? Madison studied the small, bright eyes. He probably realized that an arrest with everything that went with it implied a considerable change in lifestyle. Whatever happened here tonight and whatever charges would be laid against him, his days in Conway's crew were over. The latter had been fanatical about keeping himself out of the reach of law enforcement, and he had largely succeeded by making sure he worked with men who would not turn up in AFIS and CODIS searches – once prints and DNA were in the system a man was useless to him. Madison blinked; that was something worth remembering.

Spencer was talking and she tried to pay attention except that her focus was on Sullivan's hands, on the way he held his shoulders, on the involuntary eye movements that followed Spencer's words. Sullivan stared at the mirror and ignored the two detectives in front of him.

He didn't reply to a single question and seemed utterly unconcerned about the proceedings.

To Madison he looked like a guy who's holding a great hand in a hard game: he knows it and everybody else at the table knows it, but they all play on because they want to see what in the sweet name of everything holy he's holding.

Sullivan drummed his fingers once on the table. It was all the movement he had allowed himself.

After an hour, Spencer and Dunne stood up.

'I want a lawyer,' Henry Sullivan said. His voice was Brooklyn with a hint of Jersey.

The processing officer had told them that Sullivan had turned down the standard offer of a phone call: he was cut off from his people and drifting in dangerous waters. When the detectives left the room his behavior didn't change and his eyes remained on the mirror.

Madison arrived home at 3 a.m. She had been up for twenty-four hours straight and the darkness she had left in her windows looked exactly the same. The hot shower relaxed her and she wrapped herself in her comforter as her mind wandered through the last hours of this long day. They had upset Conway's plans for sure when they had broken up his crew; nonetheless, so far he'd followed a clear plan and nothing said that his systematic destruction of everything and everyone connected to the Hoh River case would stop just because he had one less pair of hands to do his killing and his slaying.

Chapter 46

Madison woke up at 7 a.m., not exactly late enough for a restorative sleep. *Well, it's the thought that counts.* She made coffee and promised herself a trip to the supermarket – a real one, with aisles and freshly scrubbed groceries. She could survive without food in the house but a lack of ground coffee for her stove-top machine was an eventuality that she could not face.

The sun had decided to toy with Elliott Bay and dawn was making promises it might not intend to keep. Madison dressed quickly and badly missed her Glock in the shoulder holster. She wrapped the strap around the holster and brought it with her. Her back-up piece was in place but her body felt strangely unbalanced.

She finished her coffee looking at the notes she had made on Timothy Gilman, the pages still spread on her dinner table. Conway would have finished Gilman with the same ease with which he'd finished the others. One was a sadist and a bully who enjoyed hurting little children and the other a cold-blooded murderer who killed for money. Madison checked the date Gilman had last been seen alive out of curiosity: Conway would have been a boy somewhere on the East Coast at that time, if he had ever been a boy.

*

Henry Sullivan had been assigned a public defender from the King County's Office of Public Defense. Spencer decided to give him a couple of hours' grace and then resume the interview. The Crime Scene Unit had been working non-stop in the Silver Pines Motel and an unofficial list of their initial findings had been mailed over. It was a very brief list and aside from the illegal weapons it made for very dull reading. Sullivan's wallet had contained a driver's license – fake – and $357.23 in cash. No credit cards, no plastic of any kind, and none of the insignificant receipts that chart the existence of a person from when they get up in the morning to when they go to bed at night. Henry Sullivan had materialized at the entrance of the Silver Pines Motel and the rest of his life was a blank.

Madison was on McMullen's duty: though the man had been in jail for years he must have associates who could organize a clean-up operation of that size on his behalf. It was not the kind of thing that can be handled by a stranger; if McMullen asked someone to do this for him it would be someone he knew before his arrest, someone he trusted implicitly with his life, because that was exactly what was at stake here.

There was an issue that had bothered Madison from the beginning and there really was no way around it: Conway was expensive, very expensive. Whoever had hired him had paid top dollar for his services. Madison scanned McMullen's file and looked for signs of potential wealth. Most, if not all, of his capital would have been frozen and then impounded as illegal gains as soon as he had been sentenced.

'I want to talk to McMullen,' she said to Kelly, hoping to God he had some previous engagement that could not been cancelled.

'Why?'

'Because I need to see his face when I ask him about the Hoh River case.'

'Why?'

'Because on paper he has all the credentials to have been involved in it at the time, but I don't see how he would have the capital to pay for Conway's crew.'

'If your neck is on the line you find whatever money you need to shake off the noose. We don't know that he wasn't owed favors by people who could take care of the bill.'

'He's divorced – twice – with three kids, none of whom have visited him unless they've done it under an assumed name. At the time he cut a deal with the prosecution and delivered at least four wanted felons. None of it would have created instant goodwill in jail and he spent some time in administrative solitary for his own protection. I'm saying, I looked at this file and he doesn't seem to me like he has the pull to do this. That's why I need to see him.'

'Okay.' Kelly shrugged, stood up and grabbed his coat.

'Okay,' Madison replied.

The McCoy State Prison, also known as The Bones, sat in a valley north of Seattle. They had called ahead and were expected. Officer Starecki met Madison and Kelly and led them through the labyrinth that housed over a thousand convicts.

'You know his parole is coming up in days, right?' he said over his shoulder as they proceeded down the corridor.

'We know,' Madison said. 'What's your impression of the man? You've been dealing with him since he arrived.'

Officer Starecki stopped, clearly rather surprised that someone was asking his opinion on the matter of Jerome McMullen. 'He's a model prisoner,' he replied. 'Never any trouble, never gets involved even if other people want trouble, if you know what I mean.'

'I know what you mean.'

'He's older than a lot of the guys here and some of them look up to him a bit but I've never heard him take advantage of it. He should sail through the hearing. What do you need to speak to him about?'

'He might be able to help us with a cold case.'

'I'm sure he will if he can. He's found religion too after his heart attack two years ago.'

'Right. Good to know,' Madison replied.

Jerome McMullen stood up as they entered the room. He was wearing immaculate prison clothing and his salt and pepper hair had been slicked back. Madison's first impression was that the man had been carved out of bone: he was lean and tall, his eyes were brown and striking against his pale skin. He was sixty years old and looked ten years younger – within the jail population that was highly unusual. They sat around the table. He was ramrod straight and took measure of them.

'How can I help you, Detectives?' Jerome McMullen said, and Madison knew instantly that once he was out of that parole hearing and far away from the walls of The Bones, religion and good manners would be shed like a cheap suit. I know you, she thought, and sat back in her chair.

'Mr. McMullen,' she started, 'we'd like to talk to you about your business dealings in 1985.'

McMullen smiled and the effect was not pleasant. 'That's one way to put it, Detective, but the Lord Jesus says that the truth will set me free – how apt – and we both know that in 1985 I was a foul, violent, unremorseful man who'd hurt anyone who got in his way and made his money stealing it from others.'

'The Lord Jesus?'

'Yes. I had a heart attack two years ago and when I woke up the world around me had changed because I had changed. I had accepted His Word, the only Word that matters.'

Madison felt Kelly shifting in the chair next to her.

'I will not ask you if you have been saved, Detective,' McMullen continued. 'After all, that's none of my business and you're not here to talk about my spiritual journey.'

'No, but thanks for sharing,' Kelly commented.

'We're here because in 1985 the kind of felonies you were involved in meant you extorted money from small businesses and made sure they knew what would happen if they didn't pay,' Madison said.

From the first moment she had been clocking him for any signs of apprehension and concern, anything that might tell her he had been expecting their visit and knew what they wanted to ask him. She saw none. He was calm and collected and his hands rested on the table before him.

McMullen frowned delicately as if the effort of thinking back to those times and the person he was then was physically painful. 'Go on,' he said.

'Are you aware of a restaurant on Alki Beach called The Rock?'

'Yes. Is it still there?'

'Yes, it is. Did you approach them at the time? Did you ever speak with the owners or did any of your men ever speak with the owners to indicate that you would hurt them and hurt them badly if they didn't pay you protection money when you asked for it?'

McMullen nodded. 'I understand. You're asking me if I had any part in the kidnap and in the death of that poor, poor child.'

'No, I'm asking you if the foul, violent and unremorseful man you were then paid four men to snatch three boys. And it wasn't an accidental death, it was murder.'

McMullen shook his head. 'It was terrible thing.'

'Well, that's what you can say now with the benefit of a heart attack and your ongoing spiritual journey. What would you have said then?'

'I can tell you that it would have been right up my kind of business, and the reason why I didn't approach them was because the kidnap happened before I had a chance to. And afterwards, you couldn't have gotten anybody to go near it. As far as I know no one ever approached them and, of course, in more recent years no one would anyway considering who the present owners are.'

'John Cameron and Nathan Quinn.'

'Yes,' he replied, and the brown watery eyes travelled to the fading scar on Madison's brow. 'but I don't really need to tell *you* anything about them, do I?'

'Do you have friends out in the world, Mr. McMullen? Family, people who will help you when you're out – should you get out – to restart your life?'

'My path was not one that encouraged friendships or the loving support of a family. I will do everything I can to make things right with my children and hopefully join a volunteer group that creates gardens and positive environments in areas that need them.'

Madison felt Kelly practically combust next to her.

'Gardening sounds nice. Have you ever met a man called Timothy Gilman?'

McMullen narrowed his eyes in concentration, his mind flipping through a mental Rolodex of names he'd rather forget.

'I'm afraid not.'

'Did you order the kidnap?'

'No, Detective, I did not. And I don't think I could live with myself if I had done so.'

'Now what do you think?' Kelly said as they reached their car in the parking lot.

'That weasel could find whatever funds he needed to pay off Conway,' Madison said. 'If we don't get to the end of this in time, he will be out on parole breathing free air and potting azaleas in community centers for as long as his probation lasts. After that, he's in the wind.'

'Azaleas?' Kelly snorted.

'Whatever,' Madison replied.

Chapter 47

August 29, 1985. Ronald Gray waited in the shade of the alley opposite Gilman's front door. He had been there since 8 a.m. and it was almost midday. It was nearly impossible to get into the squalid block and into his apartment to search it while he was out, and Ronald didn't fancy his chances. With the kind of luck he'd had recently Gilman would double back for whatever reason, find him in his rooms, and end his pathetic excuse for a life there and then.

In the last four hours Ronald had repeatedly cursed the first time they had ever met in his old neighborhood, and the first time Gilman had ever offered him fifty bucks to stand lookout on the street while he was having a conversation in a garage with a late payer.

Ronald had not been in the business of all-out lethal violence but he knew enough about it to be sure that Gilman would have received a slice of cash as a retainer before the kidnap and the rest of the payment would have to be settled soon. Men like Gilman don't take cheques: someone would have to meet him with a bag of cash at some point and Ronald would be there to find out who it was.

The front door opened and Ronald shrank even deeper into the shadows. Timothy Gilman stepped out in the late August sun and started walking.

The first day brought him nothing but a lingering headache and a sense of frustration. Gilman had gone into a local bar, parked himself there for hours, and then returned home. It was dingy and seedy; however, too many people had greeted him when he walked in and it was clearly not the place for some private and discreet business.

The News had not stopped talking about the case for an instant: the surviving boys had been found alive. Thank God for small mercies, Ronald had muttered to himself. The yearbook pictures had punctuated the reports on television, which repeated the little information they had and did not come within a mile of the truth.

Now Ronald knew the boys' names, the names of their parents, the name of the restaurant they owned. He knew that the scrap of paper he had salvaged from the fire was David Quinn's yearbook photo and he had suffered from congenital cardiac arrhythmia. And Gilman had known that too.

The second and the third day brought nothing more except for more footage of the rangers and the local law agencies spread around the forest and looking for the child – the body of the child. Gilman woke up late, went to the bar and returned home. On the fourth day he drove to a local supermarket and bought TV dinners, and all the while Ronald followed him and kept a bag in the car with five threadbare baseball caps in different colors and three jackets that he would switch as often as he could. Gilman had seen his 1979 Toyota a few times and he had borrowed a car from a mechanic friend, saying he wanted to keep an eye on a girl who might be cheating on him; the friend had handed him the keys without question.

The boy's funeral was on the fifth day. Gilman didn't even leave the apartment and Ronald began to believe that maybe it was pointless, this crazy idea he'd had would lead to nothing.

Every morning he would leave the house and come home late at night and he would find Vincent curled up in his bed exactly as he had left him. He would try and feed him some of the foods he liked and Vincent would take three forkfuls and then go back to bed; he had said maybe five words since the forest. Ronald had called the supermarket where Vincent had his part-time job and told them he was ill and would come back as soon as he could. Or never, he thought, looking at the shape under the bedcovers.

On the sixth day all the papers carried articles about the boy's funeral. Ronald couldn't help himself: he bought every paper and watched every report. He read the words, he stared at the pictures, and every detail pulled a thick rope tighter around his chest.

Gilman stayed home sleeping, smoking, getting drunk or watching soaps. Ronald didn't know and didn't care – he just wanted him to go out and get his darn money. He fell asleep at the kitchen table: *The Seattle Times*, the *Seattle Post-Intelligencer*, *The Washington Star* and the *Elliott Bay News* spread like a thin, ineffective pillow for a sleep that carried no peace and little comfort.

The seventh day began with as much blue sky as it had a week earlier. Human beings are trained to measure life in well-defined, pre-packaged portions, and when Ronald opened his eyes his first thought was that only a week ago his life had been an ordinary mix of dull, okay and pathetic and he would do anything to have it back as it was. *A week ago.*

He dressed quickly and made a couple of ham sandwiches for Vincent in case he got hungry when he was out. He left them on the kitchen table inside his lunchbox, next to a bag of Cheetos and half a packet of Oreo cookies, his favorite.

He sat on the side of Vincent's bed.

'Hey, Vin.'

The younger man opened his eyes.

'I'm off. I've got some things I need to do,' Ronald said.

'It's not safe.'

'It's okay, honestly, man. So far, so good. I've left you some food in the kitchen. How are you feeling today?'

Vincent closed his eyes.

'Right. Good,' Ronald said. 'You rest here and I'll be back later. Eat something, will ya?'

Ronald got up and left. He shut the door gently and managed to feel both guilty and resentful. He didn't catch Vincent's whisper in the empty house.

'It's not personal, it's business.'

He knew it the moment Gilman set foot out of his front door. Ronald had had more than a good chance to become familiar with the man's moods and how he carried himself. Timothy Gilman glanced left and right before he got into his black Camaro and Ronald knew in his bones that he was not going to the supermarket and he was not going to his bar, and Ronald was afraid. To follow and be found out was suicide, to turn around and go home – well, he thought, it would just be another kind of death. Slower maybe, but only marginally less painful.

Gilman took the I-90 and drove east, crossed Mercer Island and I-405, and continued through Eastgate first and then Issaquah. Five cars behind him, covered in a film of perspiration and wearing a pale green baseball cap, Ronald followed him.

Gilman kept a steady pace, just under the speed limit, and they soon went past Preston and North Bend. Ronald couldn't even bear to keep the radio on: his eyes were fixed on the Camaro and his hands gripped the steering wheel. When there were only three cars between them he would slow down and fall back; when he couldn't see Gilman for more than a minute he would pick up speed until he saw the black car again. There was enough traffic for camouflage, nonetheless Ronald could not allow himself to relax even for a second as exits came and went – Gilman could leave the Interstate at any time.

Finally, Gilman turned off just before the Olallie State Park and took the SE Homestead Valley Road due east. The woods were thick on both sides and Ronald slowed down as much as he could while still keeping Gilman in sight.

The Camaro turned left into a narrow lane and Ronald had no choice but to drive on, slouch in the seat and throw a quick glance as he drove past.

Shit. He had stopped. Gilman had stopped only fifty yards into the dirt road and there was another car parked there. The canopy of trees made it dark and he had hardly been able to see clearly, and yet he was sure of one thing: the black Camaro had stopped and there was another car there too.

Ronald looked around: the Homestead Valley Road was empty in both directions. He braked as softly as he could and reversed until he was seventy yards from the mouth of the lane. He prayed no one was watching and did a U-turn, as he fully expected whoever he was going to follow would get back onto I-90 after the exchange.

Ronald left the car in a pullout and stepped into the forest. It was cooler under the shade of the firs; he went ten foot deep and then proceeded to walk parallel to the road until he was on the same level as the lane Gilman had turned into. He dropped and crouched and crawled behind a bush that kept him covered but gave him a view of the two cars and the two men talking.

Ronald laid flat on the dusty ground and pulled out a pair of binoculars he had bought at REI three days earlier for $19.95. He wouldn't be able to see eagles flying around Mount Rainier for sure but he could see this, and this was enough.

He brought the lenses up to his eyes and held his breath. There they were. The other car was a midnight blue BMW and the hood was up. Good idea, Ronald thought; anyone driving past would just think *engine trouble*. Both men were facing the other side and looking at the engine; he could see Gilman gesticulating and the other man listening.

Ronald breathed and a puff of dust from the ground rose and fell; a small cloud of insects had found his exposed skin and were taking full advantage of it. He didn't care. His eyes stayed on the two men whose faces he could not see, and just then he understood something. That dreadful day a week earlier had not gone as he had expected; however, it had not gone as Gilman had expected either. The kid was supposed to die of his condition; he was not supposed to wake up and see them and make it necessary for them to kill him. What was Gilman telling the man? Was he telling him the truth?

No way. Gilman was a nasty piece of work and he wouldn't give himself any extra grief when he didn't need to.

Ronald shifted on the forest's floor as his body began to ache. The men turned and for an instant he really was afraid that it had all been for nothing and this was an accidental meeting with someone whose BMW had blown a fuse.

The other man was wearing a smart, dark suit, and suddenly Ronald saw him clearly like he was standing right next to them. Clearly enough to recognize him, and when he took out a leather satchel from the trunk and passed it to Gilman Ronald couldn't blink as his breath caught in his throat. All was lost, all was gone. His puny little binoculars could only show him a hell that had no end because it was worse than he could have ever imagined.

He lowered the binoculars and rested his brow on his wrist. First one engine and then the other came to life, and he heard the Camaro and the BMW leave.

In a haze Ronald drove back into Seattle and a beautiful September afternoon, and knew without a doubt that his troubles were only starting.

Chapter 48

Spencer called her cell as Madison and Kelly were crossing the city limits: there had been a break-in at Ronald Gray's apartment and the place had been ransacked.

When they arrived the super was still on the fourth-floor landing, waiting for the emergency locksmith to finish his job on Gray's front door. A patrol officer stood by.

'What happened?' Madison asked the super.

'I went in an hour ago because I wanted to check his gas was turned off – there's a tap by the stove and I couldn't remember if I'd turned it off. Anyway, I found what I found . . .' He gestured and Madison stepped inside.

'Any of the neighbors told you they heard anything?' she asked the police officer over her shoulder.

'No. Most of the people on this floor are still at work but the lady next door is home with the flu and she said she heard nothing all day.'

The whole place had been gutted, quietly and systematically gutted. A sharp blade had shred the sofa cushions, the padding on each chair and the mattress. The filling was spread all over the place like ugly snow. Every single item that had been on the bookshelves was on the floor. The kitchen cupboards were open and empty, their contents spilled out in the sink. Floorboards here and there had been ripped up and laid askew against the walls. Drawers had been pulled out and emptied on the ripped-up mattress.

'When were you here last?' Madison asked the super, her eyes still taking in the devastation.

'Early yesterday afternoon. I came in with the guy from the insurance company.'

'And everything was normal?'

'Yes. Well, creepy because of the murder, but normal. I guess the insurance guy will have to come back. We rent the property furnished and decorated, you know.'

Madison nodded. She saw Peter Conway steal into the building and inside the apartment, seeking and destroying without making a sound, until all that was left of Ronald Gray's life had been torn inside out.

Seeking and destroying. *He wants the Gilman link, that's what he's been searching for: the proof that Gilman was involved and how that information somehow ended up in Quinn's hands. He couldn't get to Foley and he came back here.*

The cold measured violence of what was before her was beginning to seep into her bones when Madison turned and left. Conway was getting angry: they had taken one of his men away from him, Vincent Foley was still alive and still he had not found what he was looking for.

The sky was wide and purple above them as Madison and Kelly got back into the car and drove to the precinct without a word.

Henry Sullivan, lawyered up and rested, had stuck to his vow of silence and neither Spencer nor Dunne had been able to engage him in any kind of conversation. A few hours earlier Ballistics had confirmed that the bullet that had killed Thomas Creed had not come from Sullivan's Beretta. Thus the prisoner sat in Buddha-like repose in his cell, calmly waiting for what the legal system might throw at him next.

Chapter 49

Nathan Quinn had waited until he was sure his firm's offices on the ninth floor of Stern Tower would be empty. He needed to check some legal reference tomes he did not have at home and he could not yet face the well-meaning kindness of his colleagues. He felt jagged: as if just as the scars on his body were healing well, the cracks in his life were getting deeper and sharper. The photographs of Harry Salinger's injuries came back from time to time. There he was – Cameron, his brother in all but blood – comprised and contained within the twist of that blade. Did it matter that Salinger had done much, much worse? How do you measure those acts? Were there scales that could weigh one against the other?

Quinn had arrived in the underground parking lot, driving himself for the first time, and had ridden the elevator to the ninth floor; he had waved to the camera and to the security guard monitoring his progress from somewhere in the building and had put the key in the lock of this place which had seen all his battles and all his victories in the last decade.

He had hoped for relief, or maybe just the comfort of familiarity, but none had come. The smart offices and elegant furnishings felt alien and he didn't know whether he would ever feel at home here again.

Quinn made himself coffee and brought his cup and saucer into the library. He had felt so proud when Quinn Locke & Associates had first opened its doors to the world. His eyes scanned the shelves for the books he needed; he found them and laid them open on the massive table. He wondered what Rabbi Stien would make of this, whether there was anything in the Torah that explained to a man how to take the Law and shape it like clay with his own hands and still keep his soul.

Quinn decided to put the existential questions to one side and got back to the issue at hand. Self-defense was all very well if you had an intruder in your own home, but Cameron had been in the middle of a forest and *the requirement to evade* or *the duty to retreat* played no part.

He was deep into a Supreme Court Opinion from 1989 when a gentle knock on the library door startled him out of it.

'I thought I just imagined you sitting there,' the man said. 'I honestly thought it was my imagination playing tricks after all these weeks.'

'Conrad,' Quinn said and he stood up.

Conrad Locke.

'Nathan.' Locke grabbed him in a quick hug. 'It's good to see you – it's so good to see you.'

'Thank you for your note when I was in hospital, for your support. For your kind words.'

'Please, don't mention it. We respected your wishes not to have visitors and writing was the very least we could do.'

Locke was nearly seventy years old and carried his age easily and with grace. The hair was now completely white and the eyes had more lines around them, but he was the same man who had known Quinn since he was a boy, who had stood by him without giving platitudes on the day of David's funeral.

'Let me look at you,' Locke said, his hands on the taller man's

THE DARK • 331

shoulders. Quinn didn't look away; the older man's eyes sparkled with affection.

'Now you're hitting the books for Jack,' Locke said. 'What's the latest news?'

'The hearing with Judge Martin is tomorrow morning. The whole thing has been expedited because of Salinger's insanity, the guilty plea and the bleach attack in KCJC.'

'How strong is our case?'

'Difficult to say.'

'If there's a man on this planet who can get him out of there, it's you.'

'Thank you.'

'I'm assuming that's what will happen. What then?' Locke had been a phenomenal litigator; he could turn water into wine in front of a jury and convince them that it had been wine in the first place.

'Jack will stay with me until things have sorted themselves out,' Quinn replied.

'Good. That's good. I have never given you any advice in all these years, Nathan, and I'm not going to start now. All I would say with regard to the Honorable Claire Martin, whom you have had the pleasure to argue before many a time, is *keep it simple*. Find the core strength of your case and hammer it home. Make it so it's an inescapable truth. Scott Newton is a solid attorney but he cannot prove what happened on that river bank.'

If anyone sees the photographs he will not need to prove much, Quinn thought, but he nodded. 'I'll bear that in mind. Judge Martin is somewhat unpredictable – I don't want to under-prepare.'

'Nonsense,' Locke said and he moved to leave.

'How come you're here so late?' Quinn said.

'I've left some theatre tickets on my desk. I'll spend the day out at the estate tomorrow and I didn't want to have to come back for them.'

At the ranch. Quinn smiled. 'Give Grace my regards.'

'I will.'

Quinn heard Conrad Locke's steps recede in the hallway and the lift that carried him downstairs. He thought about simplicity and about the times he'd heard Locke argue a case in court. Then he picked up each book and put it back on the shelf. At this point he knew what he knew. The case would not be resolved with something as prosaic as a precedent.

Nathan Quinn drove home and poured himself a measure of bourbon. Tomorrow night he'd be drinking one with Jack.

Chapter 50

Madison arrived home with three bags from Trader Joe's. Her phone went as she was walking in the door.

'Hey.' Rachel said.

'Hey.' Madison smiled.

'Do you want to know something funny?'

'Always.'

'Neal and Tommy are asleep and I was surfing the net – you know, reading about the recent developments in the world of psychology.'

'Sure, which is code for cats doing yoga.'

'Right. Did you know . . .'

Madison twisted the cap off a beer and started unpacking while listening to Rachel's soothing tones. Later she couldn't have been sure what they'd talked about except that it had taken the edge off a hard day. Rachel always did that. And Madison missed Tommy, missed being part of a six-year-old boy's life. Soon enough he would be seven and she ought to be there when they brought out the cake and sang to him. Madison had sung to him; she had sung 'Blackbird' to him in the forest that night she thought he'd die. She wasn't sure she could sing to him again.

She sautéed a chicken breast in the pan with some garlic and crushed chili and had it on the sofa with her feet on the coffee table, watching *The Fortune Cookie* on DVD.

She had gone for a run which had at least partially done its job, and yet as long as her brain was still capable of thought all thinking flowed in one direction. What did she know today that she didn't know yesterday? Well, for one thing Jerome McMullen was a creepy piece of work and she had no doubt that he would manage to weasel his way through the parole board and out the other side. And Conway was getting antsy, if the destruction inside Ronald Gray's apartment was anything to go by.

Madison took a sip of her beer. Timothy Gilman was lucky that all he got for his troubles was a fall into a bear's trapping pit: whether he fell or he was pushed, his death would have been instant, according to the autopsy report. God knows what Conway would have come up with for him had he been alive today; still, Conway was all the way on the other side of the country and he was just a kid at the time. Madison closed her eyes and there it was: the notion that a kid could take on Gilman and use a bear's trapping pit as a weapon against a man who was bigger, stronger and infinitely meaner. A boy. A young man who had never before done anything remarkable or been in any kind of trouble with the law.

Madison stood up too quickly and felt rather dizzy with it – or perhaps it was the idea, the sudden understanding. And it wasn't about the mechanics of it, it wasn't about the plain sequence of events. It was dark shapes changing and shifting and locking into each other to form something so big she could hardly conceive of it.

Madison flipped through her notes on the table. There it was: the last time anyone had seen Gilman alive, in a bar in his neighborhood. Madison already knew that date; she had been staring at that date for days last December when John Cameron was the prime suspect for the murder of James Sinclair and his family. It was the date on Cameron's arrest sheet for drunk driving. It went with his picture:

a somber young man with longish hair wearing a sheepskin jacket. For a long time it was all she'd had of Cameron to imagine what he'd look like, and she remembered now what she'd thought then: he didn't look drunk, he looked serious – deadly serious.

Could a boy do such a thing? The questions wound around the idea faster than any of the answers. That boy with the sheepskin jacket, what had he done? What in God's name had he done? No, not in God's name, but in the name of a child who never got to see his fourteenth birthday.

Madison checked the time and it was too late to go visiting. The bar where Gilman had done his final night's drinking did not exist anymore; however, the bartender was still alive. What he might remember twenty years after the fact Madison could not find out until morning, and morning seemed a very long time away.

She dragged herself to bed and lay there wishing for sleep like a blanket of nothingness that would stop the questions at least for a while.

Chapter 51

Madison walked into the detectives' room at 7 a.m. and went to work on what she needed. She studied the Gilman file and found what she expected to find; a quick internet search confirmed her suspicions. By the time she left an hour later it was still early but a decent enough time of day to call her only witness and invite him out for a cup of coffee.

She had taken four hours of personal time – considering the sheer number of days off missed and unpaid overtime, it was not a problem.

The bartender had not been a bartender for many years. Morris Becker was fifty-three years old and ran his own sandwich bar on Mercer Island. The coffee would be on him, he said.

The previous day's sunshine had been a blip: the day had dawned dark and stormy and meant to continue that way. Madison drove under heavy rain to the address he had given her and they sat at a table in the window, the pane already steamed up.

'I kinda thought someone would show up sooner or later,' Morris Becker said. 'After I heard that name in the news, after the appeal.'

'Why did you think that?' Madison said.

'The way things were left – as far as I know – no one was ever charged with his murder. Someone was bound to start asking the same questions all over again.'

'You think it was murder?'

'You never met the man himself, did you? No, you'd have been too young to be in the force then, but he was the kind of person who looks for trouble and brings trouble to your door. Whether you like it or not, whether you're ready or not. I was sorry to hear he'd died that kind of death, sure, but surprised? Not really.'

'You seem to remember that business very clearly though it was twenty years ago.'

'It was the most exciting thing that had ever happened in that dump. I'm not ungrateful for that job, you understand, but I was really glad to move on when I did.'

'I understand. My questions are mostly to do with the witness statements that were taken at the time.' Madison had gone through the testimonies in the precinct and knew what she had not found. It was no more than a hunch. 'I didn't find the statement from a kid – dark hair, late teens, sheepskin jacket. You remember him?'

The man blinked twice. 'I'm telling you what I told the other guy: the kid was hanging around the bar for weeks before that night and then nothing. I never saw him again. They didn't take his statement because I had no idea who he was, he was just a kid with a fake ID. It's not like we'd never had one of those before.'

Madison's brain had latched on to the first thing the man had said. 'What *other guy*?'

'A few weeks after they found Gilman's body this fella turns up at the bar and he asks me the same questions you're asking so I give him the same answers.'

'What did this fella look like?'

'Tall, dark hair, suit and tie. I'd say *lawyer* if you're asking me, and I'm not usually wrong about those things.'

Madison nodded and somehow found a small smile to go with

the nod. 'Say I have some pictures with me, would you mind having a look? See if anyone looks familiar?'

'Pictures of the guy? I'm good with faces but I only saw him the once.'

'No, not the guy. The kid.'

'Sure, go ahead.'

Madison took out a brown envelope from her rucksack and laid ten photographs on the table. She had spent some time printing just the right kind: the young men were all of a similar age and the photos had been taken around the same time.

Morris Becker leant forward as his eyes moved from face to face. 'Him,' he said.

'Are you sure?'

'No question about it. He's even wearing the same jacket he wore in the bar.'

'You're absolutely sure?'

'Look, Detective, I can even tell you about his hand thing.'

'What hand thing?'

'All the time he came to the bar his right hand was always in his pocket. I figured there was some kind of problem with it. Twenty years later I can still remember what anybody used to drink and he drank beer or coffee with bourbon.'

His finger tapped on John Cameron's picture.

Madison wanted to be nowhere specific doing nothing in particular. She needed to think the way she could when she was little, sitting in the back seat of her grandfather's car and watching the landscape flow by. Her thoughts would come up and float past in the same way.

She drove to Pier 52 and boarded the ferry to Bainbridge Island, left her Honda on the car deck and found a spot by a window. The return journey was one hour and ten minutes, not as much time as she needed but as much as she had.

Her legs were stretched out under the table and the cup of coffee steamed before her. She felt like she'd been hit by a boulder. She reached for her cell and was almost ready to speed-dial Brown when she stopped. She couldn't drag him into this; this was for her and her alone to know and to decide.

Now she had the answers that Nathan Quinn had refused to give her: why he trusted his source and why he would not tell her how he had found out about Gilman. The truth, however, had given her more answers that she had even thought to ask and she wondered what kind of world John Cameron and Nathan Quinn had lived in this past twenty-five years, what had been the real cost of this justice bought by a trapping pit dug by a boy?

The rain had not stopped as the ferry began its return journey. Water above and water below and Madison in between, making a decision that could change the lives of all involved and would define her forever as a police officer and a human being.

Chapter 52

The hearing was closed to the public and considering the kind of ghoulish interest the case had produced in the media, no one was surprised at the fact.

John Cameron had arrived at the courthouse earlier and had changed into the clothes that Nathan Quinn had provided for him. He felt very much like himself wearing black trousers and a cashmere roll neck, and that was a good thing and a bad thing: a good thing because, looking in the mirror, he saw a free man out of the KCJC jumpsuit, a man who could do as he pleased and go where his will might take him; a bad thing because he had no intention of wearing that jumpsuit again and – should Nathan fail – he would have to take some extreme measures to ensure that he would not.

John Cameron was a prudent man and as well as a home in Seattle that not even Quinn knew about, he had provided for himself four packages in different locations in the county which contained the necessary items for a quick trip to safer grounds and a permanent exile from his city.

Cameron looked around the waiting room: this was the smallest number of locked doors and armed personnel he'd had between himself and freedom in weeks. Once he was in court there would be even fewer. He was not armed himself but that was really not an issue: once he had decided on a course of action there would be little that could stop him.

Nathan Quinn had hardly slept. He felt Cameron's restless energy as if he could see him and knew that he had this one chance at making things work his way. If he didn't – Quinn couldn't bear to think about the consequences.

Conrad Locke had advised simplicity. He had suggested that Quinn should find one single inescapable truth and use it to pierce the prosecution case. In his heart he knew he had found it and it was the same truth he had found twenty years ago. Today the Honorable Claire Martin would decide whether he had been right.

The side door opened and John Cameron was escorted into the court. He stood next to Quinn as if it was the most natural place for him to be.

'All rise,' the usher announced.

Judge Martin took her seat at the bench. Her hair was up in her customary bun and her bifocals sat on the tip of her nose. She wore Hermès silk scarves under the gown, her rulings were never, ever, overturned, and any attorney underestimated her at his peril.

Judge Martin looked around her. 'Mr. Newton,' she said.

Newton nodded. 'Your Honor.'

'Mr. Quinn.'

'Your Honor.'

'We're here to talk about Mr. Cameron's bail, gentlemen.'

'Your Honor?' Quinn said.

'Go ahead, Counselor.'

'In view of the new circumstances, recent events and the present state of the prosecution's case, I move to file a motion for the immediate dismissal of all the charges against my client.'

'What –' Newton was on his feet.

'Keep your hat on, Mr. Newton. You've thought this through, Mr.

Quinn? You do know how much I hate the intentional waste of docket time.'

'I do know that, Your Honor.'

The judge sighed and stood up. 'In my chambers.'

Quinn turned to Cameron. 'I will see you in a few minutes,' he said.

Cameron held his friend whole in his amber eyes.

'What are we dealing with, Counselor?' Judge Martin sat at her desk.

'The charges against my client are totally spurious. The prosecution does not have even the beginning of a case and the continuous incarceration of Mr. Cameron as a result of the denial of bail has led to an attempt on his life.'

'One thing at a time. Your client has been charged with Attempted Murder, hence the denial of bail. What are the new circumstances?'

'Your Honor, the prosecution does not have a case for Attempted Murder; they don't have a case for Assault or Reckless Endangerment or even Jaywalking against my client. They cannot prove intent and they don't have a weapon.'

'Mr. Newton, where's your lethal weapon?'

Scott Newton had experienced numerous degrees of unhappiness on the job, but he knew when he walked into court this morning that this day was going to take the cake.

'We don't have one, Your Honor.'

'You've been looking since December, Counselor.'

'I'm aware of that, Your Honor.'

'*How* is the defendant supposed to have accomplished his Attempted Murder, Mr. Newton?'

'We don't know yet.'

'I sense I'm going to hear a lot of that today from your side of the room, Scott. What about intent?' The judge turned to Quinn and he hoped she had not seen the photos of Salinger's injuries.

'The injuries sustained were dreadful but they were entirely consistent with trying to restrain a man who had just admitted to four murders and the kidnapping and murder of a little boy. Harry Salinger has just been found legally insane and has pleaded guilty to four counts of Murder, one of Kidnapping of a Minor in the First Degree, and two counts of Attempted Murder. He confessed at the time in the presence of my client, Detective Madison and myself. All my client did was try to stop this man before he fled, and given the clearly proven violent and irrational nature of Mr. Salinger he found himself struggling for his own life in the process.'

'You're calling it a *citizen's arrest*?' Newton's voice cracked.

'My client waited for the authorities to arrive and gave himself up without question. He has no felony record and has been a model prisoner while on remand. Mr. Salinger has a previous Assault record and has never denied any of the charges brought against him. He's a dangerous man, and had my client not stopped him when he did we have no idea what other horrors he might have committed.'

'Mr. Newton, where is your case?' the judge asked him.

'Your Honor, have you seen the records of the injuries inflicted on Mr. Salinger?'

John Cameron sat at the Defense table. There were two guards by the side door, one by the door to the corridor. The stenographer stole a glance at him every so often, then quickly lowered his eyes.

All these people have done wrong today, he reflected, was to wake up and come to work.

'I have seen the pictures, Mr. Newton. What is your point?' Judge Martin said.

'There was an extreme use of violence not warranted by—'

'He was defending himself,' Quinn interrupted him. 'Was any kind of weapon found on my client at all?'

'No.'

'Was there any other weapon recovered at the crime scene?' the judge asked Newton.

Newton sighed. 'A handgun with Mr. Salinger's prints was found on the scene.' It was almost too painful to continue. 'And a hunting knife with Mr. Salinger's prints was also found nearby.'

Quinn turned to the judge. 'Detective Madison's testimony says that there were stains on Salinger's shirt that appeared to be blood – the blood of the little boy who had been kidnapped. And all the weapons on the scene belonged to Mr. Salinger. What do you think was the state of mind of my client at that point? He was trying to stop a murderer from running away and ended up fighting for his life. That was the only intent.'

'What does Mr. Salinger say about all this, if anything?' Judge Martin asked Newton.

'He says he didn't put up a fight at all.'

The statements had been taken, Quinn had read them. 'What else, Scott?' he said.

'Counselor?' The judge was fast reaching the end of an already extremely short tether.

'In his statement my client says that he didn't start fighting Mr. Cameron until he realized that Mr. Cameron did not intend to kill him as he had hoped he would.'

'He fought him so that Mr. Cameron would kill him in the fight?'

The prosecution attorney nodded.

Judge Martin looked from one to the other. She was angry about at least twelve different things going on with this case, and nothing was worse to her than the feeling of justice not been properly served in her court.

'Give me something, Mr. Newton. Right now. I'm begging you,' she said. 'Anything.'

*

Time had stretched brittle and thin and John Cameron waited in his seat. He waited because his desire to be away from these walls came up against his trust in Quinn and the next step, once taken, was irreversible.

The door opened and the judge and the attorneys returned to their places. Quinn looked blank and ashen; then again, so did Scott Newton.

Quinn turned to Cameron and nodded.

'This case is dismissed and Mr. Cameron is free to go, Mr. Newton,' Judge Martin said. 'Not a great day for the Office of the King County's Prosecutor, I'd say. This case should have never gotten this far with what you had. And what you didn't have, you should have found by now. Mr. Quinn?'

'Your Honor.'

'I'd congratulate you on winning your case but *you* didn't win it – *they* lost it. It was a mess from start to finish and you just turned up today and told me all about it. But I will congratulate you on still being alive. Today that's all you get from me.' Judge Martin stood to leave. 'Mr. Cameron, I'm not really sure what to say to you, except that I hope I'll never see you in my court again.'

They left the courthouse and went directly to the underground parking lot where Quinn had left his car. Neither one of them said a word.

When they stopped at the traffic lights on 5th Avenue, Cameron wound down his window and stretched his hand out in the freezing rain, so sharp against his skin and so welcome.

Chapter 53

Deputy Warden Will Thomas replaced the handset on the telephone. The call had been from the Inmate Transport Department, who had in turn received a call from the Seattle Courthouse to say their van would be coming back minus its prisoner and they'd have one more empty cell tonight. The paperwork would follow.

Will Thomas sat back on his chair and closed his eyes. He was not a man who had ever looked for the easy ride in his life, for the paycheck with medical and the weekends off but, Sweet Jesus, was he glad to be rid of that man.

That detective had been right: they had not apprehended him, they had not caught him, he was just staying with them for as long as it pleased him. And now he was gone, and so was the infernal drumming. And even the violent incidents would go back to their usual numbers in a couple of days.

Thankyouthankyouthankyou, he whispered to the deity who watched over prisons and their harried staff. He clicked his pen and prepared to sign a number of requisition orders.

Officer B. Miller waited until the metal door to D Wing had slid open and walked through. News had travelled at roughly the speed of light and he knew that his 4 a.m. strolls with the inmate residing in Cell D-37 were over.

The door to Cameron's former cell was locked; no one had been inside it since. He had stripped the bed, disposed of his toiletries in a small wastebasket, and no personal items were in sight anywhere. Son-of-a-bitch knew he wouldn't be coming back. And a voice Miller didn't like at all murmured in his ear, *one way or the other*.

In his cell, Manny Oretremos waited until he knew he would be alone for a few minutes, without a guard walking past and checking on him through the bars. His life, such as it was, had been over the minute he had not sent his vial of bleach flying toward John Cameron. It was just a question of when his destiny would catch up with him. And he'd had enough. Enough of everything and everyone. Most of all he couldn't bear the constant fear any longer, fear that had rubbed against his skin for years and worn it paper-thin.

He was in solitary and what he had in mind was not easy to accomplish. If he had a well of undiscovered determination now it was the time to find it.

He prayed to the Virgin Mary and asked forgiveness for his sins.

Twelve minutes later a guard found him on the ground: he had crammed toilet paper into his nostrils and stuffed the thin blanket on his cot into his mouth down to his throat. The medics tried to revive him but he was pronounced dead at the scene. They notified the Deputy Warden of the situation. The paperwork would follow.

Chapter 54

Madison, back at her desk, flipped through a small pile of messages and picked out Dr. Takemoto's. She called her back.

'I just wanted to let you know that I've emailed you some notes about my first session with Vincent and I'll be seeing him again tomorrow, all being well,' the doctor said.

'Thank you,' Madison replied.

'You know, even when he's not there Ronald is very much a presence in his life. Vincent's thoughts definitely spin around his brother.'

After they said goodbye Madison opened her mail and read the transcript and everything Vincent had said to the doctor. The words seemed to have a life of their own on the page, suspended as they were between reality and Vincent's own separate world.

Lieutenant Fynn came out of his office and spoke to the detectives' room in general. 'The Honorable Claire Martin has just dismissed the case against John Cameron. He's out.' It was a statement of fact and they could do with it what they wanted.

Madison felt Kelly's eyes on her back. They were all aware she had given a statement and that statement said that she did not remember seeing the knife Cameron had allegedly use to attack the victim, or any other weapon, in his hand.

At that point, half-crazy with grief and anger as she was, she couldn't be sure of what she had seen, and she had not lied in the statement. Had there been a flash of gun metal in the light of the flashlights? Probably. Did she believe Cameron carried a knife? Definitely. Did she want to swear under oath on either of those facts? No, she did not. There was a deeper truth there and she might as well face it because it wasn't going to go away: Madison had never committed perjury, which was why she had told Cameron not to say a word to her before the police had arrived that night; however, something in her moral compass found it impossible to begrudge Cameron his freedom. She had experienced on her skin what it was like when Harry Salinger made you his personal project. If the prosecution had not been able to present a case, then she wasn't unhappy about it. *Not unhappy* was not *happy*, it was what it was.

Cameron was out and Quinn could breathe a sigh of relief. Until his favorite client got busy again, that is.

Her cell started vibrating. It was Amy Sorensen.

'I thought I'd bring you good tidings,' the CSU investigator said. 'Spencer already knows.'

'What is it?'

'We matched DNA from Mr. Sullivan to one hair on the bag over Warren Lee's head.'

'That's excellent news.'

'Spencer said the guy isn't talking. Maybe that'll give him a nudge.'

'Thanks, Amy.'

'Something else. There were prints on the scrap of paper from the yearbook.'

'David Quinn's picture?'

'Yes. We recovered a thumbprint belonging to one Timothy Gilman, and the index finger on the back was matched to Ronald Gray's.'

'Great. Anything else?'

She heard the hesitation in Sorensen's voice. 'There's a smudge.'

'How big a smudge? What kind of smudge?'

'It's a layered mess of more than one print. The original piece of paper is small. If more than one person held it the likelihood is that their prints overlapped in most places, so that it's already pretty darn lucky we have one for Gilman and one for Gray.'

'Amy, somewhere in that mess there could be the print of the man who copied the yearbook photo for Gilman.'

'You're asking me to analyze, separate and match maybe four or five overlapping prints on the chance that one of them might belong to someone else?'

'Is that something you can do?'

'No.'

'Oh.' Madison's heart dropped to the floor.

'I mean, I can't do it but there is a particular software which uses a new algorithm to separate overlapped fingerprints estimating the orientation field of each individual component.'

'Amy, you are the bright center of my universe.'

'Yeah, yeah, that's what you say now. I'm making no promises, Madison. It's an experimental technique.'

'If we had anything at all to match to our prime suspects it would be a huge help.'

'I heard you've got one guy in California and one about to fly the coop.'

'Yes, that's pretty much what we have.'

'I'll do what I can.'

Locard, Madison said to herself. *I believe in Locard.* Every contact.

Fynn had rejected her idea of a blank recall of all the yearbooks as inpractical, which she disagreed with but could understand. However, it was still a potential avenue to explore once they could narrow the pool of suspects down from the hundreds who had bought it in the first place.

*

Madison chugged down some yoghurt drink that she had remembered to bring in from home and read Kelly's report: he had gone through most of McMullen's previous associates and it seemed unlikely that any of them had the contacts or the capital to get Conway on board. Still, where there's a will, she thought . . . The problem with organizing anything from inside a prison is *communication*, and the bulk of McMullen's seemed to be letters to and from voluntary groups and charities.

A television monitor was turned on with the sound muted in the corner of the detectives' room. The news anchor started his next item and John Cameron's arrest picture flashed behind him. Madison read the title line on the bottom of the screen and did not need to hear his commentary. Then they played Nathan Quinn's appeal from start to finish. *One down, three to go.* Except that now the count had changed. Madison knew those words well and what evil spirit they had conjured up: two nights ago she had looked straight into his dead eyes.

The sky had rolled out a blanket of heavy rain clouds and wherever they were coming from, it looked like they'd never run out. Madison turned up the collar of her jacket and felt the fat raindrops splash over her hair before she could make it into her car.

Lieutenant Fynn had given her his blessing, Kelly had given her his customary sour look, and Spencer and Dunne had wished her good luck with it.

The downtown traffic faded around her as she hit I-5 due south and picked up speed toward Seward Park.

Nathan Quinn opened his front door. He was still wearing the suit he'd worn in court and the result of the hearing seemed to have done little to lighten his mood.

Madison walked in and took stock of the brand new alarm system that had been installed since she had been here last. She had called him from the precinct parking lot. 'Now that Cameron is out we need to talk: no guards, no visiting room regulations. I have news you want to hear and I need his help. I'm on my way.'

Quinn had his hands full with carrier bags packed with plastic containers that had just been delivered from The Rock.

'Mr. O'Keefe's good work?' Madison said.

'Yes. He got food delivered to me in hospital every day without fail. Would have done the same for Jack in KCJC but apparently it's not allowed.'

Donny O'Keefe was the head chef at The Rock; Madison had met him weeks earlier. He was fiercely loyal and had been a player in the regular poker nights at the restaurant. They had played their last game in December, late at night after closing time, and James Sinclair had been there – only days before his murder.

For a moment Madison asked herself what it would be like to play poker with these men who hid so much and risked so much. Probably not very different from what she was about to do.

Although the rain made it impossible to see across Lake Washington John Cameron was standing by the floor-to-ceiling window and looking out. He'll do a lot of that for a while, Madison thought. Even one afternoon inside a jail made her feel claustrophobic.

When he turned he was the man she had first met in her home, who had looked over the books on her shelves while she made coffee, before they'd talked about death and madness and how it had crept into their lives. The convict was gone.

'Detective,' Cameron said. 'Nathan had not told me about the break-in before we came back here today. What did you make of it?'

'They were looking for any evidence he might have that connected Timothy Gilman to the kidnap. They wanted to find out if Lee or Gray had spoken to him and what they'd said. They didn't find what they were looking for and they left.'

Cameron nodded: it was a puzzle that he turned around in his hands, seeing how the different color squares fit together. By now she had seen him in her home, in the forest and in jail, and still she was not used to his presence.

Good. Don't get used to it. Never get used to it. One day down the line you'll be glad you didn't.

'What is your news, Detective?' Quinn said.

They sat around the table.

'We recovered a print from an item that came with your brother's medal. The print is Gilman's,' Madison said. 'If you ever questioned the validity of your original source, Mr. Quinn, or the legitimacy of that accusation, now you know it was valid.'

She managed to keep her tone flat. There was a beat of silence.

'I've never questioned the validity of my source,' Quinn said quietly, 'but I'm glad you found the print.'

If something passed between the men it was too subtle for Madison to notice.

'What other item?' Cameron asked her.

The question was always the same: how much can you give John Cameron and still keep the investigation safe and the suspects alive?

'I will tell you about the other item if you answer a question I have for you. And I can be as exhaustive about it as you wish but I will expect the same in return.'

'That depends on your question.'

Madison was sure that the boy Cameron had never told anyone, and by the time he was a young man it would have been too late. 'I need you to tell me exactly what happened the day of the kidnap.'

'Why?'

'Because we have one of the kidnappers in custody, and I can't tell whether what he's saying is a result of the years in a psychiatric institution or there is something there – a thread I can grasp that will get me to the truth.'

Cameron didn't look away and his gaze was as direct as always. 'You're asking a lot of me, Detective.'

'Yes, I am.'

Quinn, sitting between them, seemed to be barely breathing. If Madison was right he had never heard the story either.

Madison wouldn't even guess what could sway Cameron's opinion one way or the other: maybe it was the fact that here they were, sitting pleasantly in Quinn's living room, because she had signed a statement that said she'd never seen the handgun he had pointed at Salinger's head or the knife he had held against his brow. Maybe it was something else she couldn't even fathom.

'Okay,' Cameron said. And, minute by minute, John Cameron told them exactly what had happened on August 28, 1985. He began from the moment the blue van turned up at Jackson Pond up until the run onto the Upper Hoh Road at dawn when a trucker saw him and stopped.

Madison listened, absorbing the story and creating a space for it inside herself almost as if it had been her own, although she knew that Cameron wasn't really telling her, he was telling Quinn. After twenty-five years he was finally telling his friend the only story that had ever mattered between them.

Cameron had not held back the details and Madison didn't need to ask him any questions. She had heard what she needed to hear.

'The other item recovered with the medal was a fragment of a photocopy,' she said. 'The top corner of the page of a yearbook with David Quinn's school picture. It was circled in pencil and it had Timothy Gilman's and Ronald Gray's prints on it.'

'For the kidnappers to identify you,' Quinn said.

Cameron nodded. Madison had no doubt his memories were as sharp today as they had always been; the worst moments of her own childhood had hardly lost their fine, bitter edge.

'I think a drink would be appropriate.' Cameron stood up. 'Coffee or bourbon, Detective?'

'Coffee, thank you.'

Quinn opened the door to the deck and went outside. Madison let him be. All those years ago he had probably begged that little boy to tell him what had happened; it didn't make it any easier to hear it today, even knowing that this time something would come of it.

She busied herself studying the telescope until Cameron came back with their drinks and Quinn returned indoors – the rain had spattered his suit, his hair was damp and he looked ready to walk barefoot to hell.

'What can you tell us about the fire the other night?' he said to Madison.

She gave them what details she could, which excluded the conversation with Vincent in the gardens and the fact that they had Sullivan – or whatever his name was – in custody.

'This man from the clinic,' Cameron said. 'How sure are you that he was involved?'

'He's too damaged to be of any use to you, Mr. Cameron. Either as a witness or a source of whatever retribution you might seek.'

'How sure are you?'

'I'm sure,' Madison replied. 'But all his mind has kept are the scraps of his memories. He barely knows his own name at this point.'

'And yet you mean to use him, do you not? To wring what you can out of this poor soul?'

'We're interviewing him, yes.'

'And after you're done with your questions? What will happen then? Will he get a pass back to a life of soft foods and plastic cutlery?'

'I honestly don't know. And I can't begin to imagine what your feelings on that matter might be, both of you. But if you saw him, if you saw that strange eerie creature, you would get no joy from killing him with your own hands – if that's what you have in mind.

I think vengeance is trickier than that, and if you are going to do it the subject should at least be aware of the reason he's about to die. Killing this man would give you nothing. He's defenseless and so slight you'd break him with a harsh look.'

She had their full attention and she continued. 'On the other hand, take someone like Timothy Gilman, someone who had spent his life dispensing evil. Maybe finally someone caught up with him, someone who had the knowledge of Gilman's crimes, but it would never stand up in court. So, he dealt with him. Alone, quietly, and in a very tidy manner.'

'He *dealt* with him?' Cameron said.

Madison took a sip of her coffee. 'Yes. Alone, quietly, and in a very tidy manner. Because to do it any other way would bring more damage and pain than he could bear to inflict on Gilman's surviving victims.'

Madison looked from one man to the other. Quinn's scars looked livid against his skin, his eyes darker than she had ever seen them.

'That's my theory,' she said. 'I have no proof and in all likelihood I never will. My feeling is whoever caught up with Gilman is long dead too. Maybe he's Gilman's last true victim.'

'Maybe,' Cameron said, the truth resting on a single word.

Madison finished her coffee and left. Even though there had been an exchange of information she wasn't sure which side had gained the most. She arrived home and changed into her running gear, her back-up piece fitting easily under the cotton sweatpants. The rain was seeping through the hood and her hands were freezing. There are no sides, she thought – not about this. Not anymore.

Her feet bounced on the wet concrete and in minutes she was drenched. She kept running because it was easier to think about Cameron's story while she was moving. The streets around the neighborhood were empty and she followed the road parallel to the water.

The black tarmac was strewn with leaves and twigs, slippery and snapping underfoot.

Madison ran and let the words come as they wished because some stories take you and change you and will not let you get hold of them whole. Some stories splinter and the shards dig themselves deep under the skin.

What she'd heard stayed with her while she showered and put on clean, dry clothes; while she cooked herself a steak and ate it at the table, adding to her notes and sipping from a longneck; it stayed with every breath she took until she slipped at last into a broken sleep.

Nathan Quinn listened to the wind rattling the windows one by one as the rain gushed against the glass. He had drunk a measure of bourbon with Jack tonight, as he had promised himself only twenty-four hours earlier, and another one after that.

He hadn't known when he'd woken up this morning that by the time he went to bed many of the questions he'd been asking himself for years would be answered. It had been nearly impossible to listen to the story. Madison's steady calm had helped him: she hadn't interrupted, she hadn't asked questions, she had listened with focus and compassion.

He should have known that she would work out what had happened to Gilman, that she wouldn't give up until she did. One day, if Jack continued his life on the path he had chosen, Detective Madison would be the most serious danger that he would face. But not today and not about Gilman. In the same night she had managed to be both a threat and a source of comfort.

He was awake in the darkness for a while then got up and went to the living room.

Cameron was staying in the guest bedroom: the door was open and the room was empty. As soon as they'd arrived home from the

2222222222222222

courthouse he had altered the alarm system so that Jack could come and go without him. His Ford Explorer had been parked in Quinn's garage.

Quinn didn't need to check to know that the car was gone too.

Chapter 55

John Cameron drove fast on the deserted road due east toward the neighborhood of Admiral above Alki Beach. One of the advantages of a ride at 2.30 a.m. was that a tail would be easy to spot. After leaving the house he had spent forty minutes making sure that he was not trailing any unwanted parties. Once he was sure he was not being followed he took a turn and headed for his destination.

About twenty-four hours earlier he had been running around in the main yard of a jail with the red dots from the rifle scopes dancing on his back. They might even be there tonight, looking down from their towers at the empty yard and aiming their rifles at the shadows. We all have our jobs to do, Cameron thought as he breathed in the salt air and the pine trees.

He keyed in the entry code for an unassuming gate and waited until it swung open, drove in, and waited again to make sure that it would shut properly behind him.

There was a lot of ground around the house, a simple three-bedroom house on the top of Duwamish Head – probably more ground than usual for the area. Cameron had bought it in another man's name and no person alive or dead knew of its connection to him.

He put his key in the door and turned off the alarm. His hand hovered above the light switch and he decided against it. In a few steps he was in the living room and there was the real reason he had bought the house: one wall was entirely glass. Elliott Bay and downtown Seattle, the lights glimmering in the distance in spite of the early hour. The cloud cover was still hugging the city close and it reflected back a sickly orange glow. The room itself was bright with it.

Cameron went to work: he needed to pack a bag and pick up a few items without which he felt *underdressed*. The clothes went into a soft weekend leather bag. The rest needed holsters and sheaths. A slim knife with a 6-inch blade found its place next to his inner arm, a snub-nose Glock .38 into an ankle holster by his foot, and a Smith & Wesson semiautomatic .40 in its holster went on the bottom of the bag among the clothes together with extra ammunition for both weapons.

The drive back to Seward Park went just as smoothly. Cameron disarmed the alarm system and went to his room. When Quinn woke up a few hours later, Cameron had already made coffee.

Chapter 56

Alice Madison sat at her desk at 7 a.m. and started her day with take-out coffee and a granola bar. She read through the overnight reports in case any witnesses had suddenly and unexpectedly come forward. None had.

She composed an email to Fred Kamen at the FBI and attached Henry Sullivan's arrest file.

> We have this man in custody. He's part of Peter Conway's crew and has been involved in at least three murders and an arson attack on a psychiatric clinic. We know him as Henry Sullivan, he's lawyered up and he's not talking.

The reply came back in minutes:

> I'll let you know if he's been active around here.

Madison didn't hold much hope but they had to spread their net as wide as possible: just because Sullivan was not in the system it didn't mean someone wouldn't recognize his face from somewhere. People have lives: they live in neighborhoods, shop at supermarkets and gas up their cars. Someone somewhere must know his real name and where on this Earth he called home.

Madison thought about the man she had observed from behind the mirror and his behavior with Spencer and Dunne. How much of Conway's brand of evil was in this man? And how much did Sullivan know of Conway's plans?

At 8 a.m. Dunne had brought donuts and good news: Sullivan's room had been booked on a credit card registered to a Peter Curtis, fictitious resident of Missoula, Montana. They could trace each payment on the card and see where it would lead them, and even though it had not been used from the moment that Conway had been warned off coming back to the Silver Pines, it was their first proper lead.

The weather had gone from grim to morose and under the drizzle the detectives split the credit card payments and began to check each one, travelling from petrol station to diner to outfitters and piecing together the movements of Conway and his men. Some of these establishments had closed-circuit cameras, and some of those cameras worked.

Madison was getting rained on in a petrol station forecourt in Everett when a call came through her cell.

'It's Deputy Walbeck from Pierce County.'

It took Madison a second to remember. *Jerry Wallace.*

'Deputy,' she said.

'I've got some news and it's pretty bad. Did you know the man?' the officer said, trying to gauge how to best deliver the information, whether she was talking to an acquaintance or a stranger.

'No, I've never met him.'

'Well, we found human remains. The body of a man had been doused with lighting fluid, set alight and then dumped in South Prairie Creek. What was left didn't look human at all. Only good thing I can say about it is that he died of two GSWs to the head and didn't feel a thing after that. The daughter identified a ring he was wearing.'

'Deputy, we're holding a man who might have been involved in it. He's just been arrested and goes by the name Henry Sullivan. You might want to check any trace evidence found in the house against his DNA. He's already been connected to a murder here.'

'Will do.'

Out of the blue the sharp scent of petrol from the pumps hit Madison. *Lighting fluid and a match.*

Chapter 57

John Cameron finished reading the last document and replaced it on top of all the others. They had spent the day going through Hollis's files and matching Cameron's account of the events with the reality of who these men were.

'Nathan,' he said abruptly, 'do you remember that last Fourth of July when we went to Conrad Locke's estate?'

Quinn nodded.

'David, Jimmy and I went off wandering by ourselves in the woods and Jimmy said something. He said that he'd overheard his father talking to someone on the phone and saying that he would use his bat to put a dent in their future if they ever came back to the restaurant.'

'Jimmy's father said that?'

'Yes.'

'What else?'

'Nothing. That's all he'd heard. We thought it was pretty grown-up stuff and decided to keep our ears open and see what was going to happen. Did David ever mention it to you?'

'No.' Quinn had left that night before the fireworks and had not come back for days.

They were both thinking the same thing and Cameron said it. 'Is it possible that something happened between Jimmy's father and one of these men who'd come around like jackals sniffing for easy prey?'

'Jimmy's father was not the kind of man who responded to threats with a baseball bat.'

'Like I would? People do strange things when they're afraid.'

Quinn didn't reply. He was thinking about Jimmy's father – always kind, always ready to play with the younger kids. Had the jackals threatened the boys?

Later, while Quinn was on the phone to the alarm company, the doorbell went and it was the daily delivery from Chef O'Keefe. Cameron opened the front door and walked up to the gate. The chef was a world-class poker player and it was their luck that he was just as good in the kitchen. During the weeks in KCJC his senses had been dulled by the quality of the prison food and O'Keefe's clam chowder had been a fitting return to life.

The gate opened and he moved to take the packages from the delivery man – a busboy he didn't know wearing whites under a leather jacket, his motorcycle helmet on the bike's seat.

The movement was subtle: perhaps a shift in the man's eyes, perhaps a rushed move forward to pass him the bags. Cameron's heartbeat was as slow as his instincts were quick. If he held the bags both of his hands would be full. And then he saw the Taser gun ready to fire.

Cameron let go of the bags as he lunged forward faster than the man could step backwards. The busboy pulled back his gun hand to have enough room to fire but Cameron had already reached for his knife and struck in one swift movement. The man's white throat was exposed and vulnerable. A single lethal slash and the blood flew in a red arc. The man fell backwards, eyes wide and taking short ragged breaths. *It's never just one man.* Cameron turned snake-fast and the blade hit a soft target behind him, then Taser wires found him and his muscles tensed and cramped as the electric shock traveled through his body.

Three men in total: one down, one injured.

Hands cuffed him behind his back and snapped tape over his mouth. Hands lifted him off the ground and pushed him into the back of a van. He saw two men grab the body of their dead comrade off the tarmac and throw him roughly next to him on the van.

They shoved the door closed and were off. It had lasted seconds, it had happened in complete silence. Cameron's last thought, as a needle in the arm sent him to sleep, rang out from the overwhelming darkness: *Nathan's not here, Nathan's safe.*

Nathan Quinn's call from the alarm company had ended unexpectedly: he noticed the front door open and heard car doors slam shut and the screech of tires on the asphalt. He was already dialing 911 when he reached the gate and saw the Taser gun on the ground in a pool of blood – more blood than he thought a human being could ever contain. Quinn spoke to Dispatch as clearly and calmly as he could. His second call, moments later, was to Madison.

Chapter 58

John Cameron awoke in the half gloom of the back of the van. He gave himself a couple of seconds for his awareness to come back fully and then took stock of his body. He was blindfolded with a strip of fabric. His hands were cuffed – plastic cuffs – behind his back. A larger cuff had been locked just below his knees and a third above his ankles. He couldn't move his feet apart but by lifting them an inch off the floor, he could tell that the holster where his snub-nosed Glock had been was empty. There was bunched-up fabric rough against his cheek and they had placed him on his side in the recovery position. It made it more difficult for him to choke on his own vomit if he reacted to the drugs. All in all, an efficient and professional job.

The men had laid a thin cotton sheet over him: if someone took a look inside, and he was still sedated, they'd see a lump of white wedged between the usual debris of a working man's van.

Cameron felt the tiny bumps and shudders from the van floor and he knew they were travelling fast on a tarmac road. He listened for voices but no one was talking in the cabin.

He relaxed his muscles as much as he could to counteract the odd spasm as a consequence of the Taser hit and because being tense would bring nothing useful to the situation. He wasn't physically hurt, he wasn't bleeding, and the fact that they'd used a Taser gun meant that, at least for the moment, they wanted him whole and intact. A burning ache radiated from the spot on his side where the darts had hit, but that was all. On the other hand, he had seen their faces and that meant that at some point he wouldn't stay whole and intact.

And what had they done with the body of their dead colleague? Cameron shifted a little and felt a shape next to him on the floor. Just then the van turned into a dirt track and the vibrations became harder.

After a few minutes he heard voices whispering in the cabin, the engine slowed down and the brakes came on. They had stopped.

Cameron couldn't see and couldn't move and wisdom told him to stay still and let them think that he was sedated. He was curious about these people who had managed what many others hadn't, and he would learn a lot more about them if they thought he was unconscious.

The door slid open with a rush of cold air. The van creaked as the men climbed in the back. Each took hold of one extremity of the dead body, and they climbed back out.

Cameron listened hard: no traffic and the men's steps pushing their way through undergrowth and bushes.

'Here,' one said, and a heavy burden thudded onto the ground.

Steps walked back to the van and someone picked up something off the floor. Something fluid splashed inside a container. The man stopped where he was and Cameron felt his eyes crawling over him. He kept his breathing regular under the sheet and let his chest rise and fall and rise and fall. After a beat the man moved away.

'Awake?' one asked.

'Don't think so,' the other replied.

The smell of lighting fluid is unmistakable: Cameron heard the match and the first flames lapping the body of the dead man. It didn't take long for the sweet and acrid smell to hit and the remains to be consumed.

A few minutes later the men came back; one of them lifted the sheet and felt the pulse on Cameron's carotid with two fingers. Cameron didn't move. His heartbeat kept its slow, steady rhythm. The man measured one minute and then left; the door slid shut and the engine came back to life. They were traveling again.

John Cameron lost track of time. The only thing he knew for sure was that by that point his kidnappers had spent a lot more time with him than they had with either Warren Lee or Ronald Gray. If they wanted from him the same kind of information they had asked of the others, there were plenty of places that didn't require traveling and would do just fine.

The van stopped and this time he couldn't fake or they'd know. The voices were whispering and John Cameron prepared himself to meet his abductors. Someone lifted the sheet.

'I can see you're awake.' The voice was East Coast, not a mile south of Jersey. 'We're going to stretcher you out of the van and if you try to move, try to speak, try for anything but complete immobility, I will Taser you again and this time it will be much worse. Do you understand? You stay calm and we stay calm.'

I am calm, Cameron thought. *I am serene.*

They lifted his body with some difficulty and strapped him to a stretcher. One of the men groaned as they carried him off the van. Probably the man he had injured, Cameron thought. Under the blindfold the air was sharp and clean and felt miles away from the city. Trees whispered in the breeze and the rest was silence.

They brought him indoors and down the steps into what could be a basement. He would know soon enough. John Cameron relaxed his body against the military-style stretcher: he wasn't afraid to die even if his pragmatic nature told him it was a real possibility. The men had already made a few mistakes and they were bound to make more. In his company, even one could be fatal.

Someone ripped the tape off his mouth and removed the blindfold, and he saw them. The leader was early forties, about 6 foot tall and skinny. Dead eyes in a sallow, hawkish face. The other was a little younger, just as tall, and built like ropes of muscle wrapped around bone. A large bandage on his side told Cameron where his blade had made contact.

The basement was one large room with a dirt floor; a dank coppery scent permeated the walls. A few hooks hung from the ceiling and in a corner stood a table next to a large sink. A hunter's cabin, rented by the day or the week, deep in the wilderness. Men come here to do their hunting and their killing.

A number of bare light bulbs had been strung up and connected, which made their one half of the room brighter than the other. The younger man approached Cameron and wiped the blood of their dead partner off Cameron's face with a wet wipe. His eyes were blank and did not meet the prisoner's.

The leader took out a cell phone from a pocket of his black cargo pants and pointed the tiny eye of the camera at Cameron. He walked around him and Cameron realized he was not taking photographs, he was shooting video. The man made sure he had footage of his prisoner front and back, then he grabbed a ski mask from his colleague, pulled it down, turned the camera toward his own covered face and said: 'Alive and in full working order.'

Chapter 59

Alice Madison stood over the glossy pool of blood by the gate. Under powerful lights Frank Lauren from the Crime Scene Unit was collecting some of it with a swab to compare it against John Cameron's DNA. He had already picked up the Taser gun and placed it in a paper bag.

The vehicle – Madison and everyone else assumed it was a van though they didn't know for sure – had disappeared into the traffic and so far no witnesses had come forward with a description. The motorbike of the fake delivery man had been abandoned – it would probably turn out to have been stolen somewhere in the county. The bags with the take-out food containers had been collected and tagged.

Madison had decided to avoid platitudes altogether. Quinn wouldn't thank her for the clichés and the words felt awkward on her lips. He knew what was going on, he knew who had Cameron. The only thing that mattered was to find him before his name was added to the list. Just then Madison wished she hadn't been present at Warren Lee's autopsy and seen first-hand Peter Conway's handiwork.

'How do you read the scene?' Quinn asked her.

They were in the living room and Tod Hollis had just arrived too.

'The vehicle was hiding behind the brick wall,' Madison replied. 'One of the abductors was dressed as the delivery man and his job was to Taser him while he had his hands full. My guess is he badly underestimated Cameron and it was the last thing he ever did.'

Quinn nodded. He had reached the same conclusion but wanted to see the blood test result anyway. The difference was between Cameron captive and healthy, and Cameron captive and seriously injured. It was different degrees of awfulness.

Madison didn't know what to make of the Taser gun: it had not been used on the other victims and it left Cameron intact after a bad shock. The notion that they wanted him in one piece to accomplish what they needed was not a reassuring thought. She didn't need to express it, she could see it in Quinn's eyes.

Normally a kidnap might involve a ransom, a call for money to be offered in exchange for a life. No one in the room expected a call. All they had to anticipate the next event was to look at the pattern of Conway's past actions. And that told them that the next thing that would happen was the recovery of a body.

Hollis went outside and Madison approached Quinn. The front door was still open, with police officers coming and going.

'Where did you put his things?' she asked him quietly.

'What things?'

'Mr. Quinn, there were detectives in Cameron's room and all they found was a bag of clothes.'

She could see he was debating within himself – ever the defense attorney.

'Do you think I care about an illegal possession charge? I just need to know what he might have had on himself, if anything,' she said. 'I think we can safely assume he had a knife and that he used it.'

They were crossing too many boundaries for Quinn to keep track, or to care. He had to trust her now or regret it forever. His words were measured: he was giving Madison enough ammunition to get him disbarred.

'Before the patrol cars arrived I removed a Smith & Wesson semiautomatic .40 in its holster. It was in the bag of clothes,' Quinn conceded.

He had hidden from the police a potentially illegal weapon whose serial number had been filed away and which could have been used in a number of felonies.

'Where is it now?'

'In the attic, in a box.'

'With ammunition?'

'Yes.'

'Okay,' she said. 'Do you know if he wore an ankle holster with a back-up piece?'

'This conversation is surreal.'

'Yes, it is. Did he wear an ankle holster?'

'In the bag there was also ammunition for another weapon. Why does it matter?'

'Because Conway is very experienced but he has never dealt with anyone like Cameron, and we don't know how he's going to negotiate this particular situation. And Cameron does not make for the ideal hostage, especially if he's armed.'

'He will never give them what they want,' Quinn said. 'And they will not be able to make him . . . afraid, like the others.'

Madison nodded. And, if Conway was a sadist, it was the worst thing that Cameron could do.

A detective from the South Precinct arrived to take Quinn's statement and Madison let her get on with it. She watched Quinn as he spoke without emotion and gave her the details she asked. Madison could see the shadow of his fear: he was keeping that door locked and bolted but she felt the weight pressing against it. He spoke with the detective but his black eyes stayed with Madison.

Madison drove to the Seattle jail without taking much notice of the road. She stopped at the right times and started at the right times but her mind was elsewhere and her heart was in the Hoh River Forest, by the pit that had held the body of a child. Now the hidden man wanted to finish the job that he'd started twenty-five years ago and Madison would not – could not – let him.

She had considered – briefly – a phone call to Fynn or Spencer or maybe Brown, then she'd realized that she couldn't drag them into this.

She showed her badge and asked the custody officer on shift to bring out Henry Sullivan. Whether he wanted to wait for his attorney to speak to her was up to him – Madison didn't care one way or the other.

Thirty minutes later, Richard Bowen trudged through the door. 'Do you know what time it is?'

'Sorry, Richard. This couldn't wait.'

'What couldn't wait?'

They entered the room. Sullivan was already there; his small eyes went to Madison. They had not met before. Bowen sat down heavily next to the prisoner and Madison took her place on the other side of the table.

'What is this about?' Bowen started. 'We have already had interviews with Detectives Spencer and Dunne.'

'That was before,' Madison said.

Thirty minutes waiting for the lawyer were that all she'd had and all that she'd needed. Thirty minutes on a wooden bench in a corridor to focus and find the voice of the Lost: the voice Henry Sullivan would recognize, the only voice he would hear.

'Mr. Sullivan's colleagues have kidnapped a man,' she said to the attorney. 'It is possible that one of the abductors was fatally injured; however, what we have here is a kidnap that your client knew was going to happen but did not nothing to help us prevent.'

'You don't know that he knew—'

'He knew. It was planned and they were just waiting for the victim to be within reach to snatch him.'

Henry Sullivan didn't react. Madison knew he wouldn't: he had been well trained and had probably seen more horror working with Conway than even the worst jail could conjure up.

'Here's the thing,' Madison said. 'We have evidence to place you at the crime scene and connect you to a murder, possibly two. We have the criminal possession charge for that small arsenal that we found in your hotel room. But none of this has made a dent. Is that right, Richard?'

The attorney was not sure where the wind was blowing.

Madison sat back in her chair and thought about the years passed watching her father play poker: with poor players, with good ones and with great ones – the ones who flow with the game like it's white water.

'This is what I've been thinking about – we've never met before tonight but I watched you with Spencer from the box,' Madison said. 'And I asked myself, *What is this man afraid of? What does this man want?*'

Henry Sullivan didn't speak but she had his full attention.

'You haven't asked for a deal to make things easier for you. Why is that? A little information to keep the King County Prosecutor's Office happy would go a long way to keep the needle from your arm. It's a long list: Warren Lee, Ronald Gray, Jerry Wallace, Thomas Creed.'

'Detective—' Bowen interrupted.

Madison stood up and made to leave. 'I just wanted to tell you that tomorrow morning every single media outlet will carry an item to the effect that Henry Sullivan – not your real name but who cares, Conway will know it's you – is helping the Seattle Police Department with our investigation, and in fact you are being so cooperative that we are considering giving you immunity for all your charges. And if your lawyer denies it, it will only look like you're trying to protect him from the only thing that he's afraid of: Peter Conway.'

'You cannot do that,' Bowen said.

'Maybe I *should* not do that, but I sense that the time of *should* and *shouldn't* has come and gone. Do you have a family, Mr. Sullivan? By that I mean, do you have a family Conway knows about? A wife, children, old and vulnerable parents perhaps? Once he's done here, once he's finished what he started, where do you think Conway will go next? What if your family becomes his next project?'

'Stop right now.' Bowen stood up.

Madison thought of the eyes that had stared at her in the burning building and sought to find that place without humanity or regret in herself. She spoke and her voice was low and her words distinct.

'I will find their pictures, their addresses, the place where your kids go to school and your wife does her hair, and I will put it all in your file. Protected, yes, but not so well that someone with a will wouldn't find a way. And if, by any chance, you've kept your private life hidden from Conway, in the end he will know so much about you you'll think you have a twin. Prison will not protect you and anybody else in your life – well, that's just collateral damage.'

'Stop talking right now, Detective. This interview is over.'

Henry Sullivan blinked.

'You have one hour to decide. I want the place where they're holding John Cameron, the name of the man who paid you to do this. I want everything you know, and God forbid you should hold anything back and I find out about it. A trial by jury is the last thing you should worry about. One hour,' she repeated and left the room.

Richard Bowen followed her into the corridor. 'Have you lost your mind? You can't—'

'Go back in there, Richard, and convince your client that the sane thing to do is to share every little scrap of information he has with us.'

'You've just threatened his family.'

'I don't even know whether he has a family but Jerry Wallace had a daughter, and he's dead. Thomas Creed had two daughters, and he's dead. I'll be happy to forward you the autopsy reports for Lee and Gray. He's not afraid of anything we wave in his face because the man he works for is much, much worse than anything you or I or a maximum security prison can ever do to him. And that man's holding a live hostage right now this minute. Do you want to keep playing legal tic-tac-toe or do you want to help me get the hostage back alive?'

'I want to protect my client's rights.'

'If you want to help your client, tell him to talk to us.'

Bowen shook his head and went back in.

Madison leant against the wall: she had found the voice alright or maybe it was the other way round. A wave of clammy coldness rose in her gut and she barely made it to the nearest restroom just a few feet away.

Madison splashed water on her face and drank from the faucet, and when she went back Bowen was waiting for her.

'Some things he knows, some things he guessed, others Conway just kept to himself because this is how he works.'

Senior Deputy Prosecuting Attorney Sarah Klein walked through the doors of the Seattle jail a few minutes after midnight. Madison was waiting for her. Klein looked like she always did: whatever hour of the day or night, Madison knew that she would be immaculate in silk and Italian wool. Klein was sharp and crazy enough to dare argue against attorney–client privilege in front of Judge Martin, and win one for the team. Madison was glad to have her on board.

'Tell me you didn't threaten the suspect's family,' Klein said as they stepped into the elevator.

'I didn't,' Madison replied. 'I told him if he didn't give us what we needed I'd tell the media that he was helping us. What happened after that would be out of my hands.'

'And were you prepared to go through with it if he didn't?'

'What do you think?'

'I think you're glad you don't have to make that decision.'

'There was never going to be a decision. What we know of the kidnapper is that by this point his hostages are usually dead, after torture and evil we can't even imagine. There was no time for subtlety: Henry Sullivan has seen it happen and he knows what human beings are capable of. I just used it against him.'

'Well, Jeez, he sure believed you well enough because he doesn't even want you in the room when he tells us.'

'Here.' Madison passed Klein a list of questions. 'Something to start him off.'

The elevator's door opened.

'Bowen said you called his family *collateral damage*.'

'I did.'

The words had come out of her mouth before she could stop herself.

'Well, whatever you said . . . here we are, though I wouldn't expect a medal for it. I think Bowen needed a change of pants.'

They had reached the room where Sullivan was waiting. Madison went into the observation box.

Richard Bowen sat with his client on one side of the table; Spencer and Dunne sat on the other. Sarah Klein took a seat at the head and her eyes found Madison on the other side of the mirror.

Chapter 60

John Cameron breathed through the blindfold: the bindings were tight around his wrists and legs and his body needed to shift position. They had left him in the basement, lying on the stretcher, and he had taken stock of the house around him, following their heavy steps above him as he became familiar with their gait, their bearing and the weight and speed behind their movements. The younger man limped a little on the side he was hurting; the older one moved lightly and with purpose.

Cameron had kept track of time as best he could: it must have been just before dawn judging from the bird calls. He didn't think about what the future might bring, he thought only of the present and of this man who had not yet revealed to him the turn of his soul and the bend of his heart.

Cameron didn't think about the night he had spent tied to a tree next to James Sinclair: Madison was right, the boy he had been was long dead and the man who lay in the basement today had made more enemies and ended more lives than that boy would have ever thought possible.

He heard the door open and steps coming down. His blindfold came off and Peter Conway stood above him.

'I think you should know who you're dealing with,' he said, and he injected Cameron in the arm.

The effect was immediate: a numbing of the body and the instant realization that he could not breathe, that his chest could not rise and his lungs would not take in air, that his body had turned to stone.

Conway clicked a stopwatch then he took out a knife and cut through the plastic cuffs that bound Cameron's wrists, calves and ankles. 'It's Suxamethonium Chloride and it's a muscle relaxant used for anesthesia. It induces instant paralysis.'

Cameron knew exactly what it was and that his body was dead to him: he could not move and he could not breathe.

'You see, when they give it to patients they have to breathe for them otherwise they suffocate.' Conway stood over him and his eyes were a blank empty nothing.

He must have injected him on the exhale because Cameron's lungs were empty and every cell of his body was already slamming and crashing against a brick wall.

Cameron's mind kept a calm vigil while his whole being fell into an inescapable panic. He was shutting down: this strange death travelled up his body shutting down the system as it went like the lights in an empty house. Soon, so soon, he wouldn't be able to think anymore. How long had it been?

'Do you understand?' Conway said and he watched his prisoner.

Cameron's body screamed for air while he lay on his back utterly still, his limbs unbound, his eyes open and tears streaming down his cheeks because he couldn't blink.

'Do you understand who you're dealing with?'

Conway wiped a lock of hair away from Cameron's brow.

Thoughts came in blinding flashes. How long had it been? How long before permanent damage? Cameron focused on a dark mark on the wooden ceiling straight above him. There was pain, excruciating pain – different from anything he had ever experienced – but there was no fear.

'They say it's like being buried alive,' Conway said.

His body was burning and his heart . . . Cameron grasped at one last thought and hung on to it in the thickening darkness: a stopwatch. Conway had a stopwatch. *And my body lies on a distant shore* . . . Cameron was drowning . . . *at the end of the longest night.* He wasn't afraid because he wasn't anything anymore, he was out of that tomb of flesh and stone.

Then the bag closed over his mouth and Conway began to ventilate him with the bag-valve mask that pushed air back into lungs. It flowed in like water over scorched earth and Conway kept the puffs steady and regular.

How many times has he done this?

After one minute, like some kind of miracle, Cameron blinked and twitched the fingers of his right hand.

'Easy come, easy go,' Conway said.

It took some time for Cameron to start breathing naturally; when he did Conway pulled the mask away. There was no question of the prisoner even being able to sit up, let alone put up any kind of resistance. Conway sat back against the wall and studied Cameron as his body slowly came back to him.

After a while, when Cameron was barely able to stand, Conway walked him to a bathroom in a corner of the basement. Cameron put his head under the cold water and drank. He was too weak to take the opportunity and fight Conway, and the man knew it. He lay back on the stretcher, dizzy with the effort and seemingly disoriented. Conway replaced the cuffs on his wrists and on his ankles, and this time Cameron's hands rested on his front.

Conway left without a word.

How ridiculous, Cameron thought. How sad and pathetic and utterly ridiculous to die in a silly little cabin from the administration of a perfectly mundane drug used every day in every hospital and by the hand of a complete stranger.

The death Cameron had dealt from his hand had been to men he had known well and who had known him. It was the only way it made sense to him. This, this was a bloodless death to satisfy the itch of a petty executioner.

Cameron turned his body to one side: his head pounded and his eyes throbbed but he was not in the least disoriented. He didn't know how long he had before Conway came back or what would happen when he did: this was the basement of a hunter's cabin, a place where men brought their prey to be gutted, bled and skinned. Cameron sat up. Maybe this basement had been waiting for him for a long time, like the trapping pit had been waiting for Gilman.

It was dawn. Cameron heard it clearly now in the bird calls. He imagined it, seashell pale and freezing cold, unfolding over the cabin's roof: the tips of the Douglas firs would be black against the glow and the ground would crunch underfoot. The best time of day, his favorite.

Cameron stood up, his legs shaking a little. He raised his hands, tapped the bare bulb and it swung its light into the darker half of the basement. Above him, heavy footsteps crossed the floor.

Chapter 61

Alice Madison stood in the observation box alone. Henry Sullivan spoke of what they had done and what Conway was about to do and Madison was glad she was not in that room, glad she could not reach in through the glass and sorry, so sorry she had not shot Peter Conway through the window in the Walters Institute. She could have lived with it if she had known what she knew now. At some point Dunne looked up and straight at Madison through the mirror; she nodded at him even if he couldn't see her.

Madison met them in the corridor when they came out. Spencer and Dunne started on logistics; Klein and Bowen were quiet – attorneys had little to offer when it came to breaking down doors without warrants. There was never any question about what Madison would do.

'And you should take my car,' Dunne said.

'Thanks, Andy,' she replied.

Spencer would brief Fynn and inform the state troopers and the sheriff's office.

Dawn found Madison driving fast due north on I-5. Dunne's car was a red four-wheel-drive Chevy S10 pick-up truck – where Madison was going her Honda Civic wouldn't be much good. They had swapped keys in the parking lot after she had grabbed her emergency kit in a gym bag from the trunk.

Madison's eyes were glued to the road and yet she saw nothing. Her cell was on the passenger seat and she forced herself to pick it up. She had to keep it neutral and calm: she should tell him about plans and contingencies and search groups. She should tell him about what they were doing, what they could do, and hope that he wouldn't hear the shrill voice that kept repeating that it was already too late, much too late.

'Where is he?' Quinn's voice sounded scratchy.

'Sullivan doesn't know. Conway had been setting up a safe house somewhere north-west of Seattle, a cabin in the woods, where he'd take Cameron. Sullivan didn't know where but he knew which agency Conway was using because he glimpsed the name on Conway's laptop.'

'*Somewhere* in the Northwest?'

'I know it sounds feeble, but we're tracing the payments on Conway's credit card to tell us where he traveled, where he pumped gas and bought groceries.'

'How are you going to find him?'

'They are sending me the details of the agency's rentals and we're going to be working with local law and check each cabin. I'm on my way there now. Spencer's waking up the agency's booker and getting what information he can out of him.'

Quinn might have been exhausted, but his mind worked as well as it always did. 'I don't understand. Why is he going to all this trouble? Why is he taking Jack to a cabin hours away from Seattle when he took care of the other men quickly and locally?'

Madison held the phone close to her. 'Conway wanted a cabin that would be close to an abandoned airstrip – there's a whole bunch of them from the 1940s and 1950s dotted all over the state. He didn't kidnap Cameron to get information out of him and eliminate a witness – that was only the starting point.' Madison didn't know how to say the words. 'Peter Conway is going to *sell* Cameron to the drug dealers Cameron cheated and murdered in California. Last December Cameron killed three of them in LA from the same cartel and Errol Saunders here, and years ago there was the Nostromo.'

Quinn didn't say anything.

'When Conway got the details of the Seattle job,' she continued, 'he realized that Cameron was much more valuable to him alive than dead, and he made a deal with them. They're coming to fly him out. That's why they used a Taser gun: he needs to deliver Cameron in one piece.' Madison regretted her words immediately because she knew what Quinn would think. So *they* can rip him apart.

For a beat there was no sound at the end of the line. Madison kept the cell close and drove on.

'I'm coming with you,' Quinn said finally.

'No, you're not. I need you in Seattle going over everything you have because McMullen could be getting paroled very soon. I'll keep in touch.'

'Are you alone?'

'I won't be. The locals will be involved too but I'm the only one who has seen Conway.'

'I'm coming, I'll help with the search.'

'Quinn, listen to me. I need you to stay put. I need you to be where I know you're safe.' As far from Conway as humanly possible, she wanted to add.

Quinn didn't reply. Madison hoped his common sense would kick in: the man walked with a stick, for Chrissakes.

'Keep in touch,' he said.

And then it was just Madison alone in the car flying through the gray early morning toward Bellingham, the mountains and a promise of death.

*

If Madison had noticed the landscape she would have seen flat fields leading to water on her right, the beginning of rolling hills on her left and a lot of pallid sky – a huge dome pressing down on everything within sight. Small knots of housing developments and warehouses streaked past, neither city nor rural, suspended in a charmless urban planning limbo.

She crossed the Skagit River at Mt. Vernon and the hills on the left were a bluish smudge in the distance as if in training to become real mountains. She took Exit 255 and East Sunset Drive to get to the 542; after Deming and the turn into the Truck Road she pulled into a small rest area with a pretty diner. The woods were thick on both sides of the road and the air felt sharper. A handful of cars were parked by the wooden building, including a white Whatcom County Sheriff's Office Unit. A deputy climbed out when he saw the red pick-up. It was mid-morning and the last hours had passed in a blur.

The deputy carried a thick wad of papers and a plastic bag. He was tall and skinny with a short blond buzz cut under the hat, and didn't look a day over nineteen. Madison would have preferred someone with more than a couple of weeks' experience and possibly the ability to grow a beard.

'We were sent these by one of your people,' he said after introductions were dealt with.

Madison spread the printed sheets on the hood of the patrol car: a list of addresses for the cabins, and pages of maps with the location of local airstrips and the cabins and the stores where Conway's card had been used.

The deputy followed the line of Highway 542 with his gloved hand. 'Far as we can see we have addresses spread out in three counties: some are here in Whatcom County, but then you have a bundle in Skagit which is south, and even a handful in Okanogan all the way west. And we have the border with Canada just a rock's throw from here.'

'How many in total?' Madison looked through the list.

'Twenty-five, but we're also looking at the ones which were not booked up – just in case.'

Madison swore under her breath.

The information sheet had been filtered by the day the booking had been made and whether it was a repeat customer.

'We've eliminated some but there's still fourteen on the list, depending how close to the airstrip your man wanted to be. We've got Kendall and Riverside – they're privately owned and open for business.'

'I think our man wants something more discreet.'

'Well, we had a number but some pretty much died out and were reclaimed by the woods. Sumas – up toward the border though no one caught a glimpse of it for years – and Pasayten, Marblemount and Blankenship, but I can't tell you whether they're still in working order, and they're well spread out.'

Madison looked at the map. An airstrip in the mountains, a *turf* airstrip, was little more than a ribbon of grass surrounded by trees, wide enough for a small plane to land and take off: no control tower, no air traffic controllers and, most importantly, no lights. Whoever was flying in had to rely on natural light and that could cut the day pretty short if the weather didn't cooperate.

'Here,' Deputy Andrews said and passed Madison the plastic bag.

Inside there was a thermos, a few sandwiches, a bottle of water and candy bars. The kindness of law enforcement officers working a 2,500 square miles precinct.

'Your people said you've been driving since before dawn and, I quote, you wouldn't have stopped for red lights, let alone food and drink.'

'Thank you, that's very kind.'

The deputy blushed full crimson. 'This guy you're looking for, he's the real deal, isn't he?' he said, changing the subject.

Which guy are we talking about?

'Yes, Peter Conway is a killer – he kills people for a living. At least four in King County that we know of in the last weeks, and he has one accomplice with him.'

'We don't get many of those around here.'

'I guess not. Have you . . .' Madison didn't want to be discourteous but this was not a learn-on-the-job day and she had to know just how green he was. 'Have you dealt with this kind of situation before?'

'No.'

'Okay.'

Better to know in advance and plan for it, she thought.

'I mean, not here. But I have done a couple of tours in Afghanistan. Infantry sniper. Seen plenty of stuff there to last me a while. Some hostage situations too – that's why they sent me to meet you.'

'Right.' Madison said, feeling like a very old fool.

They went back to their respective cars and headed north-west. Behind the cloud cover the sky was light and bright. A good day to fly.

Miles and miles away, in a small room without natural light, Dr. Takemoto watched as Vincent patted the wall after drawing the latest of his lines. Vincent had not spoken to her today; he had ignored her. It looked as if soon there would be no bare wall left at all. The nurses looking after him had confirmed it: Vincent had stopped speaking almost completely. His main interaction with the world was through the worn green crayon in his hand.

Dr. Peterson studied him from the open door – Vincent's hand was shaking a little but was still capable of drawing a straight line. No one had said anything to him and he had not even asked about the night of the fire and yet, somewhere in the folds of his consciousness, the doctor was sure that Vincent had realized that Ronald was never coming back.

'What are you drawing, Vincent?' Dr. Peterson said.

Vincent turned: fear had lived with him for so long, it had been the measure of the hours and the minutes of his days, and Vincent looked exhausted by it. In spite of the constant vibration within his body he tapped the wall gently with the crayon. 'The trail,' he said.

Chapter 62

The man smoothed the bandage on his injured side: it hurt every time he breathed but at least it had stopped bleeding. *Shouldn't have gotten that close* had been Conway's only comment. It was the fifth time Conway had hired him for a job and the first he had been wounded by a target during the pick-up. This hostage did not behave like hostages do and that fact bothered the man a great deal.

He slid open the lock on the basement door – a simple bolt that Conway had installed days earlier – and went in. From the top of the stairs he could see the prisoner clearly: he lay on his side on the stretcher, wrists and ankles bound with plastic cuffs. The hostage's eyes were open and tracked him as the man walked down the stairs, suddenly conscious of his uneven gait.

Conway had left his hands tied at the front because after the Sux injection he didn't want muscle spasms or a choking fit to spoil his wares.

Shouldn't have gotten that close. The man lifted the .22 caliber handgun and pointed it at the hostage's head as he approached him. The prisoner didn't even blink: his pale brown eyes followed the man's movements and spotted the awkward lump under the shirt where the bandage was and his limp. It was like being watched by an animal.

The man came close, placed the muzzle of the gun against his brow and felt his carotid pulse with two fingers of the left hand. At that distance he wasn't going to miss the shot. The prisoner's heartbeat was steady, not even a little jolt for the inconvenience of having a gun to his head.

'Feeling better?' the man asked him.

John Cameron didn't reply.

'Any breathing problems? Muscle spasms?'

He took Cameron's silence as a negative reply, stood up and backed away. Everybody's life would take a turn for the better as soon as this package was delivered.

The lock slid back into place.

Madison glanced at the map on the passenger seat. The cabins had been split between the teams: they had three on their list. She followed Deputy Andrews's unit along the Mt. Baker Highway. He had picked up his partner on the way and had given her a radio to keep in touch and listen to the calls from the other officers, and their voices crackled and sputtered through the speaker.

After Maple Falls a bend in the road opened onto the North Fork Nooksack River: deep green flowing past the white pebble bank before the woods closed in.

Pretty, Madison thought.

Conway's old picture from Kamen's file had been handed out together with a brief but comprehensive catalogue of his achievements as a human being. John Cameron's photo had also been released with the warning that there would be a second abductor working with Conway. The sheriff's office had called in off-duty deputies and the search party was spread out all over three counties.

The first cabin on their list was ten minutes' worth of negotiating a steep narrow lane toward the border. They couldn't just roll up to the front door without an excuse and the sheriff had come up with the pretext of a missing hiker who might be injured.

Madison held back. She scrunched her hair up into a ponytail and threw a Whatcom County Citizen On Patrol green T-shirt for camouflage over her new ballistic vest. The old one could not be saved after its last engagement. As she tightened the side straps the flutter of a memory came and went. Madison checked her piece in its holster and left the pick-up.

The car parked in front of the cabin was a brand new silver SUV. The deputies knocked on the door and a minute later a woman opened the door with a toddler in her arms. They spoke briefly and then the deputies came back.

The SUV had been a give-away: whatever Conway was driving there would not be see-through windows. They were looking for a van or a small truck – it was not going to be a showroom model with kiddie toys in the back seat.

Back on the highway Madison listened to each and every word that came through on the radio as one after the other the cabins were checked and crossed off the list. The Sheriff had dispatched one unit to each airstrip known to be in the area and so far there had been no unusual traffic.

Madison kept watching the sky: every dot that could be a plane, every cloud that might mean rain and a delay in the flight. Her brain was in ticker-tape mode and would not stop: an airstrip up in the mountains required a small, agile plane and an experienced pilot; a small airplane wouldn't have enough fuel to fly up from California and back without refueling; a small airplane might take off from a British Columbia airport fully fueled, pick up its cargo and continue on to California. And if the big pay-off for Conway was the selling of his hostage then that was how McMullen had been able to afford his services – he wouldn't be paying him, the LA dealers would. *McMullen. Sweet Jesus, it was McMullen.*

Madison left a message on Dunne's voicemail to check McMullen's contacts within the jail and whether there was a chance he had met someone inside who was connected to the right people. Forget the gardening groups and the compulsory probation period: if McMullen got out, he would be gone.

Nathan Quinn picked up his cell and called Conrad Locke. He picked up on the second ring.

'Nathan, is there news?'

'No, not yet.'

The kidnapping had been all over the media since the early morning.

'Conrad, I need to ask you something,' Quinn continued. 'It's something the boys talked about that Fourth of July, 1985, when we were at your estate. I know it's a lifetime ago but you might remember about this.'

A beat of silence. Conrad Locke, friend and colleague of Quinn's father, had been present and part of all the bleak and dreadful moments of that year.

'Anything I can tell you, Nathan, I will, of course.'

'Jimmy had overheard his dad making a threat on the phone. As if someone had come around the restaurant and Jimmy's father was going to make sure they wouldn't do it again. Does that mean anything to you?'

Locke thought about it. 'I remember asking your father whether everything was alright with Sinclair and your father said there had been *issues*. He didn't say more than that and I didn't press him. Maybe I should have.'

'I know you were interviewed by the police at the time, like everybody else, but were names mentioned between you? Did my father mention anybody just between the two of you?'

'What's going on?'

'I think we're getting close. There are links between two men who were in Seattle at the time and one of the kidnappers.'

Locke sighed. 'I'm so sorry, I don't think names were ever mentioned.'

Quinn wasn't expecting a different answer but he had to ask.

'Nathan, what's happening about Jack? Are the police doing anything useful?'

'They're looking,' Quinn replied and his words sounded dead and empty.

Madison drove up and down the Mt. Baker Highway as they spoke to locals and checked the cabins on their list, and one after the other all the addresses were cleared. She felt gritty and raw from the lack of sleep.

There were so many unknowns: maybe Sullivan had been wrong and Conway didn't hire a rental from that agency or maybe he did and it was one of the empty ones they had found. Empty because the transaction had already happened and John Cameron was on his way to California or wherever his fate awaited him.

The red pick-up and the patrol car parked by the side of the road. The deputies were busy on their radios and Madison stretched her legs and thumbed through the papers mailed by Spencer.

Conway was a prudent man: he had gassed up in Bellingham where his trace would be quickly lost and bought groceries in the Kmart on East Sunset Drive – too big for anyone to remember him. The only possible bone he had thrown them was a single transaction for bottled water – a pack of twelve – at the Cross Roads Grocery & Video in Maple Falls. And all of this had happened before the remains of David Quinn had even been found. McMullen had gone into damage control mode as soon as the police had started sweeping the area where he knew the body to be buried.

Madison drank a cup of coffee from the thermos: it was warm and tasted of plastic but the gesture had been the only good thing the day had brought. She showed the map with the highlighted grocery store to Deputy Andrews.

'This place,' she said. 'This is close to the Kendall airfield, right?'

'Sure, just minutes away.'

'Okay, so what else do we have around here?'

'What *else*?'

'Yes, I'm looking at the other airstrips and they are way to the west so, if we take this grocery store as the center of a circle of, say, 20 miles, what do we have around here that's a place flat enough and long enough to land a small plane?'

'We don't have—'

'We've ran out of strips. I'm talking about a field, big and flat and long enough.'

The deputy narrowed his eyes. 'How long?'

Madison's knowledge of aeronautics was limited to the air shows her grandfather had taken her to when she was a child.

'I don't know. I'd say 700 feet if it's clear and at least double that if you have trees around it.'

Andrews thought about it for a moment. 'North of Silver Lake there's a field where people camp in the summer,' he said. 'The whole place will open up for business next month but it's still shut for the winter season.'

'Are there cabins near there? And I mean really close?'

'Yes.'

Madison flattened the map on the car's hood. 'Where is it?'

'There.' The Deputy pointed at a flash of light green on the map above the blue of the lake.

A single road dropped from the lake to Maple Falls and at the end of that road sat the Cross Roads Grocery & Video store.

Chapter 63

The Silver Lake Road snaked up between Red Mountain and Black Mountain, heading north toward the Canada border. The road left behind the residential area and started climbing quickly, thick woods on both sides alternating with fields.

Madison wanted to kick herself: she had not been thinking straight. The most important factor had to be the proximity of the place where they held Cameron to the landing field: Cameron was a dangerous hostage to move and lethal if unfettered. They had to keep travelling time to a minimum and even then getting him from A to B was going to be a complex operation.

She looked out of the window: a bright sky, and somewhere not too far away men were preparing to fly a human being toward an ugly death.

The patrol car travelled fast and so did Madison behind it. Lights and shadows flickered on her windscreen as she drove in and out of the canopy of trees.

Her cell vibrated on the passenger seat: it was Quinn's number. She watched the small screen light up and, after a beat, fade back to black. She couldn't talk to him, not really. There were no words she could offer him to describe what she must do.

*

The deputies' car pulled into a clearing with three cabins lined up and no other cars parked out front.

'There's another set of three further on,' Andrews said.

Madison and the deputies approached the first: a wooden porch jutted out and it backed straight onto the woods. Her instincts said *empty*. The door was locked and there were no lights from the side windows. They moved on to check the second.

Just then, in the shadow of the firs, the front door of the last cabin seemed to move.

'Wait,' Madison said and pointed.

There it was again – a quiver. All three took out their weapons. No sound came from the cabin, only the rustle from the top of the trees and their steps on the dirt.

There were fresh tire marks by the entrance.

Madison took her place on one side and Andrews on the other. The door was ajar and it moved in the breeze as if the house was breathing. Madison leant the tip of her Glock against it and pushed gently. She didn't know whether she was prepared for what she would find.

Someone caught his breath behind her: the room had been almost destroyed – chairs upturned, supplies spilled everywhere, a table pushed against the wall and to one side. Someone had fought a battle on every inch of that floor. On their immediate left another door was open, leading into a basement, and her eye caught the brand new bolt on it. Madison took the first step down and saw the body, her heart lurched and she ran.

The body lay on a stretcher: a tall, heavily muscled man in his late thirties with a gaping wound in his neck and slashes to his chest. He was covered in blood and he was not Peter Conway – she was sure of it. Madison checked his pulse and the man groaned.

'Do you have first aid in your car?' she said without turning round. Behind her someone hurried up the steps.

The man's hands were trying to stem the flow of blood from his neck wound. Madison knelt by his side and his eyes fluttered open.

'Where are they? Have they gone to meet the plane?'

The eyes shone unfocused.

'Where are they?'

Andrews's partner came back with bandages and got busy around the main wound. Madison stood up: signs of the struggle were all over the basement too and plastic cuffs lay in pieces on the ground. Cameron had been cuffed and managed to get away. The man – as far as Madison could see – was not armed but it probably had not started that way. Cameron had attacked him and freed himself, at least for a while. However, the way the upstairs looked and the absence of Conway's body did not bode well. The man on the ground could barely breathe; he wasn't going to tell them anything about anything.

'I'm going to the field. Is it straight on from here?' she said.

'I'm coming with you,' Andrews replied but she was already halfway up the stairs.

Madison had reached her car when Andrews caught up. 'Ma'am, what's really going on here?'

She turned to him. 'The hostage is about to be sold to men who will torture him and keep him alive just so they can inflict further excruciating pain and suffering. Right now this minute that's all I have.'

Andrews backed away one step. 'Okay.'

Madison climbed into the pick-up. 'Straight on from here?'

'Yes.'

The pick-up screeched its way out of the clearing and back into the road. In her rear-view mirror Madison saw Andrews's patrol car speeding after her and the man talking quickly on the radio.

If there were decisions to be made then she should make them now because later – should there be a later – in the midst of things she would only have time to react, not to think and certainly not to feel the ragged pain in her chest. Anything that might slow down her reaction time had to be put to one side because one thing she knew for sure was that they were going to be outnumbered and outgunned.

They made it there in minutes: Madison glimpsed it behind rows of firs and pulled in on the side of the road, almost into the ditch. The field was a long, thin, rectangular swathe clear of trees and the sky above it was just beginning to darken.

Andrews pulled in behind the pick-up. Madison racked back the slide on her Glock – one bullet in the chamber and ready. Through the trees she caught sight of the van parked at the bottom end of the field and a sound hummed in the air around them: it could have been the engine of a small plane.

She looked at the young man in the olive green uniform: Andrews had worn his ballistic vest and shouldered a sniper rifle with a scope. It wasn't the soft armor protection worn by most: it was hard-plate reinforced, just like her own. They were a hostage rescue team of two. The engine buzzed louder above them.

The white plane glided onto the field and came to an easy stop after a turn that left it in position for take-off; about 50 feet from Conway's vehicle. Madison, belly on the cold ground and elbows digging in the dirt, crawled across the last few feet to get into place in the shadows. Conway's van was 15 feet in front of her in the open and she had a clear view of the back and the driver's side. She tucked her head behind a bearberry shrub. Her eyes had not moved from the truck: no trace of Conway or his hostage as yet. The windows were rolled up and it was impossible to see inside. Madison guessed Conway was in the driver's seat and Cameron bound in the back. She had briefly thought about rushing in and storming the van before the plane landed but there hadn't been enough time and the mirrors covered the back view of the vehicle. Conway would have spotted them straightaway and cut them off at the knees.

The plane was a smart six- to eight-seater and whoever had landed it knew what he was doing. The question was how many men would be needed to escort the prisoner. Madison was a veteran of drug busts and stake-outs since her time in Vice and had seen all sorts of changes made to the inside of planes. If they took out some of the seats they could easily strap in a stretcher, which would be the safest way to transport Cameron. It meant the plane could carry the pilot and three to four men, all carrying weapons. And Conway would be armed too – one in his hand and at least one back-up. He was alone now, handling both the deal and the prisoner at the same time. It wasn't ideal and he would be wary of being jumped. Wary and watchful.

Madison reviewed her thinking: Conway was already in the back with the hostage, waiting, and they'd come out together; otherwise the dealers could waste him on sight, pick up their delivery and take off.

The doors opened at the same time and Madison held her breath. There he was, Dead Eyes, tall and skinny like a malevolent eel. He moved awkwardly – maybe Cameron had got to him too. He guided his hostage out of the van, the prisoner blindfolded, cuffed behind his back and barely able to walk. Madison thought of the inside of the cabin, saw he could stand on his own two feet and let herself be glad of that simple fact.

Three men came out of the plane: one had a narrow face and wore a suit, the others were wide in the shoulders and looked like bodyguards in matching long leather coats and jeans. Madison shifted on the ground to get a better view – the van stood between her and the group.

She trained her binoculars on the guards and, sticking out from the leather folds, she saw the tips of two MAC10 with suppressors pointing at the ground. Madison forced herself to breathe and listen.

This was the job right now – just to breathe, listen, and be ready. She felt a spike of fear like a bitter taste in her throat.

There were no introductions and no greetings; it wasn't a coincidence they were all in that field. The buyers had clocked that Conway was alone and didn't overplay it, nevertheless Madison was sure they were wondering if he could be taken without killing their prize in the process.

The man in the suit took out a cell phone from his breast pocket. Madison had asked herself how Conway would receive his payment and the easiest method seemed to be a call from the payer to someone somewhere who'd do the electronic transfer once the merchandise had been inspected, and the bank would send Conway a confirmation message. *The merchandise.*

Madison scanned the four men and saw the body language of power, threat and the straightforward trading of goods between businessmen. She read them like players at her father's table and knew which bodyguard couldn't wait to get his hands on Cameron and which couldn't care less.

Their California tans looked out of place in Washington State and they seemed too bulky to move fast but they did carry heavy-duty gun metal. The man in the suit was the deal maker: Madison watched and listened.

Conway pulled Cameron forward with the muzzle of his gun against his temple and moved him toward the three men. The man in the suit approached them and Madison steadied herself. He pulled off Cameron's blindfold. Conway's gun pressed against his skin and Madison hoped Cameron wouldn't do something idiotic because he thought he had nothing to lose.

Maybe he was strong enough in body and mind to stay still and bear it, strong enough to look Suit in the eye and not react. Cameron looked pale and weak but he didn't so much as blink, and for a surreal moment Madison felt proud to know him. Suit examined him and apparently looked pleased with his condition. He replaced the blindfold.

Madison felt the adrenaline tremble through her arms and legs. By now Andrews should have had enough time to get into place. She slid out from behind the bushes and the truck gave her ten strides' worth of cover. They didn't see her as she slipped along the side of the van, heart slamming in her chest, stopped just before the driver's window and peeked through it and through the windscreen, the metal of the bodywork cold against her skin.

Suit lifted the cell phone to his ear and she made her move.

A shot in the air from the Glock .40 exploded like cannon fire in the open field and Madison was out from behind the van.

'Down on the ground! Down on the ground!'

Heads spinning toward her and Cameron recognizing her voice. Conway turning his body around fast and putting Cameron between them. One guard twisting to lift the MAC10 and a shot cracking from the treeline hitting him like he was shoved hard in the back, and he was buckling forward. The other guard backing into the tail of the plane, the muzzle coming up, and Madison shooting him twice in the chest. The man sliding backwards against the tail and Madison already swinging back. Shots fired from the plane doors shattering the windscreen by her side, a tire bursting in the rear of the van and her cheekbone stinging as she's pulled back behind cover. Three quick rounds blasting from the treeline toward the plane door and Conway on the ground, holding Cameron tight, putting two rounds into the side of the van and two toward the treeline. A bullet glancing Conway in the neck, another hitting him in the back and, behind him, the man in the suit lowering his revolver and crawling to get to Cameron, blindfolded and bound on the ground. The engine of the plane coming to life with Madison's voice shouting above the racket, 'Hold your fire! Hold your fire!' Catching her breath, ears ringing, the air around her thick with cordite.

The man in the suit stood and dragged Cameron up with him, his body as a shield between himself and Madison and the sniper. Conway was face down and bleeding on the ground. Madison wanted to step over and kick the gun away from his hand but she was locked on the man in the suit.

'Thanks for this – couldn't have worked it out better myself,' the man said and started toward the plane's door, pulling Cameron backwards.

'No,' Madison said.

'Shoot him,' Cameron said. 'Just shoot him.'

'Come on!' someone hollered from inside the plane.

'Shoot him,' Cameron said.

The man was calm: his soldiers might be lying dead a few feet away, but this was a much better outcome since no money had changed hands.

'We're leaving,' he said, and Madison knew it would be the last voice Cameron was ever going to hear, strapped to a chair or hanging from a ceiling hook somewhere in a locked room. The voice that tells you it's almost over but not quite.

Madison's vision had shrunk to her two-handed grip, three dots aligned in the sights. 'I can't let you leave.'

'Yes, you can,' the man said, his revolver hard against Cameron's temple.

Madison tried to find in herself the last shreds of stillness. The woods creaked around them and a puff of breeze soothed her burning cheek.

All the time she would ever have was right now. It's not about gun metal, it never is. She was frayed with exhaustion and dread and sanity seemed a lifetime away. It always comes down to the same question, over and over.

The man lifted his chin, a ferrety version of a human being, and narrowed his eyes for effect. 'Time to fly.' There was a long trail of horror behind those words, years of basements and deals and prisoners begging to die.

Madison drained her voice of all that was good. 'Let him go,' she said.

She sought and found the still core that she needed and looked the man in the eye.

How far are you prepared to go?

Her voice cracked. 'Do you trust me?' she said, and in her mind she started the Fibonacci sequence. *0, 1, 1, 2, 3, 5, 8, 13, 21, 34, 55, 89 . . .*

'What?' the man said.

. . . 144, 233, 377 . . .

'Stand up,' Madison said.

. . . 610, 987, 1597 . . .

'What?'

Cameron shifted and Madison squeezed the trigger. *G-64.* Her shot slammed into him and almost spun him out of the man's grasp, blood spreading on his front. Cameron's body was too heavy to hold and he slid onto the ground.

'He's no good to you anymore,' Madison said. 'He will die on the plane.'

Her Glock against his revolver now: both of them dead or both of them alive.

'You're insane,' the man said, glancing at Cameron face down on the ground and the blood pooling on the dirt.

Andrews crashed through the undergrowth trying to get a clear shot, but the wing was in the way. Under the rumble of the plane's engine, the rotors of the county chopper sliced the air and sirens wailed somewhere down in the valley, climbing from Maple Falls toward Silver Lake.

Madison wanted it over and she didn't care about who blinked first.

'Leave. Now,' she said, counting in her mind how many rounds she'd fired and how many she had left.

Go and let me see to the dying and the dead.

The man held her in his pale eyes and knew she would manage to get out one fatal shot even if he shot first.

'Go,' she said.

The man disappeared inside the plane and it was rolling before the door was shut, picking up speed as fast as the engine would allow and away into the purple sky. Her Glock stayed on it until the wheels left the ground.

'Check on Conway – he might have a back-up.' She pointed behind her as Andrews ran across the field.

Madison dropped to her knees by Cameron's side and turned him over, hands awkward and not knowing where to touch. She took off his blindfold and cut off the cuffs with her knife. Red was all over the lower right side of his chest and his eyes were closed. *Liver, kidneys, intestines.* G-64 was the shooting target with the illustrated human organs and a scoring system for hitting the most vital: Madison had aimed to score 0.

She pulled up his shirt tails and gently lifted the fabric off the skin. The tear in his side was three inches long and weeping but her bullet had glanced off the skin without entering the body.

She heard Andrews opening the truck's door and a second later the headlights came on; he spoke on his radio, a soft and steady stream of words she couldn't catch.

Madison took off the green T-shirt and pressed it as a thick wad on the wound; she lifted Cameron's hand and laid it against it. His eyes came open.

'Keep some pressure on it,' she said.

'Conway,' he replied.

She nodded and stood up. In the beams of the headlights the bodies of the guards lay where they had fallen; Conway had turned himself over; his breathing was ragged, but his eyes were clear.

'I've taken off him his main, a back-up, a knife and three filled syringes and needles. There's more in the truck,' Andrews said and gave Madison a look. *If you want to talk to him use short words and speak them quickly.*

Conway was wheezing; the exit wound from the shot in the back had done a lot of damage.

His eyes found her against the sky and he coughed.

'Is McMullen your client?' Madison said.

His lip curled up. He would gladly row himself into hell rather than tell her.

Madison got close to him. 'You failed; let *that* be what you take with you from this field.'

Conway died between breaths and his eyes didn't look any different.

As far away as possible from them in the open the county chopper landed in a spray of dry grass; the sirens were almost there.

Madison knelt next to Cameron and took out her cell. He was still conscious. She dialed.

'Hello,' Nathan Quinn said.

'We found him,' she said.

'You have him?'

'I have him,' she replied, and passed the cell to Cameron.

The entire field was a crime scene and there were statements to give, weapons to surrender and evidence to collect, both there and at the cabin.

Cameron was airlifted to Bellingham. To Madison's untrained eye he looked pale and drugged up: she gave the medics Conway's syringes to test to find out what he'd given him and it concerned her more than the chunk of metal that she had shot into his chest.

Deputy Andrews knew everybody on the ground and introduced Madison to everyone, including some civilian volunteers who had turned up to help.

Madison felt numb: she gave a clear and efficient statement, matched by Andrews word for word, but as the adrenaline dropped to nil she found herself nearly incapable of speech. One of the bodyguards had died of two gunshot wounds to the chest; Madison had fired those shots. She stood by the dead man as the medics did their job; it felt right that she should know his face. She had never killed a person before.

A nurse checked her over, cleaned the nick on her cheekbone from the broken glass and left it to dry in the air.

Madison woke up with a start. She had taken a ten-minute break from going over Conway's cabin with local officers, sat down with her eyes closed in the pick-up's driver's seat and had slept for an hour. The clock on the dashboard said it was almost one in the morning.

The stars were out in full and she wondered whether celestial navigation might lead her in the direction of the man who had hired Conway, whether there was some cosmic residue of a man's actions maybe visible only to one of Sorensen's devices that could lead her to him. It was easy to think such thoughts away from the city lights when it seemed that every single astral body was present and accounted for and there was no black left between the dots of light. Madison shook her head: she was tired, she was hungry, and she was away from home.

She pulled her gloves back on and returned to the chaos of the cabin. When she looked up from the floor a while later Spencer and Dunne were standing in the doorway.

Chapter 64

Vincent Foley woke up early and the tips of his fingers caressed the texture of the wall, still so unfamiliar. He saw his work of the past few days all around him and felt sure Ronald would approve of it. He hadn't seen Ronald for a while. Weeks, it felt like, but he had trouble keeping track of time. When Ronald would come to visit him next they would find windows like the ones in the Institute and Ronald would tell him things as he always did.

Vincent was not sure what it was they talked about but he felt better afterwards and those nights his fear was not as bad. He reached under the cot and picked up the crayon; it was exactly where he had left it the previous night. He cradled the green crayon in his hand and fell back into sleep.

A nurse found him three hours later. After a brief and unsuccessful effort to resuscitate him, they called Dr. Peterson to make the necessary arrangements as he was his next of kin and they needed Vincent's room cleared as soon as possible.

Chapter 65

The main lab of the Crime Scene Unit clicked and whirred like a living thing. Amy Sorensen and her team hustled around the tables and the instruments, analyzing and connecting different items of evidence. In a corner of the room, ignored by all, a monitor showed a three-dimensional perspective of what at first looked like a shapeless lump in varying shades of gray. The algorithm that had created it marked each second with a green tick and each tick went to create an individual fingerprint, separating it from the gray block.

It was time-consuming and there were no guarantees of success; nevertheless, one tick at a time, the software was separating the overlapping fingerprints on the scrap of photocopy paper with David Quinn's school picture. Sorensen lifted her eyes from the piece of glass she was examining and glanced at the monitor: it got on with its job like every other member of her team and she couldn't really ask for more.

Madison gripped the baseball bat and looked around the room. It was her Friday Harbor bedroom on San Juan Island, her last address with her father, the last place in this world that held memories of her mother. She caught herself in the mirror: she was not twelve and she wore the heavy ballistic vest with the ceramic plates. The moon was high in the window and she knew her father had stolen her mother's things. She also knew that she was dreaming but somehow that did not seem to matter because her grief was real and her rage was like a wave about to hit. It was about to break and she hunkered down ready for it. The first swing of the bat found her bookshelf and the second struck the mirror. One part of her mind – the part that recognized she was asleep – was glad that her father was not home and still, even deep in her dream, Madison was aware that she had shot and killed a human being. She swung the bat and the shattering glass woke her with a start. She was lying in the back of Spencer's car, they were crossing the West Seattle Bridge and the sky was bright in the window.

Madison stood under the shower for a long time and let the cut on her cheekbone sting in the heat. She had called the hospital in Bellingham twice. The attending doctor in charge of Cameron would not speak with her at first and it took a call from the sheriff to get him to tell her what was going on. Cameron had been injected by Conway with a number of tranquilizers and quite frankly, he said, they didn't exactly know how he had been able to walk and talk. The syringes had contained Ketamine, which Conway had not used, and were probably meant as a parting gift. The gunshot wound had been cleaned and bandaged, and if he didn't plan to be lifting elephants anytime soon he would heal very well. Madison smiled a little. The doctor apologized for not taking her call at first but they'd had reporters camping outside the hospital. A private ambulance had been booked to fly Cameron back to Seattle in a few hours, once they had washed the drugs out of his system.

Madison turned off the water when it began to turn cold; she wrapped herself in a towel and sat on the sofa with a cup of coffee. Upcoming attractions in her future included a very long conversation with the Office of Professional Responsibility regarding the shooting, a standard investigation into the death of the bodyguard and – something she particularly looked forward to – an explanation of how she had deemed it appropriate to shoot the hostage she had been trying to save. Madison sipped her coffee. And the obligatory session with a Psych counselor, of course.

She was trying to think things through and focus on the next step but she kept going back to the gunshot wounds in the guard's chest. She called Sorensen for the comfort and the dependability of physical evidence.

'I heard you shot up Whatcom County,' Sorensen said.

'Well, it was . . . I don't know what it was, Amy, except pretty awful. I was wondering if you had any news.'

Any other day Sorensen would have reminded Madison that she would have called her if she had any but that day she didn't. 'I'm throwing the odd glance to the corner of the room and I swear to you sometimes I think the machine is moving faster just because I'm watching it. However, the answer is not yet. We recovered a print that matches Timothy Gilman – which didn't surprise anybody – and the rest is just waiting.'

'Thanks, Amy.'

'Look, I heard you had to shoot one of the felons involved.'

'Yes, I did.'

'My advice is, talk to someone about it. Even when you've done the best you could and that was the last resort, you're going to feel all over the place about it. Talk to someone who's gone through the same thing, someone you trust.'

'I will. Thanks for that.'

It wasn't the right moment to mention that the only other person she knew for sure had killed another human being was the hostage she had been trying to save. And Madison didn't know exactly where the issue of trust stood between her and John Cameron.

She finished her coffee and got dressed. One of the consequences of the shooting was that she was now on administrative leave until the investigation of what had happened in Whatcom County had reached its conclusions, and even so tomorrow Jerome McMullen would have his parole hearing.

One of the sheriff's deputies had collected her Glock, and Madison wrapped the strap around the empty holster and laid it on her dresser. She cleaned, oiled and dry-fired her back-up .38 and holstered it on her ankle. She had seen Peter Conway die and yet his presence had saturated the whole case to such a degree that if she hadn't seen the medical examiner doing his checks and asking her for his time of death, she'd have been left wondering.

The drive to Seward Park took little time in the midday traffic. It was strange to be back in her Honda after all the miles in the pick-up – Dunne had driven it back to Seattle himself – and Madison was suddenly aware of being that much lower on the road and closer to the ground.

Chapter 66

Nathan Quinn looked like he'd had as little sleep as Madison. She wondered if he was still on medication and what effect all this had had on it.

He showed her in and she almost smiled: his dining table was an exact replica of hers – notes, clippings, the files Hollis had dug out, everything jostling for space with a large cardboard box.

He didn't need to tell her that he thought he'd never see Cameron again and she didn't need to hear it. They sat at the table and she told him about the field and the plane. Cameron would fill in the rest.

There was great relief there certainly, and yet behind it there was something else too. It was proof of how much the last weeks had taken out of Quinn that Madison could even glimpse at anything behind his *officer of the court* face.

'Are you going to get in trouble for shooting him?' he said.

'A little trouble, probably, but not much. The SPD cannot be seen giving me a pat on the back for shooting a hostage but the situation was what it was and I doubt Cameron will sue me.'

'Can you identify the man in the suit?'

'Yes. The DEA, the FBI and the BATF are all suddenly keen to get to know me and spend time with me. I've already made appointments to brief them and I'm sure they'll bring pretty pictures for me to look at.'

'What about Conway's property?'

Madison sat back in her chair. Standing next to Conway had been the closest she had ever been to a real-life link with the hidden man, and now Conway was dead.

'The sheriff's people have collected three cell phones, five credits cards, four different fake IDs and driver's licenses and about $3,750 in cash. Most of it in a hiding place inside the van. We have already done the paperwork to work on the evidence from here and I know they'll cooperate. McMullen had motive and a way to pay for his services. Somewhere in there there must be a phone call, a current account, some kind of link to his client. We'll be getting some numbers later today.'

Madison thought of Sorensen's machine and imagined it working through its own set of numbers, night and day and night, as tick after tick the fingerprints were separated.

'Did Jack say anything to you about Conway? About what happened in the cabin?'

'No, there was no time. The medics just grabbed him and left. The drugs were a real concern until they found out what it was he had swimming in his system. Did he speak to you?'

'No, but he'll be back in a couple of hours – we'll speak then.' Quinn stood up. 'I'm getting coffee, if you'd like some.'

Madison nodded.

Quinn stopped – awkward now, one hand on the cardboard box on the table. 'You might want to look at this: before the field and the plane, before the Hoh and the forest and everything else, there was a boy who was brilliant and funny and annoying and incredibly stubborn.'

Quinn left the room. Madison studied the old box and carefully lifted the lid. David Quinn's things. She had seen his photo, she had seen every piece of paper to do with his death, but she had never seen *him*. She heard water running in the kitchen. Nathan Quinn was not going to thank her for saving Cameron's life because words were a scant reward for what she'd done for him: he was sharing with her all he had left of his brother. And just then Madison was glad he was out of the room.

She held the baseball mitt: the smell of leather so rich and deep. There was a lot of life in that box, of places he'd been and things he'd done.

Madison picked up a small book of photographs: it was a summer party around a pool, the sun was shining and the water caught it with every swell. The day seen through David's eyes. Madison turned the pages and saw the small dark-haired boy diving into the pool and she knew who he was without asking. And a group of children kidding around for the camera while an older boy looked on – long hair and the beginnings of a beard. The flags and the cake for the Fourth of July. And every rock and every squirrel in the garden. Life, after all those years, coming through stronger than all the death that had followed.

Jerome McMullen looked around his cell: he owned so very little. He could pack everything he had in less than ten minutes. Which was probably how long the parole board would take to decide whether to let him out or not. He felt this puny cell would not house him for much longer because his spiritual journey was bound to continue on the outside.

He had not seen the news or spoken to anyone today. He wanted to keep his mind entirely on one single thought: freedom. He had done so much to make sure it would be a reality.

Chapter 67

Carl Doyle, Nathan Quinn's assistant, had received the call and done what he was asked because he trusted there was a reason. There was always a reason. He took the elevator to the street level as its twin left for the ninth floor. He had been asked to go home for the day but he didn't – instead he sat down on one of the plush armchairs in the lobby. It was dark outside and for the first time he felt afraid in the way he had been as a boy.

Nathan Quinn opened the door of the library of Quinn Locke & Associates, laid his coat on the long table and leant his walking stick against a chair. Funny that he should seek the comfort of books at this time when the law they contained had let him down before. He felt as he had the day his father had called him to say that David had been kidnapped, the same anguish as if it had barely happened. The strength he needed could not be bought by a law degree, he knew that much, and his thoughts turned to the time before all this when he'd believed that it was possible for justice and the law to be the same thing. He stood there and sought that scrap of belief that he had buried a very long time ago. He sought it in his father's name; he sought it in his mother's name.

He heard the steps behind him and turned. Conrad Locke stood in the door, elegant charcoal gray suit and white hair.

'Nathan, how's John? Is he back?'

Quinn was as pale as he had ever been in his life. 'He's back. I haven't seen him yet.'

'Thank God he's alright.' Locke stepped into the library, his eyes holding Quinn.

'He's not – we're not,' Quinn said. 'We spoke on the phone and he told me that the man who had abducted him told him who his client was. He thought Jack was going to be killed and he told him who had paid him to take him and to kill the men who had kidnapped him twenty-five years ago. It was his final taunt just before the plane arrived.'

'Who was it?'

'Jack said he should take care of it himself.'

'Nathan—'

'I couldn't stop him.'

'How can you be sure the man knew?'

'He said he'd done his homework,' Quinn said. 'He knew.'

Conrad Locke stepped closer. 'Where's Jack?'

Madison had not found the super at Ronald Gray's apartment block. She ran up the stairs and Ronald's door was as she'd left it, the new lock shinier than the rest of it. When she'd realized she wouldn't have a key she'd gone back to her car and got the crowbar out of the trunk. A neighbor peeked out when she gave the first kick.

'Seattle Police Department,' Madison said, holding up the badge on the chain around her neck without turning.

It took her five minutes of loud and unsubtle work but in the end the door gave up and Madison was inside.

Dr. Peterson's call had found her at Quinn's and the news of Vincent's death had been a moment of shock and sadness in a day that seemed already full to the brim of both. Afterwards, Madison had spoken to Dr. Takemoto and there she was, with a crowbar in her hand, looking over the hastily tidied-up apartment.

Ronald Gray had lived there: a quiet life spent in a drab office job, filing paperwork for the Walters Institute and visiting his foster brother. Visiting and talking to Vincent. *Talking to Vincent.*

Madison stood by the threshold; she could see almost the whole apartment from there. When Ronald had left his home for the last time he knew he was, in all probability, going to die; he had delayed his escape to make sure all the traces of Vincent's existence were destroyed and had made sure that, should the worst happen, someone who was looking in the right places would find David Quinn's medal and the scrap with the yearbook picture.

Madison scanned the room: the furniture, the floors, the walls. Conway had been here and she knew he had not found what he was looking for. But Ronald, who had done so much to give them a start in the investigation, had done more than Conway could ever imagine.

The little broom cupboard was intact – a few domestic cleaning products, a tin of white paint, a paintbrush, a roll of plain wallpaper.

We rent the property furnished and decorated, you know. The super had been quite clear about that. Madison walked through the bedroom and the kitchen and found herself back in the living room. Ronald had left them a message. Her eyes travelled over each nook of the simple room and she went to stand in front of the IKEA rip-off bookcase.

Vincent had never been inside the apartment. If he had, Madison would have expected to see something that was not there – the walls were pristine. Vincent would have drawn his long twisty lines because *the trail was the wall.* Madison ran her fingertips along the surface; once she arrived at the bookcase she lifted the crowbar and wedged it behind the empty shelves.

With a silent apology to the super, she applied the right amount of pressure and a loud crack told her that the spackle and the screws had surrendered their hold and she pushed the bookcase away until it was at a right angle.

Behind the shelving it had been invisible: Madison pulled on a pair of evidence gloves and took out the switchblade knife from her back pocket. She felt the change in the thickness of the wallpaper and cut along the edge. The square was three feet by three feet. Madison cut the top off as if it was a flap, pulled it down and stood back: legal-size sheets of notebook paper covered in small, neat writing had been taped to the wall and protected by a layer of wallpaper that had not been glued down. In the bottom corner, a thin, flat memory stick. Ronald had left them a message and Vincent had delivered it: the trail.

The writing jumped out at her. *If you are reading this . . . my name is . . . on August 28, 1985 . . .*

A photograph from a newspaper had been taped to a page. Madison knew it well: it was the picture taken right after David Quinn's funeral. The family and their friends walking away from the grave, frozen in the worst moment of their lives, and young Cameron with his arm still in a sling attacking the photographer for his intrusion. By now Madison was familiar with all those faces: they had become part of her life like distant relatives. Ronald had drawn a circle around one of them and Madison knew why.

'You knew Timothy Gilman,' Nathan Quinn said to Conrad Locke.

'Who?'

'You were Timothy Gilman's attorney when he was up for an assault charge with Leon Kendrick. You represented both of them and you managed to get the charge dropped because you're the best litigator I've ever met.'

'Maybe I did – I don't know. Do you remember every case from thirty years ago? Why does this matter now?'

'I'd remember Gilman. He was the one who hired the others to kidnap the boys. You met him when he was just a young, mean, violent bully.'

'I don't remember him, Nathan, and I'm terribly sorry for this connection but we didn't know this at the time. You yourself didn't know he had been involved until much later.'

'My father always said you had a mind like a shark in water: it never stops and it eats everything that crosses its path. If you had defended him, you'd remember everything about him – like the fact that he had no problem hurting children.'

'What did Jack tell you?'

Quinn took a folded piece of paper from his inside pocket and spread it on the table. It was a yellowed page from *The Seattle Times*. He took a photograph from the same pocket and laid it next to it. Locke edged closer.

'Where is everyone?' he said, looking around – the corridor and the offices were empty.

'I told Carl to get everybody out. I thought we shouldn't be disturbed.'

A line had been crossed, neither could back down, and each recognized the other.

'I want to talk to Jack,' Locke said.

'Jack asked me if Bobby still worked at Harborview.'

'My son Robert?'

'Yes. They have not spoken for years and Jack asked me if Bobby still worked there. He's a cardiologist, right?'

'What did you tell him?'

'I said yes, as far as I know, Robert was still at Harborview.'

Conrad Locke took out his cell and dialed a number on speed-dial. It went to voicemail.

'Robert, call me as soon as you hear this.'

Nathan Quinn stared at his old friend.

Locke tried another number and found another voicemail. He left the same message.

'Where's Robert?' he said.

Quinn's voice was quiet in the large room and it carried with it the hell of years of rage and grief. 'You won't find him,' he said. 'You might never find him. Jack has Robert.'

'This is madness.'

'Jack is not in the mood for sanity today and neither am I. Have you seen the pictures of what he did to Harry Salinger?'

'Whatever you think happened, you can't believe the word of a killer.'

'Who are you talking about now?' This was the closest they would ever be to arguing in court against each other.

'This,' Quinn continued, 'is an article about the investigation on David's death. It's from the beginning of September. And this photograph,' Quinn lifted it for Locke to see, 'was taken by David on the Fourth of July. You're in the picture. It must be somewhere in the woods of the estate . . .'

'What . . .'

'. . . and this man next to you is Senator James Newberry. They found his body the second week of August. And his photo is in *The Seattle Times* right next to David's.'

'Who have you spoken to about this?'

'Except that the senator had been missing since the end of June. He was about to testify in a corruption and racketeering trial against defendants *you* represented, and by the Fourth of July he had been missing for over a week. You knew him from before because you knew *everybody*, and he must have come to you that day because he knew you'd be at the estate. At the inquiry about his death you swore under oath that you had not seen him since the end of June. That's perjury,

Counselor. Did he come to you asking for help, for assurances? Had you introduced him to your clients in the first place?'

'Who have you spoken to about this?'

'Did you tell him that everything would be alright? That he could lie on the stand? And that night, after the cake by the pool and the fireworks, did you call your clients – all good *family* men – and tell them where they could find him? How much have you helped them over the years? You sit on committees, you broker deals, you make connections between interested parties. What was your fee for giving them Newberry?'

'Who have you—'

'*Spoken to*? You think I'm going to go to the police with this?' Quinn felt a reckless energy that burned through his common sense. 'Me? The attorney who represents John Cameron, alleged murderer of nine? Jack has Robert, Conrad. How the hell do you think this is going to end?'

'It was *war*,' Locke said. 'You have no idea with your corporate law, your civilized criminal cases, your intellectual property disputes. You have no idea what I had to do to win at least some of the times against those animals, and the only way you could do it was with the help of other animals just like them. You don't like to think about that when you sit in this library with the mahogany table and the pretty books. Your brother was an innocent victim in an awful war and I wish he had not been there with his damn camera, but he was. As soon as I got back to the house I managed to get Bobby and the other kids all hyped up and they pushed David in the water with the camera as a joke. I thought it was the end of it and I bought him an identical one the next day. He was really upset because it was a present from you. You had already left and they never told you. I thought that was the end of it.'

Quinn held the photo; it was all he could see. 'I had already changed the film by then.'

'Where's my son?'

'Did you call Gilman after Newberry's body was found?'

Locke did not reply. There was nothing left there of the person Quinn had known.

'Did you think that David might recognize him from the pictures in the paper?' Quinn said.

Locke stepped forward. 'You have no idea what you're dealing with.'

'People like Conway?'

Locke didn't look away. 'I want my son back.'

'And I want my brother back, but apparently neither of us is going to get what we want today.'

'Nathan, you will call Jack and he will release Robert and you will both live through this. If you don't, everything and everyone you care for in this world will be burnt to the ground.'

'It's a short list,' Quinn said. 'Shouldn't take your people too long.'

'Conway is not the worst of them by far.'

Quinn looked around, took in everything he had built in the last twenty years. 'Is that why you asked me to join you?'

'You are a brilliant and dangerous attorney, my boy. Much better for you to be where I can see you. Now, call Jack.'

'Your son will die knowing what kind of man his father is. And if that is the only measure of justice we can have, then so be it. Do you know what Jack is capable of? I thought I did but it wasn't until I saw those pictures that I really understood. You'll get pictures too in the end, I'm sure. Something to remember us by when Robert has a closed casket, which is more than David ever had. Tell me to my face, you son-of-a-bitch; you told Gilman to make sure my brother's death looked like an accident, didn't you? Didn't you?'

'Of course I did! There was no other way: Newberry's picture was everywhere. They couldn't even get rid of his body properly. David was a very bright boy. And so are you. You don't want it to end this way.'

'Yes,' Quinn said, 'yes, I do.' He took the cell phone out of his coat's pocket and laid it on the table.

Conrad Locke turned and standing in the door was a younger version of himself – the eyes of the younger man were wide with shock.

'I asked Detective Madison to pick up Robert at the hospital,' Quinn said. 'They went back to his house and he dug out his old school yearbook from the seventh grade. You'd circled my brother's picture. You told Gilman to torture Jack or Jimmy Sinclair so that David would get agitated and it would bring on an episode of arrhythmia. You had to make sure that it would be bad enough to kill him. When it didn't, Gilman forced one of the other men to finish the job. After that, their silence would be certain. It's not personal, it's business.'

'Robert . . .' Conrad Locke said.

Madison had stood next to Robert Locke in Nathan Quinn's darkened office for the last half hour and thought the man wouldn't manage to go through with it. They had given him a choice after the yearbook page had been a match: be there and support his father – whom he still believed to be completely innocent – or stay home and let them get on with it.

Robert Locke had been an irritating, spoilt little kid who had grown up to be a kind man and found his path in life fixing people's hearts, and he said he'd be there to prove them all how wrong they were. He had stood quietly in that room next to Madison, Lieutenant Fynn, and Sarah Klein from the Prosecutor's Office, next to John Cameron – whom he hadn't seen since middle school – and had listened to his life unravel.

And then the offices filled with people: Spencer, Dunne and Kelly poured out of the elevator with two uniformed officers and, behind them, Carl Doyle. Cameron moved through them without a sound to stand next to Quinn. Detectives and officers regarded him warily. His amber gaze rested on Locke. Nathan Quinn leant back against the edge of the long table and watched as Spencer read Conrad Locke his rights. Locke, who was first and foremost an attorney, didn't say a word.

Considering the number of people present, the offices of Quinn Locke & Associates were quiet as the arrest was dealt with and the suspect led away.

'Thank you for earlier, Carl,' Quinn said.

Carl Doyle shook his head. He needed to do something, to organize something or file something. He felt bereft. 'What can I do to help?' he said.

'Nothing. I'm done with this place for tonight.'

It seemed to Madison that Quinn couldn't stand to be within those walls one second longer.

They turned off the lights, locked the office and took the elevator down. Doyle left at street level; Madison, Quinn and Cameron came out in the underground parking. Their cars were among the few still there. There would be statements to the police, sworn declarations, and the documents left by Ronald Gray would be authenticated. The page of the yearbook would be officially matched by Sorensen and the recording of the conversation with Locke would be entered into evidence. But all that was for another time. Even talking about what had just happened seemed too much. Quinn's eyes held Madison's. 'Would you join us for a drink, Detective?'

She saw through the old-fashioned courtesy: he was exhausted.

'Rain check,' she said. 'How's the . . .' She indicated Cameron's injured side.

Cameron shrugged – a boyish gesture that told her how far from themselves they all were.

They nodded to each other and got into their cars, Madison trying to make sense of the last few hours and Quinn and Cameron of the last twenty-five years.

Madison drove. She was numb and watched herself park and walk into Husky Deli. She bought a bowl of French Onion Soup and a Chicken Cashew sandwich. At home, she had both sitting on the sofa with her feet on the coffee table and the television muted. She wanted to speak to Brown and to Rachel but she just couldn't, not yet. She would call them in the morning.

Her one call was to Maryland. 'Detective Frakes, I have some news . . .'

For as long as she lived Madison would never forget the moment she had seen David's picture of Locke and Newberry in the woods, and then finding buried in the file the fact that Locke had represented Gilman. She hoped Quinn would manage to sleep tonight; she hoped she would never see that hurt on the face of another human being.

Madison fell asleep remembering the soft rain in the forest as she'd walked with the ranger to the place where a child had been buried. Among the sorrows of the day, she had fulfilled her promise.

Ronald Gray looked around at his untidy apartment. He had done what he could: the acrid scent from the stove was evidence of it. He glanced at the bookcase. Five times in the past twenty years – each time he had moved house – he had done the same thing. When he first started memory sticks didn't even exist. At least he'd gotten better with the wallpaper.

With each letter he had written the words had changed a little, as he had gotten older and the landscape of his life and his heart had changed. He didn't feel proud of what he was doing as he wasn't proud of what he had done. It had started as a way of protecting Vincent and himself and had ended up as a mission.

Time to go, he thought as he closed the door. He had a bus to catch.

Chapter 68

Nathan Quinn woke up in the darkness and knew without looking at the clock that it was hours to go before dawn. Sleep had been hard to come by and brittle once there.

He slipped out of bed and padded downstairs. Cameron was sitting in one of the armchairs – with the lights off, looking out into the gloom toward where Lake Washington would be.

Quinn sat down in the other chair. They had hardly spoken since they had returned home and neither had been able to stomach any food. Cameron had been driven back by the chauffeur after his ambulance flight to find a different world, and since then things had moved too fast to take stock.

Quinn was glad to see his friend was wearing a T-shirt and sweat-pants and had not been out for one of his night drives. So much between them was still unspoken.

'Are you in any pain?' Quinn asked him – Cameron's bandage was visible under the cotton fabric.

His friend shook his head and stood up. 'Drink?'

'Yes, I think so.'

Cameron poured them a double measure of bourbon each and then, without asking, he went into the kitchen, opened the fridge and took out a carton of eggs. He was his father's son, Quinn thought, and took out a couple of plates while Cameron pan-scrambled six eggs and served them golden and still soft, his hands nimble around the stove.

They had them at the breakfast bar because the table was covered in papers, and neither mentioned the things that Quinn had told Locke about Jack. It was the truth and it didn't need explanations.

Back in bed, Nathan Quinn closed his eyes and the music came back to him as it often did on the point of falling asleep, and for the first time since that night in the forest he knew that it was Madison's voice, cradling the boy on one side and holding his hand in hers through the bars of Salinger's cage. *Blackbird*.

Chapter 69

The hush that had begun in the offices of Quinn Locke & Associates pushed itself into the crevices of the following days. Madison spoke to Brown and to Rachel – the rocks at the opposite ends of her life – but she didn't read any papers and generally kept to herself except for the obligatory meetings and debriefings.

She ran on the beach, cleaned the house and cooked food from scratch. The gunshot wounds and the face of the bodyguard in the field came back to her every so often and she let them. Sometimes she woke up in the middle of night, sometimes she slept through. She didn't speak to Quinn or Cameron but they were never far from her thoughts.

It was a bright February afternoon and the sky was a clear sheet of silver. Madison walked down the rickety pier at the end of the pebble beach at the bottom of her garden and dropped her kayak into the water. She wore her yellow REI life jacket and was not armed.

She paddled toward Three Tree Point and almost expected to see a fourteen-year-old Rachel paddle toward her in her kayak. After a while, she stopped and leant as far back as she could. A few gulls were busy in the afternoon shift but for the rest it was quiet. After the initial numbness, feelings were coming back like blood to her limbs. Some she could live with, some confused her, and some she had to find a permanent way of dealing with otherwise they would damage her like a broken bone left untreated. Good friends, good food and Billy Wilder could only get her so far, and Madison made her decision. She paddled for three hours and felt blissfully tired by the time she was done.

The call came as she was drying herself after the shower.

'They'll never want me for Special Weapons And Tactics, but for Homicide I'll do.'

Brown.

'Sarge, that's just . . .'

'I know, same here. I'll be back in the precinct as soon as the paperwork is through.'

'As long as I'm on leave you're going to have Kelly.'

'Every silver lining . . .'

The following morning, Stanley F. Robinson PhD took the elevator to go up to his office. When the doors slid open Alice Madison got up from the carpeted floor where she had been sitting with her back against the wall, waiting for him. She felt like she was asking him to prom. 'You said I could come up and look at the view.'

'So I did,' he replied, hardly breaking stride. 'How was your week?'

Later on that day Madison drove home, took off her back-up piece and her holster and walked to Rachel's house. The door was festooned with balloons with the number 7.

'He's in the garden,' Rachel said and hugged her tight. 'I'm so happy you could make it.'

The house was crammed with children and adults, most of whom Madison knew already.

'I'll call him in,' Rachel said.

'No, don't. I'll see him when he comes.'

Tommy was seven. He was seven today because a man's courage

had prevailed over another man's insanity. She watched the boy run around and play and squeal with delight. When he saw Madison he waved at her and she waved back.

That night Madison slept through.

Chapter 70

Conrad Locke never made bail; he was too much of a flight risk and had the means to disappear. Every single law enforcement agency in the land wanted to speak with him and Madison trusted they wouldn't give him immunity for his testimony against his many clients. There were lots of out there, people with a set of skills similar to Cameron's, who would be following very closely the progression of the case.

Henry Sullivan – arrested in the Silver Pines Motel – and Conway's accomplice – who had survived Cameron's attack – would be charged with a number of Class A felonies and would never in their life be free again.

Jerome McMullen was given parole and spent his probationary period volunteering for good causes in King County. He went on to start his own support group for ex-convicts.

Nathan Quinn adjusted the knot on his tie. He had shaved off the stubble and his hair was almost as short as it had been in December. He didn't notice the scars anymore – other people might but that was not his problem.

It had been a few weeks since Conrad Locke had been arrested and the slow recognition that nothing would ever be the same. Jack had spent quite a bit of time on his boat, which had been moored in Poulsbo while he had been in jail. And they had spoken about some things even though others they would probably never discuss. It was enough. It was a start.

Quinn didn't know what had stayed with Cameron of those hours when death had come so close. Jack seemed to absorb everything and somehow compute and deal with it like a rock deals with the weather. And yet the time spent on the boat, sailing around the San Juan Islands, had to be a pause for reflection, for finding his balance after that disorienting moment of vulnerability. That was what someone else would have done, and Quinn realized yet again that the inner workings of his friend's mind were an unknown country and it was one of life's twisted pleasures that this man, a brother to him, should be so very hard to read.

When he told Cameron what he had decided to do, his friend had smiled.

'You understand the implications of this,' Quinn continued. 'I will never be able to represent you as an attorney again.'

'I know, but it's where you should have always been,' Cameron said.

'There won't be any attorney–client confidentiality, Jack.'

'We'll just have to take it as it comes. When do you start?'

'In June.'

'Good. The sooner, the better.'

And that was all that had been said between them on the matter.

Nathan Quinn picked up one of the nautical compasses that had belonged to his father and slipped it into the pocket of his dark suit.

David Quinn's funeral took place under soft rain on a March afternoon, the sky unsure of itself and letting sunshine through anyway. Rabbi Stien spoke of a boy who had been a bright light for all who had known him, and he spoke of hope. Four people were present:

Nathan Quinn, John Cameron, Alice Madison and Carl Doyle. It was a brief ceremony and at the end Quinn placed their father's nautical compass on David's coffin and his hand rested there for an instant. John Cameron stood by his side.

Madison hung back a little and thought of the baseball mitt and the Sonics jersey; she thought of the seashells in the cardboard box. When Rabbi Stien hugged Quinn, she looked away.

Around them the cemetery was deep green and lush as they walked through quietly, and none of them noticed the photographer with the long lens.

Andrew Riley, heart pounding, took twenty pictures in mere seconds, got back into his car, and drove away. One of the photographs would be sold by his agency and make most of the front pages the next day. Some would print it next to the one from twenty-five years ago. It was a sweet victory for Riley, who would make enough to move out of his studio apartment. This one, he reflected with his professional eye, was probably not as dramatic as the old one but it was infinitely more interesting. *Attorney Nathan Quinn, brother of the victim, flanked by a killer on one side and a cop on the other.*

After the funeral, all except for Doyle went to The Rock, where Chef Donny O'Keefe had given the staff the rest of the day off and for once enjoyed the run of the empty kitchen.

Madison went to grab a breath of fresh air on the deck, sharp salt almost crackling in the breeze and the wide sky over the water.

She turned and Cameron was there. They had not been alone since Whatcom County.

'One thing I've been meaning to ask you, Detective,' he said.

'Ask away,'

'That night, you were never going to let me get on that plane alive, were you?'

It felt like a lifetime ago. It was the decision Madison had taken on the drive up to the field, and the reason why she had not picked up Quinn's call.

'No,' she said. 'I wasn't going to let them take you away alive. If there was no other way . . .'

She didn't need to finish her sentence.

'I knew you wouldn't.' Cameron leant on the rail.

'Why did you trust me?'

'Because you couldn't come back and tell Nathan you'd lost me.'

So it was, Madison thought, and she was glad Cameron didn't say any more about it.

In the deserted restaurant, the three of them around a table, Madison told them that Amy Sorensen's machine had separated all the fingerprints from the scrap of paper but none were Conrad Locke's. It was one piece of evidence they were not going to have. She still believed that every contact leaves a trace, even if it's not the trace we expect. In the end Locard always wins, beyond machines and software and trace analysis.

'Vincent Foley,' she said, 'carried the message that his brother had coached into him, word after word, even if he didn't understand what the message was.'

'Vincent Foley,' Cameron repeated.

All their ghosts had names now. These men's lives had grown around a single event like pearls around a piece of grit and Madison felt the very air in their world had changed.

'When are you going back to work?' she asked Quinn.

'I'm not,' he replied. 'The junior partners will take over and change the firm's name. I was offered the position of Special Counsel to the US Attorney of Washington State, and I said yes.'

'You're going back to being a prosecutor?'

The clock was going back twenty years and the men's friendship was about to test new boundaries.

Just then O'Keefe came back from the kitchen with drinks and coffee. 'Since we don't know when you gentlemen will be in the same neighborhood again, we should have our game now and let it see us through the long night.'

'I'm going to do some traveling,' Cameron explained to Madison.

'Business or pleasure?' Madison said.

'Bit of both.'

California, Madison thought, and her eyes met Quinn's. Those tests might come sooner than expected.

O'Keefe had already prepared the table and brought out the deck of cards.

'I don't play,' Madison said.

'You might not, but you sure can,' Cameron said.

'How do you know?'

'Does it matter?'

A silver dollar appeared between the chef's quick fingers. 'Heads, you play. Tails, you don't.'

'Stay and play, Detective,' Quinn said. 'Just this once.'

Madison turned as the silver coin spun high up into the air.

Acknowledgements

Some of the locations in the story are fictitious because I'm reluctant to set murder and mayhem in a real house in a real street. Also, the various precincts and jurisdictions of the Seattle Police Department have been slightly adjusted.

There's a wonderful website called www.lostairports.com and I have spent quite a lot of time there working out where to land a small plane in North Eastern Washington.

Some people have made this adventure possible and I'd like to thank . . .

My family in Italy for all their amazing cheerleading and tireless P.R..

Cori, Francesca and Claudia Giambanco for sisterly support across various oceans.

Sheyla Ravan for good thoughts and the memory of her arepas.

Kezia Martin and Anita Phillips, who read each chapter as I wrote it, and gave me the occasional elbow in the ribs if I was taking too long.

Clair Chamberlain for wisdom and margaritas when they were needed.

The Berglund family in Seattle for taking us into their hearts and their home.

My mother, for more than I could ever say here.

Gerald, for his indispensable advice on ballistics and d.i.y..

There would be no book without Teresa Chris, my agent, whose energy, humour and wise counsel are irreplaceable.

Jo Dickinson and Stef Bierwerth, my editors at Quercus, for their passion as they shepherded this novel to publication and worked out exactly how much blood my name could take on the cover.

And finally, the brilliant team at Quercus, who has given Madison and Co. a happy home, including Kathryn Taussig, Hannah Robinson and Mark Thwaite – who valiantly tried to drag me into the 21st Century by introducing me to something called 'Twitter'.